OCEAN
of
STARS

OCEAN
of
STARS

GINA MAGEE

TRIGGER WARNING

This story contains content that might be troubling to some readers—including but not limited to depictions of and references to substance abuse, child abuse, child loss, theological conflict, adultery, violence, and death. Remember to practice self-care before, during and after reading.

*This book is for those
who dare to love beyond the limits.*

Playlist

1) "Flames" — WILDES
2) "Catch" — Brett Young
3) "Like Real People Do" — Hozier
4) "Nightingale" — Norah Jones
5) "Hurt Nobody" — Andrew Belle
6) "One of These Nights" — Eagles
7) "River" — Bishop Briggs
8) "From Eden" — Hozier
9) "Heart of Mine" — The Peter Malick Group & Norah Jones
10) "Code Blue" (From "Fifty Shades Darker" Soundtrack) — The-Dream
11) "Dress" — Taylor Swift
12) "Bom Bidi Bom" (From "Fifty Shades Darker" Soundtrack) — Nick Jonas & Nicki Minaj
13) "Movement" — Hozier
14) "Sara" — Fleetwood Mac
15) "Dusk Till Dawn" — ZAYN (feat. Sia)
16) "Lady Marmalade" (From "Moulin Rouge" Soundtrack) — Christina Aguilera, Lil' Kim, Mya & Pink
17) "Nothing's Gonna Hurt You Baby" — Cigarettes After Sex
18) "Two Tickets to Paradise" — Eddie Money
19) "Waves of Blue" — Majid Jordan
20) "What Am I To You?" — Norah Jones
21) "Ocean of Stars" — Paul Sills
22) "Deep Water" — Haley Reinhart
23) "Something Heavens" — H.U.V.A. Network
24) "Landslide" — Fleetwood Mac

25) "Hanging On" — Active Child

26) "Tree Song" — Dylan Wheeler

27) "Ghost" — WILDES

28) "Beyond This Moment" — Patrick O'Hearn

29) "You There" — Aquilo

30) "Heavenly" — Karley Scott Collins

THE PLAYLIST ON PANDORA
(http://pandora.app.link/3gqCHT4ZSwb)

I have found the one whom my soul loves.

Song of Solomon 3:4

1
#choices

Stevie

"We can do this the hard way or the easy way, Graham. Your choice. If you choose to take this to court though, I'm gonna fuck you over in every way that I can. You know— since you fucked me over by fucking someone else. And you can bet on me embarrassing the hell out of you too," I said.

"I'm not taking this to court. I just wanna be free of you, Stevie, so draw up the divorce papers and I'll sign them. Take everything. I do not care."

I glared at Graham and he glared at me. He was furious and so was I, and we were both done with our ten-year marriage. He and I were hurting so much but for completely different reasons. And Graham's reasons? They were something that I'd never be able to accept because if I did, then I'd be giving him a pass for what he did.

After I confronted him with the evidence of his affair only minutes ago, he'd looked me straight in the eye, owned up to it, and then accused me of neglecting him, emotionally and phys- ically. He also accused me of being married to my job at the district attorney's office and not to him. Those were his excuses for deciding to turn to another woman.

Graham and I had been together since we were juniors in high school. Two years after graduation, we had a gigantic

1

wedding and everything moved in fast forward after that day. It seemed as if I'd always been married to him and for much longer than ten years. Of course the passion in our relationship waxed and waned like the moon but that was to be expected. That was a normal occurrence in marriage as years passed by, careers took off, demands increased, etc. I didn't neglect Graham. I gave him the best of myself all these years.

I looked at my watch and then met his glare again. "You have twenty minutes to go pack your shit and leave," I said, feeling nauseous.

"I won't need that much time."

I followed Graham into our bedroom and watched him pull two of our suitcases out of the closet and begin packing them with his clothes and toiletries. While he was walking back and forth, grabbing his belongings, he kept cutting his green eyes over at me and shaking his head. I wasn't letting up, though. He deserved how I was treating him. He'd be the same way if I'd not only had an affair but had also chosen his best friend to have it with, like he had with mine.

Graham was right about not needing the twenty minutes that I allowed him. He was done packing in less than ten. Then he walked straight up to me and looked over my face with disgust showing on his.

"I hope this wakes you up," he said.

"Wakes me up?"

"Yes, Stevie. Wakes—you—up. You'll eventually find someone else and when you do, I hope you treat them better than you did me. Especially during these past four years."

I half-laughed. "Deflect and project. You are the king of that bullshit and you know it doesn't work with me, so save your breath."

"I'm not deflecting or projecting anything. What I said is the truth. You know exactly how you've been toward me and I also know exactly how I've been toward you. I've done everything that I know to do to make you happy again and nothing has worked. You're like a robot—emotionless, no affection, thoughtless automatic replies to whatever I say to you. All business. I've needed you, Stevie. I've needed my wife. Not a goddamn roommate and that's exactly what you became to me. You are a shell of the girl that I fell in love with and for your sake, I hope you find her again."

I didn't say another word because I didn't know what else to say.

Graham stepped around me and then left our bedroom with his suitcases in hand. I continued standing where I was and waited to hear the front door slam. Once it did, I walked over to the window and watched the only man I ever loved hurry to his Chevy truck parked in the driveway. He threw his suitcases into the back, got inside the cab, and then rolled down the windows. Before he drove away, he looked back at our home and wiped his eyes. So did I. And when I could no longer see his truck in the distance, I turned around, took one step, and then fell to my knees.

Fuck my life.

2
#elixir

Stevie

"I hear the ice clinking in your glass from over the phone, daughter," my dad said.

"You're absolutely right. It is. This is my first gin and tonic of several that I plan to have today."

"I understand why you feel like doing that, but do me a favor. Just enjoy the drink that you're having now and talk to me."

I took two big gulps of said drink and then a deep breath. "Okay. Well—Graham admitted to his affair with Emma and also told me that he wasn't gonna fight me, legally. He doesn't want anything other than to be free of me. After he said that, I told him to leave, he packed his stuff, said a few more things to me that I don't care to talk about right now, and then he walked out the front door."

"Did Graham say where he was planning to live?"

"No, and I didn't ask. It's gotta be at Emma's, though. Common sense."

"Let him go, Stevie. Let them both go and do whatever they feel like they need to do with their lives, and you do the same for yourself."

"Dad, I don't know what I'm supposed to do with my life now. Graham is all I've ever known."

"I know he is, but you also know exactly who you are and you're my daughter. Your mother's too. You'll be back on your feet before you know it and journeying down a new road to new adventures that you can't even imagine at the moment. But they're there and they're waiting for you."

"I know I don't ever wanna go on another adventure like the one that I'm on now because I couldn't take it. My heart is hurting so much," I choked out.

"And you just keep crying out all those emotions that you're feeling. I'll stay on the phone with you for as long as you need me to. I can even drive over, if that's what you want, and let you cry on my shoulder."

"No, Dad, don't come over, but thank you for offering." I grabbed a handful of Kleenex out of the box on my nightstand and then wiped my eyes and nose. "What I could really use is one of Mom's hugs."

"So could I."

"I miss her so much and still can't believe she's gone."

"I can't either, but she's still with me."

"Yeah, she's still with me too."

"When did she last come visit you in your dreams?"

"A week ago. On the full moon, of course."

My dad softly chuckled. "That's your mom."

"In that dream, we were sitting on a beach close to the shoreline and we were just talking to each other. I can't remember what we were talking about but I do remember how vibrant and healthy Mom looked. It all felt so real, too."

"It is real, Stevie. Our spirits live on and God allows our deceased loved ones to visit us in different ways, such as in dreams."

"Or by making their presence known around the house like Mom does with you."

"Yes—like she *frequently* does with me. It was just yesterday I smelled her perfume in the air again."

"Are you still finding things moved from where you left them too?"

"Sure am."

I smiled to myself. "Mom can't help but mess with you. Even in the afterlife."

"She always enjoyed picking on me, but I picked on her the same."

"Oh, I remember well. You know, I really believed Graham and I were gonna grow old together and be just like you and Mom were."

My dad grew quiet and then finally said, "Stevie, I wanna ask you something and I hope you don't take it the wrong way."

"What is it?"

"I've listened closely to everything you've had to say about Graham in this sad and unfortunate situation. Can you think of anything that you did, though, that might've played a role in your marriage falling apart? And before you answer me, please let me say I'm not justifying Graham's affair. I'm just pointing out the reality of it taking two people to make or break a marriage. By the end of it—yes, the majority of the blame usually lies on one person's shoulders more than the other's, but somewhere along the way, *both* people began doing things that eroded away their love's foundation."

I sighed at hearing what my dad said because I wasn't planning on talking about matters to this degree with him. Not today. Regardless, it was about to happen anyway.

"Well, Dad... I will tell you what Graham said to me before he left our house earlier. He told me that I was married to my job and not to him. He also accused me of neglecting him, emotionally and physically, especially during the last four years. That's why he turned to Emma."

"Do you feel there's any truth in what he said?"

I took another sip of my drink. "No, I don't feel like I *neglected* him—not as he described it. Like I was intentionally being mean or something. I've just been so busy at the D.A.'s office with all the cases. They take so much of my time and Graham always gave me his understanding about it."

"Looking in from the outside, you two have seemed more like roommates than husband and wife for a good while now."

"Jesus, that's exactly what Graham said we'd become."

"I never said anything to you about it, but because we're talking about all of this now, I feel like I can and should say something."

"Dad, I wish you had when you first noticed."

"Sticking my nose into someone's marriage is a fine line to walk. Even my only daughter's."

"You counsel people at church all the time."

"But they come to me for help. You've never asked me for any with your marriage."

"I just didn't think it was that bad."

"As the saying goes, hindsight is 20/20 and as time goes on, I think you'll start seeing matters with Graham more clearly. You two will both see the wrong steps that you took and hopefully, you'll learn from them too. I don't wanna see either of you go down this hurtful pathway again, and hear me on that. Again, I'm not excusing Graham for turning to another woman."

"I know you're not. But of all people, why did he have to choose my best friend?"

"Human nature. We tend to go to what's familiar and seemingly safe. He's known Emma since high school just like you have and there's an automatic trust that comes with such a long history."

"I still feel like confronting her. She betrayed me in the worst possible way, and I don't know if I'm angrier at her or at Graham. No, it's her. She broke the number one rule of the woman code. You don't have an affair with your best friend's husband. Ever."

"Don't confront Emma. It won't change a thing and you know it."

"But it would be extremely gratifying to walk straight up to her and blast her. She deserves it. You know, Dad, I've replayed in my mind every occasion that she came over here to my house to hang out with me and also spend the night. Graham was usually here when she was, and knowing about everything now that's been going on between them, I can't help but wonder when their affair began. Graham said they started seeing each other three months ago but I bet it's been longer than that."

"It probably has been. When a friendship between two people first starts leaning toward a romantic relationship—forbidden or not—there's a teetering of sorts that happens. It's a period of tests to see what the other is feeling and also willing to allow, intimately speaking. Sometimes, it only takes a few tests before the relationship moves fast-forward into the next stage. Sometimes, it takes several tests. So, yes—Graham and Emma could've very well started seeing each other much earlier than three months ago but in their minds, probably, their affair didn't begin until they slept together the first time. Some people don't equate lingering looks, evocative conversations, secret texts, phone calls, or even kissing with having an affair. That first lingering look is where it all begins, though."

"And I've also wondered when that happened between Graham and Emma, just like I've wondered when their first secret conversation took place, and their first kiss. Another thing that I've wondered about is if Emma came over here to my house to see Graham on any of the occasions when I was out of town at a conference. She probably did, and she and Graham probably had sex in our bed. I'd bet on that too."

"Suggestion?"

"Go ahead."

"If you really believe that happened, then throw away all your bedding. Get new sheets, a comforter, and pillows. Even get a new mattress if it'd ease your mind."

I took the last sip of my gin and tonic and then set down the empty glass in my kitchen sink.

"A new mattress and bedding. I can certainly do that. I can also go throw my old mattress and bedding in Emma's front yard and set it on fire."

"Now, Stevie—you know you can't do something like that, even though feeling like doing it is understandable. Save your 'get even' emotions for your court cases where you can constructively use them."

"Dad, I'm not gonna do anything crazy. I'm just venting to you. But I will say that indulging in my evil thoughts feels really good right now."

"Just don't indulge in them for too long, okay?"

"I won't."

"One more question and then I'll let you go. I figure you're wanting to get into that pool of yours to escape your overloaded mind for a little while."

"Yes, I do want to and I'm going to as soon as we hang up. Water is my church and heals me in every way," I said, looking out the window at my backyard.

"It's always been your church but you could still come to listen to your old dad preach a sermon at *his* church sometime. I'd love to see you sitting in the front pew like you always used to do."

"I may just surprise you by doing that one day soon."

"I hope you do."

"What did you wanna ask me?"

"If you'd think about taking some time off from work for yourself."

"No, I can't do that. There's way too much going on."

"I know Melissa would let you take a short leave of absence and I also know your fellow assistant D.A.s can handle the caseload without you for a little while."

"Dad, I just..."

"Please think about it. Take some time for yourself so the deep wound inside your heart can start healing. It's so very important that you do."

"I know, and yes, I'll think about taking some time off even though I don't want to. Okay?"

"Okay. I love you, daughter of mine."

"I love you too."

"Hang in there and call me if you need anything."

"I will."

"Bye."

"Bye, Dad."

After we hung up, I put on my swimsuit, walked outside into the backyard, and then jumped into my pool. Swimming my usual laps wasn't going to happen on this day—this incredibly shitty day. All I wanted to do was float on my back and stare up at the blue sky, so that's what I did. I also began examining my role in the ending of my marriage to my high school sweetheart. A man who said I didn't love him enough. Then I began crying out all the tears that I'd been holding inside.

3
#theoldme

Stevie

Three weeks later

"You're really taking back your maiden name?" Melissa asked me.

She was the district attorney of Austin, Texas, she was tough as nails, she was my boss and also a close friend, and the two of us were sitting in my office.

"Yes, a clean slate all the way around. Besides, I'm a Sinclair through and through. Not a Jones," I said.

"You're gonna have to change your driver's license, social security card, bank accounts, credit cards. Everything."

"I know, and one by one, I'll start marking off that list."

Melissa glanced down at my left hand. "What'd you do with your wedding ring?"

"I didn't flush it down the toilet or pawn it like you're thinking I did."

"Good."

"Why *good*?"

"Because you can always have it melted down and made into something else."

I shook my head. "No, I don't think so. I'm just gonna keep it put up until I decide what to do with it."

"Alrighty then. I'll let you get back to work. Let me know if I can do anything for you, though."

"I will, and thanks."

Melissa gave me a sympathetic smile and then turned to go back to her office, but not before I called her back to mine.

"I wanna ask you something and I need you to be completely honest with me," I said.

"Ask away."

"Would it be possible for me to take some time off? I thought I was doing fine with everything, but it feels like the walls are closing in on me. I need to step away from what's happened so I can regroup."

"I've been wondering if you were ever gonna ask and the answer is yes. You should take some time off to take care of yourself. We'll handle things up here while you're gone."

I sighed. "I just feel like I'll be leaving you, Brittany, Evan, and Jonah hanging."

"No, you won't. So why don't you go on home now? See how you feel in a couple of weeks and if you need more time, then let me know. Also, will you do me a favor while you're out of the office?"

"What?"

"Don't you fucking dare guilt-trip yourself for taking some time off."

I chuckled. "You know me too well."

"Stevie, we all love you being here and kicking ass on these cases, but we've got it, so don't worry."

"Easier said than done, but I hear you. Thanks for understanding where I'm at right now. My brain is so fuzzy and I'm just... Well, if you only knew how tempted I am to pack my bags, catch a one-way flight to St. Croix in the Virgin Islands, take up residence there, get the best tan ever, and maybe even run into Kenny Chesney walking down the beach. He could strum his guitar and sing a heartbreak song for me while my tears fall into my glass of rum."

"But you're a gin girl. Not rum"

"In a tropical paradise like St. Croix, my tastes could very easily change."

"I highly doubt it."

Melissa and I shared a smile, and then I said, "As soon as I finish up what I'm doing here with the Bradshaw case, I'll go let my teammates know my plan for taking off."

"Okay. And if you decide you want a little girl time while you're off work then shoot me a text. We can go get pedicures or a massage or go grab a bite to eat at Hoover's, Joe's Bakery, or wherever you wanna go."

"Maybe. Right now, though, I just feel like I need to be alone to really think about my life and what I wanna do with it now that I'm single for the first time since I was sixteen."

"I understand, but you know where I am if you change your mind."

"I do. Melissa, thank you for not only being the best boss ever but also for being such a great friend to me."

"You make it easy to be both."

After being away from the D.A.'s office for two weeks, I had to go back because I was crawling the walls of my too-quiet house. When Graham and I were together, he'd always had music playing when he was at home, or he'd be watching some kind of sports game. It was all background noise to me and I never thought I'd miss it. I did, though. I missed it a lot.

During my time off from work, I didn't take up Melissa on her offer to get together. I just stayed at home and slowly went through all of Graham's belongings. Little by little, I boxed them up and stacked them in the garage. I didn't trash them, although the thought crossed my mind several times as wave after wave of emotions kept slamming into me.

Other things that I boxed up were all the pictures of Graham and me. Technically, they belonged to both of us, but I didn't want them and decided to leave it up to Graham to make that choice for himself. The pictures included a collage from our wedding that had been displayed on one of the walls in our bedroom. Before putting it into a box, I studied each picture while remembering who Graham and I used to be. We were so young and so happy and so ready to tackle the world together. We believed we could conquer anything as long as we were together but life ended up conquering us.

Another thing that I did while away from the D.A.'s office was draw up divorce papers and then mail them to Graham at his office address. He signed and mailed them back to me with a yellow sticky note on the front page. He wrote "Thank you, Stevie" on it and I knew exactly what he was thankful for. I decided to split everything down the middle with him instead of financially ripping him to shreds.

After doing some deep soul-searching about my role in the dissolution of our marriage, crying even more tears, and also drinking probably too much gin and tonic, I finally accepted what Graham accused me of. I'd neglected him emotionally and physically. We hadn't had a real conversation in months, although I remembered him trying to initiate several after I thought about it. The typical exchange of words between us had become nothing more than chit-chat. A daily checking in with each other and then separately going about whatever it was that we wanted to do inside the house or outside of it.

Graham and I also hadn't had sex in almost a year even though we still slept in the same bed. We hadn't really kissed each other either in that length of time. Just an occasional peck on the lips that usually came from him to me when saying goodbye before he left home in the mornings to go to work. I'd truly thought we were just going through that phase I'd witnessed other couples go through after being together for more than a few years. I also thought it'd eventually pass. I never worried about it because I was more worried about taking care of my caseload at the D.A.'s office. Graham was right. I *was* married to my job instead of him and it was my mistake. My huge, regrettable, fucking mistake that was too late for me to do anything about.

After receiving the signed divorce papers from Graham, I texted him about picking up the boxes of his belongings that I'd put in the garage. When he showed up, he looked as drained as I knew I did. We politely spoke to each other, I helped him load the boxes into the back of his truck, and then I asked him about getting his half of what was inside the house. He shook his head no and told me to keep it.

Standing in the driveway with him on that late afternoon, I watched him turn to leave but then called out his name. When he turned back around, I walked up to him to do what I'd been wanting to do. I apologized to him for how I'd treated him—for being a roommate instead of his wife.

"Stevie, *I'm* sorry," he said. "I am so damn sorry for what I did. You being wrapped up in your job was no excuse for me to have done it."

"Graham?"

"What?"

"I understand why you did. It still hurts like hell, but I understand you were lonely and all that goes with it. You're human."

He searched my eyes with his and I didn't miss the tears forming in them. I could feel them in mine too.

"Please forgive me," he choked out.

"Only if you forgive me."

We both started crying, and then he pulled me into his arms and hugged me. After a long minute, we stepped back from each other, wiped off our faces, and then smiled matching weary smiles.

"Before you leave, will you tell me one thing?" I asked.

"No, I'm not in love with Emma."

"How did you know I was gonna ask you that?"

"Because I would wanna know if I was in your position."

Graham leaned down, kissed me on the forehead, and then started walking to his truck. I didn't call out his name like before, though. I just watched him go. But right before he pulled out of the driveway, he rolled down his window and looked back at me.

"Stevie, I'm still in love with you and always will be," he said.

Then he drove away.

4

#changeofscenery

Stevie

"Have you got a few minutes, Melissa?" I asked, peeking my head into her office.

"Absolutely. Come on in."

I closed the door behind me and then sat down in one of the chairs next to her desk.

"I can't do this anymore," I sighed out.

Melissa's eyebrows pulled together. "Can't do what anymore?"

"Be here at this office, in my house—in Austin. I need to leave. I need to start over someplace else."

"Stevie, please don't make any major decisions without really thinking things through."

"But you see, I have. I've been thinking about a change of scenery for the past three months."

"Is it your divorce that's made you feel like doing this or is it something else?"

"It's my divorce plus the fact that I keep running into Graham and Emma. I've seen them at the grocery store, the mall, the carwash, the post office, the oil and lube place that I've always gone to and they've even been at the park where I take my runs. I should've known that was gonna happen since we all live in the same area of Austin."

"I wish you'd told me about those run-ins happening sooner than today because I would've rerouted you to my side of town and happily gone shopping with you."

"I appreciate it, but there was no point in telling you or anybody about it. Here's the deal, though. I cannot handle running into Graham and Emma again. Every time I do, it feels as if I'm being stabbed through my heart, and I don't wanna feel that kind of pain anymore. I can't."

Melissa walked around her desk and sat down in the chair next to mine.

"Have you thought about where you'd like to relocate?"

"Yes. Dallas."

"Big D, huh?"

"It's a great city."

"Great D.A.'s office too."

"And that's where I wanna work."

Melissa looked over my face and then stuck out her bottom lip. "But I want you to stay here. You've done so much good."

"I've certainly tried."

"Have you talked to your dad about what you're wanting to do?"

"I have and he supports me. Austin and Dallas aren't that far apart. It's an easy road trip for me to take to come back here to see him or for him to come to see me."

"So how much notice are you gonna give to me?"

"How much do you need?"

"A year's," Melissas chuckled. "Seriously, though... If you can, give me a month to get all your cases reassigned and all the loose ends tied up."

"A month is fine. It'll give me the time that I need to put my house on the market and also look for a new place to live in Dallas."

"Besides the fact that your house is so beautiful, it's gonna sell fast because the market is so hot right now."

"I hope it does sell fast. There are too many memories of Graham and me inside it for me to continue living in it *or* this city."

"If you're really serious about doing all of this, Stevie, then know you have my total support, my blessing, and my love."

"I am completely serious."

"Then I'm gonna make a phone call to the D.A.'s office in Dallas. I know the whole group there and I have no doubt they'll immediately want you to come on board." Melissa gave me a backward smile and then shook her head at me. "They're gonna be getting my Joan of Arc and I'm gonna miss her so much."

I reached over and grabbed her hand, squeezing it. "I'm gonna miss you too, as well as everybody else up here at this crazy, wonderful place."

"If you ever think you might wanna venture back down this way and put down roots again then let me know. Our door will always be open to you. Okay? Don't forget us."

"I could never forget you."

Six weeks later

"Yes, I have everything unpacked and put up in its place," I told my dad.

"I still can't believe how quickly your house sold. On the market two days and boom!"

"I'm so thankful it happened like that because it pushed me to get everything done to get moved."

"How's that pool at your new house?"

"Heavenly. I've gotten in it every day since I've been here."

My dad chuckled. "It's really strange to think you're not a ten-minute drive away from me anymore."

"I know, but Dallas really isn't that far. Why don't you come to see me in the next couple of weeks and spend the night?"

"Let me know which day works best for you and I'll be there. Any day but Sunday, of course."

"Yes, Dad, I know."

"So are you ready to tackle your new position on Monday?"

"I am. I met the whole group at the D.A.'s office last week and they're fantastic. There's a real camaraderie between them too. Good energy."

"You sound like your mom talking like that about energy."

"Well, it's a real thing and you know I've always been hyper-sensitive about it whenever I'm around people."

"And whenever you're around animals too. You read them and they read you. I remember all the times your mom and I took you to the zoo when you were little and the animals were always drawn to you. They'd come right up to you like you were an old friend."

"Animals can sense who's safe to be around and who isn't. Humans can do that too if they pay attention. So many of them don't, though, because they're too busy rushing through life and lose their instinct. I did that for a while but never will again. Believe me when I tell you that my eyes are wide open after everything that happened with Graham."

"I know they are, Stevie."

"Listen, I'm gonna let you go for now so you can put those finishing touches on tomorrow's sermon. Before we hang up though, you've gotta tell me which sin you're gonna be preaching about this time?"

My dad paused and then finally said, "Adultery."

5
#lifeistricky

Stevie

Brooke Murphy. Dallas's district attorney. My new boss. Mid-fifties. Divorced. Had a grown son and daughter. Brooke was high energy, straightforward, sharp-witted, and also good friends with my old boss, Melissa Landry. They actually reminded me a lot of one another in appearance and also personality. Both women were tall and had shoulder-length sandy-blond hair and hazel eyes, as well as backbones made of steel. They also had huge hearts.

Today was Friday—the end of my first full week at my new job—and sitting here at my desk and looking around at everything inside my office, I smiled. All was organized; I'd already been assigned two court cases and was ready for more. I knew it wouldn't be long before my desk was covered with stacks of files, but there were two things that I would always save space for. They were a framed picture of my mom and dad on their wedding day and a framed quote from Shakespeare's play *Hamlet*. The quote was: *To thine own self be true.* It was my mom's favorite.

"Hey, Stevie," Brooke said, knocking on my open door.

"Hey! Come on in."

"I'm just checking to see how you're holding up with everything. I know it's been kinda nuts around here this week."

21

"I'm doing fine. It feels great to be back in the swing of things again."

"That's music to my ears."

"Oh, I meant to tell you that I checked out the running trail you told me about and it is really nice. It isn't too far from my house either, which is an added bonus. I've also felt safe every time I've gone out there for my run."

"Still carry your pepper spray with you, though."

"I do. You can't be too careful no matter where you go nowadays."

Brooke nodded and then said, "My other reason for stopping by your office is to see if you have plans this evening."

"I was just gonna go home and take a dip in my pool. That's my hot date for this Friday night," I chuckled.

"If you feel like ditching those plans, then come out with all of us for drinks after work. Because of how this week has been, your teammates and I are ready to let our hair down and relax for a while."

"You certainly don't have to twist my arm. I'd love to go."

"Wonderful! This is gonna be fun. Plus, you'll get to meet some of the other attorneys we know."

"Defense attorneys?"

Brooke grinned. "Yes."

"Fraternizing with the enemy, huh?" I said, wrinkling my nose.

"They're not all assholes, Stevie. There are a couple of them who we've allowed into our circle because they're an exception to the rule."

"That's a tricky path to walk. What happens when you find yourself in court against one of them? Because you probably have, right?"

"You are correct, but business is business. None of us let the personal side of things get in the way of doing our jobs."

I searched Brooke's eyes and then asked, "So where am I to meet all of you this evening?"

"Mystic Bar. I'll text you the address or you're welcome to ride over there with me. After we call it a night, I can drive you back here to get your car."

"I'll ride with you. You can familiarize me with this city a little more. I swear, it's a crazier maze than Austin."

"You'll get used to it and know it like the back of your hand in no time. And speaking of Austin. Do you miss it?"

"Yes and no. I miss the vibe of the city and also my dad, but I don't miss running into my ex-husband and ex-best friend who are still there, shacked up together."

"Understandable."

I heard someone clear their throat, and Brooke and I looked over to see Jason. He was one of my fellow assistant district attorneys and he was standing in the doorway with a thick file in his hands.

"Hey, ladies," he said, walking up to my desk. "Stevie, here's another case for you to dig into if you think you're ready for it."

"Of course I am. Give it here."

Jason smiled while handing me the file.

"Is that the case that Buchanan is on?" Brooke asked Jason.

"Yep, it is."

"I see," she said, looking back at me and grinning. "And he's about to meet his match in you."

"What makes say that?"

"Zac Buchanan is one of the defense attorneys we allowed into our circle because he really is an exception to the rule. Great guy, and he's also a warrior in court just like you are."

"Shit, he's an old man, isn't he? A king at what he does because he's been doing it forever."

"No, he's not an old man. Zac is only thirty-seven."

Brooke held my gaze for several seconds without saying anything and I wondered if something was wrong. I was about to ask her when she suggested I take a look at the case file and then told me to be ready to leave here at five and not a minute later.

After she and Jason left my office, I started reading over all the legal documents—several with Zac Buchanan's neat signature on them. As of now, the man was still one of my enemies. An attorney from the shady side of the tracks. A man who chose to make a career out of defending the slime of this world instead of defending the helpless. An attorney whom Brooke and my new team of assistant district attorneys considered a friend. When the time came for Mr. Buchanan and me to meet, I would know within seconds if he and I were going to be able to pull off opposing one another in court while also remaining on friendly terms outside the courtroom. I'd know it by his handshake but especially by the look in his eyes. Both held energy, and I was ready to read Mr. Buchanan's.

After I finished going over the entire file, I leaned my head back against my chair and took a deep breath. This case involved a four-year-old little boy who'd endured abuse from both his parents. Abuse fueled by their illegal drug use. Mr. Buchanan was representing the father.

There were a lot of things that I had no tolerance for and one of them was a parent abusing their child. It didn't matter if the abuse was verbal or physical. They both left scars and now, I was going to do all that I could to leave my legal scar on the father of this little boy that I'd just read about. A boy who was the same age as mine had he lived.

6
#chemistry

Zac

"Hello, Ms. District Attorney," I said to Brooke as I walked up to the table where she was sitting.

"Hey, Buchanan! How are you doing?"

"I'm doing well. Today. Thanks for asking."

"Is Bash coming?"

"He said he was but who knows what he'll end up doing."

"I hope he shows up because I want you both to meet our new teammate."

"Where's he from?"

"*She* is from Austin and worked at the D.A.'s office there."

"Why would anyone wanna leave Austin? It's the best city in this state and also the most fun."

Brooke raised an eyebrow at me. "As you know, a shitty marriage can ruin a lot of things for a person and make them feel like starting over somewhere else."

"So your newbie is divorced then?"

"Yes, she is—and very recently."

"Well, if I happen to come up against her on a case, I'll take it easy on her. One time only, though."

Brooke grinned. "You're already against her. She got the Ferguson file this afternoon and I'm gonna go ahead and warn you that she's tough. Really tough. The Austin office calls her 'Joan of Arc' and I can't wait to see her in action against you."

"I ain't scared," I chuckled. "So will your whole crew be joining us on this fine summer evening out here on Mystic Bar's patio?"

"Yes. They're all in need of a breather and a strong drink after the week it's been."

"Yeah, I'm in need of both too. May I get you something to drink?"

"Thank you, but I've already placed my order and so has Joan of Arc—who just so happens to be walking back from the restroom as we speak," Brooke said, pointing behind me.

I looked over my shoulder and did a double take at the same time my breath caught in my throat. I recognized Dallas's new assistant district attorney. Last Saturday morning, I'd seen her while I was out taking a run. As I was approaching her on the trail—her coming from one direction and me from the other—her eye contact with me never ceased until after we passed by each other. Once we had, I stopped running altogether and kept watching the stunning woman until she disappeared in the distance.

I turned around to face Brooke's new teammate directly and smiled at her. She returned it and then came to a standstill a few feet away from me while keeping her deep blue eyes glued to mine.

"Stevie, this is the guy I was telling you about earlier this afternoon. Your new frenemy, Zac Buchanan," Brooke said. "And Zac, this is Stevie Sinclair—my new assistant D.A."

"It's nice to meet you, Stevie," I said, extending my hand, "and I'm not your enemy in any way. I'm happy to be your friend, though."

"I saw you at the running trail last Saturday," she said, firmly shaking my hand.

"I remember seeing you."

"How long have you been a runner?"

"Since high school. I was in track and cross-country."

"Same here."

"How often do you run?"

"Three to four times a week, weather permitting."

I smiled at her again. "Same here."

Stevie and I were still holding each other's hand but the shaking had stopped and her firm grip had loosened. We both looked down at our clasped hands at the same time and then quickly let go of each other.

"What a small world," Brooke said, looking back and forth at us. "You two come on and sit down. Relax. The waitress will be back in a minute, then you can order that strong drink for yourself, Zac."

Not knowing which chair was Stevie's, I motioned for her to sit down first. Once I did know which chair was hers, I planned to pull it out for her, but she quickly walked around to the other side of the table and sat down next to her new boss. I then took the seat directly across from Ms. Sinclair.

"How's that adorable little boy of yours doing?" Brooke asked me.

"Malcolm is doing great."

"I'd steal him away from you and Avery if I could get away with it."

I chuckled. "You'd never get away with it. He's mine."

"So is he with Avery or your parents this evening?"

"He's currently getting spoiled even more by my mom and dad."

Without directly asking me, I knew Brooke was really wondering how things were going between my wife and me. The scratch that she'd put on my face last night told the whole story, but only Brooke and Bash were aware of what that story was.

"Here you go, ladies," a waitress said, walking up with a tray of drinks. She placed Brooke's usual glass of Chardonnay on the table. Stevie's drink came next and it looked familiar. "Would you like to order something from the bar, sir?" the waitress asked me.

"A Hendricks and tonic with extra lime would be great."

"Got it. Would you like to order something to eat?"

She held out a menu but I didn't need it. I already knew everything that was listed on it since I'd been here so many times.

"Let's do the Mystic cheeseburger."

"Curly fries or onion rings with it?"

"Curly fries."

"Anything else?" she asked, looking up from her notepad.

"No, that'll do it."

"Then I'll go put in this order and will be back with your drink in a few minutes."

"Thank you."

"You're welcome."

As soon as the waitress walked off, I looked back at Stevie. "Is that a gin and tonic you're having?" I asked, nodding at her glass.

"Not just any old gin and tonic. I'm enjoying some Hendricks like you're about to do."

What she said surprised me. "I think it's the best gin there is."

"Same here. I love the cucumber and rose flavors mixed with the juniper berry, and I also love that Hendricks is made in Scotland."

"That's my second reason for drinking it. Ancestry."

Stevie softly smiled. "Same here."

"You're of Scottish descent?"

"Very much so. According to my DNA test result, plus the extensive research that I've done apart from it, I'm seventy-eight percent Scottish with some Norwegian and English blood mixed in."

Stevie surprised me again. "Same here. Exactly, in fact. And the world just got even smaller."

I glanced over at Brooke, then immediately turned my focus back to Stevie. She smiled at me once more and then she and I continued staring at each other, studying one another's faces. I didn't know what she was looking for in mine but I was looking for traces of *something* in hers that would clue me in to more of her story. I could tell there was a whole lot more to it than what I'd already been told.

"Have you ever tried any of the limited-release gins that Hendricks makes?" I asked my new friend/fellow runner/fellow gin drinker/kinswoman.

"Yes, I've tried all of them."

"Do you have a favorite?"

"Neptunia. It's really refreshing and has a crisp, citrusy finish. The woman distiller who makes it does such a great job of blending coastal botanicals with the gin."

"It does sound really refreshing and now, I believe I'm gonna have to try some Neptunia."

"I think you'll be pleasantly surprised by its taste."

I was already pleasantly surprised and it had nothing to do with gin.

"Do you have a favorite limited-release?" Stevie went on to ask me.

"The only one that I've tried is Midsummer Solstice and I liked it. A lot."

"It's a good one too. Really floral and smooth."

"It's like summertime in a glass."

"And that's the perfect way to describe it," Stevie said, pointing at me. "I feel like Neptunia is the ocean in a glass. It's hard to find it, though."

"Have you gone to Specs or to any of the other liquor stores around here?"

"Yes, but every place that I've been to didn't have it in stock. Regular Hendricks like you and I are having this evening? Always. But no Neptunia."

"Huh. Well, I'll keep an eye out for it."

"Thank you, but you don't have to do that."

"It's no problem. If I happen to come across a couple of bottles, then I'll grab one for you and one for me. I'm sure you and I are gonna see each other again since you're hanging out with Ms. District Attorney here," I said, glancing over at Brooke again. She was grinning from ear to ear, looking straight at me.

"We all usually meet up at least once a week so we can decompress from the demands of our jobs and life in general."

"Well, I appreciate it, Zac. If I happen to find a couple of bottles of Neptunia, then I'll grab one for you. You've gotta try it."

"I'm looking forward to doing that."

"Okay, you two gin connoisseurs," Brooke said, grabbing Stevie's attention and mine. "Incoming trouble is almost to our table."

I already knew whom she was talking about. It was Bash. Then I felt his hand on my shoulder.

"It's about time," I said, looking up at him.

He jerked his head back. "What? I'm early!"

"Hell, I can't believe you actually showed up. Before you sit down though, I wanna introduce you to Brooke's new teammate here. Stevie, this is Bash Campbell. Bash, this is Stevie Sinclair."

He reached across the table to shake her hand. "Hi, Stevie. It's nice to meet you."

"It's nice to meet you too. Is 'Bash' short for Sebastian?"

"It is. Only my friends call me Bash and I expect you to do the same."

"I'll do that."

Stevie and Bash smiled at each other. Then he sat down beside me and continued talking to the beautiful woman sitting across the table from me.

"Are you from Dallas?" he asked her.

"No, I'm from Austin. I worked at the D.A.'s office there."

"I hope you don't mind my asking, but why did you leave it to come to this one? Did something unsavory happen down south?"

Stevie took a sip of her Hendricks and tonic and then set the glass back down on the table. "Something unsavory did happen but not at my job, Bash. My husband had an affair with my best friend, so I divorced him and talked myself out of burying her. An all-around change of scenery was something that I needed to do for myself and that's why I'm here in Dallas, Texas now."

"Oh damn... I did not see that one coming. I am so sorry you went through that."

"Don't worry about it. I'm fine, and really excited to be here," Stevie said, glancing at me. I was staring straight at her.

"Well, welcome to Dallas. I'm glad you're here, Stevie Sinclair. Let our legal dance begin!" Bash said.

We all started laughing, and then the waitress walked up and sat down my drink in front of me. While she was taking Bash's order, I noticed Brooke watching me again. Then she grinned and picked up her cellphone off the table. Less than twenty seconds later, I felt my cellphone buzz in my pants pocket. When I looked at the screen, I wasn't surprised to see Brooke's text notification. I didn't read her message right away, though. I waited, and when Bash and Stevie became wrapped up in a conversation about the best beach destinations, I took that opportunity to see what Ms. District Attorney had to say to me.

Brooke: Careful, tiger.

Me: Careful about what?

Brooke: Don't mistake Stevie's soft appearance, sweet voice, and sad divorce story for weakness. This beauty sitting beside me will happily drink your blood for breakfast.

Me: I don't think she's weak. It's quite the opposite. Clearly, she's a very strong woman.

Brooke: Yes, she is. But I can already tell by the way that you two keep looking at each other what both your weaknesses could become if you aren't careful.

I cut my eyes up at Brooke, shook my head in disagreement, and then looked back down at my cellphone.

Me: Not gonna happen. I'm not that kind of man and you know it.

Brooke: After what Stevie has been through, I know she's not that kind of woman. But there's always that one person who comes along that you didn't see coming and they'll make you wanna break all the rules that you never thought in a million years you'd break.

Me: No woman is worth what it'd cost me if I did.

Brooke: At least admit to what I already know.

Me: And what is that?

Brooke: Chemistry is fucking powerful.

I looked up at Brooke again, then slipped my cellphone back into my pocket. Stevie and Bash were still going back and forth with their beach talk and they kept going until my burger arrived. It was at the same time that the rest of Brooke's team of assistant district attorneys showed up. Everyone found their seats and placed their drink and meal orders, and then a mix of conversations commenced, going around the table.

While eating my burger and fries, I noticed Stevie kept eyeing my plate. I pointed at it and said, "You're welcome to have some of this."

"When I got here, I wasn't hungry in the least. Not until I saw those fries of yours. They look delicious."

"Here, grab as many as you want."

I pushed my plate toward her and watched her pick up one of the curly fries with her slender fingers. Then she took a bite and smiled.

"Yeah, I'm gonna have to order some of those."

"Seriously, Stevie—help me finish all this. Please. These Mystic burgers are huge and the fries are always piled high like this."

She side-eyed me. "Are you sure?"

"Hundred percent."

"I appreciate it."

"Of course."

Together, she and I cleaned my plate, and in between the bites that we took, we continued talking to each other. Stevie was a captivating woman. Intelligent. Direct. Funny. She was also feisty, and with the way that she spoke to Bash about her love for the ocean, she had to be part mermaid.

I felt my cellphone buzz in my pants pocket again and checked it, but the text message wasn't from Brooke this time. It was from my wife, Avery. She was asking me to pick up a gallon of milk on my way home. Malcolm loved having a cup of chocolate milk every night before he went to bed and I was going to be sure that little nightly ritual of his continued without fail.

I texted a thumbs-up to Avery to let her know I'd get the milk and then waved down the waitress for my check. After paying for my meal, I told the group that it was time for me to leave the party. When I stood up from the table, Stevie did too; then she stepped around it and came up to me.

"It was a pleasure meeting you, Zac," she said, standing so close that I could smell the sweet scent of her breath.

"The pleasure is all mine."

"Thank you again for feeding me."

"You're most welcome. You're a kinswoman and that holds a lot of weight with me."

"Same here, kinsman. I'll see you in court on the Ferguson case next week."

"Looking forward to it," I said, glancing down at her mouth. Her pouty, glossed lips made it hard not to.

I reached out to shake Stevie's hand and she immediately received mine. As I was letting go of her, I had a strange sensation come over me and I was still feeling it. It was a *pull* to Stevie that I was experiencing. A physical urge to keep touching her that I didn't understand or need to follow through with.

Before I turned to leave, I said, "Be careful driving home, Sinclair."

"You too, Buchanan."

I glanced at Stevie's lips one more time and then started heading toward Mystic Bar's exit. Right before I reached it, I looked over my shoulder. The jovial group, which I greatly enjoyed being part of, had gone back to talking and laughing. Every person except for Stevie. She had her eyes on me while sipping on her second Hendricks and tonic with extra lime. The same way that I preferred mine.

7
#backgroundcheck

Stevie

"Okay, Brooke. What is Zac's story?" I asked her. She was driving me back to the D.A.'s office so I could pick up my car and go home.

"A complicated one. Why do you ask?"

"Between seeing him last Saturday at the running trail, officially meeting him tonight, talking with him, drinking and eating with him, reading his body language, picking up on the vibe that he was giving off, and also listening to his conversations with others—well, things aren't adding up. Not to me anyway. Although Zac is certainly a lot of fun to be around, his spirit is restless and conflicted about something. I sensed a major tug-of-war going on inside that man."

"So that's the reason you couldn't take your eyes off him! You were trying to figure out his story just like he was trying to figure out yours, and that's the reason why he couldn't take his eyes off you. That and also his obvious attraction to you. Would your attraction to him happen to be another reason why you kept staring at him?" Brooke cut her eyes over at me and grinned.

"I was just trying to make sense of what wasn't adding up about him."

35

"So you're not attracted to Zac? Did I really just read every-thing wrong back there at Mystic Bar?"

I sighed out a smile. "I cannot deny that Zac is a very attractive man, because he is. I'm divorced, Brooke. Not dead."

She chuckled. "I know you're not. I'm just teasing you about all of this."

"Seriously though... I was mainly trying to figure out what Zac's deal was. I hope I didn't come across as rude with the way that I kept watching him."

"You both came across as being innocently curious about each other. And about Zac's story? I'll tell you exactly why his spirit is restless and also what he's conflicted about, if you're really ready to hear it."

"Why wouldn't I be?"

"You're about to find out."

"I'm listening."

"As you know, Zac is married and has a little boy."

"Yes, Malcolm. I remember Zac mentioning his name."

"Right. Well, long story short—Zac's wife, Avery, is a thunder-cunt from hell."

I jerked my head back. "What?"

"You heard me. There's no nice way to describe her. She's a raging alcoholic and she's also a narcissist. I don't throw that term around loosely, either, because it's so overused nowadays. But Avery is a narcissist and she's a mean one too."

"Okay."

"She's volatile, especially when she's drinking, and she takes out her anger on Zac. Did you happen to notice the scratch on his face?"

"Yes, I did. After finding out that he had a son, I just thought maybe he and Malcolm had been play-wrestling like fathers and sons do."

"No. That scratch came from Avery."

"How long have incidents like that been happening be-tween them?"

"Most of their marriage."

"And how long have they been married?"

"Ten years."

"Same as I was. I cannot imagine living with such an awful person as Zac is. And what about Malcolm? Has Avery ever harmed him?"

"No, or Zac would've killed her. Malcolm is Zac's entire world. His pride and joy."

"Why doesn't Zac just get a divorce?"

"He doesn't wanna split custody of Malcolm with Avery. He's told me that he'll never be a part-time father no matter how bad things get at home."

"You and Zac seem to be really close. You know so much about him."

"We are really close, Stevie. He's like another son to me."

"Does anyone else know about Zac's home life?"

"You mean from our team?"

"Yes."

"I'm sure they know some of Zac's story through the legal community's grapevine, but I've never discussed it with any of them."

"Then why are you discussing it with me?"

"For some reason, I felt like you needed to know about it. Don't ask me why I felt that way because I can't explain why."

"I understand that kind of feeling, and I appreciate you being open with me about Zac. Tell me about Bash, though."

"What do you wanna know?"

"He and Zac are best friends, right?"

"Yes."

"And Bash is single?"

"He is."

"Has he ever been married?"

Brooke cut her eyes over at me again. "No. He did have a partner for several years, though."

"Gotcha."

"And about Bash... He and I both feel so sorry for Zac, and we also have the greatest respect for him."

"So you two have discussed Zac's home life."

"We have. Bash is like my third son. I would adopt him *and* Zac if they'd let me," Brooke chuckled. Her motherly affection toward them was sincere and heart-warming.

"They'd probably let you if you asked them."

"They both have great moms already. I just miss having my son around is what my deal is, and Zac and Bash help to fill that void."

"How long has your son been in Germany?"

"Three years. He's made four trips home, but it's not enough for this momma bear."

"I'm so sorry."

"That's the military for you, but my son loves it so I'm happy for him."

"Zac and Bash aren't the only ones who have great moms."

Brooke smiled at me. "Thank you for that."

We both grew quiet for about a minute, and then I brought up Zac again. I told Brooke how blown away I was by everything she'd shared about him and his wife.

"It's a lot to take in, Stevie," she said.

"What you told me this morning about the attorney side of Zac combined with my personal impression of him from at the bar... Well, I would've never guessed he's dealing with so much bullshit behind the scenes. Looking in from the outside, he appears to have his life together."

"He's holding it together in the best way he knows how."

"Now that I know his background, I understand what I was sensing about him. But tell me this. Is a scratched-up face the worst that Avery has done to him?"

"No. She's done a whole lot worse than that."

"Such as?"

"She's clawed up his neck, chest, arms, and his hands. I've also seen bruises on Zac. The very worst thing that happened was when Avery threw a glass of vodka and orange juice at him. It hit his left ear when he turned his head and shattered. Zac had to go to the hospital to get stitches in the deep gash it left."

"Holy shit, that is insane. And knowing that Zac has had scratches on his hands and arms tells me that he's literally had to fight off Avery to defend himself."

"Exactly."

"Has he ever hit her back, pushed her, or anything that you know of?"

Brooke had started shaking her head no before I finished asking my question.

"Zac has never laid a hand on Avery, and he won't, because he isn't that type of man. If he did knock the hell out of her—which I think she deserves—there would be legal consequences for Zac. He doesn't need that, and he doesn't want Malcolm to ever be told that his father hit his mother. Your new defense attorney friend is so far from being a violent man. Avery has tried baiting him into becoming violent toward her so many times but it's never worked. She's insulted him, cussed, yelled, and physically attacked Zac but he just deals with it."

"Has Malcolm ever witnessed any of those incidents?"

"He has, but he's so young that he doesn't understand them. They just scare him and he cries. Zac tries really hard to shield Malcolm from everything. Several times, he's loaded up Malcolm into his car and the two of them drive around for a while or they go stay with Zac's parents. It's all to give Avery time to sober up and calm down."

"Brooke, have the police ever been called in to handle her?"

"Yes, but not by Zac. His neighbors have called the police to intervene on three different occasions."

"So the neighbors must've heard the arguing and fighting going on inside Zac's house."

"They have, and they've also heard and witnessed it happening outside his house. Avery likes playing the victim in front of everyone, but we all know better. Even the police do."

"What I'm about to ask you may seem like it's coming out of left field, but there's a reason behind my asking it."

"Go ahead."

"Considering how horrible Zac's marriage is and how long it's been that way, do you think he's ever stepped outside of it and had an affair?"

"No, Zac has been true to Avery. I would understand, though, if he chose not to be."

I paused for several seconds while thinking about his heart-breaking situation and then started telling Brooke more details about the infidelity in my marriage.

"When I found out about my ex-husband's affair, I was so hurt. The sense of betrayal that I initially felt was devastating, but after my anger subsided, I took a hard look at my marriage. I examined the way that Graham—that's my ex's name—and I had been living for some time, and finally accepted my role in pushing him into someone else's arms since I'd pretty much pushed him completely away from me. I'm not excusing him for his affair, but what I am saying is that it's understandable. And like you, I would also understand if Zac had an affair. He's gotta be lonely."

"He is lonely, but he's not open to having an affair because he feels like it'd cost him everything if Avery found out about it. He believes she'd file for divorce and also split custody of Malcolm. Becoming a part-time father is Zac's worst nightmare."

"Brooke, you know as well as I do that the courts have changed their view of marriage, affairs, divorce, and parental rights. To me, Zac already has plenty of ammunition to legally go up against Avery and quite possibly get full custody of Malcolm. The well-being and safety of children are the main concerns of the court system. Not a good man turning to someone outside his marriage for companionship because his wife is a damn psycho."

"I've told Zac the very same thing but he just isn't willing to roll the dice. He will not gamble on his son."

I sighed and shook my head. "It's such a sad, sad deal."

"I know. And here's one more sad thing about it: Zac and Avery have been sleeping in separate bedrooms for over four years now. That happened months before Malcolm was born, and it was Avery who made the decision to sleep apart from Zac."

"Why did she wanna do that?"

"Two reasons. She decided she wasn't attracted to him anymore and she also blamed him for getting her pregnant, as if she wasn't a willing participant in the occasional sex that they were still having at the time."

"Okay, I do not understand how her attraction to Zac just suddenly died and I have to laugh about her blaming him for her pregnancy. Good grief."

"I know, it's ridiculous."

"To me, it sounds like she was looking for an excuse to pull away from him."

"She looks for any excuse to mess with his head and his heart. It's all about control for her. Tear a person down, weaken them and then you've got them right where you want them."

"A true narcissist's M.O."

Brooke nodded in agreement. "You've got that right."

"So did Avery *not* want to have children? Because that's the impression that I'm getting."

"No, she didn't."

"Like ever?"

"No, but she didn't tell Zac that until after they were married. The whole time they dated and also after they became engaged, she really talked up wanting to have a family one day, but she didn't mean it. She just wanted Zac and what he could financially provide for her. He really wanted to have children, though."

"Why do you think he stayed married to Avery after finding out everything was a ruse? He could've so easily left the marriage, and with little complication, since there were no children at the time."

"The number one reason is Zac fell in love with the Avery that he initially met. He told me that she was wonderful and so loving at that time. After she revealed her true colors, Zac kept hoping the *old* Avery would return. That's who he so desperately wanted to believe she was at heart, but she wasn't. The second reason he stays in the marriage is because of the vows that he took. He meant them for better and for worse."

"I simply cannot fathom someone putting on such an act and playing such a cruel emotional game like Avery has done and must still be doing with Zac."

"Oh, she's still doing it for sure. I'll tell you what tops the long list of cruel things that she's done."

"What?"

"On the day that Zac and Avery brought Malcolm home from the hospital, she told Zac that she didn't want anything to do with Malcolm. Not even after carrying him all those months and feeling his movements. It didn't change a thing for her. Zac pleaded with Avery to give motherhood a chance and try to bond with their beautiful new son. She reluctantly agreed but only put forth minimal effort—until family and friends came over to see Malcolm. Whenever they did, Avery acted like mother-of-the-year in the way that she tended to Malcolm and talked about him in front of everybody. As soon as the company left, though, she'd hand Malcolm back to Zac or put him back in his baby bed."

"Hearing all of this is nauseating."

"Yes, it is but I want you to know one positive and very touching thing. Something that's gonna make you give Zac a five-star rating as a father."

"Okay."

"He is who cared for Malcolm after he was born. Zac took six weeks off from work to stay at home with his son. He got up with him during all hours of the day and night to feed him, change his diaper, bathe him, and just hold and rock him, all while Avery kept her lazy ass in bed. Zac's love, care, and concern for Malcolm have never wavered, either."

"Yep, a five-star rating for him for sure. But who took care of Malcolm after Zac went back to work?"

"Zac's parents did and still do. Zac takes Malcolm to their house each morning before he goes to work."

"I can only imagine how his parents feel about Avery in all of this."

"Disgusted with her is how they feel, but they've never let their personal feelings about her get in the way of doing all they can for Zac *and* Malcolm."

Brooke and I both grew quiet again as she continued driving through the maze of Dallas streets. Although neither of us was making a sound, my boss's mind was just as loud as mine was as we mulled over Zac's dark reality.

"Back to Zac and Avery sleeping in separate bedrooms..." she said, breaking the deafening silence. "Obviously, his sex life has been non-existent but I don't believe Avery's has been."

"What makes you say that?"

"Because she makes frequent trips to see her family and friends in Lubbock and whenever she's there, she blows up her Instagram and Facebook pages with pictures of herself shopping, eating out, and partying with all of them. And in that group, there's this tall dark-haired guy who's always standing beside her, smiling just as big as she is. My guess is he's someone that Avery has known for a long time. The thunder cunt's first love maybe. The one that got the hell away from her as fast as he could way back then but has since forgotten why he did," Brooke chuckled.

"Do you know if Zac is aware of that possible situation?"

"I doubt it since he's not on any social media platforms."

"And you've never mentioned the pictures to him?"

"No, I haven't, because he's already dealing with enough, day in and day out. If it ever becomes necessary, though, I will not only tell him about the pictures but I'll also give him the thick file of them that I have. It's full of copies of those pictures plus screenshots that I've taken of red flag posts that Avery has made along with her family and friends' comments. There are dozens of back-and-forth comments between Avery and that guy that are borderline inappropriate."

"You've really done your investigative work on her."

43

"I enjoy investigating people like her and then watching the effect of how they treat others boomerang back around to them. It's coming for Avery Buchanan one day. Wait and see."

"Brooke, what do you think Zac would do if he found out that she was having an affair?"

"Nothing."

"Nothing?"

"That's right. Because if he did something like filing for divorce, then he'd be in the very position that he doesn't wanna be in concerning sharing custody of Malcolm with her."

"I just see an affair on her part as being even more ammunition for Zac to use against her in court *and* not have to be a part-time father. I think he'd win."

"Oh, I agree."

"I wonder what it's gonna take for him to finally get enough of Avery and take that chance in court. I would've done it a long time ago."

"Stevie, you've dealt with an affair in a marriage but you've never had a child involved in the mix. It complicates matters so much more. Unless you've been there, you can't understand what it's like, or know what you'd do, until you're faced with a situation like that."

"You're right about me never having had a child involved in a situation like that—but I have had a child. He died from SIDS when he was two months old."

"Oh my God," Brooke said, reaching over and squeezing my hand. "I am so very sorry that happened."

"I'm sorry it happened too."

"How long ago did you lose him?"

"Graham and I lost him four years ago. A strangely coincidental thing about my little boy and Zac's is that I also named my son Malcolm. It's a strong, Scottish first name and that's why I chose it."

"That's why Zac chose it for his son, too."

8
#boundaries

Stevie

"I wanted to give you a quick call to let you know I'm about to get on the road and head your way!" my dad said.

"Sounds great! Be very careful and I'll see you around seven."

"Okay. I love you."

"Love you too."

My wonderful dad, Steven Sinclair, was driving up from Austin today to see me and he was going to spend the night. It was Friday afternoon and my second full week at my new job was coming to a close in less than an hour.

The court case that I was supposed to go up against Zac on had been rescheduled due to Zac's client having some kind of health issue that landed him in the hospital the day before court. Conveniently. I'd witnessed other defendants pulling stunts like that to get out of having to face the karma of their illegal actions. Zac's client had bought himself some time, but it wasn't going to change one thing about the case. The asshole was still going to have to face the music for the abuse that he did to his little boy. I was determined to make it happen.

Earlier today, Brooke invited me to join her and my teammates at Mystic Bar after work again. Because of my plans with my dad, I had to turn down her invitation, which she completely understood. I would've gone, though, if I didn't already have plans. I very much enjoyed the new group of people around me, which included Zac and his friend Bash. If I had to guess, both of them were going to be at the bar this evening—Zac sipping on another Hendricks and tonic and possibly enjoying another Mystic burger and curly fries while Bash sucked down the frozen margaritas and munched on a plate of beef fajita nachos.

Zac and Bash were funny together and appeared to have been best friends for a long time. While Zac was clearly over six feet tall, with a slender yet muscular build and lighter features, Bash was maybe five feet ten, stocky, and had wavy brown hair, plus brown puppy dog eyes. He was so cute and Zac was—well, attractive was an understatement. I hadn't seen either man since I'd met them last Friday. I'd thought I might run into at least one of them while taking care of my other cases at the courthouse this week, but that didn't happen. I'd also thought I might see Zac at the running trail since I'd been out there three different times. That didn't happen either, though.

I hadn't been able to get my mind off everything that Brooke had told me about him and his home life with his wife, Avery, and little boy, Malcolm. Like Brooke and Bash, I felt sorry for Zac and I also respected him. Tremendously. I understood the catch-22 that he was caught up in and it was a hell of a thing for him to have to shoulder.

I needed to stop by Whole Foods after work to pick up some groceries for dinner with my dad this evening. I planned to cook some salmon fillets, make a salad, and bake some garlic bread. Dessert was going to be my dad's favorite: key lime pie. I was so excited about him coming to see me this soon. I'd thought it was going to be at least a month. Although he and I regularly talked on the phone and texted each other, it just wasn't the same as being able to see his face and hug his neck.

At Whole Foods, I found everything that I needed to make dinner and dessert, and as I was walking up to one of the checkout lines, I found something that I didn't need but wanted. I couldn't resist getting them because they reminded me of my mom. She loved all kinds of flowers, but Galaxy orchids were her favorite and the bouquet that I was holding had them. The orchids' blue-purple color was so pretty and went perfectly with the white Calla lilies.

I was walking across the parking lot when I heard someone call out my name. I looked to my left and as soon as I saw who it was, I smiled.

"Hey, Zac! How are you?" I said as he was approaching me.

He didn't have on a tailored suit, white-collared shirt, tie or dress shoes like he did last Friday at Mystic Bar. Today, he was wearing something similar to what I'd seen him wearing on the running trail that first time: a tank top, shorts, and Asics running shoes. Also like before, he had earbuds but this time they were hanging loose around his neck.

"I'm doing well. How about yourself?" he asked, reaching out his hand to shake mine.

"I'm doing well too. Did you get off work early?"

"Yes, I worked for only half a day. Met with some new clients. No court appearances, though."

"That explains why you're wearing your running attire instead of your professional attire at..."

I started to check my cellphone for the time and realized Zac's long, warm fingers were still wrapped around my hand and my fingers were still wrapped around his hand. Zac also realized what we were doing, and then we slowly let go of each other. The shy smile on his face mirrored mine and so did the quiet deep breath that he took. We'd done it again. Just like when we first met, we immediately got caught up in our conversation and didn't realize we were still touching.

I cleared my throat and then pulled my cellphone out of my pocket to see what time it was. "Um, five-forty in the afternoon," I said, looking back up at Zac.

"Yeah, I just finished taking a run. It felt great too. Always a stress reliever."

"It certainly is."

I pushed the button on my key fob to open the hatch on the back of my car and then Zac asked me if I had weekend plans.

"Yes. Actually, unexpected plans. My dad surprised me by calling me early this morning and asking if I wouldn't mind him driving up from Austin to come to see me. He's on his way here as you and I speak, and it's gonna be the first time I've seen him since I moved to Dallas. I'm really excited."

"Sounds like you're gonna have a great weekend then."

"Half a great weekend. My dad is staying with me for tonight only. He has to go back home tomorrow so he can attend church on Sunday morning."

"He won't miss a sermon to spend a full weekend with his daughter?"

"He can't because he's the pastor of the Methodist church that he goes to."

Zac's eyebrows shot up. "Oh! I understand now."

I glanced at the mostly healed scratch on his face and then quickly looked over his neck, arms, and hands. There were no fresh marks from Avery. At least not any that I could see. For all I knew though, there could've been some underneath Zac's clothes.

"Do you have weekend plans?" I asked.

"I do. I'm taking my son to the zoo in the morning. He loves going there and is like a magnet for all the animals. It's like he has his own language with them and it's the funniest thing to watch, especially at the petting zoo."

"I've always been like that with animals too. They're drawn to me, I'm drawn to them, and yes—we do speak our own language. My parents were always taking me to the zoo when I was little and I'd just go play with my furry friends there."

"When was the last time you went to a zoo?"

"I was around eleven or twelve."

"Why so long ago?"

I shrugged. "Outgrew going, I guess."

"Nah! We're never too old to go to a zoo."

I smiled at Zac. He was clutching the side of my buggy with his hands now and his blue eyes were sparkling. They reminded me of the sky.

"You really should check out the Dallas Zoo sometime. It's nice," Zac went on to tell me.

"I may just do that."

I picked up a couple of my grocery bags and started loading them into my car. Without hesitation, Zac began helping me with the rest.

"So do you have Sunday plans?" I asked. "Going to church with the family?"

"No, I'm not a churchgoer any longer, and for reasons that I won't waste your time or my breath listing. My plan on Sunday is to get all the yard work done at my house. Will you be attending one of the many Methodist churches around here? You can literally take your pick."

"Like you, I'm not a churchgoer any longer either."

"A pastor's daughter who doesn't go to church. Do you mind my asking how your dad takes that?"

"He understands because he knows all about the downside of organized religion and how it, as well as some of its members, can leave a bitter taste in someone's mouth—as it has mine."

"Some of its members? You mean the hypocrites?"

I sighed. "Yeah. It seems you've had dealings with them too."

"I have—and I got tired of dealing with them. I got tired of listening to their judgments of any and everybody when they've committed their own wrongdoings and continue committing them."

"I got tired of the same thing. The icing on the cake for me was finding out the assistant pastor at my dad's church was abusing his wife. While at the salon that I used to go to in Austin, she came in and sat down in the chair next to me. Of course we recognized each other and started talking and the longer we talked, the more heart-to-heart our conversation became. Before I knew it, Cathy—that's her name—had broken down crying and told me all about the hell that she was living in. It finally made sense to me why she was so meek whenever I saw her at church and also why she would so often quietly cry to herself while sitting alone in one of the pews, listening to her husband deliver his sermon. My dad allowed him one Sunday a month to hone his preaching skills."

Zac huffed in obvious disgust. "Yeah, that would've done it for me too. I would've said something to the guy, though, or to your dad."

"I did. To both. I confronted the assistant pastor about everything and will never forget how red-faced he got. I told him that I was going to my dad about what I knew and I also told him that if I found out he'd laid another hand on his wife or spoken another cruel word to her, then I was going to the authorities. The man was dismissed from the Methodist Conference a week later."

"Do you know what happened to him and his wife afterward?"

"They got divorced and Cathy happily moved on with her life. We still keep in touch and she's remarried with three beautiful kids now."

"Good for her. I like happy endings."

"So do I."

Zac and I paused our conversation and just stared into each other's eyes. And the longer we did, the faster my heart beat and the deeper the breaths I was having to take. Zac swallowed hard and then turned his attention to my bouquet of flowers. They were the only thing left in my buggy.

"Speaking of happiness..." he said, picking them up. "These look like some really happy flowers to me."

"I think they look that way too. And by the way, these were my mom's favorite," I said, pointing at one of the Galaxy orchids.

"*Were* her favorite?"

"Yes. She passed away last year from breast cancer."

Zac's jaw dropped. "My God, Stevie. You have been through so much in the last year and I am so sorry."

"It's just life but it's all good again now. My moving here to Dallas was a wise choice."

"Well, I for one am glad that you're here, and I'm glad that life is good for you again."

"Thank you."

Zac smiled and handed me the bouquet.

"I won't take up any more of your time. I'm sure you need to get home so you can get ready for your dad's arrival," he said, glancing down at my mouth. Twice. The second time, it was a bit more than a glance. It made me wonder if there was something on my lips that shouldn't be there, so I reached up and lightly touched them with my fingertips.

"Okay, Zac, what's on my lips? You keep looking at them but I can't feel anything."

He smiled at me again and then shook his head. "There's nothing on your lips other than that sparkly lip gloss."

"Is that why you keep looking at them? Because of my lip gloss?"

"No. That's not why."

"Then what is it?"

"It's your lips."

"What about them?"

"Stevie, I already feel like I've spoken out of place here and I apologize if you feel that I have. We really don't need to be talking about your lips."

"Zac, seriously... Is there something wrong with the way they look?" I asked, touching them again. "I know they're full and maybe I shouldn't wear this kind of lip gloss on them. It just draws attention to them, doesn't it?"

He put his hands on his waist and looked down at the ground, grinning, then cut his eyes back up at me. "Nothing's wrong with the way your lips look. Nothing at all. And don't stop wearing that lip gloss because it looks really nice on you."

Another pause between us and another lingering look from Zac that filled my stomach with butterflies. *Again.* It happened when he and I first made eye contact on the running trail and it happened too many times to count when we were at Mystic Bar. It also happened to me each time I walked into the courthouse this week, thinking I might run into Zac, although I never did. And it happened to me today when I first looked across this parking lot and saw him after he called out my name.

"Thank you," I said quietly.

"You need to get going and so do I."

"Okay."

"Enjoy your time with your dad."

"I will. Enjoy your time with your little boy at the zoo tomorrow and also that yard work on Sunday."

"I will enjoy my time with Malcolm. But the yard work? Not so much."

"Do you have a big yard or something?"

"I do."

"Mine is medium-sized so it's not too much to keep up with. My swimming pool actually takes more maintenance, but it's worth it to me."

"I have a pool too, and mine is also worth the maintenance. I enjoy the water."

I looked over Zac's unshaven face while debating whether or not to ask him the question that had just popped into my mind. I wasn't sure how he'd take it but decided to ask him anyway.

"What would your sign happen to be?"

"My sign?"

"Yes. Your zodiac sign."

"Oh, I'm a Taurus."

"You're an earth sign and the only sign in the zodiac that has the ability to touch another without using your hands. You use your eyes."

"I do?"

"Yes—you do."

"That's interesting. I had no idea."

"Another thing that's interesting about a Taurus is they're one of the most sensual signs. Water must feel that way to you. Sensual, soothing, calming and the like."

The corners of Zac's mouth curled up. "It does feel that way to me."

"Same here."

"Since you asked me what my sign is, you've gotta tell me what yours is."

"I'm a Pisces."

"A water sign."

"Yes."

"So where does your sign land on the sensual scale?"

"According to astrologers, people who are born under the sign of Pisces are the most sensual *and* passionate."

Zac glanced down at my lips again. "I see. Well, I will say that with you being a water sign, and the most sensual and passionate of the zodiac, it makes total sense for you to have a swimming pool and to also love the ocean as much as you do."

Right then, Zac steered away from talking about the kind of sensuality and passion we both knew I was referring to. Yes, I was extremely passionate about my love for the ocean, and like Zac, water felt sensual to me. Whether it was trickling over my skin or I was completely immersed in it, it always felt like an aquatic heaven.

When it came to sensuality and passion in the sexual sense—the kind that I'd been talking to Zac about—I knew exactly how I used to be. It'd been a long time since that part of me had been ignited. A long time until now.

Standing here and looking up at this tall and extremely handsome man in his running attire, sweat shimmering on his tan skin, about a three-day scruff on his face, sparkling sky-blue eyes, and a bright white smile... Well, I could feel a deep stirring going on inside my body. It was a stirring that was wrong for me to be feeling and I was well aware of that fact. I couldn't help myself, though. This illicit arousal that I was experiencing somehow felt invigorating to me, and all I wanted was to have this one little, sinful taste of it because I'd never tasted anything like it before in my life.

"My conversation with Bash last Friday," I finally said.

"Yes. The back-and-forth bantering between you and him about the best beach destinations was fun to listen to *and* watch."

"I like Bash. How long have you been friends with him?"

"Since law school."

"Where'd you go to law school?"

"Texas Tech. What about you?"

"U.T. Austin."

The words between us stopped yet again and we just stared at each other. Although Zac had mentioned that we both needed to get going, we'd fallen right back into talking to each other without any hesitation or his mentioning again that we needed to go our separate ways. When my cellphone started ringing, Zac and I both jumped and then I checked to see who was calling me.

"I'm sorry but I need to take this," I said, looking up from my phone. "It's my old boss at the Austin D.A.'s office."

"You take that call and I'll see you later, Sinclair."

I smiled at hearing Zac call me by my last name again and said, "See you later, Buchanan," to see what his reaction would be at hearing me do the same to him. He smiled so big that his eyes squinted and crinkled around the corners and a cute little dimple appeared on his right cheek. I hadn't noticed it until now and something about it made me feel like reaching out and touching it with my fingertip. I didn't, though. I just admired it along with everything else about Zac.

After glancing down at my lips one more time, he stepped around me and started heading toward the entrance of Whole Foods. I answered Melissa's call by quickly telling her that I'd call her right back and after she said okay, I hung up and looked back in Zac's direction.

"Hey, Buchanan!" I called out.

He stopped walking and then turned around to face me. "Yeah?"

"This that you've got going on..." I swirled my finger around my mouth, along my jawline, and then pointed at Zac. "It looks really nice on you. Don't shave it off."

Another huge smile from him, a nod, a thank you, and then he took off walking again across the busy parking lot. I carefully laid the bouquet of flowers in the back of my car and as soon as I closed the hatch, I looked back in Zac's direction again. He was looking over his shoulder at me. No smile from him this time and no smile from me either. Just another curious look that we shared. A look that filled my stomach with butterflies all over again. When Zac disappeared through the entrance of the store, I got inside my car and cranked it, then called Melissa back.

"Hey there," she answered.

"Hey! How are you?"

"I'm fine. Just calling to check on you again. I've been wondering how your second week has been."

"It's been good. I really do like living and working in Dallas."

"I'm relieved to hear you say that."

"Listen, I apologize if I came across as abrupt when I answered your call a few minutes ago. I was a little distracted at that moment."

"You didn't come across as abrupt at all. But what were you distracted by?"

I closed my eyes and shook my head at myself. "Chris Hemsworth's doppelgänger."

"What a yummy distraction to have."

"He is yummy and he's also married. Evidenced by the shiny gold band on his left ring finger."

"Girl, run in the opposite direction of that married man and run fast!" Melissa chuckled.

"No need for me to run. I just enjoy being around him because he is so handsome and kind and engaging."

"Oh, I didn't realize you were talking about someone that you actually knew. I thought you spotted a good-looking man just now, wherever you are. And where are you, by the way?"

"Sitting in my car in the Whole Foods parking lot where that *someone*, that I met last Friday, just left my company."

"He was with you when I called?"

"Yes, but he's inside the store now. We happened to run into each other when I was walking out to my car with my groceries."

"So tell me a little more about Chris Hemsworth's doppelgänger."

"Well, he's a local defense attorney who Brooke accepted into her circle because of how great of a person he is—and he really is."

"What's his name?"

"Zac Buchanan."

"Brooke has mentioned him to me many times. Zac is like a son to her."

"She told me that too."

"Did you meet him at court?"

I half-laughed. "No, we met at a bar."

"What?"

"Last Friday, Brooke invited me to join her and my new teammates for drinks at a bar after work. Zac was standing by our table and talking to Brooke when I came back from using the restroom and that's when he and I met. It wasn't the first time that I'd seen him, though."

"When was the first time?"

"The Saturday before on a running trail that isn't very far from my house."

"After you and Zac met, did you mention that you saw him on the trail?"

"I did, and he said he remembered seeing me. We talked about running and several other things, and we were both so surprised by how much we have in common."

"Other than running, what else is there?"

"Like me, Zac is a huge fan of Hendricks gin. We're also both of Scottish descent and share the same deep reverence for our ancestry. He also has a four-year-old little boy named Malcolm, believe it or not."

"Wow on all of that, but especially his son's name and age. I'm sure that really tugged at your heartstrings. It tugs at mine."

"Yeah, it did. Still does. I didn't tell Zac about my Malcolm, though, because it wasn't the right time."

"I understand," Melissa said. Then I heard her sigh.

"What is it?"

"Stevie, my dear friend and Joan of Arc, whom I greatly miss being here... Going by everything that you just told me and also the lightness that I hear in your voice, I can tell you're interested in Zac."

"I'm intrigued by him is what I am. He's such a refreshing soul to be around, but I'm well aware that he's romantically off-limits to me just like I am to him. Because of that gold band on his finger, it's more than safe for us to be around each other. Besides, you know me. I'm not the type of woman to pursue a married man and never will be. I'd be the hypocrite of the year if I did that after what I went through with Graham."

"I'm not worried about you in all of this. But who's to say Zac wouldn't try pursuing you? I have no doubt that he's as intrigued by you as you are by him."

"He may be, but we will only ever be friends. On top of that, Brooke and I had an in-depth talk about him after we left the bar and it is crystal clear to me that he is not the type of man to be unfaithful to his wife. Not even if his home life is miserable—and his is very miserable."

"Brooke has never directly said anything to me about it, but I've homed in on little comments that she's made about Zac's wife over the years. They made me wonder what Zac's marriage is really like behind the scenes."

"Well, it's volatile. His wife, Avery, is an alcoholic and when she starts drinking, she goes after Zac—cussing and yelling at him, clawing him up, hitting him, and throwing things at him.

According to Brooke, Zac either just tries to defend himself or he completely gets away from Avery. He's taken Malcolm and left his house before to drive around. He's gone over to his parents' house too, to give Avery time to sober up, simmer down, or whatever."

"That's really sad, and let me guess... Zac stays in that marriage because of his little boy, right?"

"Yes. He doesn't wanna have to split custody of him and be a part-time father."

Melissa sighed again. "Stevie, do me *and* yourself a favor."

"Okay."

"Be cautious of that entire situation."

"What makes you say that?"

"Your greatly respected desire to swoop in and help any and all who are caught up in a harmful environment. I'm not just talking about children, either. I've witnessed you help plenty of adults too. Remember?"

"I know."

"What I don't wanna see happen is you falling into a messy trap due to you trying to help Zac and his son. I can easily imagine you getting legally involved, but it's up to Zac to help himself and Malcolm. Not you."

"Yes, it is up to him, and I'm not falling into any trap. Zac doesn't even know I'm aware of his home life. Melissa, believe me when I tell you that I'm very clear-minded about what's happening here and I know where all the boundary lines are."

"But you see, it's the boundary lines in that big ol' heart of yours that I worry about. It's obvious to me that it wouldn't take much for them to blur—not only because of sweet little Malcolm Buchanan but also his handsome, kind, and engaging father with whom you happen to have a lot in common. And you're right—he could pass for Chris Hemsworth. Easily. I Googled him while we've been talking."

"What picture did you see?"

"The one on his website."

"I haven't seen it because I didn't even know he had a website. All of that aside, I assure you that I'm in complete control of what's going on here so don't worry about me. I'm fine and I appreciate your concern. I know it's coming from a place of love and I love you for it," I said.

"I love you too. I just know everything that you've been through over the past four years and there are things about this scenario with Zac that could easily and understandably weave their way into your heart even more than they already have. I don't wanna see you get hurt again is all."

"I'm not. My sword and shield are ready."

9
#eyeofthebeholder
Stevie

I had just saved the picture of Zac from his website to my cell-phone when I heard my doorbell ring. I knew it was my dad and could hardly wait to see his face, so I tossed my phone onto the kitchen counter and then ran to open the front door.

"Hey!" I said, grabbing my dad and hugging him so tight. He chuckled and wrapped his arms around me.

"Hello, daughter of mine! It is so good to see you," he said, kissing me on the cheek. "Look at you."

"What about me?"

"You're glowing—your eyes, your skin. You look really happy, Stevie."

I smiled up at him. "I am. You're here."

After giving my dad the grand tour of my new home and backyard, I began setting the dining room table.

"What can I do to help?" he asked.

"Nothing. I've got it covered."

"Well, I appreciate you having me stay here and cooking dinner."

"Of course!"

"Eating a homecooked meal is gonna be great. I cook for myself but it's just not the same."

"I know what you mean. I cook full meals for myself maybe twice a week; otherwise, I just graze on different things. Tortilla wraps, mixed nuts, cheese, fruit, raw vegetables."

"Nutritionists say that's better for us anyway. It's supposed to keep our blood sugar level even."

I finished placing the silverware onto the napkins and then walked up to my dad. "I have a bottle of Pinot Grigio in the fridge if you'd like to have a glass with dinner."

"Are you gonna have a gin and tonic?"

"After we eat."

"Then I'll wait. It'll be a real treat to have some wine. It's been a good while."

"Why has it been a good while? You enjoy drinking it."

My dad teetered his head back and forth. "It's the pastor in me."

"You're a Methodist pastor and drinking in moderation is accepted by the Methodist Conference. Like I need to remind you of that, as well as the fact that Jesus drank wine. He also turned water into wine at a wedding and the party was on!" I chuckled.

"Oh, I know. But remember, I was a Baptist preacher before switching sides, and drinking is not accepted by that Conference. Old habits die hard."

"You know what?"

"What?"

"We're gonna bury that old Baptist habit of yours once and for all. Right now. You're gonna have a glass of wine with dinner and also one after we eat and maybe even another."

My dad side-eyed me and grinned. "Okay. But only if you drink with me."

"Deal. Besides, you coming here to see me is a special occasion, so let's celebrate."

"Yes, let's."

I walked into my kitchen and got the bottle of Pinot Grigio out of the fridge, then popped the cork and poured my dad a glass of the dry white wine. Not the regular serving of five ounces. A serving that nearly reached the rim. When I handed the glass to my dad, he shook his head at me and started giggling. Then he asked me about my drink.

"I'm about to go make mine, but you go ahead and start enjoying yours," I said.

"I believe I will. Thank you."

"You're very welcome, Dad."

As soon as we sat down at my dining room table to eat, my dad held out his hand for me to take. Then he lowered his head, closed his eyes, and began blessing our meal with a prayer. I kept my eyes open and watched him—and I smiled to myself. When I was a little girl, I used to peek at my dad like this whenever he prayed at home or at church. Even back then, I saw and also sensed the sincerity in every word that he spoke to God, and it always warmed my heart so much. Just like now.

By about midway through our meal, we had talked even more in-depth about my new job, colleagues, and also the running trail that I'd been going to, when my dad asked me how I was doing in my healing process since my divorce.

"I would say that I'm about eighty percent along. I wish I was a hundred percent over everything but I'm just not. Memories of Graham and me keep coming up out of nowhere and they never fail to set me back," I said.

"That's a normal part of the healing process. You're grieving your personal loss while also learning to let go. Stevie, do you ever find yourself missing Graham?"

"I miss the old him, just like I'm sure there are days when he probably misses the old me. The first six years of our marriage were so wonderful and we were so in love, but everything went downhill after we lost Malcolm. It went downhill quickly, too."

"You and Graham did the best you could to fight your way through that storm. Your mother and I both witnessed it, along with Graham's family and all your friends."

"We were so ill-equipped to fight our way through it."

"No one's well-equipped to handle the loss of their child. Nothing can ever prepare you for it. Not even if you saw it coming."

I set down my fork and then looked back over at my dad.

"Malcolm is who I really miss. I dream about him so often. I've even dreamt that I was carrying him again," I said, rubbing my hand across my abdomen. "On my first night here in this house, I dreamt about him having lived and what he'd look like now. He was such a beautiful baby, and the four-year-old version of him that I saw in my dream was just as beautiful. Cotton-white hair, the brightest blue eyes, a little round nose, and apple cheeks with a dimple in the right one. Perfect. And the strangest thing about that dream was Malcolm talked to me in it. I clearly heard his sweet angelic voice."

"What did he say to you?"

I wiped away the tear that was rolling down my cheek. "Mommy, I love you and I'm still here."

My dad reached over and rubbed my shoulder to comfort me.

"When he said that," I continued, "I remember thinking how he spoke older than a four-year-old would have."

"Malcolm's soul may be old, like his grandpa's here, and that's what came through when he talked to you."

"Dad, do you *really* believe someone who has died can visit us? I know we've talked about Mom doing that, but sometimes I wonder if it's all in my head. I wonder if I'm just so desperately wanting to see Mom again, and Malcolm, that my mind manifests them whenever I'm asleep. It's not really them in my dreams, though. It's just me missing them, combined with my imagination, that's made an image of them appear."

"Yes, I really believe the soul of a loved one has the capability to visit us. It's human nature, though, to rationalize away supernatural occurrences—which includes vivid dreams like what you've had, things such as my smelling your mom's perfume in the air, and also items being moved from where I *know* I put them. The thing about the spiritual realm is that our logical minds can't make sense of it. Science can't prove or disprove it. There are no definitive answers and I believe that's by God's design. What we have to do is close the door on that part of our brain that's hellbent on making sense of something that it will never be able to make sense of. Then we have to fully open the door to our soul's intuition, listen to what it's telling us—and trust it."

"Right now, mine is telling me that Mom's soul really has come to see me in my dreams, and so has my precious son's."

My dad smiled and then nodded. "And my intuition is telling me that you are correct."

I searched his blue-gray eyes and thought to myself how much my mom would've loved to have heard everything that he'd just said to me. He spoke like she used to about the spiritual realm and listening to our intuition. Not once, though, had he ever addressed those topics from his church pulpit, because they were thought to be New Age, too out there, too controversial, and too dangerous by the Christian body.

It had always been a fine line that my dad walked being a pastor who not only believed in the supernatural but was also married to a woman who very much did. I could so clearly remember all the stories that my mom shared with me about the beliefs and practices of our ancestors. She said their religion was the "Old Religion" which honored the spiritual realm, and another facet of it was living in tune with nature, the seasons, and the moon cycle. My mom used to privately laugh at people who believed doing all of that was something new when it was actually so ancient.

"I'm curious about something," I said to my dad.

"What are you curious about?"

"If you noticed what's sitting on the nightstand next to my bed."

"I did notice it, and I think Malcolm's urn is exactly where it should be. Close to his mother when she's resting at night."

"Since it's just me now, I felt comfortable setting it out in the open instead of having it put up in my closet like at my old house."

"I know Graham didn't like seeing it."

"No, he didn't. Not at all. It has never bothered me, though, because it's all that I have left of Malcolm."

My dad rubbed my shoulder again and then we went back to eating our dinner. When we were done, I surprised him by pulling the key lime pie out of the fridge.

"Is that what I think it is?"

I chuckled. "Yes."

"Given the chance, I'll eat that whole thing, daughter."

"Let me have one slice of it and the rest is yours."

'No, but I will take a large slice, please."

"And what hasn't been eaten by tomorrow, you're taking home with you."

"Deal."

After slicing two large portions of the pie and putting them onto dessert plates, I sat back down at the dining room table with my dad and we began savoring the tart sweet treat. That and also another glass of Pinot Grigio for him and another Hendricks and tonic for me. When we were done eating, I brought up something that I was compelled to talk about because my dad and I had discussed Malcolm.

"I know it's really soon for me to say what I'm about to say to you, considering how little time has passed since my marriage with Graham ended, but I have to say what's on my heart."

"By all means, Stevie. What is it?"

"I've wondered if I'm ever gonna get another shot at marriage and having a child. I wanted so much to be a wife and a mother. I wanted a sweet little family of my own and still do."

"I know you do and yes, you'll get another shot at marriage and having a child. You forget how young you are and how many years of living are ahead of you."

"Some days, I feel so much older than thirty, though."

"Like my age?" My dad chuckled and then so did I.

"You know what I mean."

"Yes, I do."

"You've always been young at heart, Dad, and I'm so glad to see you haven't lost that."

"Right after your mom and I met each other, she told me that I had an old soul but a young heart. I know it was her, though, that made and kept me young at heart all those years that we had together. Everything was an adventure with her. Even the simplest things like grocery shopping. She made living our daily lives so much fun and she was always making me feel like I was in my twenties all over again."

"You and Mom were the cutest couple. I remember well the giddiness between you two, the way you flirted, as well as the way that you used to look at her and the way that she used to look at you. Neither of you ever lost that spark for each other."

A wistful smile stretched across my dad's lips. "Your mom set my soul on fire from day one, Stevie. It happened the moment I looked into her beautiful eyes."

As soon as he said that, my mind went spinning back to when I saw Zac on the running trail. I'd stared at him from the moment we first made eye contact until we passed by each other *because* of his eyes. The light in them got to me. It was so bright and warm and inviting. Now I realized that on that early Saturday morning, *my* soul had been set on fire just by looking into Zac's eyes. That was what I'd been feeling and not understanding. I did now, though, and it was wrong for me to be feeling this way. So wrong—yet something about it felt so right.

"I can imagine you seeing her that first time," I said, refocusing on my dad.

"She walked into my church, sat down in the front pew, and kept her eyes on me during my entire sermon."

"And she was a visitor, not a member."

"That's right."

"I've never asked this because I've never thought much about it until now, but was Mom a member at some other Methodist church when she came to yours?"

My dad searched my eyes and then let out a long sigh. "Stevie, there's something that you don't know about your mom and me. Something that I never thought I'd tell you, but I'll do it now. I'm sure it's all this wine that I've had that's making me feel like spilling the beans and I'm just gonna do it because the time feels right."

"Okay."

"I met your mom at the Baptist church that I used to preach at. Not at the Methodist church that I was assigned to after leaving the Baptist Conference. Your mom is the reason why I left."

I jerked my head back. "What?"

"Yes, it was because of her. I *had* to leave."

"Go on."

"Before I tell you the rest of this story, would you mind refilling my wine glass, please? I'm gonna need it."

"Of course, Dad. You stay here and I'll be right back."

I got up and hurried to my fridge to get the bottle of Pinot Grigio. As soon as I made it back to the dining room table, I filled my dad's glass nearly to the rim again. He chuckled, shook his head, and then took a big gulp of the wine.

"Okay, let's do this, daughter."

I had no clue what he was about to tell me about his history with my mom, but I had the feeling that my dad had needed to confess to whatever it was for a very long time.

"I'm ready to hear it," I said, reaching for his hand. It was trembling.

"I was married before, Stevie. My marriage with your mom was my second one."

My mouth fell open. "Wh-what?"

"I was married to another woman when your mom and I met."

"Oh my God, you and mom had an affair, didn't you?"

"No, we didn't have an affair, but my ex-wife thought we did. She convinced herself of it."

"What made her think you were?"

"For starters, I could hardly keep my eyes off your mom and she could hardly keep hers off me. She joined my church one month after she began attending it and then jumped right into serving the congregation in every way she could because that's who she was. As you know, she was a giver and also a healer, and the members of my church immediately embraced her. They loved her. Everyone but my ex-wife."

"It sounds like she was jealous of Mom."

"She had a right to be. Although your mom and I were strictly friends at that time and had never spoken to or touched each other inappropriately, our eyes had. They told the real story, and right or wrong, we fell in love with each other. I couldn't help but fall in love with your mom. I fought my feelings for her until I no longer could."

I picked up my Hendricks and tonic and finished off what was left in the glass.

"Do you need another one of those?" my dad asked.

"No, I'm okay. I just need to hear the next chapter in this story."

"My ex-wife asked me for a divorce six months after your mom joined my church."

"And what was your response?"

My dad shrugged his shoulders. "I got divorced as quickly as I could and once it was finalized, I went to your mother and confessed my feelings to her. I told her that I was in love with her and wanted her to be mine. All mine. She told me the same thing, we got married by a justice of the peace, I switched to the Methodist Conference, was assigned a church and the rest is history."

I took a deep breath and stared at my dad while trying to process everything that he just told me.

"I don't understand why you switched conferences," I finally said.

"Because in the Baptist Conference, you can't be a preacher if you're divorced but you can be in the Methodist one."

I took another deep breath.

"Are you okay?" my dad asked.

"Um, yeah. My mind is just a little blown at the moment is all."

"I thought that might happen. So what do you think of me now? Your sinner dad."

I reached over and held his face in my hand. "I think even more of you for being true to yourself. In my eyes, you did nothing wrong by falling in love with Mom and she did nothing wrong by falling in love with you. I can see why you two fell for each other and I also understand why you were so conflicted about it at first, considering your circumstances at the time. It wasn't the ideal scenario, but it doesn't matter. There's no point in fighting what keeps your heart beating."

"I tried to, but..."

"I know, Dad. I believe you and Mom were destined to meet and make a life together. People from your old church may have cast their judgment onto you two, but so what. They're all hypocrites."

"Actually, no one from my old church judged us. No one except for my ex-wife. She also tried to stir up things by spreading the rumor that your mom and I had been having an affair since she first started coming to my church. It was a flat-out lie that ended up reaching some of the members in that first Methodist church that I pastored at but everyone there ignored it."

"Good."

"The members embraced me but especially your mom. They loved her and she served that church just like she did the Baptist one."

"And just like the church that you pastor now."

"Yes."

"How many years have you been there, again?"

"Eight. I hope to stay at this one until retirement, but you never know with the Methodist Conference. They tend to move pastors around."

I leaned over and hugged my dad. Then I told him that I loved him.

"I love you too, Stevie."

"Thank you for telling me about the true beginning of you and Mom. It means more to me than you know."

"You're welcome."

"I just had it in my mind that you two met at your first Methodist church, fell in love with each, got married, had me, etc."

"No, it wasn't that simple."

"Tell me this one thing. Do you have any regrets about it?"

"None at all. My life was never the same after I met your mom. I lived a dream with her for nearly thirty years and I'd sin a thousand times over just to have her by my side again. She made a believer out of me that soul mates are real—and I have no doubt that she was mine."

10
#pictureperfect

Stevie

"Text or call me as soon as you get home. Okay, Dad?"

"I will. And thank you again—for everything. I love your new house, I love that you're happy with it *and* your new job, I love the dinner and drinks that we had last night, I love the talk that we had and I love that I get to take home what's left of this key lime pie," he chuckled, glancing over at it, sitting in the passenger seat of his car.

"I told you that I was gonna send you home with whatever was left of it and you better enjoy it."

"You know I will!"

"Yeah, I do."

I hugged my dad and he squeezed me tight. "It makes my heart so full to see you shining again, Stevie."

"I'm really happy with where I am and what I'm doing," I said, pulling back to look at him. "I needed this change. It's been like a breath of fresh air."

After my dad left, I went back inside my house and checked the time. It was only two o'clock in the afternoon. I thought about taking a dip in my swimming pool but then another thought came to me.

I grabbed my cellphone off my kitchen counter and Googled the Dallas Zoo. After checking out the website and seeing

71

all the pictures of the different animals and attractions, I decided to do what Zac suggested I do. Something that he'd said we're never too old to do. I was going to the zoo today.

When I arrived, the parking lot was packed but then again, it was Saturday. After paying for my ticket, I walked through the entrance and then began exploring the different attractions. When I saw the sign that pointed in the direction of the petting zoo, I smiled and started heading toward it. I felt like a little girl again doing what I was doing right now. The only thing missing was having my mom and dad here.

I could see the petting zoo several yards ahead of me and as I was nearing it, butterflies filled my stomach. Not because of the animals, though. Zac was standing inside the fenced-in area with a little boy beside him. I knew at once that it was his Malcolm because he looked just like Zac. I was surprised to see the two of them here at this time of day because Zac told me they were coming to the zoo this morning. Their plans had obviously changed.

I glanced around, looking for Avery, although I didn't know what she looked like. I figured if she was here, then she'd be hanging around close by, but there was no attentive-acting woman anywhere near Zac or Malcolm.

I decided to *not* enter the petting zoo. Instead, I walked along the fence line and then stopped to lean against it so I could continue watching Zac with his son. They were both so cute in the way that they were interacting with all the animals and also with each other. It was easy to see how much Zac loved Malcolm and how much Malcolm loved his father.

I still had my eyes on them when Zac unexpectedly looked up and stared straight at me. Then he smiled and waved. After I waved back, he leaned down to say something to Malcolm, picked him up into his arms, and then the two of them started heading in my direction.

"Hey, Sinclair," Zac said as he reached the other side of the fence.

"Hey, Buchanan."

"I see you took my suggestion to check out this zoo."

"I did and I love it here. But who is this precious little boy you're holding?"

"This is my son, Malcolm. And Malcolm, this is my friend Stevie. Can you say hi to her?"

He leaned his head down onto Zac's shoulder, acting shy, but he kept watching me while sweetly smiling.

"Hi, Malcolm. Are you having fun petting all the animals?" I asked.

He nodded yes and then surprised me by reaching out his arms for me to take him. I looked up at Zac and he nodded that it was okay.

After he passed off Malcolm to me over the fence, I held Zac's mini-me on my hip. He was a solidly built little boy with white-blond hair, bright blue eyes, a little round nose, and apple cheeks with a little dimple in the right one. Then all at once, it hit me. Strangely, Zac's Malcolm looked identical to the Malcolm in my dream. The dream that I had during my first night in my new house. The dream where I saw my son at four years of age. The dream where he told me that he loved me and was still here.

Standing in the middle of the Dallas Zoo, holding Zac's son in my arms and looking down at him smiling up at me now, I could feel myself getting choked up. That was something that didn't need to continue, though, because Malcolm nor Zac would understand. So I took a slow, deep breath to pull myself back together.

"What's your favorite animal, Malcolm?" I asked.

He didn't say. He just kept staring into my eyes and smiling, then he wrapped his little arms around my neck and clung to me. I looked at Zac, and he grinned and shrugged his shoulders. Neither one of us knew what was going on with Malcolm behaving like this toward me but we were both more than okay with it.

"Will you take me to see the fish?" Malcolm said, pulling back to look at me again. His voice was like an angel's.

"If your daddy is okay with me doing that, then of course I'll take you."

Malcolm and I looked up at Zac at the same time and he smiled so big that it made his eyes squint. They also crinkled around the corners and that dimple in his right cheek appeared, just like it had yesterday as he and I stood in the Whole Foods parking lot talking to each other.

"Mind if I join you?" he asked me.

"That's what I meant—for all three of us to go. Unless someone else came with you."

"It's just my boy and me. It always is."

Zac knew what I'd been asking without asking. I'd wondered if Avery was here, hanging out somewhere, and I just hadn't seen her. She wasn't, though, and I was relieved.

"Then let's go to the aquarium and see some fish."

After Zac exited the petting zoo and walked over to Malcolm and me, I started to put Malcolm down so he could walk with his daddy and me, but he clung to me even tighter. He wanted me to carry him and I was all too happy to do it. I was enjoying the feeling of this little boy in my arms. A little boy who could've so easily been mine.

After reaching the aquarium, I kept holding Malcolm while walking around and looking at all the different aquatic life. Several times, I caught Zac watching me with his son, and then he'd smile at us. I knew he was just as blown away as I was by the way Malcolm had taken to me. I still didn't know what to make of it, and Zac still didn't seem to know either.

"What a beautiful little boy," an older woman said, grabbing my attention. She was standing a few feet away from Zac, Malcolm, and me. "He's a perfect blend of his parents." She looked back and forth at Zac and me a couple of times and then her eyes went right back to Malcolm.

"Thank you, ma'am," Zac replied.

The woman nodded and started making her way over to the stingrays. I met Zac's gaze and held it, not knowing how to feel about what the woman had said or if I should've responded to her in some way. I was so caught off guard by her statement and couldn't think of a proper reply, but then Zac had handled it. A "thank you" was all that was necessary. Not explaining that only one of this beautiful little boy's parents was present, along with a woman that he met at a bar eight days ago.

Zac grinned and shrugged his shoulders at me again, and then I went back to showing Malcolm the different fish and telling him everything I knew about them.

"You should've been a marine biologist, Stevie. You know so much," Zac said.

"I just enjoy marine life is all. I could never make a career out of it."

"I have no doubt that you could do anything you set your mind to accomplishing."

I paused and looked over Zac's face. He still hadn't shaven, and I was again wearing the sparkly gloss on my lips that he said looked really nice.

"Same to you," I said, but the words came out in a whisper.

Zac kept staring at me, and I finally made myself look away from him. I had to. He'd touched me once again, but not by using his hands. Like a true Taurus, he used his eyes—those beautiful sky-blue eyes of his that spoke volumes. They also had the power to unravel me and most certainly would have if I hadn't looked away.

What I was feeling toward Zac was so confusing. It was also exhilarating. I couldn't keep allowing myself to go there, though, with my attraction to him. It was as strong as it was wrong.

I had just finished telling Malcolm about stingray barbs when Zac leaned down closer to him.

"Guess what, son? Stevie is really a mermaid. During the day, her tail disappears, but at night, it comes back and she goes swimming in the ocean."

Malcolm's eyes got big as he looked back up at me. I was already smiling about what Zac had just said. He was a kid at heart who enjoyed playing make-believe with his son.

"Do you wanna know what color Stevie's tail is?" Zac went on to ask Malcolm, and he nodded yes. "It's the same color as her eyes. What color are her eyes?"

Malcolm looked up at me again and then put his hands on either side of my face, squishing my cheeks. "Blue like yours, Daddy!"

"They are blue, but Stevie's are a little bit darker than mine. They're really pretty, aren't they?"

"Yes! So pretty, pretty, pretty!"

Malcolm leaned closer to me, placing his forehead against mine, and my heart melted. He didn't move from where he was for several seconds and neither did I. When he pulled back, he smiled and just gazed into my eyes. Looking into his, the thought came to me that Malcolm had an old soul just like my dad said my Malcolm did. He spoke like he was biologically older too.

He, Zac, and I continued making our way through the aquarium and came to a section that I hadn't known was here. There was a large glass tank with a woman inside it who had long blond hair, a white seashell bikini top, and a fake blue mermaid tail. She was swimming around underneath the surface of the water and waving at all of us watching her.

Malcolm looked back and forth from her to me and then said, "Go swim, Stevie."

"I wish I could, but remember, my tail only comes out at night. That's the only time I can go swimming, but let's go look at her tail," I said, pointing at this zoo's mermaid.

As soon as I stepped up to the glass, she swam up and waved at Malcolm. He waved back at her and she smiled at him, then pressed her hand against the glass. Malcolm reached out and pressed his against it—his hand and the pretty mermaid's hand mirroring each other's. Before she swam away, she blew a kiss to Malcolm and then he blew one to her. I had a little Romeo in my arms and if I could have, I would've kept him.

After we'd seen everything inside the aquarium, Zac said, "Stevie, I hate to leave, but it is time for me to take Malcolm back home and get him settled in."

"I understand."

"Are you gonna leave now, too?"

"No, I'm gonna stay for a little while longer. I wanna go back to the petting zoo and see my furry friends, then go check out the rest of this place."

"Do you like what you've seen so far?"

"Very much so. You were right. This is a really nice zoo."

"I'd never lead you in the wrong direction," he said.

I watched his eyes trickle down to my lips and linger there, then he met my gaze again and held it. Zac was who looked away this time, though. Not me. And as soon as he did, I turned my attention to his son still in my arms.

"I'm so happy to have met you, Malcolm. You're such a sweet boy and I hope to see you again sometime," I told him.

His bottom lip started quivering and tears filled his eyes. Then he wrapped his little arms around my neck and clung to me again. I looked back up at Zac and this time, I was unable to hide my emotions. I was just as choked up about this goodbye as Malcolm. Zac stepped even closer to us and rubbed our backs to comfort us while staring straight at me with a mix of sympathy and amazement written all over his face. What was happening with his precious son was uncanny, yet I welcomed it so much.

After about a minute, Malcolm loosened his arms from around my neck and looked at me again. I smiled at him and he smiled back. Then I wiped the tears off his face and kissed one of his apple cheeks. I set him down on the ground after that and he was okay with it. He, Zac, and I said our goodbyes, and then I watched the two Buchanans begin making their way toward the zoo's exit. Zac was holding Malcolm's hand and the vision of the two of them was picture-perfect, so I took one with my cellphone.

11
#backytoreality
Zac

Malcolm was asleep in his car seat before we'd even made it to the interstate. His day had been a full one and so had mine. It had started out with an early morning run as the sun was coming up. It felt good being outside, breathing, sweating, and letting all the fucked up things that Avery said to me after I got home from picking up Malcolm from my parents yesterday fade away.

As soon as I realized she was drunk on her regular fix of vodka and orange juice, I texted my mom to let her know what was going on. Then I asked if she and my dad wouldn't mind keeping Malcolm overnight. I hated to ask them for yet another favor, since they babysat him for me all week while I was at work, but I felt I had no choice. I didn't want Malcolm to be around Avery in the intoxicated state that she was in.

My mom texted back that she and my dad were happy to keep Malcolm overnight for me and to bring him back over as soon as I could. I was relieved and I was also thankful. My parents were the best and they loved Malcolm as much as I did.

After dropping him off at their house, I drove around and listened to the radio, wishing there was a way that I could escape the hell of my marriage without having to split custody of my son with Avery. She was such a miserable person, and the alcohol just brought out more of her true colors.

The woman had blindsided me after we got married by telling me that she didn't want to have children. That wasn't what she said when we began dating and then became engaged. During that time, she was all for having a family. It was what I had always wanted and was excited about our future together. Then Avery pulled a Jekyll and Hyde act on me that I was still so hurt by.

Despite the friction within our marriage that began after she told me about not wanting to have children, I made the decision to stay committed to her. Not only did I not want a divorce on my track record, I also kept hoping Avery would change her mind about having a family. But she never did, and I finally stopped talking to her about it.

Our years together hadn't all been bad. There'd been occasions when we had fun, laughed, took trips, enjoyed the getaways, and also times when we enjoyed our home life. The joy was always short-lived, though. It was like a cycle that Avery was in with her happiness and then her misery. It was one extreme to the other and it exhausted me, always trying to gauge her mood.

We were in our fifth year of marriage when I finally asked Avery to go see a therapist because I was convinced something was chemically off inside her brain. I had a strong feeling that she was bipolar or something along those lines. To my surprise, she agreed to my request, and after going to several therapy sessions that I was also part of, and also going to see a medical doctor for testing, Avery was found to be "normal." But the therapist said something to Avery *and* to me during our last session with her that completely opened my eyes concerning my wife.

She said, "Avery, you are the most self-centered woman that I've ever counseled. You're selfish, manipulative, spiteful, and vindictive. And Zac? I feel sorry for you. You deserve so much better in life and I hope you find it one day. Now it's time for both of you to leave my office and don't call me again. We're done here."

After the therapist said what she did, Avery told her to fuck off and then stormed out of her office, slamming the door behind her. I apologized, paid the therapist for the session, thanked her for trying to help Avery, and then left, not knowing what in the hell I was supposed to do next.

Avery didn't say a word to me on the drive home. A week later, she still hadn't spoken to me, but the next day, she started talking and acting as if nothing had happened during that last appointment with the therapist. It was like she stuck her head in the sand and just moved on. When I realized that, I decided to move on too, because I was mentally and emotionally wiped out.

The on-and-off friction between Avery and me continued and I just dealt with it the best that I could. When things were good, we had a lot of fun. We went places and did things together. We still had sex during those times too.

One night, Avery and I started partying at home by drinking and listening to music while lounging by our swimming pool. We ended up getting into it completely naked and then we started kissing. Before I knew it, we were fucking each other and neither of us had thought about using protection until after we were done.

As I was pulling my cock out of Avery, she snapped, "I better not be pregnant after this, Zac! If I am, then it's your fault!"

Still intoxicated from all the Hendricks and tonic, I laughed at Avery for what she'd said to me. Then I told her, "You were part of this too. I didn't make you fuck me. You clearly wanted to, and now here we are fighting about it. And if you do end up pregnant after tonight, then I'll be happy to take care of our child. You don't have to worry about a damn thing."

I got out of the pool after that and went inside to go to bed. Avery slept in the guest bedroom that night and also the next. When I asked her on the third night if she was going to continue sleeping apart from me, she said yes. A month later, we were still sleeping separately and also living every other part of our daily lives in that way.

By that point, I'd thrown myself into my job even more while Avery continued doing what she'd already been doing. She'd sleep until noon or later, go lay out by the pool, go out with her friends in Dallas, make trips to Lubbock to see her family and friends, and spend money like it grew on trees. I never complained to her about any of that, though, because her being able to come and go as she pleased equated to peace for me.

It remained that way for several weeks until I came home from work one day to find Avery sitting on the couch and crying. I ran to her to find out what was wrong and when I touched her shoulder, she shoved my hand away and then held up a home pregnancy test that she'd taken. It was positive. She was pregnant with Malcolm. I sat down at the opposite end of the couch and then asked her what she was going to do.

"Have this damn child!" she yelled. "What did you think I was gonna do?"

"It wouldn't have surprised me to hear you say you wanted an abortion, Avery."

"I do! But because of you, I'm not gonna get one. I'm gonna go through with this pregnancy, ruin my body, give birth and you're gonna owe me when it's all over."

"Owe you?"

"Yes, Zac. You're gonna owe me."

"Let me remind you that you had a role in getting pregnant. Again—I didn't force you to have sex with me that night in the pool and you didn't think about using protection any more than I did. But if you're gonna insist on blaming me, then go ahead. Blame away! You can believe I owe you all day long. I don't care, Avery. Have fun with that."

I got up from the couch and had just started walking off when Avery screamed, "Fuck you! Fuck everything about you! You are the biggest disappointment of my life, Zac Buchanan, and you're never touching me again!"

I turned around, walked back over to Avery, pointed my finger in her face and started to blast her with some cruel words that I'd thought to say to her before—but decided not to. I started thinking like an attorney and held my tongue. I thought about what I'd advised clients of mine to do before, and that was to begin documenting heated incidents between them and their spouses or whoever. So that's what I began doing with Avery.

As weeks passed, morning sickness became something else that she bitched about. When her regular clothes no longer fit, she bitched about that too. After she'd reached the fourth month of her pregnancy, I asked Avery about getting a sonogram to find out what the sex of our baby was and to no surprise, she bitched about that as well. She didn't want to get one. She refused to do it, and it wasn't until the day she gave birth to Malcolm that I knew I was the father of a son.

I was in the delivery room when he came into the world and I cried the moment I saw him. Avery just looked pissed off. When one of the nurses asked her if she wanted to hold Malcolm, she replied, "No, that's my husband's job." From that point on, I took over total responsibility of Malcolm and never looked back.

In the four years since his birth, Avery had shown random interest in him as he'd gotten older. She'd even spent what seemed to be quality time with him. I'd caught her smiling at him and him smiling at her, as well as the two of them laughing. But as usual, it was short-lived and cyclical. I understood what was happening but Malcolm didn't. He didn't get it when his mother was affectionate toward him one day and then wanted nothing to do with him the next.

Malcolm was still asleep when I exited off the interstate. My house was only a couple of miles away but I wasn't ready to go back yet because I didn't want to deal with Avery. There was no telling what state of mind she was going to be in and I didn't want it to spoil mine.

I was so surprised to see Stevie at the zoo. Seeing her again, talking to her, the way that Malcolm interacted with her and also the way that she interacted with him made my day. It was unreal how my son responded to Stevie. I chalked it up to his instinct. He instantly knew she was a good person. No—a *great* person. Although she didn't have any children of her own, she was obviously a natural with them.

I decided to keep driving around, so I got back onto the interstate. This way, Malcolm could get a good nap in and I could keep letting my thoughts about Stevie flow while listening to the radio. Thoughts that I knew I shouldn't be having but allowed myself to have anyway.

Although she and I were newly acquainted, I'd already seen enough of her and had heard enough of everything she'd said to know someone like her would perfectly fill the lonely void in my life. I couldn't help but question why I couldn't have met someone like Stevie ten years ago. I also questioned what it was that God was trying to teach me by my being married to Avery.

It was when my dream of being happy with her started disintegrating into nothing that my faith in God had begun to waver. For all I knew, my toxic marriage was the price that I was paying for something I did in a past life. Karma had come back around. But how long was I going to have to pay this hurtful and disillusioning price?

Malcolm started waking up from his nap just as I was exiting the interstate again. I reached behind me and patted him on his leg and my little buddy smiled at me. Whenever he did that, it somehow made everything okay.

He was still groggy when I parked my car in the garage, so I got him out of his car seat and carried him into the house. The heavy scent of garlic was in the air and I realized Avery was cooking. My guess was some kind of Italian dish. When Malcolm and I made it to the kitchen, Avery was in the process of handwashing some dishes. She looked up and then smiled at us.

"Hey, you two," she said.

I breathed a sigh of relief: she was in a good mood today. When I'd left the house to take my run this morning, she was still asleep, so I couldn't gauge her emotions. When I got back from my run, she was still asleep and that didn't change even when it came time for me to leave the house again to go pick up Malcolm from my parents to take him to the zoo.

"Hey," I said, watching her closely for the slightest shift.

"I hope you're hungry. I'm baking lasagna and it's almost done."

"It smells good. Thank you."

"How was the zoo?"

"Packed but fun. Malcolm really enjoyed seeing the aquarium this time."

As soon as I said that, he lifted his head off my shoulder.

"I saw two mermaids, mommy," he told her.

"You did?"

He nodded yes and then Avery asked him what the mermaids looked like.

"Pretty," he said.

"All mermaids are pretty. What color was their hair?"

"White."

"Both had blond hair then."

Another nod from Malcolm, and then Avery asked him what color the mermaids' tails were.

"Only one mermaid had a tail, mommy. It was blue."

Avery frowned. "Only one had a tail?"

"Uh-huh."

"Then the one that didn't have a tail isn't a mermaid."

"Yes, she is."

"No, Malcolm—she's not. A mermaid has to have a tail."

"Stevie's goes away."

Avery looked at me and shrugged. "Stevie? Who is he talking about?"

"There were two mermaids at the aquarium today and one of them was named Stevie," I explained.

"How do you know that?"

"Because Malcolm and I met her."

"I'm confused. If both mermaids were inside the tank at the aquarium then how did you meet the one named Stevie?"

"She wasn't swimming in the water like the other one. She was walking around inside the aquarium and interacting with others."

"A mermaid with no tail. How confusing to a child."

"Not to mine," I said, glancing at Malcolm. "He understood that she was still a mermaid—with or without a tail."

Avery rolled her eyes and sighed. "Whatever, Zac."

It was right then that I witnessed the shift in her mood, and it had happened over something so small and irrelevant. It seemed that she was always looking for something to argue about and this time, she was arguing with a four-year-old about mermaids.

"I'm gonna go change Malcolm's clothes and mine," I said, and started walking off with him still in my arms.

"Aren't you two gonna eat with me? I've worked hard on this meal."

I turned around and glanced at the empty box sitting on the counter, then looked at Avery. "Worked hard? You popped a frozen lasagna into the oven. Yes, I appreciate you cooking because it's so rare that you do, but you didn't work hard on preparing a meal for the three of us to eat."

"Thanks for that."

"It's true, Avery. You're seeking credit when credit isn't due. I can't help but wonder what you want from me now. I figured out a long time ago that when you're being exceptionally nice, then you want something. So what is it this time?"

"Fuck you, Zac!" she snapped. Then she threw down the plate that she was holding. It shattered in the bottom of the kitchen sink and made Malcolm jump and hold on to me tighter.

"It's okay, son. Mommy is just tired so we're gonna let her rest. Would you like to go swimming with me?" I asked him.

He searched my eyes and then said a shaky, "Yes."

"Okay, let's go put on our swimsuits."

"Can Stevie go swimming with us?"

I looked over at Avery still fuming next to the kitchen sink. "I wish she could. It'd be so much fun to swim with a mermaid," I said.

"I'm going back to Lubbock tomorrow, Zac."

"Big surprise there."

"I need you to transfer some money over to my debit account before I leave."

"And there it is. That's what you want from me. Don't worry, I'll have it in your account tonight. And next time, Avery—just tell me what you want and spare me your wifely theatrics. They aren't necessary—just like your presence here at this house."

She flipped me her middle finger and then left the kitchen. I already knew she'd be in the guest bedroom for the rest of the evening except for coming back to the kitchen to make herself another vodka and orange juice. The less I had to see her, the better.

After getting Malcolm and myself dressed to go swimming, I took the lasagna out of the oven and left it sitting on the stovetop. My stomach was in knots and I couldn't have eaten if I tried. Malcolm wasn't hungry either, so the two of us walked outside into the backyard and got into the pool.

He had on his floaties even though he was capable of swimming without them. He was like a little fish and water was his natural habitat—then it hit me. He was a Pisces. A water sign. I hadn't ever thought about the significance of that until now, and it was all due to a beautiful blond mermaid named Stevie Sinclair.

12
#eavesdropping

Stevie

When I woke up, I was shocked to see that it was after 9:00 a.m. I'd never slept in this late before. My body apparently needed the rest and I did feel refreshed. I also felt like taking a run. It'd been three days since my last one and I didn't like going any longer than that if I could help it.

It was Sunday morning and I didn't expect the trail to be as busy as I'd seen it before during the afternoon and evening. I preferred it when I didn't have to keep an eye on so many people as we passed by each other. Especially those who ran around me from behind. When I arrived at the trail, I immediately took off running, looking forward to getting a runner's high. I loved it when my body's stamina kicked into overdrive like that. It always made me feel as if I could run forever.

After clocking two miles, I called it quits. That was enough exercise for today, but I didn't stop moving. I kept walking along the trail, allowing my heart rate to slow down and my body to cool off. I'd just taken another sip from my water bottle when I heard a voice in the woods ahead of me, on the right. It was a man's voice, and even from this distance, I could tell that he was angry about something. His tone made that very clear.

I kept walking until I came to where he was, although I couldn't see him due to the density of the trees blocking my view. I probably shouldn't have done it, but I stopped to eaves-drop on the conversation the man was having with someone on his cellphone, which he happened to have on speaker. After lis-tening for only a handful of seconds, I quietly gasped because I recognized the man's voice and I also realized whom he was arguing with because he called her by name.

It was Zac who'd walked off the running trail and into the privacy of the trees to have a heated conversation with his wife, Avery. I could hear her screaming at him, telling him that she hated him, hated her life with him, and also that she didn't know when she was coming back from Lubbock. Zac told her to do whatever she felt like she needed to do and that he was going to do the same for himself and Malcolm.

I didn't know if it was Zac or Avery who hung up first, but their conversation ended—evidenced by their back-and-forth hurling of words coming to a sudden stop. Then I heard Zac blow out a heavy breath, followed by him saying, "Fuck my life." It was the same thing that I'd said after watching Graham drive away from our house after I confronted him about his affair with Emma.

I gave Zac a moment to gather his composure and then started making my way to where he was standing among the trees. As soon as he saw me, his eyes got big with surprise, and then he perched his hands on his waist and looked down at the ground. He was embarrassed. I continued approaching him anyway and came to a standstill directly in front of him.

"Zac, are you okay?" I asked.

He cut his eyes up at me and shrugged his shoulders. "I don't know what I am right now, Stevie, but I am so sorry about you hearing however much it was of the conversation that I just had with my wife. I didn't intend for anyone to hear a word of it. That's why I'm back here."

"I'm the only one who heard your conversation and I hap-pened to walk up during the last part of it. There's no need to apologize, either."

I searched his troubled eyes and could see traces of anger still in them. Then I noticed something else. It was his bottom lip. There was a small, puffy cut on the left side of it that wasn't there yesterday, and I had a good idea of where it came from.

I dropped my eyes down from Zac's mouth and then noticed a long, irritated scratch on the left side of his neck. There was also one peeking out from underneath the neckline of his tank top, as well as four scratches close together on his left bicep. After seeing all the evidence of what I now had no doubt was Avery's volatile aggression toward Zac, I took both his hands into mine and then turned them over. To no surprise, there were more marks. Either yesterday or sometime this morning, some kind of argument/altercation took place between Zac and Avery, she physically came after him again and he defended himself against her.

When I looked back up at him, he licked his lips and it caused the cut on his bottom one to come open and start bleeding. I reached up and gently wiped away the droplet of blood with my finger. It was an automatic response to what I was seeing and Zac didn't try to stop me. He just stood still and watched what I was doing to him.

"Try not to lick your lips so the cut can clot again," I said, showing him my fingertip and then wiping his blood onto my shirt. He swallowed hard and nodded. "All of these marks that I see on you are your wife's handiwork, aren't they?"

After a long pause, he mumbled, "Yes."

As soon as he confirmed what I already knew, I stepped the rest of the way up to him and wrapped my arms around his neck. It was another automatic response that I couldn't help because my heart was breaking for Zac. When I hugged him, he didn't move at first, but then I felt him slowly embracing me around my waist.

"It's gonna be all right," I whispered into his ear.

Zac drew in a deep breath and so did I—the two of us hidden away from the prying eyes of strangers, secure in where we were and in what we were doing. It was needed by him as much as it was by me. I was being a consoling friend to one of mine who was hurting and I wished there was more that I could do for him.

When I started letting go of Zac, he hugged my body against his even tighter and said, "Not yet. Please."

Right or wrong, I wrapped my arms around his neck again and rested the side of my face against his. Listening to him breathing, feeling his warm skin on mine once more, I closed my eyes and allowed myself to linger within this moment.

When I started stepping away from Zac this time, he let me go and then softly smiled.

"Thank you for hugging me. Twice. I needed it," he said.

"I know you did and you're welcome."

"Stevie, you know things about me now that I never intended for you to know. I don't want you to feel sorry for me."

"Too late."

"I'm not a weak man."

"I know you're not."

"I stay in my marriage only because of my son."

The cut on Zac's bottom lip had another droplet of blood on it, so I wiped it off with my finger like before.

"You may have to stop talking to me to get that to stop bleeding," I said, nodding at his mouth.

"I don't wanna stop talking to you. The cut can bleed. I don't care."

I studied Zac's eyes and no longer saw anger in them. Just light, kindness and—desire. Zac was starving for romantic intimacy. I could tell how much he wanted and needed to be touched, held close, cared for, and also loved. I recognized all of this in him because I felt just like he did. I was starving for romantic intimacy too, but didn't realize it until I met him that night at Mystic Bar. No, it was when I saw him on this running trail the first time. That was when I felt myself beginning to awaken from what had been a long dormancy of my emotions and also my needs as a woman. On that day, I allowed myself to be fully attracted to everything I saw in a total stranger who unexpectedly became a friend to me less than a week later and was now on the verge of becoming something more if we weren't both careful.

"Okay. So keep talking to me and I'll keep tending that cut on your bottom lip," I said.

Zac smiled at me again and then glanced down at my mouth. "Um," he said, pointing at it. "You have something on you."

He reached out and carefully wiped off my bottom lip with his fingertips and then held them up for me to see.

"*I'm* bleeding?" I asked, surprised.

"No. Some of my blood was still on your finger when you touched your mouth a minute ago. Are you grossed out now?"

"Not at all. I don't remember touching my mouth, though."

"Well, you did."

Zac wiped his fingers on his tank top and then I noticed there was a shiny look to the red stain.

"And now you have my lip gloss on you. It's mixed with your blood."

He looked down and then lifted up the bottom hem of his tank top to see what I was talking about. While he was inspecting the sparkly red color on it, I inspected his exposed, well-defined abs along with the trail of dark hair below his navel. When I looked back up at Zac, he was watching me. He'd caught me checking him out but he didn't say anything about it and neither did I. Instead, we just stared into each other's eyes.

"I don't mind having your lip gloss on me," he quietly said, but the full meaning behind his words was loud and something that I clearly understood.

"I should probably go now, Zac."

He nodded and then stepped even closer to me, to where we were only inches apart. I could feel the heat radiating from his body and knew it had nothing to do with the temperature outside and everything to do with his attraction to me. It was as obvious as mine was to him. We'd both just been keeping it under professional wraps.

GINA MAGEE

I had a choice to make right now, and that was to either walk away from this dangerously tempting situation or stay in it. What I actually needed to do was to run as fast and as far away from it as possible, but looking up at Zac, whose beautiful blue eyes were still staring straight into mine—I chose to stay. I was craving this illicit intimacy as much as he was. Although the most that we'd done was hug each other, our eyes had done so much more and they still were.

"Forgive me for what I'm about to say to you, Stevie, but I have to say it—and it's that I wanna kiss you. I've wanted to so many times since we met but knew it'd be wrong if I did. Just like now."

"Yes, it would be wrong. Just like it'd be wrong for me to kiss you back."

"Does that mean you wanna kiss me?"

I looked down at Zac's lips and then met his gaze again. "Yes."

"What if we kissed each other just one time?"

"One time wouldn't be enough for me."

"Yeah... It wouldn't be for me either."

We kept staring at each other while the seconds kept ticking by, then Zac stepped the rest of the way up to me. His chest was resting against mine and I noticed our breathing was in sync. It was deep, too, and quickly growing even deeper. Something was going to have to give—then Zac leaned his head down and pressed his lips against my cheek. He held them there, and I closed my eyes while trying so hard not to turn my head and kiss his mouth. I wanted to so badly, but I couldn't do it.

Zac slowly pulled his lips away from my cheek and as he was doing it, he stared into my eyes again. His chest was still pressed against me and his mouth was still within kissing distance from mine. I could feel his warm breath blowing against my face and it was intoxicating. *Zac* was intoxicating. Everything about him was.

He looked over my face and then took two wide steps away from me. "Stevie, you really should go now, because if you keep

92

standing here in front of me like this and keep talking to me and keep touching me and keep looking at me like you've been doing and are still doing, then I'm not gonna be able to stop myself from kissing you like you deserve to be kissed. So walk away from me before we both cross the line."

"Okay. I'll walk away from you, but before I do, I want you to know something."

"What?"

"I've never done this before. I've never allowed myself to be in this kind of position with a man."

"You mean a *married* man?"

"Yes."

"I knew you hadn't. And as a married man, I've never allowed myself to be in this kind of position with a woman. You are the exception to this rule of mine."

"Why am I the exception?"

"I can't tell you why. Nothing other than to say there's just something about you. Something different that's gotten underneath my skin and in the best way."

I smiled to myself because that was exactly how I felt about Zac. He was the exception for me as well, and there was something different about him that had gotten underneath *my* skin, and in the best way. Something that made me feel so alive. Something that made me feel like breaking all the moral rules.

"I'm gonna leave now," I said, taking a step back.

"Okay."

"Bye, Buchanan."

"Bye, Sinclair."

I turned around and started making my way through the trees, but then stopped and looked over my shoulder at Zac. He still had his eyes on me.

"When you get home, put some Neosporin or some kind of antibiotic ointment on all those places on your body. Even on that cut on your bottom lip," I said.

"I will."

"I don't want them to get infected."

"Thank you for caring."

I smiled at Zac and he lifted his hand to wave at me. I waved at him too and then headed for the trail. When I reached it, I took off running instead of walking and I ran all the way back to my car in the parking lot. Once inside, I cranked it and turned the A/C on high, blowing it straight into my face.

What in the hell are you doing, Stevie? I asked myself.

What I'd just run away from with Zac was wrong in every way, yet it felt so incredibly right. I knew I was playing with fire just like he was, and I also knew that for the two of us to continue being around each other—professionally and person-ally—I was going to have to be the one to stomp out that fire, even though I didn't want to. But if I didn't do something about it, this *thing* between Zac and me was going to continue racing down its forbidden pathway and lead us into having an affair. That was so obvious. But having an affair was not the answer to his hunger for a romantic relationship nor was it the answer to mine. It would only be a temporary fix—one that would leave us both feeling unfulfilled and lonely every time we had to go our separate, secretive ways.

Still...

I couldn't deny how alluring the thought of having a pas-sionate affair with Zac Buchanan was to me. He was the only man with whom I had ever allowed myself to picture doing that. Part of me felt terrible for thinking about him in that way, but it was only a small part. The rest of me was fine with it, because I knew Zac and I weren't ever going that far. I wasn't going to allow an affair to happen and he really didn't want it to hap-pen either. Although we hadn't discussed it, we both knew how much regret would be involved if we did. That was a no-brainer.

What was it about the "forbidden" that pulled at people so much? Why was the temptation of it so strong? Was it just about breaking the moral rules set by mankind? Another form of rebellion? When it came to having an affair with someone, was the allure of it only about having something that didn't be-long to you?

On the drive back to my house, I thought about every interaction that I'd had with Zac since the first time I saw him. The curious friendliness between us had progressed so quickly yet carefully on both our parts. After today's interaction with Zac, though, I knew he and I were going to have to be even more careful to not show exactly how curious and attracted to each other we really were while in the public eye. I would never want anyone in the legal community to grow suspicious of our friendship. If someone did, it carried the high potential of snowballing into a vicious rumor that could ruin both our careers—even if the rumor held no truth. Even if Zac and I weren't fucking each other.

That was something I was only going to allow myself to fantasize about doing.

13
#proceedwithcaution

Zac

Damn. I hated to see Stevie leave but I understood why she did. It was for her own good and also mine. We had both been tempted to cross a line that we didn't need to cross although it would've felt so good doing it. It would've felt so incredibly good to not only hold Stevie's body against mine again, but also to kiss her.

It'd been years since I'd been kissed by a woman. It'd also been years since I'd been touched in the way that Stevie touched me in the short amount of time that we'd stood here together, hidden away among these trees next to this running trail. The concern for me that she'd verbalized was unbelievable. Her caring hands on my skin were too, along with her arms that she hugged me with.

Although Stevie told me that she felt sorry for me due to how my life with Avery was, I knew her affection toward me wasn't just about that. She and I were both so attracted to each other and it was nearly overpowering to me. When she was standing here—so close that I could smell the coconut scent of her lip gloss—I came so close to giving in to my desire for her and kissing her. The cut on my bottom lip would've probably started bleeding again but it would've been worth it just to feel Stevie's lips against mine.

I needed to go pick up Malcolm from my parents' house and take him back to mine, and I was hoping and praying that Avery would be on her way to Lubbock by the time we got there. I knew she wasn't going to Lubbock again only to see her family and friends like she'd always claimed. She was going to see her college boyfriend, Justin, with whom I was certain she was having an affair. He was Avery's main reason for all the trips. Regardless, I was willing to tolerate it, along with footing Avery's traveling expenses, just to live in peace with my son.

His selfish mother was gone when he and I got home and over the next few hours, he and I played together with his Legos in his bedroom, ate some hot dogs and potato chips for lunch, then piled up in the living room on the couch to watch "The Sea Beast" on Netflix. It was the latest kids' movie and Malcolm loved it, but the little guy needed his nap and fell asleep about halfway through.

When he woke up, he said he wanted some ice cream, and so I asked him if he wanted to go to Baskin-Robbins. I already knew his answer was going to be "Yes" because he was a big fan of an ice cream they called "Daiquiri Ice," and so was I. Obviously, Malcolm didn't have a clue about what a real daiquiri was. He just loved the tart lime flavor of the ice cream.

When we walked into the store, I did an immediate double take at the same time my breath caught in my throat. To my total surprise, Stevie was standing next to the counter, looking down at the display case of all the different ice cream. She hadn't told me what her plans were for the rest of the day before she left me at the running trail earlier, but being able to see her again this soon and at this place made me smile. *Timing.*

I picked up Malcolm and carried him on my hip over to where Stevie was still standing. Her back was to us and one of the Baskin-Robbins employees was working on scooping some ice cream for her.

"Do you see who that is right there, standing in front of us?" I whispered into Malcolm's ear.

He looked at Stevie's long blond hair and then stretched away from me to see the side of her face.

"Hi, mermaid Stevie!" he said, so excitedly.

She turned around and smiled as soon as she saw him.

"Malcolm! How are you?"

He answered her by reaching out his arms for her to hold him just like he did when we were at the zoo yesterday. She looked up at me and I nodded that it was okay for her to take him. It would always be okay.

While Malcolm was hugging Stevie and she was hugging him, she met my gaze again and quietly said, "Hey, you."

"Hey, *you.*"

"Fancy meeting you here, Buchanan."

"Ditto. In the mood for some ice cream, I see."

"I am definitely that."

"My boy and I are too."

"What's your favorite ice cream, Malcolm?" she asked, pulling back to look at him.

He pointed behind her at the display case. "The green one."

Stevie turned around to take a look. "That green one?" she asked, pointing directly at the container of Daiquiri Ice, then Malcolm nodded at her. "That one is my favorite too."

Just as she finished saying that, the Baskin-Robbins employee handed her a sugar cone with a giant scoop on top of it.

"Here, you can have some of mine," she told Malcolm, and without any hesitation he licked her ice cream and then took a big bite of it. She started giggling and so did I.

When the Baskin-Robbins employee asked who was next in line, Stevie and Malcolm stepped to the side and I walked up to the counter to place my order. Once I had, I looked back at my son and the woman still holding onto him.

"So Daiquiri Ice is your favorite too?" she asked me.

"It is."

We smiled at each other and I searched her eyes—caught up all over again in what they held within them. Besides their beautiful deep blue color with little flecks of gold in them, the embers of what we'd secretly shared this morning were still burning just like I knew they were still burning in mine.

"Here you go, sir," the employee said from behind the counter, pulling me out of my enamored daze.

"Thank you."

I took the two cones from him, handed Malcolm his, and then motioned to Stevie to walk over to the register. As we reached it, she told Malcolm that she needed to put him down for a minute so that she could get her wallet out of her purse.

"I've got this," I told her and then handed the cashier the debit card I'd already pulled out of my shorts pocket.

"Well, thank you. I certainly didn't expect you to pay for my ice cream."

"I know you didn't, but I'm happy to do it. Would you like to go sit outside on the patio?"

"I'd love to go do that. It's a beautiful day."

"Yeah, it really is—and not just because of the unseasonable summer weather that we're having."

Stevie glanced down at my mouth and then nodded at me. She knew exactly what I was talking about without having to spell it out. This day had turned into a beautiful one at the moment I saw her coming through the trees at the running trail, and it became even more beautiful as we began talking to and also touching each other. When Stevie left, I didn't think my day could get any better. That was until Malcolm and I came into this place to see a beautiful mermaid standing next to the counter.

After the three of us went outside, we sat down in the lounge chairs at one of the umbrella tables but Malcolm stayed glued to Stevie. He sat on her lap, and in between his licks and bites of his scoop of Daiquiri Ice, she wiped off his mouth and chin with a napkin. Her nurturing attentiveness was something that I'd never seen in Avery before and it warmed my heart so much for Malcolm. He was eating it up along with his ice cream.

Right after we finished our frozen treats, Malcolm surprised Stevie and me both when he asked Stevie if he could go swimming with her. He then told her to make her mermaid tail grow, and she looked over at me and grinned.

"Malcolm, remember Stevie's tail only comes out at night," I said.

"I wanna see it now, Daddy."

He looked back and forth at Stevie and me, then placed his hands on her cheeks and held them there. While staring into each other's eyes, neither Malcolm nor Stevie said a word. They just looked at each other and smiled, sharing a moment the two of them seemed to understand and also need.

I noticed Stevie's eyes were welling up and then a tear started rolling down her cheek. She wiped it away, pulled Malcolm closer, hugged him and nuzzled his neck. He started giggling, and Stevie looked over at me.

"Are you okay?" I quietly asked her.

She sniffled and then shook her head. "Yes. This little boy of yours is just so precious."

"I think he is too."

Malcolm wasn't sidetracked for long. He again asked Stevie about making her mermaid tail grow so the two of them could go swimming together. Even if she really was a mermaid, there was no place for her and my son to go glide through some water.

"What are you and Malcolm doing after you leave here?" Stevie asked me.

"Going back home."

"So, is it really just you two?"

I knew at once what she was indirectly asking. She wanted to know if Avery was really in Lubbock, so I nodded yes. Yes, my self-centered, self-righteous, narcissistic wife was in west Texas—far away from here. Once again, she had run away from reality and from her responsibilities to go seek undeserved solace in the arms of her family, her friends, and also her lover.

"Zac, I know of a place where I could take Malcolm swimming if you're okay with me doing that," Stevie went on to say.

"Which place are you talking about?"

A soft smile and then a slight shrug of her shoulders. "I have a pool. Remember?"

I was surprised by her. Although her invitation to take Malcolm swimming was purely intended on her part, I knew that if I took him over to her house, Stevie and I would be getting even more personal in our relationship. Being inside her home was only going to increase the probability of the two of us stepping over the line. At least it would for me. The temptation of her was never going away. Regardless—I accepted Stevie's invitation by asking Malcolm if he wanted to go swimming with her in her pool. He immediately said yes while bouncing up and down on top of her lap. When it came down to it, he really wouldn't care if she donned a mermaid tail or not. He'd just enjoy being with Stevie.

"So it's a date then?" she asked me.

"It is."

"It's gonna be a really fun one, too."

"I agree. I need to get your address, though."

"Give me your cellphone number and I'll share my contact info with you."

I quietly drew in a deep breath because what we were about to do was yet another step that we were both willingly taking toward that forbidden line. After I gave Stevie my number, she texted me her contact info and I gave her the rest of mine. We had each other's work and personal phone numbers now, as well as each other's work and home addresses.

"I need to run by my house to get Malcolm's swimsuit and floaties," I said. "I'll text you when we start to head your way."

"Sounds good to me."

As we were getting ready to leave Baskin-Robbins, Stevie hugged Malcolm again, stood up while holding onto him, and then set him down on the patio floor. He reached for Stevie's hand and held it, and then he reached for mine, holding it too. It was the three of us linked together and the vision of it moved me. I didn't care how wrong I was for feeling like we were a family standing here. I also didn't care that taking Malcolm over to Stevie's house wasn't the best idea. Either way, he and I were going so that his wish of swimming with a mermaid could come true. I had my own wish, too, that would soon be coming true, and it was getting even closer to Stevie.

14
#aquatic

Stevie

Seeing Zac and Malcolm at Baskin-Robbins was the last thing that I ever expected to happen but was happy it did. It thrilled my heart to see that sweet little boy again—and also his kind and handsome daddy.

I could tell that Zac had doctored the cut on his bottom lip along with the other places where Avery scratched him. The wet-looking glaze of Neosporin or whatever he'd used was evident on his mouth and skin. I was relieved to see that Zac had done what I wanted him to do and I was also relieved to see that all the places already looked better.

I was at my house now, getting everything ready for the company who was going to be here soon. I knew that because Zac texted me right before he and Malcolm left his house to come to mine. Another thing I knew was where Zac lived. Coincidentally, it was only about a ten-minute drive from my house. As I was going over his contact info after I got home, I touched his address and it took me straight to my maps app. When I saw how close we actually lived to one another, I could only shake my head and smile.

When Zac let me know that he and Malcolm were on their way, I quickly texted him back to let him know about something special that I was going to do for Malcolm when it came time to go swimming and to just follow my lead. He sent back a mermaid emoji along with a red heart beside her.

The "something special" that I had planned for Malcolm was to wear my fake mermaid tail. It was a full-sized blue one my mom and dad had bought for me several years ago. I could actually wear it while swimming and it would securely stay on my body from my waist down. And amazingly, it looked real.

When I heard my doorbell ring, I took a deep breath and then went to greet the two Buchanans who were standing on the other side of my front door. The moment I opened it, they smiled.

"Hey, you and you!" I said, looking back and forth at them, then I told them to come in.

After stepping inside my foyer, Zac turned around and looked at me. "Thank you for doing this, Stevie."

"I'm happy to."

He glanced down at my lips like he'd done so many times in the short amount of time that we'd known each other and the effect was the same: butterflies in my stomach and also a sensation between my thighs that was good to feel again.

I held out my hand for the bag Zac was carrying, strapped across his shoulder. I knew it didn't have Malcolm's swimsuit in it because he was wearing it but thought for sure it had his floaties in it, as well as Zac's swimsuit. Right now, Zac was wearing his Asics running shoes, a different pair of running shorts than those he'd had on at Baskin-Robbins and also a different t-shirt. And his t-shirt? It caught my eye the moment I saw it because it had *Destin, Florida* printed on the front along with some palm trees. That locale was my favorite tropical getaway within the U.S. because of its beautiful white-sand beaches and clear blue water.

"I'm gonna go put this bag in the kitchen, and then I'll show you two around," I said. "Give me just a sec and I'll be right back."

Zac nodded and as soon as I started heading toward the kitchen, I felt a little hand grab my free one. Malcolm was walking beside me and looking up at me with his bright eyes that were the same color as his daddy's.

"I'm so happy you're here," I told him and he smiled, making that little dimple appear on his right cheek. Also the same as his daddy's.

After showing him and Zac around my cozy abode, I asked them if they were ready to go swimming.

"Yes!" Malcolm said before Zac could answer. This little boy was something else and his enthusiasm was contagious.

"Okay then, but I need you and your daddy to go use my bathroom first. It's important that you go tee-tee before you get into the water," I said, glancing up at Zac.

Those were my verbal and visual cues for him to distract Malcolm while I put on my mermaid tail. I already had on my black bikini and was also wearing a netted cover-up. It wasn't going to take me but a minute to get into costume and then I'd be ready to give Malcolm the surprise of his life.

As Zac was leading him toward the hallway, I said, "Feel free to use the guest bathroom or the master bath in my bedroom. Either is fine."

Zac looked over his shoulder at me and I watched the corners of his mouth curl up. Then I watched him keep going down the hallway toward my bedroom. It didn't surprise me that he chose to do that, either. Although he'd already gotten a quick peek at where I lay my head down at night to sleep, as well as where I took a shower and got dressed every day, he was about to get a closer look at the most personal space inside my home.

I knew he'd feel freer to look around without me standing beside him and I also knew how normal his curiosity was. I was in the same boat as him, although I knew I was never going to get to see the inside of the most personal space inside his home. I could imagine what it was like, though, just like I could imagine what Zac looked like when taking a shower, as well as laying in a bed. The bed that Brooke said he'd been sleeping in alone for over four years.

While he and Malcolm were gone, I ran outside onto the back patio, took off my cover-up, and then grabbed my mermaid tail out of the storage room. I slipped it on with ease while sitting on the edge of the swimming pool and then slid down into the water. I was floating on my back in the middle of the pool when Zac and Malcolm walked outside and saw me. Both of them had huge, surprised eyes and smiles. Malcolm ran over to the edge of the pool and started clapping his hands with excitement, and I swam over to him just like a real mermaid would've done.

"My tail grew during the daytime just for you, sweet one," I said.

"It's so pretty!"

"Thank you."

I was about to ask Zac where Malcolm's floaties were when Malcolm unexpectedly jumped into the water. I caught him before he went all the way under and then looked up at Zac. He immediately waved off my concern.

"He swims like a fish, Stevie. If you're really worried about him, though, I'll go get his floaties."

"As long as you're okay with him going without them, then I am. I've got my hands on him and I won't let him go."

"I'm more than okay with him not wearing his floaties. I know you've got him."

Zac smiled at me and then dropped his eyes down to my lips again. Then he went even lower, glancing at my bikini top-covered breasts. I kept floating in the water, holding Malcolm and watching his daddy's unapologetic display of attraction to me.

"Aren't you gonna swim with us?" I finally asked him.

"I hadn't planned on it."

"Why?"

"I thought the invitation was just for my boy."

"No, it was for both of you. I'm sorry, I should've clarified that."

"It's okay."

"You're welcome to swim in those running shorts that you have on."

"Are you sure?"

"Of course."

"Okay then. I will."

Without any delay, Zac pulled his cellphone and car keys out of his shorts pockets, tossed them over into the grass, and then took off his shoes and socks. He left them on the pool deck and then pulled his t-shirt over his head, leaving it on the deck, too. It wasn't until now—seeing him bare-chested—that I realized he had a tattoo above his heart. It was of tiny footprints along with some kind of writing beneath them. I didn't ask Zac about the black ink on his skin, though. That would come later. At this particular moment, I was more interested in letting my eyes wander over his tall, lean, and well-defined body.

After doing exactly that, I looked up to see Zac staring straight at me. He was grinning. I started grinning and then the two of us chuckled. I didn't care that he'd caught me checking him out again. I really liked what I saw and was still looking at, and Zac seemed to really like the fact that I did. After a few more lingering moments of eye contact with him, he dove into the water and swam up to Malcolm and me floating in the middle of my pool.

"Daddy, you're swimming with a mermaid too!" Malcolm cheered.

"I know, buddy! I've been wanting to swim with her just like you have. Isn't this so much fun?"

Malcolm shook his head in agreement and then I stretched out onto my back, holding him on top of me while swaying my tail back and forth. We began moving around in a wide circle. I could feel Zac watching us. Less than a minute later, he swam up beside me, stretched out on his back, and then started moving his legs—all three of us synchronized, going round and round together while swimming, talking, and laughing.

Something that Malcolm couldn't see was his daddy's arm wrapped around me beneath the surface of the water, but I definitely felt it and his hand on my skin. Zac was gently holding onto me, keeping me steady.

After about twenty minutes, he suggested we take a break, so the three of us swam over to the shallow end of my pool and I set Malcolm down on top of the steps.

"I wanna swim to you, Stevie," he said, holding out his arms toward me.

"I would love for you to swim to me!"

I backed up a few feet and then Malcolm jumped into the water, going beneath it. And just like Zac said—he swam like a fish and he did it with ease all the way to me. After catching him in my hands, pulling him above the water, and then telling him what a great job he did, I looked over at Zac to see him smiling so big. Big enough to make his eyes squint and crinkle around the corners again and big enough to make that dimple in his right cheek appear once more. This time, I couldn't help myself and reached out to touch it with my fingertip.

"What do you think about my boy's swimming ability?" Zac asked, grabbing my hand with his as I was pulling mine away from his face. Then he lowered them beneath the water—privately continuing to hold onto me with his fingers laced through mine. It was the first time a man had held my hand in years and I really liked the way that Zac's felt.

"You were right. He's like a fish in water and it really does come naturally."

After telling Zac that, I glanced down at the tattoo on his chest and then looked right back at it, keeping my eyes glued to the writing beneath what I could now clearly see were baby footprints. I took a deep breath and asked Zac what I already knew the answer to.

"Those are Malcolm's, aren't they?"

"Yes."

"And that's his birthdate, right?"

"It is."

I looked at the date again while shaking my head to myself.

"What is it, Stevie?" Zac asked.

"Malcolm is a Pisces like I am and that explains why he's so drawn to anything aquatic."

"I thought about that, too, after you and I had our talk about zodiac signs in the Whole Foods parking lot."

"There's something else that I wanna tell you, though," I said, stealing another glance at the date inked onto Zac's skin.

"Okay."

"Let's all go swim around in circles again and then I'll let you know what's on my mind."

Zac's eyes filled with concern. "Are you all right?"

"Yeah. I will be."

As soon as the three of us reached the middle of my pool and began our synchronized swimming all over again, I began telling Zac about *my* Malcolm and how I lost him. The last thing that I told him was something else that he wasn't expecting to hear: that my son died on the same day that Zac's Malcolm was born. After I revealed that fact, he remained quiet and just kept searching my eyes with his.

"Stevie, I had no idea about any of this," he finally said.

"I know you didn't."

"I am so incredibly sorry for your loss. I cannot imagine what you went through. Between losing your son four years ago, your mother a year ago, and then going through a divorce—I don't see how you're sane."

I chuckled. "Water, running, Hendricks gin, and my father, plus my old boss and good friend Melissa Landry, are to thank for my sanity."

Zac nodded and then gently squeezed my waist with his hand. I knew he intended that squeeze as a comforting gesture—and it was—but it also made me feel like crawling into his arms. I wanted to feel *both* of them wrapped around me just like they'd been at the running trail this morning. I wanted to share that same kind of intimate embrace with Zac right this second, feel his body pressed against mine and the side of my face resting against his, and I wanted it to happen here within this water that he and I both enjoyed so much.

I couldn't crawl into his arms, though, where I knew he'd immediately receive me. We weren't alone like we were less than eight hours ago. We had an audience of one at the moment, and it was Zac's mini-me, who was kicking his legs and having fun making little splashes in my pool.

"Something that I never dreamed would happen is that date on your chest becoming something positive for me, but it has," I went on to say. "The birth of *your* son has made it that way and I'm grateful."

Zac nodded at me again and remained quiet. Then he gazed up at the summer sky above us, and that's when I noticed the tears forming in his eyes, matching mine. I looked back at Malcolm, who was looking back and forth between his daddy and me. He smiled at us and then started kicking his little legs again in the water. And again—Zac gave me another comforting squeeze on my waist, but this time, after he did, he pulled my body even closer to his.

The three of us continued floating for about five more minutes, going round and round in circles, then Malcolm said, "I need to go tee-tee, Daddy."

"Okay. I'll take you back to mermaid Stevie's bathroom."

Zac reached out for Malcolm and the three of us swam over to the steps again. As the two Buchanans were getting out of the water, I told the eldest where the beach towels were. He smiled and thanked me.

As he and his mini-me stepped onto the pool deck, I noticed something. Not about Malcolm. About Zac.

Because his running shorts were wet now, they were hanging lower in the front and I could see quite a bit of his Adonis belt. They were the two V-shaped muscular grooves on every man's abdomen that ran vertically alongside their hips. And Zac's? To say they were visually appealing to me was putting it lightly.

As I watched Zac walk Malcolm over to the patio table and begin drying him off with one of the beach towels that I'd put there, I kept thinking about the name "Adonis." In Greek Mythology, he was the god of fertility and the mortal lover of Aphrodite, the goddess of sexual love and beauty. A man who was considered desirable and attractive was often referred to as an "Adonis" and I was currently staring at one named Zac Buchanan. He was so desirable and attractive and he obviously had the fertility part covered too.

"We'll be right back," he said, looking over his shoulder at me.

"Take your time."

While they were gone, I took off my mermaid's tail and put it back into the storage room. Then I wrapped a beach towel around my waist and sat down on one of the chairs next to the patio table. My cellphone was within reach and the thought of playing a music playlist that I had on it crossed my mind. I'd made it while in Destin, Florida—a solo trip that I intentionally took alone, not long after losing my Malcolm. I did it despite Graham's objection, as well as my parents' concern. It was just something that I had to do for myself and I'd never regretted it.

I could vividly remember my first night there, sitting on the beach, listening to the waves crashing against the shoreline, breathing in the salty air, and gazing up at the sky. From where I sat and as far as I could see, it looked like an ocean of stars above me.

After being on the beach for about half an hour, I decided to play some music on my cellphone and knew which song I wanted to hear first: "Nightingale" by Norah Jones. It fit the state of my heart and my soul at the time. While listening, all the emotions that I'd been holding inside began pouring out and I let them continue pouring until I couldn't cry anymore.

When I went back inside the beach house that I'd rented, I created a Pandora playlist and added "Nightingale" first. After that night and in the days that followed, I continued adding songs from all genres. Some of them helped me continue grieving my loss of Malcolm while others helped me smile. Since that trip, my feelings about all my grieving songs had evolved into something positive. I could listen to any one of them now without getting emotional. I enjoyed the songs for what they were: a beautiful gift. In the mood to hear the gift of Norah Jones again, I grabbed my cellphone and began playing the song in the number one slot on my playlist.

As soon as Zac and Malcolm walked back outside, Malcolm came running up to me with his eyes big and full of worry.

"Where did your tail go, Stevie?" he asked.

"I had to make it go away for a little while so it could rest. It was tired from swimming."

Malcolm didn't say anything else about it. He just crawled into my lap and rested his tiny body against mine. I wrapped my arms around him, snuggled him even closer to me, and then asked Zac if he was going to join us. He was still standing up and staring straight at me.

"I'd love to, but I feel like we've already taken up enough of your time," he said.

"No, you haven't. I don't have anything else planned for the rest of this day and would very much enjoy it if you two stayed here for a little while longer."

Zac paused, then finally said, "Okay, we'll stay. Thank you."

"Of course. Now have a seat."

As he sat down, he glanced over at my cellphone. "That's Norah Jones I hear."

"It sure is."

"I haven't heard her music in a long time."

"I listen to her almost every day. I love her voice."

"Yeah, it's really smooth."

"And soothing."

"And sultry."

I smiled. "Yes, that too."

"Have you ever seen her in concert?"

"Nope. I hope to one day, though. She's my favorite music artist."

"Why haven't you gone to see her, then?"

"Because I'd be attending the concert alone. I don't know of anyone who'd be interested in going with me."

Zac raised his hand and grinned. "Um...hello?"

I laughed and then pointed out what we both already knew. It'd be frowned upon if we attended anything together. As much fun as I felt like Zac and I would have, we could never take that risk.

"Unfavorable circumstances can hamper a lot of things that we wanna do," Zac said, glancing down at my lips.

Our conversation stopped right where it was, but what didn't stop was the mounting desire that I could see burning in Zac's eyes again. I knew he could see it burning in mine too. We needed to change course because, once again, we were pushing the limits. Zac and I were playing with this undeniable fire between us by the things that we were saying and also by the way that we were looking at each other. But damn, it felt so incredible to be wanted by him like this.

"So would you or Malcolm like something to drink or eat?" I asked, steering things in a different direction.

"I'm good. Thank you, though. Are you thirsty or hungry, son?" Zac asked Malcolm.

He cut his eyes over at his daddy and shook his head yes, then said he was thirsty.

"Would you like water or orange juice?" I asked him.

"Water."

I started to get up but Zac held up his hand for me to stop. "I'll get it for him. Just tell me where."

"Over there," I said, pointing at my mini-fridge next to the storage room. "I have bottles of water in there and also some bottles of Topo Chico with lime if you'd like to try one."

Zac jerked his head back, smiling. "Topo Chico with lime, huh?"

"Yeah. Have you heard of it before?"

"Yes. I have some at home, and on occasion, I use it instead of tonic water with Hendricks. It's lighter and crisper."

"Oh, I know. On occasion, I use it too."

Zac chuckled, and so did I, about this other likeness between us. Then he said, "If you don't mind, I'm gonna have a Topo Chico. I like it just by itself."

"Grab one for me too while you're at it. There's a bottle opener on the side of the fridge."

"Okay."

After getting a bottle of water for Malcolm and our two drinks, Zac sat back down across from me. We began talking again and before I knew it, Malcolm had drunk two-thirds of his water. He handed his bottle to me and then rested his little body against mine once more while his daddy and I continued getting to know each other even better with our back-and-forth questions and answers about random things while continuing to listen to my music playlist.

I didn't know how much time had passed when Zac pointed at Malcolm and I looked down to see him sound asleep in my arms. I started running my fingers through his silky blond hair, and when I looked back up at Zac, the corners of his mouth were curled up.

"What are you grinning about?" I whispered.

"Malcolm loves to have his hair played with like that."

"I used to do this to my Malcolm and he'd relax right into a deep sleep. He was born with a headful of cotton-white hair."

"So was that boy in your lap." Zac sighed and then went on to say, "Stevie, I have to tell you again how sorry I am about you losing your son."

"I appreciate it. I wanted to tell you about him before today but the timing was never right. After seeing your tattoo earlier though, I knew it finally was."

"I'm curious about something."

"So ask me."

"What made you choose the name *Malcolm*?"

"It's a strong Scottish name."

Zac nodded. "That's exactly why I chose it."

"It's a good name," I said, then leaned down and kissed the top of Malcolm's head. When I met Zac's gaze again, he was shaking his back and forth.

"I can't get over the way that Malcolm is being with you. He's totally at home," he said.

"I love children."

"And it shows."

"They're little for such a short amount of time and their childhood should be as happy and peaceful and magical as possible. Full of unicorns and fairy dust and rainbows."

Zac smiled. "And mermaids."

"Yes. And mermaids."

"Malcolm is never gonna forget this day with you."

"I won't forget it either. The look on his face when he saw my tail was priceless."

"I know. He was so excited. Thank you again for doing all of this for him. I was so surprised when you invited us over here."

"Something inside me told me to do it—that it was okay. I didn't think about it earlier, but now I'm wondering how Avery is gonna respond to you having brought Malcolm over here to swim with me. He's so smart, and I feel like he's gonna talk to whomever he can about this day."

"If he does, then he does. I'll handle whatever comes of it."

"Okay. I just don't wanna cause any issues for you."

"You're not, Stevie, so stop worrying."

"I'll try. And by the way, I see that you did what I suggested. The cut on your bottom lip and all those scratches on your body already look better."

"Thanks to you. Normally, I just let them heal on their own."

"Do you mind telling me when the altercation between you and Avery happened?"

"Last night."

I shrugged. "What caused it?"

"Nothing. Avery is just volatile, and when she drinks, it's worse. She looks for things to fight about. I usually don't engage, but last night I did because I had enough of her. I spoke my piece on the way I felt about her behavior and she started trying to claw me up and hit me like she's done before."

"And you held up your hands to block her blows, didn't you?"

"Yes. I also tried to get away from her. I've left my house with Malcolm so many times and just gone driving around to give Avery time to cool down or pass out."

"Where was Malcolm when all of this was happening last night?"

"Asleep in his bed—sleeping as peacefully as he is right now, resting there against you," he said, nodding at him. "The fight with Avery happened in our backyard. After I got Malcolm to sleep, I felt like getting into my pool to relax. I didn't wanna drink any gin which would've helped me relax, but I wasn't in the mood for it. I just wanted to be in the water."

"So you were in your pool when Avery came outside?"

"Yes. She stumbled out the back door and when I saw her, I got out of the pool. I didn't know what she was gonna try to do. Then she came up to me and started telling me how sorry she thought I was while calling me every derogatory name in the book including every four-letter cuss word there is. I didn't call her any names but I did cuss back, which I normally don't do."

"Zac, I understand why you did. You had every right to do that and to also call Avery derogatory names."

"She and I were in each other's faces when she started coming at me with her hands. She's got those fake nails and they're like weapons. She got me good with them but she also lost a few in the process. I found them later by the pool."

I blew out a heavy breath. "Wow. Avery's behavior just boggles my mind. She's a woman. A mother, for God's sake."

"I know."

"So how did things end up dissolving last night?"

"Losing that last fake nail seemed to really hurt Avery, despite the alcohol in her system. She stopped coming at me but did spit at me before she turned around and stumbled back into our house to go to bed."

I knew it wasn't the bed that Zac slept in, but he didn't know that I knew that, so I asked him.

"She went to bed and you actually got into it with her whenever it was that you finally decided to go to sleep?"

"Hell no, I didn't. And forgive my language."

I held up my hand. "I'm not offended in the least."

"Avery and I have been sleeping in separate bedrooms since before Malcolm was born."

"I'm sorry to hear that."

"Don't be. It's better that she and I stay apart from each other as much as possible."

I stared at Zac while thinking about taking this conversation to the next level. Then I decided to.

"Do me a favor?" I asked.

"Name it."

"Start taking pictures of the marks that Avery leaves on you. Start recording her too. Document the incidents."

"I already have and will continue to do so."

"Good."

"This morning at the running trail, you and I briefly talked about the reason why I stay in my marriage."

"Yes, we did. It's because of Malcolm, and I understand."

"I cannot imagine ever splitting custody of him with Avery. Not only do I not wanna be a part-time father to him but I also don't trust Avery to take care of him like a mother should. Like I know you would."

I gave Zac an appreciative smile. "It breaks my heart in two knowing you and Malcolm live in such a toxic environment. You both deserve so much better."

"My parents tell me that all the time."

"Where do they live?"

"Here in Dallas. About twenty minutes from my house. If it wasn't for them, I don't know what I'd do or where I'd be. They've been there for me from day one when things first started going downhill with Avery, and they stayed right with me when Malcolm came along. He's their only grandchild and they're crazy about him. They keep him for me all the time too so I can work, plus none of us wanna put Malcolm in a daycare."

"I don't blame you at all for that. Zac, do you not have any siblings?"

"No, I'm an only child."

"So am I." Malcolm started stirring around in my arms but then settled back down. "He's having a really good nap," I said, running my fingers through his hair again.

"He feels secure with you."

"I'm glad he does. He's a little angel."

"He's a special little boy, for sure."

"I don't know if I should tell you this, but I'm gonna do it anyway and I hope you take it the right way."

"Whatever it is, I'm sure I will."

"I had a dream about my Malcolm during my first night here in this house. He wasn't an infant, though. He looked to be around four years old and strangely, his physical appearance was like your Malcolm's. Identical, in fact."

"Are-are you serious?" Zac stammered.

"Completely."

"How did you know it was your Malcolm in your dream?"

"He talked to me. That's how I knew, plus I sensed it."

"What did he say to you?"

"Mommy, I love you and I'm still here."

Zac softly smiled. "His soul is with you."

I felt the sting in my eyes and looked down at Zac's Malcolm in my arms, hugged him even tighter, and kissed the top of his head. Then I looked back up at Zac.

"I believe it's something like that."

"Stevie, why couldn't I have met someone like you ten years ago? It's been hell living with Avery all these years and I can't help but wonder what I did to deserve it. It's like—what'd I do in a past life?"

"You think what you're going through is due to karma?"

"I can't help but think that."

"I think it comes down to blind choices that we're all guilty of making, plus the repercussions of making them. Sometimes, we see in people what we wanna see instead of who they really are. I believe that's what happened when you got together with Avery."

"I've never heard it put that way, but I think you're right."

"Looking back, do you recognize any red flags?"

"Yes, I do. There was a big one in particular that I should've paid closer attention to and asked a whole lot more about."

"And which one was that?"

"Avery was engaged to a guy that she met in college and he broke off their engagement a month before their wedding. Everything was paid for—Avery's dress, the flowers, the photographer, the caterer, the D.J., etc. And after the guy ended things, Avery and her mother went to where they bought the wedding dress, and also the flowers, returned the merchandise, and then demanded they get their money back. The florist said she couldn't refund the money because it went against the store's policy. Avery's mother became so furious that she actually grabbed Avery's bridal bouquet off the counter and threw it at the florist. Then she cussed her out."

I scoffed. "It's not hard to see where Avery learned her behavior."

"You're right about that. Of course, in her mind, all of that mess had nothing to do with her. It was all on her fiancé."

"Let me guess... She gave you a sob story, didn't she? Played the victim? Made some horrible accusations about the guy that would make one wonder why she wanted to marry him in the first place?"

"She did exactly that. And as for playing the victim? She still does that well. She's never owned up to anything that would shine a bad light on her."

"To me, it sounds like that guy decided to reexamine the red flags about Avery and when he did, he pulled the plug on everything."

"I should've done the same thing. What about you and your past marriage? Looking back, do you recognize any red flags?"

"None at all. Graham and I were high school sweethearts, got married two years after graduation, got our careers going, and were really happy and doing so well until we lost Malcolm. It devastated our marriage. I totally shut down and threw myself into my work at the D.A.'s office. Graham and I became roommates for the most part and because of his own loneliness, he turned to my best friend, Emma, for love and affection."

"The only similarity that I see between your situation and mine is the roommate part."

"Not the loneliness part, too?" I asked.

"Are you asking me if Avery is lonely or if I'm lonely?"

"I don't care about her. I wanna know about you."

Zac swallowed hard. "I was lonely, Stevie."

"*Was?*"

"Yes. Until I met you."

I swallowed hard then. "I was lonely too, but didn't realize how much until I met you. You made me start feeling things again that a woman should feel and because of you, I'm not lonely anymore, either."

Zac got up from his chair and walked over to mine, then knelt down beside me. I reached out and held his handsome face in my hand, and seconds after I did, he placed his hand on top of mine. The moment stood still between us and I didn't want it to end because it was so honest and raw and vulnerable and real.

"We're doing it again, Sinclair," he whispered.

"Doing what?" I whispered back.

"Playing with this fire between us."

"And what do you suggest we do about it this time?"

"Let it burn."

"Neither one of us could afford the cost if we did."

Zac searched my eyes, nodded once, and then stood up. I thought he was going to sit back down but he didn't. Instead, he moved over and stood directly in front of me, then leaned down and placed his hands on the arms of my chair. His face and mine were only inches apart and he was staring straight at me.

"It doesn't change the fact that I still wanna kiss you," he said. "No—I wanna do more than that to you, Stevie."

"And I want you to."

Zac drew in a deep breath then closed the little bit of space between us by planting his lips on me—but not on my mouth. He kissed me on the cheek like he had this morning in the woods at the running trail. And just like then, he didn't immediately pull back. His lips were still on my skin, and the warmth of them made me feel like turning my head and kissing Zac's mouth despite the treacherous pathway it'd undoubtedly send us flying down. I could feel myself starting to give in to the overpowering temptation of this man when his son began stirring in my arms. Zac pulled his lips away from my cheek, looked down at Malcolm, and then looked back up at me.

"You just started to kiss me, didn't you?" he quietly asked. "I felt you turning your head."

"Yes... I did. I'm sorry."

"There's nothing to be sorry about."

"I don't want you or anybody to get hurt," I said, stealing a glance at Malcolm. He'd settled back into sleeping. "All three of us most assuredly will if you and I keep playing with this fire. So walk away from me this time, Zac, because I don't have the willpower to walk away from you again."

"I'm not going anywhere."

As soon as he finished whispering those words to me, he leaned all the way in and kissed me on the lips. I closed my eyes and breathed into Zac as he breathed into me. Then he began moving his lips across mine, slowly brushing them back and forth. Moments later, our tongues found one another's. They gently touched, they tasted and they teased.

Zac pulled back and looked at me then leaned in again and started kissing me more deeply. We were both breathing faster and wanting so much more than this illicit kiss. Everything came to an immediate halt, though, because Malcolm started stirring around again.

"Daddy, I need to go tee-tee," he said, lifting his head up off my chest. Zac and I both looked down at him and he looked up at us with his sleepy blue eyes.

"Okay. I'll take you to mermaid Stevie's bathroom again. Did you have a good nap?" Zac asked him.

Malcolm slowly nodded, and then Zac picked him up and held him in his arms.

"We'll be right back," he said to me, glancing down at my lips.

"I'll be right here waiting for you."

Zac turned around and started heading toward my back door. I kept my eyes on them and couldn't help but grin when Malcolm peeked over his daddy's shoulder and gave me that dimpled smile of his. It was only a few minutes later that the two of them rejoined me.

"As much as I hate to leave, I think we probably should. The sun is gonna be setting soon," Zac said, looking down at Malcolm standing beside him. Father and son were holding hands. "I need to get this boy home and settled in for the evening, plus I have some prep work that I need to do on one of my cases."

"Would it happen to be the case you're opposing me on?"

Zac grinned. "Yes, it would be."

"I see."

"Are you ready to face off against me, Sinclair?"

"I've been ready, Buchanan."

"No surprise there. Your Joan of Arc reputation precedes you."

"And your warrior-in-court reputation precedes you."

"How are we supposed to do all of this though, after..."

He cut his sentence short, but I still knew what he was asking me. He wanted to know how we were supposed to keep things professional after becoming so personal in our conversations, with our shared touches, and especially after kissing each other as passionately as we'd done only minutes ago.

"We're gonna do what we both know is right."

"In or out of court?"

I stared at Zac already knowing what my answer was about the "in court" part of his question. I would always do what was right when it came to covering my legal responsibilities. I'd fight like hell to defend the defenseless. It didn't matter if I was going up against the sexy legal eagle, Zac Buchanan.

When it came to the "out of court" part of his question, I knew what my answer should've been, but I couldn't say it because it wasn't true to how I was feeling deep down inside. I didn't want to do "right" when it came to the personal side of my relationship with Zac. Adhering to that moral standard was something that I wasn't interested in doing any longer.

For thirty years, I'd done everything that I *should*, and look where it had gotten me. Now, this pastor's daughter was ready to travel down a different pathway. The wrong one in the eyes of others—but it was the right one for me at this stage in my life. I had no clue where it was going to lead me and that was okay. I wasn't scared and I had no expectations. I wasn't looking for anything from Zac other than this fiery companionship between us that was filling the emptiness inside me. An emptiness that the past four years had put there. Zac and I were going to have to work really hard, though, at keeping what we were doing under wraps.

"In court," I finally said.

Zac studied my eyes and then nodded. We both understood the agreement that we'd just made to do what we knew was right when it came to our jobs. We also understood the unspoken agreement we'd just made to do what was right for the two of us in our personal lives despite the moral conflict.

"May I call you later?" Zac asked me.

"I was hoping you would."

"Is nine o'clock too late?"

I shook my head no. "I usually don't go to bed until around midnight. Sometimes later."

"So you're a night owl?"

"I am. I love nighttime and how quiet it is. Everything seems so peaceful in the world when it's dark outside."

"Do you ever go swimming at night?"

"I *float* in my pool at night is what I do," I chuckled. "I lie on my back in the water and stare up at the sky. It gives me the sensation of floating in space. I know that sounds weird."

"No, it doesn't."

"Do you ever go swimming at night?" I asked, then held out my hands toward Malcolm. Without hesitation, he walked back over to me, and I picked him up and hugged him while he rested his head on my shoulder.

"I do go swimming at night and I do the same thing that you do," Zac said. "I also get the same sensation of floating in space."

"Another likeness between us, Buchanan."

"Maybe one of these nights, we can—you know."

And I did know. He wanted the two of us to go swimming together sometime after the sun had set. He didn't want to say that in front of Malcolm, though, and I understood why.

"That'd be nice."

Zac smiled and walked over to pick up his cellphone and car keys out of the grass. Then he picked up his running shoes, socks, and *Destin, Florida* t-shirt off the pool deck. After putting everything back on, I asked him if he wanted to wrap himself and Malcolm up in a couple of my beach towels for their drive home.

"I'll take one for my boy, but I'm good. My shorts are barely damp now."

I got up from my chair while still holding on to Malcolm and grabbed a dry beach towel out of my storage bench. After wrapping him up in it, I asked him if he'd had fun today. He nodded yes and then he leaned against me again. After hugging him and kissing his cheek, I stood back up straight and the towel that I'd wrapped around my waist came undone and fell onto the patio floor. Zac had already seen the top of my black bikini but not the bottoms and they left very little to the imagination. I hadn't planned on being this exposed in front of him or Malcolm, but it was too late to do anything about it now.

When I looked up at Zac, he was in the process of canvassing me with his eyes. After he was done, he let out a long sigh.

"What is it?" I asked.

He shook his head back and forth. "Nothing."

"Sure about that?"

"No, I'm not sure about *that*, but I am sure it's best that my boy and I go home now."

"And if you didn't?"

"Something might get started here between y-o-u and m-e if someone fell a-s-l-e-e-p again," he said, glancing at Malcolm and I had to smile.

The first reason was Zac spelling out his words to keep his precious little boy, still standing in front of me, out of our conversation loop. I thought it was so cute. The second reason I smiled was that I knew exactly what would get started between Zac and me if he and Malcolm stayed here and Malcolm fell asleep again. Not in my lap but somewhere inside the house, such as on my couch or in my guest bedroom. I knew Zac and I would have sex. I also knew how many times I'd already imagined that very thing happening.

Zac kept staring at me, then shifted his feet, and a low, brief groan escaped his throat. I instantly knew what he'd really just done. He shifted his cock around. Although his t-shirt perfectly fit him, it wasn't long enough to completely cover the front of his gray running shorts. I could see the beginning of his erection and even the outline of the tip of his cock. His shorts still had enough dampness in them to make what was happening beneath them that much more visible and I liked what I saw. Zac was an extremely well-endowed man.

"I'll walk you out to your car," I said, stealing another glance at the front of his shorts.

Zac bit down on his bottom lip and grinned at me. He knew I was checking out his cock and I didn't care.

"Okay."

"Are you sure you don't want a towel to wrap up in?"

"I'm sure. I've got that bag that I brought with me. I'll use it as camouflage because I wouldn't wanna alarm any of your neighbors if they saw what was going on with me at the moment—thanks to you."

"You're welcome," I giggled. "And I'm not worried about my neighbors."

"Here, let's get you wrapped back up before we walk out front."

Zac came over to me and bent down to pick up my towel. As he was standing back up, I watched his eyes trail up my body. After looking into my eyes like he could devour me, he slowly wrapped my towel around my waist and when he was done, he, the little Buchanan and I walked into my house.

While on our way to the front door, Zac kept his hand on the small of my back, guiding me, while Malcolm and I held hands. When we stepped onto the front porch, I looked over at Zac's Blazer and then back at him.

"Has your engine been running this whole time?" I asked.

"No, I auto-started it from my phone before we came out here."

"Oh, I didn't realize you'd done that."

"Gotta cool down the car for little man there," Zac said, looking at Malcolm.

After strapping him into his car seat, I kissed the top of his sweet head and then told him how happy I was that he'd come over to swim with me. He smiled, looking just like his daddy with that dimple in his right cheek showing again and those sky-blue eyes.

After I stepped away from him, Zac said, "Son, you wait right there for me. I'll get in the car in a minute. Okay?" Malcolm nodded, and Zac tossed the bag that he'd been covering the front of his shorts with into the floorboard, closed the car door, and looked at me. "Do you mind walking around to the back of my car so I can talk to you?"

"That's fine. Let's go."

When we reached it, he turned to me and asked, "Are we really doing this, Stevie?"

"Doing what?"

He sighed out a smile. "You know what I'm talking about."

"Yes, I do. *This* is the beginning of an affair, Zac. Something I never thought in a million years I'd have with someone. You know I was raised by a preacher-man and you also know my ex-husband had an affair while we were married."

"I've thought about all of that."

"After meeting you, though, and getting to know all about you—well, I've realized a person can't understand the position that you and I have found ourselves in unless they've traveled down this pathway. They can't understand why we'd intentionally choose to commit adultery knowing how wrong it is. Although you and I have only kissed, we both know it was wrong— and what I've already imagined you doing to me, long before today, is really wrong."

"What have you imagined me doing to you?"

Before answering Zac, I looked at his lips, admiring them and also the dark brown razor stubble surrounding them. Then I ran my eyes along his chiseled jawline, shadowed by even more razor stubble. After that, I let my eyes wander down the full length of Zac's tall, muscular body and then met his gaze again.

"I'm just gonna say it, Buchanan, and it's that I've imagined you fucking me in my bed, in my shower, in my swimming pool, in the woods at the running trail, on a beach. You name it. I've imagined your lips, your tongue and your hands all over my body, and also your cock so deep inside me that I lose complete control of myself."

Zac shifted his feet again, letting out a deeper groan than earlier. When I looked down, I noticed his erection was coming back. Quickly. This time, he put his hand against the front of his running shorts and adjusted his cock.

"God, what you're doing to me saying all of those things," he whispered.

"You asked."

"Yes, I did." Another adjustment of his cock then he said, "Stevie, I've imagined the same things that you have except I had you in *my* bed, in *my* shower, and in *my* swimming pool.

I've imagined fucking you in those three places and also in the woods at the running trail, as well as on the Destin, Florida beach. And every time I've imagined fucking you—hard *and* slow and easy—I made you lose complete control of yourself. I made you cum unlike you ever have and you did the same for me."

Although it wasn't showing on me like it was on Zac, I was just as aroused as he was. I could feel the wetness in my bikini bottoms.

"To answer your question about if we're really doing *this*... Yes, we are. Unless you wanna stop everything right now. And if you do, I understand," I said, glancing in Malcolm's direction.

"I don't wanna stop a thing."

"Neither do I."

"Are you nervous, Sinclair?"

"Of course I am. This is foreign territory to me and I'm not sure how to navigate it."

"Same here."

"I know. Are *you* nervous about what's happening here between us?"

"Yes. My heart is pounding."

"I have to say one more thing and it's that I have no expectations of you, Zac. I understand your circumstances and if, at any point, you feel like *this* needs to stop, then just tell me. Okay?"

His eyes danced across my face then he nodded. "I appreciate everything that you just said—but I won't be the one to stop *this*. I've waited too long for someone like you to come into my life. And as far as expectations go? I don't have any of you either. You owe me nothing, and if you feel at any point that our affair needs to end, then just tell *me*. Okay?"

"I will."

Zac gently took my face into his hands, ran his thumb across my bottom lip, and then kissed me once more.

After we told each other goodbye, I watched him get into his car and drive away. When I could no longer see his white

Chevy Blazer, I went back inside my house and made myself a Hendricks and tonic with lime. Lots of lime, just like my secret lover preferred. Then I walked outside onto my back patio with my drink, journal, pen, and my cellphone.

Sitting at the patio table now, I set my playlist to random. Another one of Norah Jones' songs didn't come on, though. One that I'd recently added to the playlist did. It was a song titled "Hurt Nobody." Andrew Belle sang it, and he did an amazing job of it, too. I loved his voice. It was smooth and also sultry—just like Zac had described Norah Jones's.

"Hurt Nobody" was a song that got to me the first time I heard it. It wasn't only due to Andrew Belle's singing ability. It also had to do with the lyrics. I'd first interpreted them as a scenario that involved a man who was crazy about a woman but the woman had never noticed him before. The man wanted her so much and he also wanted to do right by her. He didn't want anybody to get hurt.

The scenario was an innocent one but now, listening to this song again, I could see how the lyrics also applied to a not-so-innocent scenario involving a man and a woman. A scenario like the one I'd allowed myself to get caught up in with Zac. A scenario that had "hurt" written all over it. Still—I was willing to take this risk because I wanted that kinsman of mine. He was as soothing to me as the ocean had always been, and all I wanted to do was to continue immersing myself within his tranquil, deep waters every chance I got.

I was well aware that all of *this* that he and I were doing could all come to an end at any time. Even today. Zac could make it home with Malcolm, think about the risky pathway down which we'd both agreed to journey, and decide to turn back. If he did, then he did. I'd be fine either way. I felt like no matter what happened, he and I would always be good friends, even if we had to stop being lovers.

I started "Hurt Nobody" over again and by the time it ended, I'd finished my drink. Then I opened up my journal to begin making my entry for today. The only words that came to me were: "To thine own self be true." My mom's favorite quote. I wrote it down, scribbled the date at the bottom of the page, closed my journal, and then jumped into the pool to float for a while. And also wait for Zac's phone call.

15
#sohelpmegod

Stevie

By the time Zac called me last night, I'd already put a guilt trip on myself for allowing things to go as far as they had with him. Was I being true to myself? Yes and no. The way I was raised was currently sparring with the newly single me who was now viewing life through a different set of eyes that I never imagined having.

When Zac called me at 9:00 p.m. on the dot., he thanked me again for the mermaid adventure I'd taken Malcolm on earlier. Right after that, he moved into talking about us. He wanted to know when he could see me again. That was when I told him about my internal tug-of-war about what we were doing, plus how I felt it was best for everyone involved if he and I stopped *this* right where it was.

He grew quiet after I explained myself to him, then finally said, "I understand. But please don't stop talking to me, Stevie. I need your companionship."

I agreed, because I needed his too, and then we went back to chatting with each other and kept the subject matter light. It was strained, awkward and disappointing, though. It was also something I should've expected to happen. It was hard to go backward after being intimate with someone. Even if it was just kissing.

It wasn't long after our conversation became such a struggle that we ended it and hung up. I didn't bother taking a shower before going to bed. I just crawled underneath my covers with damp pool-water hair and the scent of chlorine on my skin. When I woke up this morning, Zac was the first thing on my mind. I wondered what time he'd gone to bed last night and how he'd slept. Me? I slept like shit. I tossed and turned all night, struggling with my mess of internal feelings.

After making myself a cup of coffee, the thought of sending Zac a simple "Good morning" text crossed my mind. *It would be harmless*, I told myself, but then asked myself how I'd feel if Zac sent me a text like that. It would make me feel excited was what it would do. It would also leave me feeling hopeful and wanting more.

Standing in my kitchen now, trying to fully digest the fact that I really did pull back from seeing a man that fit me in seemingly every way except for him being married, I found myself feeling an emotion that I hadn't felt in months: grief. I was grieving the loss of something that had already become so wonderful and would have undoubtedly continued to become even more wonderful if I hadn't brought it to an end. But then I reminded myself that I never really had it to lose to begin with. Or rather, I never really had Zac to lose, because he wasn't mine to have. He never would be, either, so I decided against sending that sunrise text message to him and got ready for work instead.

I needed to go pull some records from the courthouse, so that was my first stop instead of going straight to the D.A.'s office like I normally did. The moment I walked into the building, my stomach filled with butterflies. Zac was going through the security line. He'd just put what I guessed were his car keys, wallet, phone, plus any legal paperwork that he might've had into the plastic tub to be scanned by the police officer. As if he sensed my presence, he jerked his head up and looked straight at me. Then he smiled.

He was walking through the metal detector when I reached the end of the line to wait my turn. As soon as I was scanned and cleared to go to the records division, I grabbed my keys, cellphone, and purse out of the plastic tub and began making my way to the elevators. I glanced around but didn't see Zac anywhere and felt the butterflies in my stomach turn into knots. I thought he would've waited for me to make it through security and at least said hello.

I had just made it to the elevators and pushed the button to call one down to the first floor when I sensed someone standing behind me and looked over my shoulder. As soon as I saw those sky-blue eyes of Zac's, all the butterflies that'd been inside me returned.

"Hey, you," he said quietly.

"Hey."

"You doing okay this morning?"

"I'm doing okay. How about you?" I asked, turning to face him directly.

"I'm okay right now but I know I'm gonna have to bust out an energy drink later. I only slept four hours last night."

"I'm so sorry, Zac. This is all my fault. I should've never..."

"Stevie, don't," he said, cutting me off. "Nothing here is your fault. I'm the one to blame. I never should have kissed you that first time."

I glanced around us. Strangely, we were the only two people standing by the elevators despite the courthouse being abuzz. When I met Zac's gaze again, I told him that yes, he should've kissed me that first time and all the others too. Then I told him that I had no regrets and that he shouldn't either.

"Easier said than done," he breathed out. As soon as those words left his mouth, he looked down at mine and softly smiled. "By the way... After you and I hung up from talking on the phone last night, when I was brushing my teeth, I took a closer look at myself in the mirror because I noticed my lips were sparkly. Your gloss was all over them."

"Oh shit. I did not even notice that before you left my house. I was, I guess, just so caught up in everything."

"I know. Me too. And I'll tell you again that I don't mind your lip gloss being on me. Do you see my struggle going on here?"

I nodded yes. "I'm just as conflicted about things as you are."

"I keep teetering back and forth. One minute, I regret taking things as far as I did with you, but then I don't regret it. But then I do again. I just want you and me to be like we were before that first kiss happened: two people with a whole lot in common who enjoy each other's company."

"Our commonalities will always be there and I'll always enjoy your company, Zac."

The words between us stopped and we stared into each other's eyes. I could feel myself wanting to give in to him again. So much, I wanted to tell him that I didn't mean what I'd said last night. I really did want *this*—I wanted to have an affair. I wanted any pieces of Zac and his life he could give to me because even in the smallest of pieces lay such treasures.

The doors began opening on one of the elevators, instantly snapping the two of us back into the reality of where we were standing, how close we'd gravitated toward each other while talking, as well as the way we were looking at each other. Zac quickly took a step away from me as four people began exiting the elevator.

"Are you getting on?" he asked me.

I nodded and stepped into the empty space. Zac was right behind me but no one was behind him. It was just the two of us alone again, standing side by side this time. We both reached for the control panel and our hands brushed one another. I pulled mine back and so did Zac, and then I looked up at him. The corners of his mouth were curled up.

"Go ahead," he said, nodding toward the panel.

"Which floor?"

"Sixth."

After pushing the sixth-floor button, I pushed the fourth and watched the elevator doors start closing.

"I have something for you," Zac said, reaching into his jacket pocket. He pulled out a folded piece of paper and handed it to me. "I was hoping I'd get to see you today or sometime this week so I could give it to you.

As soon as I unfolded the paper and saw what was on it, I pressed it against my chest. It was a picture of a mermaid with long blond hair, a black bikini top and a blue tail. Malcolm had made this for me and he'd written his name at the bottom. I couldn't get over the detail of the mermaid nor the fact that Zac's mini-me was already able to write his name.

"I absolutely love this," I said, looking back at Zac. "This picture is going on the front of my refrigerator as soon as I get home today."

He smiled so big and the usual happened: his eyes squinted and crinkled around the corners, and that dimple in his right cheek appeared. I wanted to touch it with my fingertip like I did in my swimming pool yesterday but made myself hold back.

"After Malcolm and I got home last night, he told me that he wanted to color a picture for you. He didn't want any of his coloring books, though. He asked me for a sheet of paper, so I got it for him and then the two of us sat down at our breakfast table and I watched him draw and color that for you."

"And also write his name."

"Yes."

"He's so gifted."

"I know. He's obviously a child, but there are times when he reminds me of an old man. It's like he's got an old soul and it comes out in the random things that he says and does. He's way beyond his years."

"I agree," I said, looking at Malcolm's drawing again. "This is really special. Please tell him that I said thank you and also that I love his picture."

"I will."

The elevator reached the fourth floor and the doors opened. There wasn't anyone waiting on the other side. It was still just Zac and me. I stepped off and then turned around to look at him again. When the doors started to close, he pushed the open button on the panel but kept his arm up. I couldn't see what he was doing now but my guess was that he had his finger pressed against the hold button.

"Don't you need to go up two more floors?" I asked.

"Yes, but it can wait." He searched my eyes, looked down at my lips again, and then went lower—all the way down to my feet and back up. "What you're wearing today looks really nice on you," he went on to say.

I had on a navy blue suit with a beige silk blouse underneath the jacket. My skirt skimmed the tops of my knees and my beige high heels matched my blouse.

"Thank you."

"Your hair looks really nice today too."

"Thank you again. I threw together this low, messy bun last minute this morning but it isn't holding up very well. See? It's already loosening," I said, tugging at some of the hair that'd fallen around my face.

"Yeah, well, it still looks nice. I like seeing your hair falling around your face like that, so if you don't mind, leave it like it is."

I chuckled. "Okay. Anything else?"

"Yes. I have a question for you."

"What do you wanna know?"

"Do you always go bare-legged in your professional attire? I mean, I can see why you would with those tan legs of yours. You don't need to wear pantyhose."

"Yes, I always go bare-legged until Labor Day arrives, and then my pantyhose and I regularly spar all the way through autumn and winter until Easter gets here. That's when I start going without them again. I can't stand how restrictive they are."

"So what are you wearing underneath your skirt now?"

I looked up at the ceiling, chuckling again. Then I looked back at Zac and shook my finger at him. "You shouldn't be asking me a question like that," I said.

"Please answer me."

I paused to weigh whether or not I should tell the tall, handsome and still unshaven attorney standing in front of me, who'd kissed me several times yesterday and had also agreed to the two of us having an affair, that I wasn't wearing anything underneath my skirt. Not even a slip. Then I decided to tell him just that.

"Nothing," I said.

"Nothing?"

"No."

"No panties?"

"I never wear them."

Zac looked down at the front of my skirt, sighed, and then met my gaze again. "Well... What I'm imagining at the moment is definitely gonna help get me through the rest of this day."

"Glad to be of assistance. Is there anything else that I can do for you?" I asked, grinning.

"Yes—there is."

"And what is it?"

The playful look in Zac's eyes had grown serious. "Be my lover."

"Zac..."

"I know this thing between us is complicated and has the potential to cause a lot of pain but selfishly, I want you. Stevie, you walked into my life like you've always been part of it and everything is so easy with you. Everything fits, everything flows and feels right."

"But..."

"You don't have to give me an answer right this second. Just think about everything. Okay?"

"We talked about all of this on the phone last night."

"I know we did. But what you said to me is contradicting what's showing in your eyes this morning. They're shining and

I can see how much you want me. How much you want *this*. So please think about what I'm asking of you. Will you do that for me?"

I took a deep breath and then slowly nodded yes.

"Thank you. I hope you have a good day, Sinclair."

"I hope you do too, Buchanan."

He dropped his arm down from the control panel and the two of us continued staring at each other until the elevator doors closed. I glanced around and was relieved to see that no one was anywhere near me. In fact, the hallway was still empty. It was strange—just like it was when Zac and I had arrived at this floor and also when we stood by the elevators on the first floor, waiting for one to arrive. We were alone with each other in both instances.

Still standing here in this quiet hallway on the fourth floor of the Dallas courthouse, I had to shake my head at not only the way that things timed out with Zac this morning but also at the last part of what he said to me before those elevator doors closed. He saw right through the neutral, friendly front that I'd been trying to uphold while in his presence. My eyes told him the whole truth and nothing but the truth.

I did want Zac and I did want to have an affair with him. I had no doubt of how passionate it'd be—but I couldn't agree to go through with it. I was still concerned about Zac and Malcolm somehow getting hurt, and that was the last thing that I wanted to happen. They had so much more to lose than I did and now, I just had to figure out when I was going to tell Zac again that I couldn't be his lover.

16
#lilith

Stevie

Life would've been so much easier if it was black and white. Despite black-and-white rules, laws, and moral codes, certain situations fell within the varying shades of gray, and it was the gray that made making certain decisions in life so difficult.

"Today feels like it should be Friday but it's only Monday," Brooke said, peeking her head around my open office door. Then she leaned against the door frame.

"Yeah, it really does. It's been a long day."

"I don't know if it's the moon cycle or what, but everyone up here is frazzled. Normally, their cases don't get to them this much."

"It could very well be the moon. It's gonna be a full one tonight."

"Shit, that's gotta be the culprit then. There's no other reason for the crazy vibe in this office today," Brooke chuckled.

"Sounds like all of you are moon sensitive."

"I guess we are, but you don't seem to be."

"Oh, I definitely sense it, but it doesn't bother me."

"Are you part witch or something?"

I chuckled then. "I just enjoy the full moon is all. It's so pretty to look at and that's what I'll be doing tonight after it comes up."

"Well, that's much later. How about joining me at Mystic Bar after work? I need to unwind for a little while."

"Sure. I'll meet you there."

"Great! I'm gonna go ask the others about joining us."

"Okay. And even if they don't want to, I'll still go."

"Sounds good. By the way—I've been meaning to ask you all day how your visit went with your dad, over the weekend."

"It was wonderful, and so good to see his face. Our time together went by too fast is all. He spent only Friday night with me and left to go back to Austin after lunch on Saturday."

"That was a really quick trip for him."

"I know. I'll be going to see him next and will get more time with him because I'll be there Friday through Sunday. I may even go see the old man preach at his church."

"He'd probably love that."

"I would too."

"So did you do anything fun with the rest of your weekend?"

Brooke's question caught me off guard. "Um, I went to the zoo on Saturday afternoon."

"Did you really?"

"Yes, and I loved it. My parents used to always take me when I was little."

"You're a kid at heart."

I smiled. "In some ways."

"Buchanan is a kid at heart too and takes his little boy to the zoo all the time. It would've been something if you ran into them while there."

"Why is that?"

"Because you would've seen Malcolm and then you'd understand what I was talking about, about him being so adorable."

"I'm sure he is."

Brooke looked over my face and then nodded. "I'll see you at Mystic Bar in a little while."

"Looking forward to it."

After she left, I got up from my desk and closed my office door. Then I took a deep breath. What Brooke had said about my weekend, the zoo, and Zac and Malcolm gave me the impression that she already knew what I'd done after my dad left for Austin. There was no way that she could have, though. I was just being paranoid. I was still grappling with my guilt about everything that happened between Zac and me, too. I was also still thinking about what he'd asked of me this morning at the courthouse.

I walked over to the window and looked down at the busy city below, letting my mind wander. I replayed every interaction between Zac and me, beginning with the first time I saw him on the running trail. I thought about all the different things that we had talked about since officially meeting at Mystic Bar, as well as all the lingering looks and secret touches that we'd shared. I could hear Zac's deep, raspy voice inside my head now whenever I thought about him. I could also see his beautiful blue eyes and could clearly remember the way his hands felt on my skin. And I'd never forget the feeling of his soft lips on mine or the taste of his tongue.

I closed my eyes and sighed, then walked back to my desk and sat down. Five o'clock would be here in less than an hour, and I wondered what Zac's plans were after work. More than likely, he'd be picking up Malcolm from his parents, or he might take a run before doing that. Actually, no. He'd had only four hours of sleep last night due to my calling off our affair, so I knew a trip to the running trail wouldn't be part of his evening plan. Undoubtedly, Zac was even more exhausted by now and had probably needed more than one energy drink to get through this day.

Since we were still close friends, I thought about sending him a quick text to check on him. Then I did.

Me: Hey, you. How have you held up today? I've been worried about you.

There was no response from Zac. Not even by the time five o'clock arrived. I didn't know what to think or how to feel about it, either. I tried rationalizing that maybe he was still working on a case...or something. I just wished he'd text me back so these knots in my stomach would go away.

I'd just gotten my car keys out of my purse and stood up from my desk when someone knocked on my office door, then opened it. It was Brooke again.

"Hey, Stevie. Why don't you ride with me over to Mystic Bar instead of meeting me there? That way, we don't both have to fight the Dallas traffic."

"Um, okay."

"I'll bring you back here to pick up your car after we call it an evening."

"That's fine. Are the others gonna meet us there?"

"As soon as they can. They all have some errands to run first."

"Then let's go!"

I grabbed my cellphone off my desk and glanced at the screen to see if Zac had gotten around to texting me back. He hadn't, so I turned off my phone and threw it into my purse along with my car keys.

As Brooke was pulling into Mystic Bar's parking lot, I spotted a white Chevy Blazer ahead of us on the right and then saw Zac getting out of it. Instantly, the knots in my stomach unwound.

"There's your gin buddy," Brooke said, nodding in his direction.

"It sure is. He must've had a really long day too, showing up here on a Monday like this.

"Your guess is as good as mine, but it's obvious that he got the invite that I texted him earlier. I never heard back from Zac, but he's a really busy man so it didn't surprise me. I figured if he could make it here, then he would."

Finding out from Brooke that Zac hadn't replied to her text either was a relief, but I still wondered what he was doing this late in the day that had kept him from replying to us. I hoped everything was okay with Malcolm. I also hoped Avery was still in west Texas.

Brooke pulled towards the empty parking space on the other side of Zac's car. He was standing next to it with the driver's side door open, in the process of rolling up the sleeves of his white-collared shirt. He'd already taken off his suit jacket—and damn, he looked sexy. There was something about a professional man with his sleeves rolled up to his elbows that I really liked—but I especially liked it on the man that I was staring at now.

As Brooke began easing into the space, Zac looked up, smiled, and waved. He closed his car door and motioned for Brooke to pull the rest of the way in. Once she'd parked, Zac opened my door for me.

"Hey, Sinclair," he said. His blue eyes were sparkling.

"Fancy seeing you here again, Buchanan."

He nodded and then leaned down to look across me, at Brooke. "Thanks for sending me that text, Ms. District Attorney. Sorry I didn't get back to you. I actually woke up from taking a nap at my office not very long ago."

"A nap?"

Zac chuckled. "Yeah. I didn't get quite enough beauty sleep last night."

"What on earth kept you up?"

"Just couldn't sleep for some reason."

"I know what your problem was: the moon! Stevie informed me earlier that it's gonna be a full one tonight. Then she told me that some of us are moon-sensitive," Brooke said, glancing at me and grinning. "That means its energy not only affects us but can also start jacking with us three days before the moon is actually full and three days afterward. It seems to be jacking with you as much as it is with me."

"Who knows? I'm rested now, though, and feel great, so come on, ladies. Let's get out of this summer heat and go get a drink."

"Sounds good to me!"

The second that Brooke turned around to grab her purse off the back seat, Zac looked at me and motioned for me to get out of the car. When he held out his hand, I didn't hesitate to take it, and as soon as I felt the warmth of his skin on mine, my skin ignited all over again. My attraction to him and the arousing effect he had on me were so hard to hide, but I was still trying to, for his benefit as well as Brooke's. My boss, especially, didn't need to see what was really going on here between Zac and me. Yes, she knew that I found him attractive. Hell, any woman would. I was going to have to be really careful, though, to not look at Zac too many times or for too long while we were here at Mystic Bar or it'd give me away. It'd let everyone sitting around us know the real story of what was going on inside my head *and* my heart. Although Zac and I were just "good friends" status now, I still craved him in every way.

After stepping out of Brooke's car, I moved over to the left of Zac so he could close the door. He didn't let go of my hand, though, and I smiled to myself. He was stealing every private moment with me that he could, and he stole another one as soon as the car door clicked shut.

"I'm sorry I didn't text you back. I passed out on the couch at my office and when I woke up and saw your text and Brooke's, I hauled ass to get over here to see you again," he quietly said.

I looked over his handsome face and nodded. "I'm glad you're here."

We both heard the driver's side door close and Zac held out his arm for me to walk ahead of him. As soon as we met Brooke on the sidewalk in front of her car, she hugged Zac. It was obvious how much she cared about him and vice versa. He really was like a son to her.

Inside Mystic Bar, we grabbed a long table and I sat next to Brooke again while Zac took the chair directly across from me like before. We'd been sitting for only a handful of seconds when one of my teammates came walking up.

"Hey, Jason! You beat us here," Brooke said.

"Yeah, I decided the errand that I was going to run could wait because I was more than ready for one of these," he said, holding up a frosty mug of beer. "How are you doing, Buchanan?" he asked, playfully grabbing Zac's shoulder.

"I'm doing well. How about yourself?"

"Getting better by the second, man." Jason took a sip of his beer and then another.

"I hear you! Have a seat."

Zac motioned at the chair beside him and Jason took it. Right after he did, a waitress walked up and Zac took it upon himself to order drinks for Brooke and me. My tough yet easygoing boss apparently drank chardonnay every time she came here and probably at any other bar or restaurant that she went to, I guessed. I wasn't interested in drinking anything other than my usual either: Hendricks gin plus tonic water with extra lime—and that's exactly what Zac ordered for me. Then he ordered himself the same thing.

"Would any of you like something to eat?" the waitress asked, holding up some menus.

Zac looked over at me. "Are you hungry?" he asked.

"No, I'm just thirsty. Thank you, though."

"Brooke, what about you?"

"I'm with Stevie. Besides, it's too damn hot to eat."

Zac grinned at her, then pointed to Jason. "And you?"

"Nah, man. I'm good. Got everything I need right here," he said, taking another sip of his beer.

Zac glanced at me then looked back up at the waitress. "I'm not hungry either. Give us a little while and maybe we'll all change our minds."

As soon as the waitress walked off, the four of us began talking about summer vacations. Brooke had an Alaskan cruise booked while Jason had plans to go to Las Vegas with his fiancée, Chloe. Zac said he didn't have any vacation plans and didn't explain why. He didn't have to. Brooke, Jason, and I were all aware that he was the only full-time parent to Malcolm and didn't have the luxury to take off work to go somewhere to relax.

"What are your plans, Stevie?" Brooke asked me.

"I don't have any."

Her eyebrows knotted up. "Why?"

"Because it's not any fun going on vacation alone."

"Oh, I just thought you might've had a girlfriend or group of girlfriends that you travel with. I've taken trips with mine and it's always a blast."

"I'll bet it is."

"You should come with us next time."

"I appreciate that. Let me know when you book your next trip."

"I sure will. But seriously... You've gotta do *something* for yourself this summer. Go somewhere for a few days. I've taken trips alone several times just to have that time to myself and it's always been so rejuvenating."

"If I do anything at all, it'll be a staycation at my house. I have my swimming pool and can lay out by it while imagining I'm on a beach in the Caribbean."

"Or in Destin, Florida?" Zac interjected.

I looked over at him and smiled. "Yes."

"I remember you telling Bash that was your favorite tropical place to go to in the U.S."

"It is."

"Because of the white-sand beaches and clear blue water."

"That's exactly why. Great memory, Buchanan."

He grinned at the same time that he glanced down at my lips. "How many times have you been to Destin?"

"Several. Have you been there before?" I asked, knowing that Zac must have vacationed there at least once because of the t-shirt he'd worn over to my house yesterday.

"I haven't, but my parents took a quick trip down there last summer."

And that's how Zac got that t-shirt, I thought to myself.

"Well, I highly recommend you go whenever you get the chance."

"I'll keep that in mind."

"I highly recommend the two of you going also," I said, looking at Brooke and Jason.

"I've been, and it is a gorgeous place, but this menopause that I currently have going on demands me to go to a cooler locale for vacation," Brooke chuckled.

"I'm so sorry you're dealing with that."

"It's just part of being a woman. Enjoy the age that you are as much as you can, Stevie, because before you know it, Madame M. will be showing up on your doorstep and royally pissing you off."

All four of us laughed then, but I did pat Brooke on the shoulder.

"Speaking of Destin..." Jason said. "It's where I proposed to Chloe."

I was surprised. "Did you really?"

"Yeah. Planned it all out. I asked her to marry me on the beach at sunset, had a photographer and everything."

"Wow," I said, imagining it. "It must've been so beautiful."

"It was and thankfully, Chloe said yes!"

"That's a good thing. When do you plan on marrying her?"

"August of next year."

"Are you planning a honeymoon?"

"We are. We're flying to England to go see all of the historical sites."

"You're gonna be so close to Scotland and Ireland. You and Chloe have to go there too!"

"Yeah, we've talked about doing exactly that and probably will."

"Because of my ancestry, I really wanna visit Scotland." I looked over at Zac and he was staring straight at me. "Have you been to our motherland?"

"I haven't, but it's at the top of my bucket list."

"I hope you get to go there one day and sit in a pub, enjoy a Hendricks and tonic with extra lime while you're there, and run into one of your Scottish relatives. Have a good long chat with them, exchange contact info, and maybe even get to meet some more of your kinsmen and kinswomen."

"That would be amazing—and I hope you get to do that one day too."

"Your ancestry test results are identical, right? Same percentage?" Brooke asked, looking back and forth between Zac and me.

"Yes," he and I said together.

"Wouldn't it be something if you two are distantly related?"

I looked back across the table at Zac and once again, he already had his eyes on me. "I'm curious about something," I said to him.

"And what would that be?"

"Did you happen to trace your ancestry through records or did you just take the DNA test?

"I combed through every record that I could find online and there were hundreds of them. Well-documented records. I printed all of them too."

"Do you happen to recall reading about any clan Buchanan men marrying a clan Sinclair woman?"

The corners of Zac's mouth curled up. "Yes, I do. The first time that happened was during..."

"The fifteen hundreds. During the Renaissance when Mary Queen of Scots ruled," I said, finishing his sentence.

"How do you know that?"

"After you and I met right here on that Friday after work and talked about our Scottish ancestry, I started wondering if there was a connection between us somewhere down the line. So after I got home that night, I went back through all the well-documented records of my lineage that I printed out and found the first Buchanan/Sinclair couple that I just mentioned."

Zac gave me a full-blown smile this time. Dimple included. "I did the same thing late that night. After you and I talked about our ancestry, I also began wondering if we shared a connection."

"History is fascinating, isn't it?"

"To say the least."

"Now I'm even more fascinated," Brooke said, looking back and forth between Zac and me again. "And I challenge the two of you to pool your records sometime and compare them to see if they match. You can use the conference room at my office."

"Or my conference room," Zac said, looking over at me again.

"If we do that, you know it's gonna take a good while. There are so many records," I said.

"Well, with two sets of eyes looking over them, maybe it won't take too long to travel back in time."

"Ah! Here's the rest of the gang," Brooke said, pulling my attention away from Zac.

I waved as they were walking up to the table and after sitting down, they placed their drink orders and we all began chatting. I loved this group of people I worked with. They were all good souls and desperately wanted to do right for others. The truth that lay within their hearts was so obvious and it warmed mine. The truth that lay within Zac's did, as well. Although he and I were at opposite ends of the spectrum regarding whom we chose to defend in our profession, I knew Zac wanted to do right for his clients by upholding the law and protecting them just like I did mine. Everyone had that legal right.

Zac and Brooke began discussing some old cases with each other and while watching and listening to them, I thought about my case against Zac. It was scheduled for Wednesday and I couldn't help but wonder how he was going to be around me in a courtroom setting. Although he and I had already talked about keeping things strictly professional when working, it went without saying that it was going to be a challenge. At least it would be for me. I would make myself do it, though; otherwise, my face would show exactly how personal I'd been with Zac, and that reality was a major conflict of professional interest.

I excused myself to go use the restroom, and on my way back to the table of my comrades, I saw Zac coming toward me down the hallway. He smiled as soon as we made eye contact and when we reached each other, he stopped in his tracks. So did I. He was standing in front of me now, not saying a word, and just gazing into my eyes. The sexual tension between us was palpable and thick and heated.

"I'm really happy to see you again," he finally said.

"Same here."

"Whenever you're around, my whole body is keenly aware of it. All my senses are heightened and all I wanna do is touch you."

Zac reached up and slowly ran his fingertips down one of the tendrils of hair hanging around my face. I kept watching him and wondered if he was going to stop there or touch me somewhere else. Then he grazed my cheek with his fingertips. I closed my eyes at feeling his touch and when I opened them, he was staring straight at me.

"So, Sinclair... Have you thought about what I asked of you this morning?"

I took a deep breath and nodded yes. "I haven't stopped thinking about it."

"Have you reached a verdict yet?"

"Yes, I have. I still feel it's best that we don't jump into the deep end of this thing between us. And it isn't that I don't want to, because I do and you know that. It's just..."

Zac unexpectedly leaned in and kissed me midsentence. I kissed him back too. I did it fully aware of the risk that we were taking by possibly getting caught. I also knew how much I was contradicting what I'd just told him. All that it'd taken to make me do that was him kissing me. Being close to him like this weakened my will, as well as my knees.

The moment our kiss ended, Zac leaned his forehead against mine and we both sighed. Then he pulled back and gazed into my eyes. "I'll see you back at the table in a few minutes."

"Okay."

"And FYI... I know it's only a matter of time before you let me take you to bed. Keep drawing out the inevitable for as long as you need to, though. I'm a patient man and I'll be ready whenever you decide to stop worrying about things so much and say yes to being my lover."

Zac kissed me again—quickly this time—and then stepped around me to continue walking to the men's restroom. I looked over my shoulder at him and right before he reached the door, I called out to him.

"Hey, Buchanan?"

"Yeah?" he said, looking back at me.

"Your lips have my gloss on them, so you might wanna take care of that while you're in there."

He reached up, swiping his bottom lip with his fingertip, and then looked at the evidence of our two secret hallway kisses.

"I'll tell you again that I don't mind your lip gloss being on me, but for security reasons I'll remove it while we're here at Mystic Bar," he said, grinning. I couldn't help but grin too. I also couldn't help but acknowledge to myself that Zac was right. It really was only a matter of time before I let him take me to bed.

Damn, damn, damn.

After he'd closed the restroom door behind him, I started making my way down the hallway again, to go back to the table. Before rounding the corner, I stopped to compose myself. In a matter of seconds, Zac had nearly unraveled me.

When I sat back down, Brooke leaned over and asked, "Everything okay?"

"Yes. Why?"

"You just took a while is all."

"Oh—when I was coming back from the restroom, I ran into Zac in the hallway and we talked about comparing our ancestry records. We both think it'd be a lot of fun."

I'd just lied to Brooke but had to say something to reroute her focus.

"No doubt it would be, and I'm serious about you and Zac using the conference room at my office. Just let me know when."

"I appreciate it."

Brooke rejoined the conversation that she'd been part of when I first returned to the table. I just sat back and listened while sipping my drink and waiting for Zac to return.

I saw him the second that he rounded the corner of the hallway and he smiled at me, then pointed up at the ceiling. Mystic Bar had music playing—some SiriusXM station was my guess—and coincidentally, the current song was "One of These Nights" by the Eagles. A decades-old classic rock song that was still so good and also fit the situation that I was caught up in with Zac. It matched his belief and also what I knew to be true: that on one of these nights, he was going to fuck me.

He sat back down at the table, still watching me as much as I was him. The song had just reached its midpoint when Don Henley sings, "In between the dark and the light. Coming right behind you. Swear I'm gonna find you. Get you, baby, one of these nights," and Zac quietly sang that last line in his sexy, deep voice but I was the only one who apparently heard him do it because no one sitting around us turned their attention to him.

Afterward, he kept his eyes on me as much as I was keeping mine on him while everyone else remained wrapped up in the group chat. Zac and I needed to reel in how much we were looking at each other, but there was something alluring about pushing the limit that made me want to do it even more. After another long and lustful moment of staring into Zac's eyes, I turned my attention to Brooke and the others. Not for long, though. I used Bash as an excuse to give all my attention to Zac again.

"Is your best buddy gonna be joining us this evening?" I asked him.

"No, he had other plans, but I'll try him again if we all come back here later this week."

"It'd be good to see him again. He's so funny."

"Bash has always been a comical guy and a lot of fun to hang out with."

I smiled and then looked away from Zac at Brooke and the others who were still chatting away. When I felt one of my feet being nudged underneath the table, I looked straight across it at Zac and he was grinning. He was messing with me and enjoying pushing the limits as much as I still was.

Our waitress returned and asked everyone about ordering another drink. My glass of Hendricks and tonic was empty now just like Zac's was and I waited to see if he was going to order another one, but he asked me about getting one first.

"I'll have another round if you are," I told him.

"Yeah, I'm having another one."

For the next half hour, Zac and I sipped on our Hendricks and tonic while talking to each other on and off. Whenever we had our attention on Brooke and the others, I still stole glances at Zac and he did the same thing to me. He kept randomly nudging my foot with his underneath the table, too. True to what he'd told me in the hallway—all he wanted to do was touch me and that was evident. I understood how he felt, because I wanted to touch him just as much.

The last time he nudged my foot, he kept the side of his pressed against mine. I looked across the table at him when he did it and saw the slight shrug of his shoulders, as well as the curled-up corners of his mouth. And here we were pushing the limit once again.

We finished our drinks at the same time that Brooke finished her one glass of Chardonnay. Then she leaned over and asked me, "Are you about ready to go?

I wasn't ready, because I didn't want to leave Zac's company yet, but went ahead and told Brooke, "Whenever you are."

"I'm ready now. I wanna go home and get out of these clothes and just walk around naked so I can cool off all the way."

I gave her a sympathetic smile. "Then let's go."

We both reached for our purses hanging on the backs of our chairs and then pulled out our wallets.

"I've got this, ladies," Zac said to us.

"Well, I appreciate it, Buchanan. It'll be my treat the next time," Brooke said.

"And it'll be my treat after that," I added.

Zac smiled at the two of us, waved down our waitress, and then paid Brooke's tab and mine. Brooke had already told our team that we were leaving, but they were staying for a while longer. I thought Zac was too but when Brooke and I stood up from the table, so did he. Then he told Jason, Ellie, Jennifer, and David goodbye.

My menopausal boss, my kinsman and I left Mystic Bar together—Zac walking Brooke and me back out to her car. He opened my door for me again and after thanking him, I took a moment to just look at him before sitting down in the passenger seat. His blue eyes were still sparkling like the sun was in them and I knew what it was time for me to do. There was no point in fighting it any longer, so right or wrong and no matter the risk or consequences, I gave in to Zac.

"Yes," I whispered, and he immediately side-eyed me like he wasn't sure about what my "Yes" was referring to, so I quickly clarified it for him while Brooke was getting into the car. "I'll be your lover."

Zac swallowed hard then quietly asked, "When can I see you again?"

"Soon. Real soon."

"Okay."

He held my hand while I sat down and then bent over to tell Brooke goodbye across me.

"Have a good evening, Buchanan, and give that sweet little boy of yours a tight squeeze for me."

"I'll do that. Ladies, you two have a good evening, and maybe we'll meet up here again sometime this week."

"More than likely," Brooke chuckled.

Before closing my door, Zac looked at me one more time and smiled, and then Brooke and I left Mystic Bar. On our way back to the D.A.'s office, she asked me about my case against Zac. She wanted to know if I was ready to face off against him.

"I've been ready."

"I just wanted to check in with you about it again because of the friendship that I see blossoming between you and Zac."

"Brooke, I've never had a problem drawing the line between the professional and personal parts of my life. Yes, Zac and I have become friends, but we both have our jobs to do. I haven't talked to him about any of what you and I are discussing, but I do believe that his gloves are gonna come off in the courtroom the second that mine do. And that's gonna happen as soon as I walk through the courtroom doors."

"I just needed to hear you say that, Stevie."

"Don't worry about me. I've got everything under complete control."

Brooke reached over and patted my shoulder. "Good."

As soon as she dropped me off at the D.A.'s office parking lot, I got into my car, but didn't leave right away. I let Brooke leave first while acting like I was looking for something inside my purse and then I pulled up Zac's contact info on my cellphone. I stared at his phone number while debating whether or not to touch the screen, then decided not to and clicked off my phone.

I wanted to call him to feel him out. I was wondering what he was doing for the rest of this evening but was certain he'd be taking care of Malcolm. If I'd known he wasn't going to be doing that, then I would've followed through with calling him to invite him over to my house. Now that I'd decided to really move forward into having an affair with Zac, I was anxious to get a full taste of him, and that was something that I'd been hoping would happen tonight. I wanted to feel his lips and his body all over mine and could so easily imagine it, just like I could so easily imagine what it'd be like to feel him inside me.

It'd been years since I had sex, and it happened with Graham. He was the only man I'd ever been intimate with. We were both virgins when we met and then began dating in high school and remained such until the day we married. After that, we couldn't get enough of fucking each other, and it was that way until right before I gave birth to our Malcolm.

I remembered how alive and vibrant sex used to make me feel. I felt like a real woman. No, I felt like a goddess and I was ready to feel that way again. But this time, I was going to be stepping into a different role. I wasn't going to be a good Christian wife anymore. I was no longer like Eve. Now I was like

Lilith, about to defy the patriarchy. I was about to become an adulteress, and strangely, I was relishing this sexual rebellion that I was holding in my hands.

17
#river

Stevie

The sun was setting when I decided to text Zac just to see what he was doing. Because it was close to 9:00 p.m., I was pretty certain that he had already tucked Malcolm into bed for the night.

Me: Hey, you.

Zac: Hey, you. What are you up to?

Me: I was about to ask you the same question. I'm sitting on my back patio, thinking about you, me—everything.

Zac: Having second thoughts again about being my lover?

Me: Not at all.

Zac: I'm relieved to know that.

Me: After Brooke dropped me off earlier, I started to call you.

Zac: About what?

Me: I wanted you to come over tonight but realized it was pointless to ask.

Zac: Why did you think it was pointless?

Me: Because you wouldn't have been able to do it, since you have Malcolm there with you.

Zac: Actually, he's staying with my parents tonight.

Me: So you're alone.

Zac: Yes. Just like you are.

Me: I'm tired of being alone, Buchanan.

Zac: So am I.

I paused my texting to take a deep breath and absorb the fact that a door had just opened for Zac to come over. Before texting anything to him about it though, I wanted to do something else.

Me: I have a song that I wanna send to you. I've listened to it several times since I've been home.

Zac: Norah Jones?

Me: No. Bishop Briggs. It's her song called "River." It's been out for a good while but it's still really popular and it's addictive too. At least it is to me.

Zac: What's addictive about it to you?

Me: The whole vibe of the music. Its energy is highly sexual, plus the lyrics remind me of us. If you listen to the song, I think you'll have a very clear picture of what I want

**you to do to me whenever the time comes for you to take
me to bed.**

Zac: Text me the song, Sinclair.

I copied the link off Pandora, sent it to Zac, and then waited for his response. Less than three minutes later, he called me and I answered my phone by asking him if he liked what he'd just listened to.

"Yes. A lot. I've heard that song before but didn't know the title or who sang it. Now, because of you, I have a great appreciation for it," he said.

"It's a great song."

"And since I've listened to it again—this time knowing that it reminds you of us and also that it spells out what you want me to do to your body with mine—I wanna ask you a question."

"So ask me."

"May I come over to your house tonight?"

"You know what's gonna happen if you do, right?"

"Yes. I'm ready for it to happen. Are you?"

"I am."

I moved my mouth away from my phone and covered the receiver with my hand. I may have been coming across as calm, cool and collected about the subject matter that Zac and I were currently discussing, but I wasn't calm, cool and collected on the inside at the moment. My heart was pounding because this affair between Zac and me was about to be in full force. We really were about to do *this*. We were really about to fuck each other. *I* was about to fuck an extremely unhappily married man who hadn't had sex in over four years. Same as me.

"Are you still there?" Zac asked.

"Yes."

"What are you thinking about?"

"That you need to get over here as quickly as you can."

"Okay. Before I do that though, I want you to understand something. This isn't just about me wanting to have sex with you. I care about you, Stevie. Tremendously. And I'm also crazy about you."

"I feel the same way about you. Even this soon."

"It is soon for both of us, yet it's not. Not when you take into account our ages, what we've been through, what we're still dealing with, what we've missed out on, and also what we're still seeking in life. I know exactly what I want in mine—and it's you."

"Then come show me how much you want me."

"I'm already in my car."

As soon as we hung up, I made a beeline for my bathroom so I could check my appearance. I'd taken a couple of dips in the swimming pool after getting home from Mystic Bar and was still wearing my black bikini. My hair was damp and what little makeup I'd had on earlier was now gone. Because I was about to get back into the pool, I didn't bother changing into something else or doing anything with my hair, but I did put on some waterproof mascara and a fresh coat of lip gloss.

Floating on my back once again, I waited for Zac to arrive. What he didn't know and would soon find out was that I didn't want the first time we had sex to happen in my bed. I wanted it to happen while the two of us were immersed in this sensual water that we both enjoyed so much.

Because I'd intentionally left my back door open, I heard Zac ring my doorbell, and I also heard my cellphone chime, alerting me that he was here. Swimming over to the edge of the pool, I grabbed my phone off the deck and opened up the Ring app so I could see and talk to Zac through the camera on my front porch.

"Hey, you. I see you," I said.

"And I'm ready to see you."

"The code to open my front door is 10987. Come inside, lock the deadbolt behind you and then walk outside into my backyard."

"Okay."

I continued watching him as he was punching in the code and when he opened the front door, I clicked off my phone and tossed it over into the grass. Then I swam into the deep end to wait for my lover to appear. The moment he stepped through the back doorway, his eyes found me and he smiled, making the butterflies that were already in my stomach flutter even more.

"Would you like for me to close this door?" he asked, pointing at it.

"Please."

After the latch clicked, he turned back around and walked over to the edge of the pool, coming to a stop straight across from me.

"In the mood for a swim tonight, I see," he said, canting his head to the side.

"Something like that."

I watched Zac take his time looking me up and down. Although it was well after dark now, the lights inside the pool were on. Zac could see me just as clearly as I could see him—but no one could see us. The privacy fence surrounding my backyard blocked my neighbors' view and that of any cars driving down my street.

"Now that I'm here alone with you like this, you'd think I'd know what to do but I don't. I mean, I know what I wanna do but I'm nervous as hell. Are you?" Zac asked.

"Yes."

"Stevie, there'll be no turning back after we do this."

"I know."

"And I have no idea of where we're headed after tonight, but I'm all in no matter what. Like I told you earlier on the phone—I want you. I want all that you're willing to give to me of yourself."

"I'm ready to begin doing exactly that for you. It starts tonight, here in this pool. So join me," I said, splashing the water at Zac and making him smile.

"Um, we didn't talk about it beforehand, but I brought some protection for us to use tonight. As a matter of fact, I stopped by

CVS on the way here to pick up some because I didn't have any. I haven't needed it because..."

"I know that too."

Zac half-laughed and then began shaking his head. "While I was inside the store, I felt like I was a high school kid trying to be discreet while looking at all the different condoms. Then, as timing would have it, an elderly woman walked up to get in line behind me and started eyeballing the box that I'd put on the counter. She even huffed at me."

"Because you picked out extra-large condoms?" I chuckled.

"Actually, yes."

I glanced down at the front of Zac's trousers. "Not surprised."

"Stevie, I'm not sure how well a condom is gonna work in that water."

"You don't need one, because I'm on the pill, but I appreciate your consideration. Now take off your clothes and jump in here."

"Okay."

Zac was still wearing what he had on at Mystic Bar and began loosening his tie. After pulling it off and dropping it onto the pool deck, he unbuttoned his shirt, dropped it onto the deck, and then took off his dress shoes and socks. When he started unbuckling his belt, he stared straight at me and I could see the anticipation of what was about to happen between us running all over him. His eyes were burning with desire and he was breathing faster. A lot faster.

After unbuttoning his trousers, he slowly unzipped them like he was doing a strip tease, although he really wasn't. I knew he was just taking his time with his clothes so he could take in every little moment, like I was doing. I also knew I was about to get properly fucked by this man.

Wearing black sports briefs now, he looked me up and down once more, then said, "I hope you're ready—because I'm about to run you like a river. Just like the song says."

He dove into the water before I could say anything and swam up in front of me. His eyes were locked in on mine, our bodies were only a couple of feet apart, and I could feel the energy quickly mounting between us. I knew the levee that'd been holding back the two of us from showing everything we felt toward each other was about to break. Then it did.

Zac pulled me into his arms and had his lips on mine within seconds. He kissed me deeply and he kissed me hard. The feeling of his hot tongue entangled with mine sent a wave of arousal rushing through me that turned my skin into goosebumps. We continued kissing each other while going round and round in circles in the water, then I began untying my bikini top from around my neck.

Zac realized what I was doing, pulled his lips away from mine, and glanced down at my partially exposed breasts. Obviously wanting to see even more of them, he reached around my back and finished untying my bikini top, letting it float away. Then he cupped my breasts in his hands and gently squeezed them, making my nipples even harder than they already were.

"You are so damn beautiful. All over," he whispered. "I love your body."

I smiled at him and then reached for my bikini bottoms. Zac watched me take them off and once they were, he pulled me back to him and started kissing me again. I wrapped my arms around his neck and my legs around his waist, feeling his erect cock pushing against my pussy through his sports briefs. I was ready to feel every bare inch of it inside me.

This time, I pulled my lips away and breathed out, "Fuck me, Buchanan. I can't wait any longer."

He slipped off his sports briefs with ease while continuing to tread water and keeping us both afloat, and then he reached down between our bodies and took his cock into his hand. When I felt the tip of it touch the outside of my pussy, I sighed in anticipation of what was going to happen next—but what I thought was going to happen didn't. Zac didn't thrust himself into me. Instead, he began rubbing his cock up and down the inside of my pussy, touching my clit with every stroke and driving me even wilder.

I'd expected him to be like Graham used to be, not knowing any better. I realized Zac was going to take his time with me. He wanted to bring me pleasure and he also wanted me to be ready to take in all of him. His consideration and attentiveness were impressive, as well as his self-control. He was so different from Graham.

Still looking into Zac's hungry blue eyes as he was making me get even wetter, I felt so open and vulnerable. I felt like a woman again. A goddess. I also felt so close to Zac, and not just in the physical sense.

"Don't stop doing that," I whispered against his face.

"Does it feel good to you?"

"So good."

"I want you to feel that way, Stevie. I want this to be the best sex that you've ever had. *I* want to be the best lover that you've ever had."

It was about a minute later that Zac stopped what he was doing to me and placed both his hands around my waist. Then he moved me to where he needed me to be and slowly pushed my body down on top of his long, rock-hard cock. I closed my eyes, leaned my head back and quietly moaned. It felt like heaven to finally have Zac inside me.

When I looked back at him, he grabbed onto my ass with both hands and held me in place against him, then began moving us into the shallow end of my pool. Once there, he stood up out of the water while I continued hanging onto him and he hung onto me. After walking us over to my pool's edge, he set me down and I loosened my legs from around his waist, letting them dangle in the water. Then I looked down between them.

Zac's cock was still pulsating inside my body and the sight of the two of us joined together like this was something I liked seeing. We both watched as he began moving his hips back and forth, sliding himself in and out of me in a slow and steady rhythm. We also stole glances at each other's faces. Zac's eyes were half-closed and his mouth was partly open as he drew in one deep breath after another just like I was doing.

"You're so tight," he said.

"And you're so big."

The corners of his mouth curled up. "How do you feel now?"

"Like my body is on fire. I feel every little thing but it doesn't hurt. It feels amazing. *You* feel amazing."

"I wanna make you feel even more. Lay back for me."

I did what Zac said and lay back on the pool deck. Then he pulled his cock out of me, got down on his knees in the shallow water, reached out his hands and touched the outside of my pussy. After spreading me apart, he leaned his head down and began sucking on and flicking my clit with his tongue. He also ran it up and down the inner part of me several times, taking turns between doing that and softly biting at me.

I placed my hands around the sides of Zac's face while staring up at the beautiful full moon and stars above us. I could feel every little movement he was making, and each thing that he did felt so good. His lips, his tongue, his teeth, and also his soft razor stubble. It kept brushing against my inner thighs, making my skin break out in goosebumps over and over again.

Just when I thought I couldn't feel any better, Zac slid two of his long fingers into my pussy and began fucking me with them while continuing to have his way with my clit. I was about to come undone, but he stood back up and pushed his cock back into me. Then he leaned over my body and supported himself by pressing one of his hands against the pool deck.

I lifted my legs out of the water and had just dug my heels into Zac's tight ass when he began doing something to me that I'd never experienced before. He pressed his free hand against my lower abdomen and as he began moving his cock in and out of me again, it felt unlike missionary sex ever had. The pressure that Zac was putting on me magnified the sensation of his cock going into my body and I could feel every throbbing inch of him.

"How's that?" he asked, searching my eyes with his.

All I could do was shake my head yes—yes, what he was doing to me felt so damn good. About a minute later, Zac raised back up, pulled his cock out of me again, and then held out his hand for me to take. After pulling me upright, he lifted me up underneath my arms and set me back down into the water. We stood in front of each other—both of us naked as the day we were born, and we were unashamed. We were bold in our skin and also in our desire for each other.

"Turn around," Zac whispered, making his deep voice sound even raspier.

I smiled and then did what he wanted me to do. I turned around, realizing that he really was going to run me like a river. He wanted to travel all over my body and I was happy to let him do it.

After pushing me by my waist over to the pool's edge, I felt Zac's warm chest pressing against my back. Then he moved my wet hair to one side and placed it over the front of my shoulder. Seconds later he was kissing my neck, and the whole time that he was doing it, I could feel his cock pressing against my ass.

Zac reached up and cradled the side of my face in his hand, then he pulled my face around to where he could kiss my mouth. Our lips met, our tongues followed, and it wasn't long after that that I ended our kiss and leaned over the edge of the pool. I was ready to feel Zac inside me again.

He wrapped his hands around my waist but before he slid his cock back into me, I looked over my shoulder and reached for every erect inch of it. Then I began running my hand up and down it, making Zac let out one low moan after another. He kept watching what I was doing to him until he couldn't take it anymore.

"I need you now, Stevie," he exhaled.

I dropped my hand, arched my back, and then he thrust himself into my pussy from behind. He started fucking me hard, gripping my hips and taking all of me he could while I held myself steady on the pool's edge. Moments later, he leaned over and pressed his chest against my back, and then I felt him reach around to the front of me. He found my swollen clit again and started rubbing little circles on top of it, bringing me even closer to coming undone. We were both breathless as we continued moving our bodies together, wanting so much for this release to happen.

Then it began for Zac.

He buried his face in the hair at the back of my neck and let out a deep, throaty groan that went on and on. Between listening to him and feeling the continued thrusts of his cock into my pussy, and also his fingertip still going round and round on top of my clit, I started to cum. And like Zac's orgasm, mine went on and on. Wave after wave of so much pleasure rushed through me, making it impossible for me to be quiet. I had nowhere to bury my face though, so I just let the full extent of everything that I was feeling come from my mouth. I didn't care if my neighbors heard.

When my orgasm ended, I collapsed onto the pool deck and Zac collapsed on top of me. After we caught our breaths, he leaned his head around mine, kissed my lips, and then raised himself back up while slowly pulling his cock out of me. I got up after that and turned around to face him, and he stepped even closer to me and put his hands on my shoulders.

"Stevie, you're trembling all over," he said, looking concerned.

"I know."

"Why? It's not cold out here."

"Because of what you just did to my body with yours. It feels like every nerve ending in mine has been reignited and it feels good. Really good. And by the way—the sex that we just had *is* the best that I've ever experienced in my life. *You're* the best that I've ever had, Zac. You're an incredible lover and you're also an incredible man."

He searched my eyes and then pulled me into his arms, resting his head against mine.

"I'm not trembling like you are but please don't think I haven't been deeply affected by what we just shared, because I have been," he said. "It felt like an earthquake breaking me open, then you and all your sweetness poured into me and filled me up. And by the way—that was the best sex that I've ever had too. *You* are the best that I've ever had. *You* are who's incredible, Stevie. *You* are an incredible lover and woman."

After a long and tender moment of just holding each other, Zac loosened his embrace and looked at me. He smiled, I smiled, and it was like we knew what the other was thinking because without saying a word, we both took off swimming toward the deep end of my pool at the same time. As soon as we made it there, Zac pulled me underwater with him and then pressed his lips against mine. When he pulled away, we stayed underneath the surface of the water, just staring at each other. Everything was so tranquil and dreamlike. The blue lights in my pool were illuminating our naked bodies, as well as the bubbles that were escaping our mouths.

This bed of water we were in was a cocooning paradise to me and I could've stayed in it all night long with Zac, but I knew our evening together had to end. The morning was going to be here before we knew it and so was our work. With our heads above water now, I decided to mention that reality even as much as I hated to.

"This evening with you has been everything that I imagined it would be. It's been amazing, but we need to get some rest. Duty calls at daylight for both you and me, Buchanan," I said, and he sighed.

"You're right. Where did the time go?"

"Magical hours always fly by."

"This time with you has been so magical, Stevie."

"Same to you."

"I haven't even left your house yet and I'm already missing you."

As soon as Zac said that, a thought came to me, but I wasn't sure if I should air it because I wasn't sure how he would react to it. Then I decided to go for it anyway.

"You don't have to leave. Stay here with me if you want to. Spend the night."

"Are-are you serious?"

"Yes. Fall asleep with me in my bed and when morning comes, we'll get up and have coffee together. Then I'll cook breakfast for us and after we eat, we can get dressed and go to work."

Zac didn't say anything back. He didn't do anything other than continue to stare at me.

"Are you okay?" I asked him.

"Yes. Um—if I stay here with you tonight, it'll be the first time in over four years that I've fallen asleep with someone beside me other than Malcolm. That reality just hit me."

I reached out and held Zac's face in my hand. "It's been a long time for me too. Let's just hold each other all night long. We both need it."

"We do. But Stevie... Don't you think we'll be taking an even greater risk of getting caught if I stay here until morning? My car is parked in your driveway. Not that any of your neighbors know me, but still."

"I've already thought about that. You can park your car next to mine in my garage. It's not a big deal."

The worry in Zac's eyes slowly diffused. Then he said, "Okay, I'll stay. My God, I want to. Before I get out of this pool and go move my car though, I need you to tell me exactly how you're feeling about everything now since we've had sex."

"It's just like you said. There's no turning back, and I have no idea either of where things are headed for you and me. But I'm all in. I'm in this a hundred percent because I want you, Zac Buchanan."

"You've already got me, woman."

18
#heavenonearth

Zac

I fell asleep in Stevie's bed last night with her in my arms, her head resting on my chest, and it was the best sleep that I'd had in years. It was peaceful, it was pure and it felt so right having Stevie by my side.

We woke up at the same time this morning, just as the sun was starting to come up. I looked down at my lover still in my arms and she looked up at me. I whispered, "Hey, you," and she smiled. Then I pulled her over on top of me and held her warm, naked body against mine. She rested her head on my chest again, right on top of my tattoo of Malcolm's newborn footprints and birthdate. We took a few minutes to absorb the newness of the day and process everything that we were feeling. It went without saying that Stevie's emotions were in the same heightened state as mine. The morning was brand new and bright, and so was the state of our two hearts.

When we got out of bed, Stevie slipped on a black, silky robe with pink hibiscus on it and I put back on my sports briefs. Then we walked down the hallway together, holding hands all the way to the kitchen. After brewing two K-Cups of French roast coffee for us and adding a splash of whole milk to each, Stevie suggested we go sit outside on her back patio, which I was all too happy to do with her.

We spent the next fifteen minutes or so just talking to each other like we'd been doing that morning routine forever. Looking at Stevie sitting across the table from me, with her ruffled long blond hair, sleepy blue eyes, and glowing cheeks, I thought to myself how breathtaking she was. She didn't have on any makeup whatsoever and she didn't need it. She was a natural beauty.

Instead of Stevie cooking breakfast for us as she'd planned to do, I took over her kitchen and made a giant omelet with cheese, then spooned some Kylito's salsa on top of it, the same kind I had in my fridge. We shared the omelet along with some toast and orange juice, and when we were done eating, I left Stevie's house to go to mine because I needed a fresh suit to wear to court today. Before I left though, I took Stevie to bed again. Not in the water but in the one that we'd slept in. I had to have some more of her.

I *needed* some more of her.

It didn't take me long to get her highly aroused again by teasing her clit with my tongue, and when I saw that she was getting close to orgasming, I raised up and moved my body over the top of hers. Then we became one again.

Before I started sliding my cock in and out of her, I propped myself up on my elbows on either side of Stevie, and then placed my hands underneath her head, holding it on top of her pillow. I wanted to watch her face when she came this time—but especially her eyes. I hadn't gotten to do that last night while we were having sex on the edge of her swimming pool because I was fucking her from behind when she lost control.

Right before Stevie lost it this morning, I felt her pussy start tightening up around my cock like before, and then she dug her heels into my ass even harder, pulling me into her that much deeper. Her hands were wrapped around the metal bars on her headboard and her breasts were bouncing up and down as I kept thrusting myself into her over and over again. Then finally, she started to cum.

When she began arching her back, I thought she was going to close her eyes the rest of the way but she didn't. She kept them open and she kept them on me. I could tell by the burst of fire in them how good I was making her feel and then she moaned out my name. As soon as I heard it, I came, and like last night, it lasted for so long. It felt like an earthquake breaking me open again.

Afterward, I collapsed beside Stevie, then wrapped my arms around her and hugged her body to mine. She was trembling again, but I knew it was the good kind, so I didn't worry about it.

After catching our breaths, I leaned my head down and kissed her soft lips, and then we got up to take a shower together. I didn't expect that but Stevie asked me to join her, and I enjoyed every second of being in the water with her again. She bathed me, I bathed her, and it didn't feel awkward at all—just like when we'd sat on her back patio, sipping on our cups of coffee and talking while the sun came up. Our intimacy came so easily and felt like something that we'd been sharing for so long, although we hadn't. Technically, it'd only been seventeen days.

After I left Stevie's house to make the short drive to mine, I turned on the radio and the song that happened to be playing instantly made me smile. I hadn't heard it in years but it was still one of my favorites by Hozier. "From Eden" was the title and the lyrics covered exactly how I felt about this affair that Stevie and I were having.

As soon as I parked my Blazer in my garage, I texted a link to the song to Stevie. Less than a minute later, she sent back a row of red hearts and also: "I know that song and love it! It's on the playlist we listened to when you brought Malcolm over."

I texted her back, commenting on how much we had in common, and she agreed. Then she sent me her favorite lyrics from the song: "Babe, there's something broken about this. But I might be hoping about this. Oh, what a sin!" After that, I sent her mine: "Babe, there's something lonesome about you. Something so wholesome about you. Get closer to me." Stevie replied with another row of red hearts and I just kept smiling.

After the incredible morning that we'd shared together, I didn't think my day could get any better. Not until now. I'd just left the courthouse after a divorce/custody hearing for one of my clients and Bash had also just left after one of his client's hearings. He and I were walking down the steps together, talking, when I noticed a sexy mermaid coming up them.

I wondered how this was going to go—how Stevie was going to be with me while Bash was present. She and I had been friendly the one time that Bash saw us around each other at Mystic Bar, but our level of friendliness had obviously increased since then. Tremendously. Her interaction with me was about to tell the tale. She was either going to be as friendly as she'd ended up being with me while at the bar that Friday evening or she was going to switch back into professional mode. Still friendly but also reserved.

When Stevie saw us, she politely smiled and waved. We returned the gestures but I was having a hard time not looking down at her black pencil skirt, knowing she wasn't wearing any panties underneath it and also knowing my face, as well as my cock, had been between her tan legs again only a few hours ago. I could still taste her juicy sweetness on my tongue and I'd never forget the sound of her moaning my name when I made her cum, nor the look in her deep blue eyes.

"Hey, Bash. Buchanan," she said as all three of us met and came to a standstill on the steps.

"How are you, doll?" Bash asked, stepping closer to Stevie to give her a hug.

I was going to have to refrain from doing that, though, as tempting as it was. I'd just caught the scent of Stevie's body lotion in the air—the lotion she'd rubbed all over her neck, chest, arms, and legs this morning after she and I took that hot shower together. I really liked the way that it smelled and when I commented about it to Stevie, she held up her bottle of "Warm Vanilla Sugar" from Bath and Body Works for me to see.

I told her that she smelled like a delicious sugar cookie and I wanted to take a big bite of her. I'd wanted to early this morning and I wanted to at this very second. It wasn't just the scent of the lotion, though, that had reignited my senses. It was how it mixed with Stevie's body chemistry and right now, the combined scent of the two was making my mouth water and was also causing my cock to get hard. Thankfully, my suit jacket was long enough to shield what was happening. I just needed it to stop.

"I'm doing well. How are you?" Stevie asked Bash.

"Fantastic!"

I hadn't taken my eyes off my lover and noticed how she was trying to *not* look at me for very long. Only a few quick glances. I wanted more of her attention though, so I reached out my hand to shake hers.

"Sinclair," I said, calling her by her last name as she had done with me. She'd chosen to take the "friendly-professional" route, so I followed her lead but I couldn't help but wonder how long this reserved approach between us was going to last.

"And how are you this morning?" She gripped my hand firmly and stared straight into my eyes this time.

"Better than Bash."

I saw her façade slip a little, evidenced by the grin that was now playing along her sparkly lips.

"Is it really possible to be better than fantastic, Buchanan?"

"It most certainly is."

"Then you're gonna have to tell me what your secret is for feeling that way."

"I will...some other time."

Just like what happened on the evening when Stevie and I officially met at Mystic Bar and shook hands, and also when we saw each other in the Whole Foods parking lot and shook hands—we kept holding on to each other after our greeting. Once again, I found myself caught up in searching her eyes like she was doing to mine right now, and in hers, I saw the fire that she was trying to contain. The fire that I'd put there.

We realized at the same time that we'd been staring at each other for far too long and had also been holding each other's hands in Bash's presence. We instantly pulled our eyes away and unclasped our hands, dropping them to our sides. I cleared my throat and so did Stevie. Then we both looked over at Bash, who was side-eyeing us.

"Did I just see something here between the two of you? Something that I wasn't supposed to see?" he asked, pointing back and forth at us.

Stevie and I jerked our heads back at the same time. "What?" we said, also at the same damn time.

"You heard me."

"No, you didn't see anything other than my respect and admiration for this lady," I said, half-laughing. I was doing my best to try to make Bash doubt what he'd clearly witnessed.

"And you saw mine for Zac," Stevie added, switching from calling me by my last name. I didn't know if that was intentional or another slip.

Grinning from ear to ear now, Bash began patting me on one cheek while looking straight at Stevie. "Okay. Keep telling yourselves that, but I know what I saw—and I get it," he said, dropping his hand away from my face. "Just be careful, my friends. Really careful. I'd hate for this to blow up in both of your pretty faces."

He turned to me while saying that last sentence, then I looked over at Stevie. Her eyes were drowning in concern.

"It's okay," I said, touching her shoulder.

I was trying to put her at ease—there was no need for her to worry about a thing. Bash would never tell a soul about the affair that he'd just figured out I was having with Stevie.

"I-I should probably go now," she stammered.

"I'll call you later."

She nodded at me, looked over at Bash, smiled nervously, and then said, "Bye, guys."

We told her goodbye and watched her as she was walking up the steps toward the courthouse, and as soon as she was out of hearing range, Bash turned to me.

"So she's the one worth risking everything for?"

"She is."

"Lilith has bewitched you."

"Don't say it like that."

"I mean it in a good way. I'd rather have a Lilith than an Eve any day. They'd just need to have a penis is all."

I busted out laughing.

"Listen, Zac..." Bash continued. "I've already told you that I get it, and I really do. I understand both your and Stevie's circumstances and can see why you two have fallen into this as you obviously have. Here's the deal, though. You're gonna have to work a hell of a lot harder to hide what's going on. Not from me but from everyone else."

"I know. Stevie just realized that too."

Bash started shaking his head back and forth, smiling at me. "Dude... The sexual attraction that I just witnessed between you and her. Shit!"

"Yeah, she drives me wild," I breathed out.

"You've gotta tell me when all of this started."

"Before I ever met her. That's when."

"Huh?"

"I saw her on the running trail two Saturdays ago. That was a week before she and I met at Mystic Bar that Friday night when you, me, Brooke, and the gang were all there. On the morning that I saw Stevie at the trail, she was running toward me and kept her eyes glued to mine until we passed by each other. I stopped running, turned around, and continued watching her until I couldn't see her anymore. After that, I had to step off the trail to go walk around in the woods for a while because of what had happened to me."

Bash's dark eyebrows pulled together. "What happened?"

"My entire world was lit up in a matter of seconds by a complete stranger, and we never spoke a word to each other. Not until we met that night at the bar. And like clockwork, my world filled with light all over again at the moment I saw her."

"Ah, the power of eye contact with a beautiful woman. It's been known to slay many a man. Even valiant ones such as yourself."

"It was more than just making eye contact with Stevie. Both at the trail and the bar, it felt like she was staring straight into the core of me. The woman literally took my breath away both times. Hell, she has every time that I've seen her. Even a few minutes ago when she was walking up these steps," I said, motioning at them.

"I wish you'd told me about seeing her on the running trail before now. I wish you'd told me about *everything* before now."

"There was no point in telling you about what happened on the trail because I didn't think I was ever going to see that beautiful stranger again. But then I did. As far as what's happened since that night at Mystic Bar? It's been a whirlwind of coincidental meetings at different places around Dallas. And I planned to tell you about *everything* when the time was right. I just didn't know it was gonna be today."

"Tell me where all of these coincidental meetings happened."

"For one, the Whole Foods that's close to my house. That's where I ran into Stevie next, in the parking lot. It happened this past Friday. We stopped to talk to each other and of course, our chemistry immediately came into play. Also, the sexual tension between us was..." I stopped talking to take a deep breath. "It was intense, and before we said goodbye, I told Stevie to keep wearing that sparkly gloss on her lips because I thought it looked really nice on her. And she told me to keep this scruff on my face because she thought it looked really nice on me."

"I've been wondering what that was all about," Bash said, glancing down at my jawline. "I just thought that maybe you'd gotten tired of appearing so squeaky-clean but that's not the case at all. You're looking rugged for Ms. Stevie Sinclair."

"Yes, I am."

"And she's keeping those plump lips of hers sparkly just for you."

I smiled. "She is."

"Damn, you two are something else."

"I'd like to think we are."

"Don't ever doubt it, man. So go ahead and tell me about the next coincidental meeting."

"I took Malcolm to the zoo on Saturday like I always do, and we were inside the petting zoo when I looked up and saw Stevie standing by the fence, smiling at us. I took Malcolm over to meet her and the crazy thing—he went right to her and hugged her. It was like he found an old friend of his or something. The three of us went to the aquarium after that, Stevie told Malcolm about all the different fish, I brought up mermaids and that's another story that I'll finish telling you about in a minute."

"God, it's like the stars keep aligning and providing all these open doors for you and Stevie to see each other," Bash said, shaking his head in disbelief.

"I know. And the next open door appeared in front of me on Sunday morning. I saw Stevie at the running trail again and the heat between us was instant like before. I couldn't help myself and told her that I wanted to kiss her even though I knew it'd be wrong if I did. She admitted to wanting to kiss me too but then agreed it'd be wrong for us to cross that moral line. I asked her to walk away from me after that because I didn't have the willpower to walk away from her and knew I wasn't gonna be able to continue holding myself back from her if she stayed—so she walked away. Stevie left me on the trail with my head spinning once again.

Bash set down his briefcase on the steps and then held up both his hands. "Okay, stop for just a second and let my brain catch up with all of this."

"I know it's a lot to take in. I'm still processing it."

"Yeah, but it's so great. What you've already told me reminds me of the first part of a romance novel. The sexual tension between the hero and heroine is building and I have a really good idea about what's coming next, so go ahead. I'm ready to hear the rest of this story."

"Well, late Sunday afternoon, I took Malcolm to get some ice cream at Baskin-Robbins and when we walked in, Stevie was standing at the counter with her back to us. I couldn't believe my eyes or the timing."

"I wouldn't have either."

"Malcolm recognized her, said her name. We talked for a minute, ordered our ice cream, and by the way—Stevie's favorite just so happens to be the same as Malcolm's and mine. Daiquiri Ice."

Bash shook his head back and forth. "You've gotta be kidding me?"

"Not at all," I chuckled.

"So go on."

"The three of us went outside and sat at one of the umbrella tables in front of the store, and kept talking to each other and laughing and during that whole time, Malcolm happily occupied Stevie's lap instead of mine. She tended to him too, wiping off his mouth and all, and he loved it."

"And I bet you loved seeing that happen, didn't you?'

"Yeah, I did. Anyone watching us would've easily believed we were a family and for longer than I should have, I let myself imagine we were. Somehow, it felt wholesome and right. Does that make any kind of sense or am I just fucked up for allowing myself to go there?"

"It makes all the sense in the world, and no, you're not fucked up. You're meant to be a family man, Zac. For as long as I've known you, you've wanted a *wholesome* marriage. You've wanted an equal and happy partner in a wife, which is impossible for you to have with the one you're currently married to since she's such a crazy bitch. You also told me from the get-go of our friendship that you wanted to be a father one day. Well, you've been blessed on that part because Malcolm Buchanan is the cream of the crop where kids are concerned."

"I agree with you. He is the only thing that motivates me to keep going."

"Not anymore. It's obvious to me that Stevie is now motivating you too."

I had to smile. "Yeah, you're right. She does motivate me, and in more ways than one."

"You dog," Bash chuckled. "So what happened after your unexpected ice cream date with her?"

"Stevie did something I never imagined she'd do."

"Which was?"

"She invited Malcolm and me over to her house so that Malcolm could go swimming with her in her pool. And now, here's the mermaid story."

"Okay."

"Malcolm believes Stevie is a mermaid whose tail only comes out at night."

"Why does he believe that?"

"Because that's what Stevie and I told him while we were at the aquarium. We were just having fun and Malcolm was so intrigued. You know how much he loves fish, mermaids, water—all of it."

"Yes, I do. Go on."

"Stevie surprised Malcolm by appearing in a full-size, fake, sparkly-blue mermaid tail. When Malcolm saw Stevie floating in her pool with that tail on, you should've seen his face. I'll never forget it. Stevie told him that she made her tail grow especially for him."

Looking around the courthouse grounds, Bash sighed out a smile. Then he focused back on me. "I'm standing here with all of these visuals of Stevie going round inside my head and... I don't know. You're just fucking lucky as hell, dude, to have crossed paths with her."

"That's an understatement."

"So what happened after Malcolm saw that beautiful, blond mermaid during daylight hours?"

"The three of us went swimming together is what happened. We floated all around Stevie's pool too, just relaxing, talking and enjoying what was left of the day. Later on, Malcolm crawled into her lap and fell sound asleep. While he was out, Stevie and I started talking about our pasts, then we started talking about everything we were feeling toward each other. One thing led to another and I kissed her while Malcolm was still asleep in her arms. I couldn't stop myself. I crossed that line, Bash."

"I don't think you crossed a line. Stevie is divorced and you're married only on paper. You and Avery have been living separate lives for the most part since before Malcolm was born. You sleep in separate bedrooms, there's no sex whatsoever, Avery still treats you like shit and she's currently in west Texas fucking that Justin guy. You and I both know it, so do me a favor and don't waste another second of your life feeling any kind of guilt for what you have going on with Stevie. You of all people, Zac, deserve to have some happiness in your life."

"I appreciate you saying that."

"Well, it's true. I don't know how long your relationship with Stevie is gonna last because of both your circumstances, personally and professionally. You two could be forced to end it at any time but while it does last, soak up as much of that woman as you can."

"I plan on it. You know what's strange, though?" I asked, thinking back to last night.

"What?"

"I had a dream about Stevie and it felt so real. I married her, Bash. It was like a sped-up movie reel. I saw the engagement ring that I bought for her, my proposal, our wedding, our honeymoon, and then I saw the house that we lived in and Malcolm was there, running around and playing. Everything was like it's supposed to be."

"The white picket fence life."

"Yeah, it was, and it was a happy one. I know my mind cranked out that dream because I want Stevie in my life and I want her full-time. Not like this. Not an affair. I want us to be out in the open. Hell, I wanna show Stevie off and let everybody know she's mine and I'm hers. I'm not ever gonna be able to have her in that way though, because of *my* circumstances. Not hers. So I'm just gonna keep doing exactly what you said. I'm gonna soak up all of Stevie that I can and for as long as I can, and when that last day with her arrives, I hope it doesn't shatter me. I think it's going to though, because I'm already falling for her."

Bash patted my shoulder. "I can tell. I'm happy for you and I hate it for you at the same time. Isn't it something that we, as humans, willingly do certain things because they feel so fucking good to us and we do them knowing we're more than likely gonna get hurt in the end?"

"Yeah, it is something. Self-torture, I suppose. But right now, what I have with Stevie is the sweetest torture that I've ever experienced and I'll never regret making the decision to become involved with her."

"I wish you'd met her years ago."

I shrugged. "So do I, but then again, it wouldn't have worked."

"Why is that?"

"Because she was happily married years ago. Time wasn't on our side then and it isn't now."

"No it isn't, Zac, not right this second. But who knows? Life can turn on a dime and maybe that dream of yours will come true one day. I don't wanna get your hopes up, but the more I listen to you talking about you and Stevie... Well, none of us know what life has in store for us until it happens. Anything is possible."

"Anything but having Stevie. Until Malcolm is grown, my life's path is set."

Bash paused and studied my eyes. "I'm not so sure about that. I used to be, but not anymore. You believe what you want, though. For now, I want you to give me the juice on everything you've got going on with that beautiful mermaid. I know you've done more than kiss each other. You've had sex. Body language doesn't lie, so go ahead and start talking."

I had to laugh. "You're right. Stevie and I have had sex. Twice."

"When?"

"Last night in her pool and then this morning in her bed, after I cooked us breakfast."

Bash jerked back his head. "This morning in her bed? Cooked breakfast?"

"Yes. I spent the night at Stevie's house. My parents had Malcolm. I parked my car in Stevie's garage. We're trying to be as careful as we can be."

"Dude!" Bash said, making me laugh again. "Oh my God! Wow. Okay. So now I need to know just one more thing."

"Yes, Stevie rocked my world."

"That's what I wanted to hear you say. I hope you rocked hers too."

"I damn sure did."

19
#pokerface

Stevie

I didn't get to see Zac again yesterday after running into him and Bash on the courthouse steps, but we did text back and forth not long after that. Zac texted me first, asking me if I was okay. I let him know that I was still a tangled mess of nerves and then asked him what we were supposed to do since Bash figured out he and I were having an affair. Zac explained to me that there was nothing for either of us to do because Bash accepted and supported it. He supported *us*. I smiled when I read that and liked Bash even more for not casting stones at his best friend and me.

I never intended for anyone to find out Zac and I were romantically involved with each other and couldn't let that happen with another soul. It wasn't going to be easy though, because Zac had the ability to melt me by just looking into my eyes. I was going to have to block him out whenever we were in the company of others such as Brooke and the rest of my team members, plus all of those in the legal community. I just wasn't sure how I was going to do that yet.

Zac and I were finally able to talk on the phone last night after he got Malcolm fed, bathed, and tucked into bed. He told me what Bash said about Lilith bewitching him—or rather, *me* bewitching Zac. My being compared to her took me aback for two reasons. The first one was due to the timing of Bash bringing up her name. It was coincidental considering I'd recently thought of myself as being in line with Lilith instead of Eve.

The second reason that I was taken aback by Bash's statement was that I knew how negatively those in organized religion viewed Lilith. Whether she was once real or a total myth didn't matter. She was known for being Adam's first wife, who chose to buck his authority by not obeying him and was then banished from the Garden of Eden, forcing Adam to take a second wife in Eve. Lilith had been called a she-demon among other awful things, but I'd always thought of her as being a strong, fiery woman who stood up for herself by essentially giving Adam and his patriarchal reign over her the middle finger. I didn't blame her either. I would've done it too.

After Zac told me that Bash meant his statement in a good way, I felt a whole lot better about it, but there was still a little twinge in my stomach by the time Zac and I hung up. I knew it was due to my being raised by a pastor-father and also having grown up in church. I was going to have to work harder to let all of that go, because if I didn't, then my underlying guilt about this affair with Zac was going to take over and cause me to pull away from him again.

And I didn't want to pull away from him.

Selfishly, I wanted Zac even knowing I'd never have him all to myself since he wore a gold band on his left ring finger. It didn't matter that his marriage to Avery was a joke, either. Zac was legally bound to her and had chosen to remain that way because of Malcolm. I completely understood that. I also understood that my time with my lover was limited.

Undoubtedly, there was going to come a day when this pathway that he and I had agreed to journey down together was going to split. Circumstances were going to cause him to go in one direction while I went in the other. Logically, it had to. Until then, though, I planned to relish every moment with Zac that I could steal from time.

The biggest challenge that I could see in this tricky game of hearts that we were playing with each other was stopping myself from falling in love with Zac. I'd already felt the early tugs of that deep emotion and had been able to stop them, but didn't know how much longer I was going to be able to continue doing that. Zachariah Dalton Buchanan was the kind of man a woman couldn't help but fall in love with.

And today—Wednesday—I was scheduled to go up against him in court.

I had less than two hours before I'd be looking into those sky-blue eyes of his again, and it was going to be one hell of a test to hold myself together, professionally. I'd never had this problem before, but I'd never been in a situation like this, either. My case was prepared and ready to go, but I wasn't. At least not yet.

"Knock, knock," Brooke said, peeking around my open office door.

"Good morning."

"Just checking to see how you're doing, Joan of Arc. Ready to kick Buchanan's ass?"

I smiled. "I'm certainly gonna give it my best shot."

"I know you will. Good luck and I'll see you after court."

"Okay, Brooke. Thanks."

She walked off and I leaned back in my chair, resting my head against it and closing my eyes. After a handful of deep breaths, I heard my cellphone buzz and picked it up off my desk to see who texted me. It was my lover.

Zac: Hey, you.

Me: Hey.

Zac: Wanted to tell you again that I'm crazy about you.

I started smiling like an idiot. Even though I was about to go up against this warrior in court, just hearing from him last minute like this helped to ease my nerves.

Me: You know I'm crazy about you too.

Zac: When can I see you again?

Me: Whenever you're free to do so.

Zac: I'm craving you, Stevie. I need another taste of you. I need to be inside your beautiful body and watch you lose control. I wanna see you arch your back and hear you moan my name again. I just need YOU.

I dropped my head and sighed. The effect this man had on me was so powerful. The way that he was in bed with me was powerful too. Both times we had sex, he knew exactly what to do to me, as if we'd been together for years. He touched my body like I needed it to be touched and God, I loved touching his. Zac was so damn sexy and passionate and he had no inhibitions whatsoever about expressing himself in front of me. The fire within him had consumed me but didn't burn me up. It just kept me longing for Zac.

Me: I'm gonna have to start wearing panties underneath my skirt if you make it a habit of texting me at work like this and talking about sex between us.

Zac: So you're getting wet right now?

Me: Do you really even need to ask? <water emoji>

Zac: <devil emoji> I'm gonna see if my parents will keep Malcolm for me tonight. If they can, then I'll come over to your house.

Me: I hope they can because I'm craving you, Buchanan. In every way. I just need YOU too.

Zac: I'll let you know what they say as soon as I find out.

Me: Okay.

Zac: See you in court, Sinclair.

I pulled into the courthouse parking lot forty minutes before the hearing was scheduled to begin. Walking toward the entrance of the huge building, I wondered if I was going to run into Zac going through the security line like before, but he wasn't anywhere around that I could see once I made it up to the line.

This court proceeding that I was going to was on the third floor, and as soon as I made it up to it and the doors of the elevator had opened, I started tingling all over. Zac was standing about ten yards away, wearing a dark gray tailored suit, white-collared shirt, a tie and dress shoes. His short dark blond hair was groomed and neat, and his still-unshaven face looked so good.

Shit, shit, shit.

He looked up from speaking to someone I presumed was his client, met my gaze and softly smiled at me. I watched his eyes fall from mine, down to my waist, and then even lower. Without saying a word, I knew Zac was thinking about the fact that I wasn't wearing anything underneath my skirt. The only thing that lay beneath the fabric of my professional attire was my bare skin.

Before I pulled my eyes away from Zac, I returned his smile. Walking down the hallway toward the courtroom where Zac and I would soon be facing off, I took a deep breath and refocused my train of thought back to my client—the four-year-old little boy who the state of Texas and I were representing. He wouldn't be here today, because of his fragile age, but his guardian ad litem from Child Protective Services would be, as well as his attorney ad litem. I'd already spoken with them on several occasions about this case and we were all three ready to see justice dispensed today. It was going to be coming from the judge, not a jury.

When I walked into the courtroom, no one was present yet. I was glad to have this time to myself to get my files out of my briefcase and go back over them. I'd just sat down at the prosecutor's table when I heard the courtroom doors open behind me, making my heart jump, and when I looked over my shoulder, my heart jumped again. Zac was walking toward me and his eyes were bearing down on mine.

"Good morning, Ms. Sinclair," he said, right before turning toward the defense table.

"Buchanan."

We'd both switched back into professional mode, but I could see that Zac was already struggling to keep it going because the corners of his mouth were curled up. But then I thought that maybe he really wasn't struggling. Maybe that grin of his was intended to weaken my front, to tease me, to toy with the boundary lines once again. The temptation within Zac to do that very thing was just as present within me. The possibility of getting away with something was definitely alluring but we simply could not go there. Not within this legal space.

I turned my attention back to the case documents in my hands and began thumbing through them. This was a good distraction from Zac and also a good way to pass the time. I looked up at the clock on the wall: twenty-five minutes left before court would be called into session. I expected others to begin filing in here at any moment.

I picked up my pen and made a note on my legal pad while keeping an eye on Zac in my peripheral to my right. He was going over documents and I wondered if he was simply going through the motions like I was—putting on a good act. Then he looked over at me, but I didn't look over at him. I kept scribbling notes. Not any that had to do with this case, though. I was actually attempting to draw what I thought I saw on Zac's tie.

He continued staring at me and as soon as I finished my drawing, I decided to turn my attention to him. I knew this was our last chance to share something intimate while inside this room, even if was only a look. And the way that he was looking at me right now was definitely intimate. His eyes were flickering with desire and they danced across my face, coming to a brief stop at my lips. Zac quietly sighed and so did I. This attraction between us was so sultry and intoxicating.

I looked back at my legal pad, took a deep breath, then asked Zac, "Is that Scottish thistle on your tie?"

"It is."

"Thought so. Nice tie, kinsman."

"Thank you, kinswoman."

I was still looking down at the thistle I'd drawn when my cellphone buzzed on the table. As soon as I saw who the text was from, I smiled.

Zac: My parents are keeping Malcolm tonight.

Me: Okay.

Zac: How about I get you and me some takeout for dinner?

Me: Or I can cook something.

Zac: Let's keep it simple. Does Chipotle sound good to you?

Me: Yes.

Zac: What do you like from there?

Me: Keto salad bowl with chicken.

Zac: That's what I get except with steak.

Me: <smiley face emoji>

Zac: I should be at your house by 6:00. Is that okay?

Me: Of course it is.

Zac: Great! I'll text you when I'm almost there.

Me: And I'll open my garage door for you.

Zac: Then I'll greet you with a kiss.

Me: Then we'll eat.

Zac: Then I'm taking you back to bed and making you lose control.

Me: I expect you to.

Zac: <tongue emoji>

Me: <cat emoji>

Zac: <eggplant emoji>

Me: <lips emoji>

Zac and I started quietly chuckling at the same time and stole a glance at each other. Then I sent him another text message.

Me: Will you be spending the night with me again?

Zac: I'd love to.

Me: Then bring a change of clothes with you for work tomorrow.

Zac: Okay, I will. Thank you for having me.

Me: You're welcome. You can stay with me any time you want.

Zac: Waking up with you beside me is something that I could get used to.

Me: Same here. I feel secure when I'm with you.

Zac: <flaming heart emoji>

Me: I love sleeping with my head on your chest too, listening to your heartbeat and your breathing.

Zac: I love the warmth of your skin on mine and smelling your hair.

Me: I love the way that you touch me and how our bodies fit together.

Zac: Same here. I love the way you look at me.

Me: Same here. I love your blue eyes. They remind me of a bright, sunny sky.

Zac: And yours remind me of a night sky full of stars. Their color is so beautiful with those little flecks of gold mixed in. They're mesmerizing. Stevie, you get to me so much and you also GET me.

Me: Same here.

I sighed again, then looked over at Zac. He was staring at me. Strangely, we were still alone in this courtroom, so I decided to quickly do something that I knew would really get to him. I was taking a chance on getting caught in an extremely risqué position if someone walked in but at this very moment, it was worth the risk to me.

I looked back at my cellphone and then swiveled my chair in Zac's direction, uncrossing my bare legs next while leaning my upper body against the table. Then I reached for the hem on my skirt, pulling up the left side of it to the middle of my thigh.

I could see Zac out of the corner of my eye and he still had his on me, so I pulled up my skirt a little more. Then I spread my legs. Not too much but just enough. Enough to let Zac see what I knew would definitely get to him.

When I heard him let out a low groan, I glanced over at him: he'd dropped his head and closed his eyes. *Got him,* I thought to myself while trying so hard not to laugh.

I closed my legs, pulled the hem of my skirt back down, swiveled my chair back to face the judge's bench and continued staring at the screen on my cellphone while waiting for the text from Zac that I knew would soon be arriving.

> **Zac: You just flashed me your treasure trove in the middle of this courtroom.**
>
> **Me: Empty courtroom. And yes, I did.**
>
> **Zac: I'm hard as a rock.**
>
> **Me: You're welcome. And is "treasure trove" really what you're calling my pussy?**
>
> **Zac: Yes.**
>
> **Me: What made you choose that name?**
>
> **Zac: The fact that what lies between your legs reminds me of a treasure trove full of gold medallions and exquisite gems. It's priceless.**
>
> **Me: So does that make you a pirate?**
>
> **Zac: If you consider my taking from you what I sexually want and need to be plundering, then I guess I am a pirate.**
>
> **Me: Although I like the idea of you being one, the truth is you haven't robbed me of anything. I've willingly opened up my treasure trove for you to dive into and explore.**

Zac cleared his throat and I looked over to see him grinning at me. Then he swiveled his chair around in my direction and lifted up the bottom of his jacket. The bulge between his legs was huge. He was so turned on right now and so was I.

Wanting to get to Zac a little more, I lifted my hand to my mouth and pushed my index finger into it. Then I slowly pulled it back out while keeping my lips wrapped around it and imagining it was Zac's cock that I was tasting. I knew he was imagining the same thing because it was written all over his face. Right before I looked away from him, he shook his head at me, sighed, and then swiveled his chair back around. Seconds later, he sent me another text.

> **Zac: I feel like throwing you over my shoulder and carrying you into the bathroom around the corner, locking the door behind us, and then fucking you up against the wall.**

> **Me: If I knew for certain that we could get away with it, then I'd let you.**

> **Zac: You and I are really pushing things here.**

> **Me: I know. Isn't it fun though?**

> **Zac: Yeah, it is. It's a real rush.**

> **Me: We're living dangerously.**

> **Zac: I'm not scared.**

> **Me: Neither am I.**

I'd just hit send on my last text when the courtroom doors opened. Zac and I both looked behind us to see who was coming in but it was only one person. A bailiff.

"Good morning," he said.

"Good morning," Zac and I said together.

"Why are you in here, Buchanan? And I apologize—I don't know your name, ma'am."

"I'm Stevie Sinclair, here for the state."

"Neither of you read the sign taped on the door, I see."

"What sign?" Zac asked.

"Judge Hammond has Covid, so he won't be here today. Judge Smith is handling his cases. Fifth floor."

"Shit! No, we didn't notice the sign," Zac said, jumping to his feet. So did I. We had less than ten minutes to make it to court.

After quickly gathering up all our paperwork, the two of us power-walked to the elevators and Zac pushed the button. Then he looked at me and blew out a disbelieving laugh. He didn't have to tell me what he was thinking. I already knew because I was thinking the same thing. Not due to any fault of our own, we were in one hell of a time crunch to get to the correct courtroom before Judge Smith took the stand.

When our elevator arrived, Zac and I hurried onto it and once again, it was just the two of us alone together. As we stood side-by-side with our briefcases in hand and not saying a word, my lover leaned over and quickly kissed me on the lips. With another floor still to go, I reached over and grabbed his crotch, making him flinch.

"You're killing me, Sinclair," he chuckled.

"Likewise."

Right before we reached the fifth floor, I looked up at Zac again and noticed his mouth. "Sparkly lips, Buchanan."

He'd just finished wiping off my lip gloss when the elevator doors opened, and the two of us took off jogging toward the courtroom. When we made it to the doors, we stopped to catch our breaths while looking around. People were everywhere in the hallway—legal personnel, defendants and undoubtedly, victims too.

"Ready?" Zac asked me.

Before answering him, I glanced down at his mouth: the evidence of our secret kiss was all gone. Right or wrong, part of me would've liked to have seen a sparkle or two still left on those soft and capable lips of Zac's. Proof of not only what we did within those sixty seconds on the elevator, but also proof that he was mine and I was his in this forbidden way.

"Ready," I said, and then Zac opened the courtroom door.

20
#joanofarc

Zac

As Stevie and I entered the courtroom, she headed straight to the prosecutor's table and I hurried over to my client, Mr. Ferguson. Thankfully, my opposing counsel and I had made it to court with three minutes to spare and in that short amount of time, we were able to prepare for what was about to take place here.

"All rise for the honorable Judge Mike Smith," the bailiff said, bringing court into session.

Every person here rose to their feet, and then the judge appeared through the doorway to the left of his bench and walked over to his chair. After telling everyone to be seated, my legal argument with Stevie began.

This was the second hearing that had come about due to my client's negligence and now physical abuse of his four-year-old son. His wife had the same charges but I wasn't representing her. Last year, this couple was charged with neglecting their little boy—the root of it being found to be their illegal drug use. At that time, they were court-ordered to go into three months of treatment for their drug problem and also into counseling on how to be proper parents while their son was temporarily placed into foster care. The couple successfully followed through with the order of the court and then had their son returned to their

home. A month later, their home life had gone back to being a
toxic environment that involved illegal drug use, plus abuse of
their son. He was again placed into foster care while his parents
were charged for their crimes and awaited the legal end result
of them. Today, I was attempting to sway the judge into giving
my client one last chance to get his life right.

After presenting my side of this matter, which included
Mr. Ferguson's agreement to go back into drug treatment and
parental counseling, Stevie had her turn at presenting her argument on the case. I watched her rise from her chair and approach my client on the stand, coming to a stop a few feet away
from him. There was something different about Stevie. There'd
been a major shift in her demeanor and the look on her face was
all business. And her eyes? They were fierce.

"Mr. Ferguson, I'm Stevie Sinclair and I'm representing
your four-year-old little boy, Jacob," she said.

"Hello, Mrs. Sinclair."

"Ms."

Mr. Ferguson smirked. "Ms."

"I need you to clarify something for me if you don't mind."

"What would that be?"

"You're listed as William and also Billy in the legal paperwork that I have on you. So which is it? Which name do you
prefer to go by?"

"What does that matter?"

"Please answer my question, Mr. Ferguson."

He sighed. "I used to go by Billy. I prefer William now."

"I see. A grown-up name for a grown man who makes ju-
venile decisions."

I stood up. "Objection, your honor."

Stevie looked over at me and raised her eyebrow. "It's for
clarification, Mr. Buchanan."

"I understand, but bullying Mr. Ferguson isn't required for
clarification."

"Oh, I'm not bullying anyone. Just stating the facts."

I looked over at Judge Smith. I expected him to call Stevie out, but he didn't. He didn't say anything. I shrugged my shoulders at him and he shrugged back, then returned his attention to Stevie. Right then, I realized he was going to let her run with the ball this morning: she was the newest addition to the district attorney's office and he wanted to see what she was made of. I also realized my hands were now tied. It didn't matter how hard I fought this case.

"Moving on, Mr. Ferguson," Stevie said, dead-eyeing him again. "Last year, you had your son taken away from you by the state of Texas due to your and your wife's negligence of him caused by your illegal drug use. You got help for it, had Jacob returned to your home, started using drugs again, and then began physically abusing Jacob. Correct?"

"Yes but I..."

Stevie held up her hand. "It's a yes or no question."

Mr. Ferguson cocked his jaw to the side. "Yes."

"And here you are again in a court of law not only having to answer for your actions but also wanting another shot at being a responsible and loving father to your son. Correct?"

"Yes."

"Is it also correct that you've gone through a second round of treatment for your drug use and also went through parental counseling again?"

"Yes."

"How many months ago was that?"

"Three."

"And you've been clean of drugs ever since?

"Yes."

Stevie walked back over to the prosecutor's table, picked up her cellphone, and pulled up something on the screen. "Mr. Ferguson, do you have any social media accounts?" she asked, approaching him again.

"Why?"

"Yes or no."

"Yes."

"On which platforms?"

"Facebook and Instagram."

"Do you have your accounts set to private or public?"

"Private."

"Are you sure about that?"

"Yes."

"Okay," she said, half-laughing. "When was the last time you posted something on either account?"

"I don't know. A couple of weeks ago maybe."

"A couple of weeks ago?"

"That's what I said."

Stevie stepped even closer to Mr. Ferguson, then she held up her cellphone in front of him. "Is this your Facebook account?"

"Yes."

"It's not set to private. Your Instagram account is, but because you linked it to your Facebook account, anything you post privately on Instagram is also posted to your non-private Facebook account. Did you get all of that?"

Mr. Ferguson cut his eyes over at me, and I knew right then that he'd fucked up again. I just didn't know what he'd done this time.

"Yes or no, Mr. Ferguson?" Stevie pressed. My client growled out "Yes" and then Stevie held her cellphone even closer to his face. "What is the date of your Facebook post on my phone screen?"

I finally stood up with another objection to the court—this time, about the apparent evidence that Stevie had against my client. Evidence that I knew nothing about. And again, Judge Smith blew off my objection. Then Stevie looked over her shoulder at me.

"Mr. Buchanan, you have the same access to social media that I do," she snapped. "It isn't my fault that you didn't do your homework."

Stevie's eyes had daggers in them while she was making that smart-ass comment to me. I sighed in frustration and then shook my head at her, trying to contain my own anger about the bullshit being allowed inside this courtroom right now.

Stevie briefly turned her attention back to my client, then looked over at Judge Smith. "Please continue, Ms. Sinclair," he said, smiling at her.

"Thank you, your honor."

I completely gave up at that point and sat back down in my chair at the defense table to take in the rest of the show. I wouldn't be objecting to another damn thing because it was absolutely pointless.

"Again, Mr. Ferguson," Stevie said, looking at him again and holding her cellphone right in front of his face. "What is the date of your Facebook post on my phone screen?"

"Yesterday."

"So you lied to this court?"

"I just didn't remember when I posted last. It's not a big deal."

"But it is—especially since the photos in your post show you smoking what appears to be marijuana with some friends of yours."

Mr. Ferguson cut his eyes over at me again and I shrugged my shoulders at him.

"No, it was just tobacco," he said.

"Your honor, I'd like to request a drug test on this defendant before we go any further with these proceedings," Stevie said.

As soon as the words left her mouth, Mr. Ferguson slapped her cellphone out of her hand, sending it flying across the room. Judge Smith and I jumped to our feet and then my client lunged at Stevie from across the witness stand. She stepped back just in time to avoid him putting his hands on her and seconds later, I had mine on him, restraining him while he screamed profanities and tried to break free. The bailiff was by my side within seconds and got Mr. Ferguson in handcuffs, then started walking him out of the courtroom. Before they made it to the side door, though, Mr. Ferguson looked back and smiled at Stevie in a way that made my stomach churn.

"Karma's a bitch," he said.

"You know that well, don't you, Billy Ferguson?"

Stevie's question, as well as the smirk on her face, were clearly meant to antagonize my client and it worked.

He screamed, "Fuck you!" at the top of his lungs and was then hauled away. Once he was out of the courtroom, I turned and looked at Stevie, Judge Smith, and everyone else present.

"My sincerest apology to all of you for my client's actions. I did not see any of it coming," I said.

"I did, Mr. Buchanan."

I met Stevie's gaze as soon as she said that and noticed her smirk was gone, along with the daggers in her eyes. All that I saw now was her concern about what had just happened. We all knew how easily and quickly the situation with Mr. Ferguson could've evolved into a much worse one. Had he been able to reach Stevie across the witness stand, he would've hurt her. He was a big man and he was strong. Yes, Stevie would've undoubtedly fought back with everything she had, but it wouldn't have been enough and I would've felt even worse than I already did now had she been injured.

I acknowledged what Stevie had said by nodding at her, then walked back over to the defense table and sat down, waiting to hear what Judge Smith had to say. Like I already expected, he ordered Mr. Ferguson to a drug test. I knew the result of it was going to be positive for marijuana and probably for other illegal substances too. I also knew Mr. Ferguson would soon be permanently losing all of his parental rights to his son and now, I agreed that it was best. He'd blown the two chances that he'd been given to be a good father and there wasn't going to be a third chance. There was no charm to be found in this unfortunate case.

As soon as Judge Smith adjourned court, everyone began filing out of the room while Stevie and I stayed to gather up our paperwork. Soon, it was just the two of us alone again.

"Are you okay?" I asked her.

She closed her briefcase and then looked over at me. "I'm fine. A little shaken up, a lot pissed off, and also relieved that Mr. Ferguson will no longer be able to hurt his little boy. That son of a bitch can rot in jail as far as I'm concerned."

"I agree. Again—I am so sorry all of that happened with him. I wouldn't have let him hurt you."

"I know."

I paused to look over not only Stevie's flushed face but all five feet seven inches of her. Then I said, "I saw a very different side of you today."

She glanced around the courtroom—to be sure we were still alone, I knew. "And why are you surprised by that? I already told you that when it comes to my job, I will always do what's right and go down fighting for justice for any victim that I represent."

"I know what you said. It was just different seeing you in action is all, Joan of Arc. You did a great job of kicking my ass and no one does that."

She grinned then. "You might've kicked mine had your client not messed things up for you."

"Who knows? But for the record, I'm done representing him."

"I'm really happy to hear you say that. I'd be even happier if you ditched all the pieces of shit you represent."

"I have a job to do, Stevie, and not all my clients are pieces of shit."

She nodded her head in agreement, then walked around the prosecutor's table and started looking around the courtroom floor in front of it.

"Did you lose something?" I asked.

"Unfortunately, yes," she said, glancing over at me. "One of my earrings. I know it's in here somewhere because I pushed the clasp tighter on it before court began. It's gotten loose over time and my hair always seems to get caught in it, which then pulls the earring loose from the clasp."

I walked over to where Stevie was standing and started looking around on the floor for an earring of some sort. I didn't see one, though.

"Okay, what does your earring look like?" I asked.

"Like this." Stevie pulled back her hair from her left ear and showed me the tiny silver butterfly. "If I can't find the one that I lost, it's really gonna suck. My parents got the set for me when I graduated from law school."

"Can you get another set?"

"No," she said, glancing up at me again. "The Austin jeweler who made them retired last year. Closed his store."

Stevie and I made a few more sweeps across the floor and even underneath the prosecutor's table, but couldn't find her earring.

"I'm sorry, I don't see it anywhere," I said, giving her a sympathetic smile.

"Neither do I."

She rested her hands on her hips and let out a long sigh. I glanced around the courtroom to make certain that Stevie and I were still alone, then walked all the way up to her. I was standing close enough to her to smell the Warm Vanilla Sugar body lotion that she'd rubbed onto her skin again and also the coconut scent of her lip gloss. She stared into my eyes while I did the same to hers, and then I pulled her into my arms and hugged her. I had to.

"Nothing can ever happen to you, Sinclair. It'd kill me if it did," I whispered into her ear.

"Nothing's gonna happen to me, so don't worry."

"I can't help but be protective of you."

"I know. I feel the same way about you."

I squeezed her a little tighter, then let her go, taking a few steps back in case someone happened to walk into the courtroom.

"Listen, I need to go back to my office but I'll come back here later to look for your earring again."

"No, you don't have to do that."

"I want to do that. It's in here somewhere, we just can't see it at the moment."

"Well, thank you—and I need to get back to my office too. I know Brooke is waiting to hear how things went today."

"I'm sure she's already heard that you won and also heard about the drama that happened. Word travels fast around these parts."

"Noted."

"Do you wanna walk out of here together?" I asked.

"Sure. I'll be back in professional mode as soon as we make it to the hallway."

"Me too."

I grabbed my briefcase off the defense table, and then Stevie and I made our way out of the courtroom. When our elevator arrived, I was happy to see that it was empty. I was about to be alone again with my lover. It didn't matter that it was only going to be for about sixty seconds.

After stepping into the private space together, we kept our distance until the doors closed. Once they were, I had Stevie back in my arms and this time, I kissed her. Right before we reached the first floor, I quickly wiped off my mouth and Stevie just giggled at me.

While walking down the courthouse steps together, making sure to stay a few feet apart, I said, "I'll see you after work with our dinner in hand."

Stevie and I glanced over at each other, but her focus wasn't on my eyes. It was on the front of my trousers.

"What if I want dessert first?" she asked.

"I can arrange that."

"Wonderful. I'm ready to celebrate kicking your ass in court today by having that big cock of yours inside me again and as soon as possible."

I was grinning from ear to ear now, and so was Stevie. We reached the sidewalk, I extended my hand to shake hers and she wrapped her fingers around mine.

"Be careful—and I'll see you later, Sinclair," I said.

"You be careful too, because it would kill me if anything happened to *you*, Buchanan."

The serious and caring way that she was looking at me right now made me feel like pulling her into my arms again, but we were in public. Instead, I gave her hand a quick squeeze, and we smiled at each other, said goodbye, and then went our separate ways. Six o'clock couldn't get here fast enough.

21
#codeblue

Stevie

I was pulling into the D.A.'s office parking lot when I noticed my cellphone screen light up, sitting on the console. Zac had texted me. As soon as I parked, I opened up his message to see a link to another song and just like before, I knew this one. It was one that I'd heard while watching the movie "Fifty Shades Darker" and I immediately liked the sound of it. I knew it was an R&B song but just didn't know who sang it, so I opened up my Shazam app on my phone that night and got my answer: The-Dream. Then I Googled the lyrics.

Before replying to Zac's text, I tapped on the link to the song and then began playing it through my car speakers while leaning my head back against my seat with my eyes closed. Hearing the lyrics again and visualizing the picture they painted, I felt myself getting choked up and I knew why.

The song was about two people who unexpectedly fell in love with each other, but even though they had, they both knew their relationship wasn't going to last forever. The reason why wasn't clear in the song, but the reason why my relationship with Zac wasn't going to last forever was very clear. One day, my heart was going to be broken again, and it was apparent that Zac felt the same way about his; otherwise, he wouldn't have sent me this tragically romantic song. Despite the obvious pain on the horizon for both of us, we were in this affair together and we were in it all the way.

By the time the chorus started playing for the second time, I was wiping away my tears. The repeated two lines of "That's what I get for loving you. Code blue," were slaying me but I wanted to listen to them anyway because in my listening, I was allowing myself to accept that I really was falling in love with Zac and was no longer going to fight it.

Because he'd sent me the song, I couldn't help but wonder if he was falling in love with me. Yes, Zac had told me how crazy he was about me and I'd said the same to him, but neither of us had dared to admit to anything more. If he was falling for me, I hoped he'd keep it to himself like I was going to do. We simply could not go there. We could not admit to being love-struck because if either of us did, then we'd automatically feel obligated to give more of ourselves and our time to each other. It just came with the territory of saying those three words, and feeling that obligation wasn't part of our plan. Zac and I had agreed to that from the start.

Although I was capable of giving as much of myself and my time to him as he wanted, he wasn't capable of reciprocating that and I never wanted him to be in the position of trying to make it happen anyway—because he would. Because that's who he was. We were already risking so much and couldn't afford to raise the stakes any higher than they were.

As "Code Blue" was ending, I dried my eyes and then re-opened Zac's text. I teetered back and forth about whether or not to reply to him now, since I needed to get up to my office to discuss the outcome of the Ferguson case with Brooke. It took me only a couple more seconds to decide to text Zac anyway.

Me: Hey, you. That's another song that I know and love. How do you know it?

Zac didn't text me back. He called me instead, and I answered my phone by asking him what he was doing.

"I just pulled away from Starbucks with a venti coffee and am about to go on over to my office. Is it a good time to talk?" he asked.

"Yes, it's fine."

"I figured if it wasn't, then I'd get your voicemail."

"No, really, it's a perfect time to talk. It's a treat getting to hear your voice again so soon."

"Yours too. I've got you on speaker and your voice is all around me."

"Same here."

"I can hear you smiling, Sinclair."

I smiled even bigger. "Same here."

"You sound a little stopped up now, though."

Shit. Zac can tell I've been crying.

"Um, I am. There's something in the air that isn't agreeing with me."

"Do you have anything to help with that? Like a nasal spray?"

"Oh, I do at home, but I'll be all right. I'm sure it'll pass."

"Okay. Let me know if I can pick up something for you."

"I will, and thank you."

"You're welcome. And hey, about your text... Tell me how *you* know 'Code Blue' first."

"The movie Fifty Shades Darker.

"Same here."

I was surprised. "You actually watched it?

"I did. All three movies."

"I can't believe what I'm hearing."

"Why?"

"Those movies are chick flicks."

Zac chuckled. "They're guy flicks too."

"So tell me what you got out of watching them."

"A mental escape."

"Don't you mean a sexual escape?"

"Yes."

"Were you alone when you watched them?

"Were you?"

"I was."

"Me too."

"Confession time. Did you touch yourself while watching the movies?" I asked.

"Yes. How about you?"

"I touched myself several times."

Zac blew out a hard breath. "We've really gotta change the subject matter—I'm starting to get hard from talking about all of this. I'm imagining you touching that delectable treasure trove of yours and making yourself cum."

I glanced around the parking lot through my car windows and then quickly turned off my cellphone's Bluetooth connection, ending Zac's voice coming through the speakers. There were people going to and coming from their own cars and I didn't want any of them to hear where I knew my conversation with Zac was about to go despite his request to change the subject matter.

"And I've already imagined you getting yourself off more times than you know," I said, holding my phone to my ear.

"Okay, I just had to adjust myself. Do you even realize what you do to me, Stevie? How easily you get me aroused?

"Yes. And I like that I can. Do you realize how easily you make me get wet?"

Zac blew out another hard breath. "I have a pretty good idea."

"You should have a really good idea by now. And the thing is—you don't have to be anywhere near me for me to get turned on by you. All I have to do is think about you."

"As a man, it feels really good to hear you say that."

"And as a woman, it feels really good to hear you tell me that I turn you on like I do. For a long time, I felt unwomanly. Undesirable. I know my feeling that way was due to me shutting down after I lost my Malcolm. It took away everything feminine about me except for my physical appearance. I just didn't see the point of struggling to keep my inner woman alive when I felt so dead inside, and it wasn't until I saw you at the running trail that first time that the woman inside me started coming back to life. During those few seconds of us running toward each other, I allowed myself to be completely attracted to you," I said, clearly recalling that moment.

"Why me, though?"

"There was something about you, Zac. Something different that I saw in your eyes. When we finally met each other at Mystic Bar, I saw it again and it pulled me right in. *You* did. I swear, it was so hard keeping my attraction to you at bay while we were at the bar that evening."

"Same here. I could hardly keep my eyes off you."

"I know, and I could hardly keep mine off you. As a matter of fact, Brooke teased me about the way that I kept staring at you."

"When did she do that?"

"Right after we left, while she was taking me back to my car."

"Well—since we're confessing things, I'll go ahead and tell you that while we were at Mystic Bar, Brooke texted me. Literally, while sitting across the table from me and next to you."

"What did she text you?"

"About the way that I kept staring at you. She noticed it and was teasing me about it."

I had to laugh. "Oh, Brooke. Was she really teasing you, or just momma-bearing you? It's obvious how close you two are."

"Yeah, we are close. She's like a second mom to me in a lot of ways. She's been an ear to listen to me and a shoulder for me to lean on during a lot of the B.S. I've gone through with Avery."

"You're lucky to have Brooke in your life and she's lucky to have you. She told me that you're like a son to her."

"Yeah, she's told me that several times too. I love Ms. District Attorney and think the world of her. She's a great soul."

"I agree."

"And to answer your question about her either teasing or momma-bearing me, she was doing a little of both that night.

One thing that she texted me was 'Easy tiger'. Then she asked me to admit to something."

"What?"

"That chemistry is fucking powerful. Quote."

"Ours definitely is."

"Without question. And Stevie?"

"Yeah?"

"What you were saying about not feeling womanly for so long... Don't ever doubt that you are all woman. You are so desirable and passionate and you're beautiful, inside and out. Also, I love how open you are about your sexuality and how you express yourself. You don't hold back."

"I love that about you too and I also love how confident you are about sex."

"Confession time again. I'm not that confident about it, and that's a result of the past four years of my life especially. It's not easy hearing repeated insults from the woman you married, telling you that she's not attracted to you, you make her skin crawl, you're pathetic, you're not a real man, and you've got a shrimp dick. The list goes on and on."

"Oh my God. Avery really said all that to you?"

"She did, and still does on occasion."

"Zac, I am so very sorry that you've had to listen to that bullshit. It's *all* bullshit. You know, Avery is one of those sad, sad women who doesn't realize how blessed she is to have a man like you in her life. A *real* man who is kind and funny and responsible and is so damn sexually attractive. The bonus on top of all of that about you is that you have a Moby Dick. Not a shrimp dick."

"I'm glad you think so," Zac chuckled.

"I know so. Avery must have a cow hooch to think you're not well-endowed and that's on her."

Zac busted out laughing then. "Well, I'll put it to you this way: she's nowhere near being like you are. Your tight little treasure trove hugs my *Moby Dick* just right."

"We fit together like two puzzle pieces, don't we?"

"We do. And not only sexually."

"I agree. And about you not feeling confident about sex... I haven't seen a lack of confidence in you when we've been together."

"The way I've been is all about you, Stevie. You make me feel so alive, and the way I want you is borderline animalistic. You make my mouth water, you make me sweat, you make my heart race, and you make me harder than I've ever gotten. While driving over to your house on Monday night, I felt just like the big bad wolf because I planned to take from you exactly what I wanted and that was *all* of you."

"I got from you what I wanted too and afterward, I felt even closer to you."

"Same here. I feel very bonded to you," Zac breathed out. "Listen, we've gone around the whole block with our conversation that started with 'Code Blue' and I wanna tell you why I sent that song to you."

The tone in his voice had turned even more serious and I braced myself for what my gut was telling me he was about to say next.

"It describes us and this affair that we're having...among other things," he continued.

"Other things?"

"Yes."

"Don't say it, Zac. Please."

"You know what I was about to say to you?"

"Yes."

"How?"

"I just do."

"Would it be because you feel the same way about me?

"Zac..."

"Stevie, I'm falling in love with you. No, I'm already in love with you. If you feel that way about me, then why wouldn't you want me to know?"

I leaned my head back on my seat and took a deep breath. What I didn't want to happen had just happened anyway and things were about to change between Zac and me.

"Are you still there?" he asked.

"Yes."

"Where are you now?"

"Sitting in my car in the D.A.'s office parking lot."

"Stevie, I had to tell you how I feel. I *needed* to tell you because my heart is on fire for you and I cannot contain it any longer. It is you and only you who has ever made me feel this way. I wanted to tell you that I love you in person but couldn't wait any longer and thought the song would be a good way for me to lead into telling you now."

I paused again and this time, so did Zac. Then I began again.

"When you and I started this affair, we agreed that we owed each other nothing. There were no obligations between us, but falling in... Going there, and also voicing it, automatically and naturally presents an obligation that we can't fulfill. Well, I can, but you can't. I can give all of myself and all of my time to you, but that's not true for you. I don't fault you for it, either. I understand. I'm still never gonna ask any more of you than what you're already giving to me of yourself and your time."

"By saying 'still', I hear you admitting to falling in love with me. At least I think I do."

"Zac, I..."

"If I'm wrong then tell me. Please. I don't wanna love you in vain, Stevie."

Feeling the sting in my eyes once again, I closed them. Then I confirmed what Zac already knew.

"Yes," I whispered.

"Yes?"

"Yes, I'm in love with you. I didn't plan on it and it's taken me by total surprise, but you—dammit, *you*! It is impossible for me not to love you."

"Same here. You are everything that I've ever wanted. I put you on my wish list a long time ago but just didn't know your name. Now, I do."

I took a moment to breathe deeply because my heart was pounding, my head was spinning and my tears were falling again. After halfway collecting myself, I asked Zac what we were supposed to do now.

"We keep moving forward into tomorrow and the next day and the next, doing what we've already been doing. The only thing that's changed is we confessed to loving each other," he said.

"But Zac—this is all gonna end one day and we both know it. Just like the lyrics in 'Code Blue' say: there's no forever, baby. Not in a situation like ours."

"I can't even consider that."

"You're gonna have to, because it is our reality."

"I'm gonna tell you something that Bash reminded me of while I was talking to him about you yesterday. He said life can turn on a dime and become something good when we least expect it. I've heard that saying so many times before but stopped believing in it because I've been burned so much by life since marrying Avery. I lost my faith in life ever turning in my favor, but it finally did—on the day that I met you. Now with all of that said, I wanna tell you one more thing."

"Okay," I sniffled.

"The pathway that you and I are now journeying down together may seem doomed to split one day and send us flying off into two different directions, but I don't believe it is. I can't explain why I feel so strongly about that other than I just do."

"Well, I feel strongly that it is gonna split. Because of the differences between your life and mine, it has to, and that's just how it is when it comes to having an affair. Besides, do you really see the two of us continuing on in secret like this for a year, two years, or even longer?"

"Stevie, I have no timeline for you and me in my head. All I see is you, though, and all I'm asking is for you to keep walking beside me down this pathway because I feel in my heart there's gonna be a door open for you and me to be together as a couple—and not in secret. Don't you know I want that?"

"Yes, just like I do. But I don't see a door opening until Malcolm is grown. That's fourteen years from now. And please don't mistake what I just said. I'm not asking you to change your situation at home for the sake of us. I'd never want you in that way. I couldn't live with the guilt of being the cause of you divorcing, but I really couldn't live with the guilt of you having to be a part-time father to Malcolm if the courts ruled in Avery's favor."

"I know that's not what you're asking of me because that's not the kind of person you are. As far as you not seeing an open door for us to be together until fourteen years from now—well, I really do believe it's gonna appear much sooner. I don't know how or when it's gonna happen but I sense it coming. I sense life turning on a dime for you and me and giving us a forever. Stevie, are you willing to wait for it with me? I need to know."

There was a tap on my driver's side window and it startled the hell out of me. When I looked up, I was shocked to see Zac standing beside my car with his cellphone pressed to his ear, staring straight at me. I wiped my eyes again and then noticed Zac's were red and his cheeks were streaked. He'd been quietly crying while on the phone too.

"Are you willing to wait for a forever with me?" he asked again.

I ended our call, tossed my cellphone onto the passenger seat, and then got out of my car. Everything around me was a blur except for this man standing in front of me who'd so unexpectedly stolen my heart away. His chest was rising and falling just as quickly as mine was and the quiver of his bottom lip matched mine.

When I nodded my head yes, he whispered, "Please say it, Stevie. I need to hear you say it."

His voice cracked as he spoke those words, and hearing that, as well as seeing the burning look in his beautiful eyes, I told my lover what he needed to hear and what I wanted to say.

"Yes—I'll wait for a forever with you."

Zac had me in his arms within seconds and his lips on mine. Our emotions poured from our eyes while we kissed and even after we stopped. I rested my head on Zac's chest while he hugged me so tightly. But as we continued standing next to my car, the reality of where we were began sinking in. That and the risk that we were still taking of being seen together in this way.

I lifted my head off Zac's chest to look around the parking lot and strangely, no one was near. No one had witnessed a thing.

"See? We just had another door open for us," Zac said, smiling down at me.

"This lot is always so busy. It was until you showed up."

Zac nodded and then began running his fingertips across my cheek. "Are you okay?"

"Yes. Are you?"

"I am now. I thought I was about to lose you."

"Like you told me right before you kissed me on my lips that first time... I'm not going anywhere."

Zac shook his head and then sighed. "I don't feel like going back to my office. I just wanna spend the rest of this day with you."

"I wish we could."

"But we can't. I know."

"It won't be too long before we get to have our dessert," I said, grinning.

"And I plan on savoring every bite of it."

"So do I."

Zac and I noticed a car heading our way and looked back at one another.

"You better go," he said, stepping away from me.

"I need to. I know Brooke is wondering where I am. It's fine, though. I'm just gonna tell her that I needed to drive around for a while after what happened with Mr. Ferguson."

"Okay."

As the car passed us by, we both waved at the driver. Neither of us knew him, though, which was a relief.

"You better go too," I said.

Zac looked around, then quickly stepped back up to me and cradled my face in his hands. "I wanna tell you in person now that I love you. I love everything about you, Stevie, and believe me, I know how crazy it is that we've fallen for each other this fast. But I couldn't help it."

"Same here."

Another car started heading in our direction and Zac stepped away from me again.

"I'll see you this afternoon," he said, glancing down at my lips.

"Okay."

"Bye."

"Bye."

I watched him start walking toward his Blazer, parked behind my car, still running and with the driver's side door wide open. Before he drove away, I wanted to say one more thing to him.

"Hey, Buchanan?"

He turned around, facing me again. "Yeah?"

"I wanna tell you in person now that I love *you*—and I love everything about you too."

He smiled and he smiled big, making his eyes squint and crinkled around the corners, and like clockwork, that adorable dimple in his right cheek appeared.

22
#bombidibom

Zac

"I can't wait to see your dress," I told Stevie.

"I think you're gonna love it."

"Give me just one hint about what it looks like."

"Not doing it. I want it to be a total surprise."

"Okay, fine!" I chuckled and so did Stevie. "We'll be at your house around eight-thirty."

"Bash really goes all-out on occasions like this, doesn't he?"

"Always, when it comes to birthdays. He's done this several years in a row for Brooke."

"She's not only got a bonus-son in you but also in Bash."

"Yeah, but she likes me the best."

"Of course she does. So do I."

"You better!"

"Do you doubt it?"

"Hell no, I don't doubt it. You not only like me best but you love me too."

"With all my heart."

I smiled. "And you've got mine, Sinclair."

"I know."

"Hang on for just a sec. My mini-me, as you call him, is walking into my bedroom," I whispered into my phone.

"Okay."

"Daddy, I'm hungry," Malcolm said, crawling into my lap.

"I know, son. I am too. The chicken nuggets will be done in ten more minutes. Do you think your tummy can wait that long?"

"No," he said, grinning up at me.

"Oh, yes it can!"

I started tickling Malcolm, making him giggle, and when I stopped, he looked over at my cellphone. I had laid it beside me, on my bed, and it was face-up with the screen clearly showing that someone was still on the other end of the line.

"Is that mommy?" Malcolm asked.

"No, it's one of my friends."

"Mermaid Stevie?"

It surprised me that he automatically thought it would be her. I was often on the phone after work, discussing a case with Bash or another one of my colleagues while Malcolm was in the living room with me or in whichever room that I happened to be in. Not only that, but it'd also been almost a week since Malcolm and I had gone swimming with Stevie. I hadn't mentioned her name since then except for telling Malcolm on Tuesday evening that I'd given Stevie his picture and that she loved it. He smiled when I told him that and then asked me about her tail. He wanted to know if it'd grown back. I said that it was resting again when I'd seen Stevie, and then Malcolm ran off to play while I cleaned up our dinner dishes. It went without saying that this story of a beautiful blond mermaid with a sparkly blue tail was just going to keep evolving between my son and me.

"No, a friend from work," I told Malcolm.

He kept looking up at me and finally said, "I'm gonna color another picture for mermaid Stevie."

And there's the next evolution, I thought to myself while smiling inside.

"Okay, buddy. You go do that and then we'll eat dinner."

He hurried down out of my lap to go to his room and when I could no longer hear his footsteps down the hallway, I picked up my cellphone off the bed.

"Are you still there?" I asked Stevie.

"Of course I am."

"Sorry about that little interruption."

"Don't be sorry. It was the sweetest thing listening to you two talking, and I'll get Malcolm's picture from you later."

"Okay," I chuckled.

"Zac, I hope you don't mind me asking, but has Avery called to talk to Malcolm since she's been gone?"

"I don't mind you asking. Feel free to ask me anything you want and I'll answer you. And about Avery calling to talk to Malcolm? No, she hasn't. But it's typical of her."

"What's the longest she's been away from home?"

"Three weeks and a day."

"And during that length of time, did she call Malcolm?"

"No."

"Not even to check in with you?"

"She has called to check in with me before, but only to tell me that she mistakenly had her Amazon order shipped to our address instead of her parents'. She wanted me to mail it to her there after it arrived, which I did to keep the peace."

Stevie let out a long sigh. "Has Avery contacted you about anything this week?"

"No. If she had I would've told you."

"I felt like you would have but I had to ask. All of this is so new to me and I want you to know I appreciate how you're being about it. I hope I'm not coming across as nosy or petty."

"You're not, so stop worrying."

"I'm just concerned, Zac, and I also cannot wrap my brain around the fact that Avery hasn't called to talk to Malcolm. I would need to hear my little boy's voice every day I was gone, as well as yours."

"Same here."

"To back that up even more—I'd never abandon you and our child as Avery has repeatedly done."

"I know. I wouldn't either."

Stevie sighed again. "Does Malcolm ever seem to miss her?"

"Not really. And when he was in here with me a minute ago and asked if it was her on my phone, I saw the worry in his eyes where excitement should've been and would've been if Malcolm had a normal mother. I could tell that he wouldn't have wanted to talk to Avery, had it been her on my phone and asked to speak to him. I wouldn't have pushed him to do it either. Shit, Bash is calling me."

"Okay, take his call and don't forget the chicken nuggets in your oven," Stevie reminded me.

"I'm on it."

"And Buchanan?"

"Yeah?"

"Thanks for talking to me about all of this."

"I like being able to talk to you about all of this, Sinclair. You're part of my life now and what goes on it is your business as much as it is mine."

"Same goes for you with my life."

I paused to think about what she'd just said to me. Or more specifically—the gift of her willingness to let me into her life to this degree.

"I really do love you," I finally said.

"I know. I really do love you too."

"I'll see you soon."

"Okay."

"Bye, lover."

"Bye, Moby Dick."

The limousine driver pulled up in front of Stevie's house at 8:30 p.m. as scheduled. Bash had rented this big black beast as part of Brooke's birthday celebration just like he did last year so that we could all ride to the party together, drink as much as we wanted, and safely make it back home. This time, instead of going to Theory Nightclub in Dallas, we were going to Candleroom. It was another upscale bar/dance club and one of Bash's favorite places to go to because of the "posh" setting, as he called it, and also the crowd and music.

Another difference between this outing and last year's was that this year, there was no chance of Avery being part of it since she was still in Lubbock. When she happened to walk into my bedroom and see what I was putting on to wear to Brooke's last birthday celebration, she'd asked me where I was going and so I told her. Because of the mostly separate lives we'd been living, I hadn't previously mentioned where I was going or why. Not only that, but I didn't think Avery would be interested in celebrating Brooke's special occasion since she never had been before. She suddenly was last year, though, and my only conclusion as to why was that she happened to be bored on that particular evening.

When it came to official events within the Dallas legal and business communities, however, Avery was always adamant about attending with me. I knew it was only because she wanted to make a show in front of everyone, acting like she was something she was never going to be.

In preparation for those events, she always had her hair professionally colored, cut, and styled, had her fake fingernails redone, and always dropped hundreds of dollars on a new outfit, along with matching jewelry. And at those events, she would always look at me, talk to me, hold my hand and lean her body against mine, behaving as if she was really interested in me, proud of me, and also loved me. I knew better but played along anyway because at the time, I was still concerned about presenting a positive family image in front of those in attendance whom I knew.

The only thing that I was concerned about doing now was continuing to uphold my hard-earned positive image in the community. Not Avery's artificial one. She was on her own and what she didn't yet know was that I would be attending all future events without her. That also included get-togethers with my friends, such as the one that I was participating in tonight.

I viewed the timing of Avery being in Lubbock as another open door for Stevie and me to see each other again. No, I wasn't going to be able to pull my lover into my arms and kiss her when I saw her in a minute. That would come later tonight. For now, I was going to have to desire and admire her from afar. Not because of Bash, of course. It was because of Brooke, her boyfriend Ian, her team from the office and their spouses/ significant others.

"Shall we go let Joan of Arc know that her chariot has arrived?" Bash asked me.

He was sitting across the aisle from Brooke, Ian, and me while everyone else was scattered around us, talking and laughing.

"Sure. Let's go," I said, playing it cool.

Bash was playing his part too. He and I had already discussed how this was going to go. Once we arrived at Stevie's house, he was to take the lead instead of me so that no red flags came close to being raised.

"I'm ready to see what the doll is wearing!"

Bash could make statements like that all night long and no one would ever think a thing about it since he was gay. Without a doubt, he was going to continue making similar statements about Stevie until this night was over and he was also going to continue shooting me a sly grin at every turn just like he was doing now.

We'd just stepped onto Stevie's porch when she opened her front door and my breath caught in my throat. She smiled at me and then looked over at Bash.

"Damn, girl! You—are—gorgeous!" he said.

"Thank you. Don't you just love this dress?" Stevie held her arms out to the side and began moving her hips around in a way I'd never seen her do before. She only did it for a few seconds and then stopped.

"I more than love it, doll! Wow!"

Bash walked up to her, grabbed her hand, raised it into the air, and then slowly spun her around to see all of her. Front *and* back.

Stevie's dress was black-sequined at the top and faded down into a mix of black and silver, hitting Stevie's bare legs a few inches above her knees. The only thing holding the dress on her body were two thin straps going over her shoulders and I could already imagine one of them slipping off, then Stevie slipping one of her slender fingers underneath it to put it back in its place.

I couldn't get over how the garment looked on her. It was like it'd been tailor-made for Stevie. It accented her waistline and hips, and also her breasts. The plunge in the front revealed inches of her cleavage, and seeing it made my cock twitch inside my pants. It'd already done that several times since I'd been standing here staring at Stevie, and with every second that kept passing by, the more I realized exactly how challenging it was going to be to keep the red flags lowered this evening. Or more aptly put—how challenging it was going to be to keep my hands off Stevie in front of everyone.

I glanced down at the black high heels that she was wearing and noticed the straps on them were sequined like the top part of her dress. I also noticed that Stevie's toenails were polished a glossy black like her fingernails.

When I looked back up at her face, I began taking in more detail about her makeup. It was more than I'd ever seen her wear before but it looked incredible. Her eyes were lined in black on the top lid and above that precise line, Stevie had applied a pearl-white shadow and then a brownish-gray one a little higher up. Her bottom lash line was shadowed with that same brownish-gray, making her eyes appear smoky, and her eyelashes were neatly coated with black mascara, making them appear even longer than they already were. Her eyebrows were more defined, her high cheekbones were contoured and her pouty lips were glossed with sparkles. And her hair? Stevie had it pulled up in the back with loose pieces falling around her face. All I could do was stare at this drop-dead gorgeous vixen in front of me and as soon as Bash stopped checking her out, she looked back at me and smiled again.

"So what do you think, Buchanan? Is all this I've done to myself too much?" she asked.

I put my hands in my pockets and swallowed hard. "No, Sinclair...it's not too much. You look amazing."

"You really like my dress?"

I dropped my head and smiled, then met Stevie's gaze again. "I love your dress. I love those high heels that you have on. I love the way that you're wearing your hair and how you've done your makeup, and I also love that black polish on your fingernails and toenails. You took my breath away when you opened your door."

Stevie kept staring into my eyes without saying anything and I wished so much that I knew what she was thinking right now. Then she finally told me.

"I did all of this for you and was really hoping you liked it. I love that you love it."

"I really do. And that dress..." I said, looking at it again. "It fits you like a glove."

"And Zac will be taking it off your body later tonight." Bash chuckled, making Stevie do the same.

I cut my eyes over at him and he had that sly grin of his aimed straight at me again. Then I asked Stevie if she was ready to go.

"I am, but before we leave, I need you to do something for me please," she said.

"Anything."

"Unbutton your shirt some more. Two more buttons, in fact. It's only fair that I get to see a little more of your skin since I'm showing so much of mine."

I smiled and then did as she asked. "Is that better?"

Her eyes moved across my chest and then met mine again. "Yes."

"Oh my God, you two!" Bash said, shaking his head at us. "Come on! We need to get this party started!"

Stevie chuckled again and grabbed her black clutch off the entryway table along with a gift bag. After closing and locking her front door, Bash and I stepped aside and motioned for her to walk ahead of us. As she was moving past me, she ran her fingertips across my stomach, making it quiver. I sighed, then looked over at Bash.

"Don't say another word," I told him.

He sly-grinned at me yet again and patted my arm, and then we stepped onto the sidewalk, trailing behind Stevie. We'd only made it a few yards when I heard whistling and hollering coming from the limo and looked over to see the windows rolled down and all the occupants with their eyes glued to Stevie. She waved off their catcalls while laughing and I just kept watching her walk in front of me while my body ached for hers.

Inside the limo, Stevie sat down next to Brooke and this time, I sat across the aisle from her, next to Bash. I was also directly in front of my lover, who'd just met Ian for the first time. I knew she was going to like him as much as everyone else here did and I also knew he was going to like her just as much.

"Okay, Sinclair and Buchanan," Brooke said, smiling back and forth at us. "If I didn't know better, I'd think you color coordinated your outfits tonight. Zac, your shirt is black like the top of Stevie's dress and your gray pants basically match the silver in the bottom half of her dress, plus you're both wearing black shoes."

Stevie and I looked at each other, shrugged, and then started laughing.

"No, ma'am, I promise, we didn't know what the other was gonna be wearing tonight," I told Brooke and it was true.

"Oh, I'm just teasing both of you. But isn't it something how perfectly you match?"

She was looking at Stevie when she asked that question. Then looked back at me.

"Just a coincidence," I said.

I searched Brooke's eyes and saw the smile still in them, but I also saw something else: a look of knowing. A womanly knowing. A *motherly* knowing. And all at once, it hit me that Ms. District Attorney knew Stevie and I were having an affair.

At least I thought she did. My gut instinct was telling me that she did, but it'd been wrong before.

If Brooke really did know about Stevie and me, then I wondered when it was that she'd found out about us. *How* did she find out about us? Stevie and I had been careful to keep our relationship a secret, but then I remembered the risk that I'd taken at Mystic Bar on Monday. When I kissed Stevie in the hallway. That had to be it. Brooke must've gotten up from the table to go use the restroom and seen me kissing Stevie. Although she'd kissed me back, I put Stevie in that risky position.

Time would reveal what Brooke knew. She would either be confronting me soon or she wouldn't. If she did confront me, I hoped that after our conversation was over, she'd understand why I couldn't help but fall into a relationship with Stevie and also fall in love with her. I also hoped that Brooke would let Stevie and me slide on the violation of professional ethics that we'd committed and were still committing by being romantically involved with each other while also being in legal opposition in the courtroom. Although I felt in my heart that she would, Brooke still had a job to do and she took it as seriously as anyone in the Dallas district attorney's office ever had.

Whatever was done was done. Whatever was known was known and whatever was going to happen would. I wasn't going to worry about it. What I was going to do was celebrate Brooke's birthday to the fullest degree tonight. I was going to enjoy the hell out of this gathering of friends and I was going to especially enjoy Stevie being here. And after the party was over, I planned to do exactly what Bash said. I was going to take Stevie's sequined dress off her beautiful body—but not only that. I was going to run her like a river again.

By the time an hour had passed, Brooke had blown out the candles on her birthday cake and opened her gifts, and every one of us present, celebrating her special day, was having so much fun and feeling so damn good. Drinks had been consumed as well as a mix of appetizers, music had been playing the whole time and the vibe tonight was electric. Then a song came on that instantly made Stevie and Bash both start dancing around where they were sitting. Bash was next to me and Stevie was sitting across the table from me, perched beside Brooke. And once again, Stevie was moving her body in a way that I wasn't used to seeing but really liked.

"You know this song?" Bash asked her, seeming doubtful.

"I sure do! 'Bom Bidi Bom!'"

"And you are correct! You can't keep still either when you listen to it."

"And you are correct," Stevie chuckled, still moving her body around. Then the strap on the right side of her dress fell off her shoulder and made the front part of her dress drop down, exposing even more of her full breasts.

Just like I'd imagined it, Stevie slipped one of her fingers underneath the strap to put it back in its place, and as she was lifting it up, the inner part of her arm pressed against the side of her breast, making it raise up. It was only a couple of seconds but I still caught a glimpse of Stevie's nipple. Yes, the lights inside Candleroom were dimmed, but there was no mistaking what I saw and there was also no mistaking what seeing it had done to me.

I moved my hand down from the table and adjusted my cock while trying like hell to wish away the growing erection that I had going on at the moment. I glanced over at Bash and he appeared oblivious to what had just happened with Stevie. He was still carrying on his conversation with her about what I knew was another song from the Fifty Shades Darker soundtrack, and it was obvious that she loved it as much as "Code Blue."

"Okay, that's it! You've gotta dance with me, doll!" Bash said, getting up from his chair. Then he motioned for Stevie to come over to him.

She looked at me, smiled mischievously, and then got up from her chair too. I kept my eyes on her as she walked around the table to make her way to Bash and he grabbed her hand. Then the two of them started heading toward the crowded dance floor.

On their way there, Stevie took the clip out of her hair, looked over her shoulder at me and then tossed the clip in my direction. I caught it in my hand and set it down on top of the table, and when I looked up, Brooke and Ian were grinning at me. I grinned back, then returned my attention to my lover and my best friend. I had no doubt they were about to put on one hell of a show.

Bash always had more rhythm than a white boy should ever have. I knew Stevie had rhythm too. The way she moved her body was always like a smooth and fluid dance. Whether she was walking, running, swimming, or moving in time with me whenever we were having sex, her natural rhythm always showed itself.

Bash turned around to face Stevie when they reached the dance floor, then crooked his finger at her to come closer to him and she did. Without hesitation, Bash wrapped his hands around her waist and pulled her all the way to him. Their bodies were pressed together, Bash now holding on to Stevie by her hips and she with her arms wrapped around his neck. Then they began dancing together while singing the lyrics of "Bom Bidi Bom" to each other. Not even ten seconds had passed when I realized exactly what kind of dance I was going to be watching for the next few minutes: erotic.

The sway of Stevie's hips matched Bash's—the two of them moving together like they were having sex while standing up—and then Bash turned Stevie around so her back was to him. She pressed her body against his and leaned her head back, resting it on his shoulder while he moved his hands around her waist and then placed them on her lower abdomen. She raised both her arms and wrapped them around Bash's neck from behind and they continued gyrating their bodies in identical rhythm.

I saw Bash lean his head down and say something to Stevie, and then she shook her head yes. I didn't know what she'd just agreed to but it only took a moment to figure out what it was. Stevie and Bash began turning up the heat on their dancing.

He reached for her neck and briefly acted like he was S&M choking her, and then he slowly ran his hand down the center of Stevie, making his way past her breasts and stomach, then coming to a stop at her treasure trove. His fingers were splayed across the front of it, and he moved his hand over to the right and clenched the upper part of Stevie's thigh.

While he was making all of those moves on her, Bash kept running his nose up and down the side of Stevie's face and neck. He continued doing it until Stevie turned her head and looked at him. She smiled, Bash smiled, and then he leaned in, bringing his lips within an inch hers. They held that position for several more beats of the song while continuing to move their bodies together. Then Bash pulled back and spun Stevie around to face him.

The next move he made on her was reaching behind her head and grabbing a handful of her hair. Then he pushed her down to the floor. Not all the way but to where Stevie was squatting down with her face in front of his crotch. As they continued writhing their bodies in front of each other, Stevie leaned closer to Bash and began snaking her way back up into a standing position while simulating running her tongue up the front of Bash's pants, his shirt, his neck and chin—finally coming to a stop at his mouth. Her tongue never touched any part of Bash but I was still about to come unglued.

I wasn't pissed off about what I had witnessed. I just had a full hard-on now because I'd been imagining it was me dancing with Stevie like that. I wished I could, but there was no way that we could even slow dance together tonight without raising those fucking red flags in front of the group.

When the song reached the part where Nick Jonas stops singing and Nicki Minaj begins, Stevie stepped away from Bash and started dancing in a way that not only made Bash's jaw drop but also brought back a memory of mine. It was when Avery and I went to Scarborough Renaissance Festival in Waxahachie,

Texas—an occasion when I would've been better off leaving Avery at home.

She and I, along with at least a hundred other people, attended the belly dancing show, and what I saw those belly dancers do on stage was identical to what I was seeing Stevie do now. The circles and figure eights that she was making with her hips, the quick and repeated snaps of them, the belly rolls, the way she was moving her head around, the fluid way she was moving her arms and also the way she was holding her hands were all the same as what those ren-festival dancers so talentedly did.

After seeing their show on that spring day, Avery's bitch side resurfaced before we'd even got up from our seats to leave. She complained about the "way" that I watched the women. I didn't watch them any differently than anybody else, including Avery. We were all fucking impressed but she just couldn't allow me to have that little bit of enjoyment.

Not in the mood to listen to another word come from Avery's toxic mouth, I left her sitting in her seat with her arms crossed and her jaw cocked to the side, then went to the tavern around the corner to buy another pint of cold beer. After getting one, I walked around the festival grounds for the next hour by myself while enjoying every sip of beer that I took and also enjoying looking at every belly dancer, bar wench, and Lady of the Court that I came across.

Watching my own personal belly dancer now, I smiled. It was like I was getting a redo of that day at the ren-festival but it was happening inside the walls of Candleroom. Here I was in a place of merriment with a good crowd, good drinks and good music. And the best part? I was going to be taking that beautiful blond belly dancer to bed later tonight.

As she continued making her sexy moves, Bash started trying to mimic her, and then the two of them busted out laughing and hugged each other. I laughed too and so did Brooke and Ian. When I looked over my shoulder at them, Brooke smiled and winked at me. I returned her smile and when I looked back at Stevie and Bash, they'd just stepped off the dance floor and were heading back to the table. They dropped down into their seats—both of them breathless and sweating. Little beads of it were sprinkled across Stevie's nose and cheeks, and also across her chest.

"Well, I have to say that was the best dance I've ever had with a woman," Bash said, holding out his hand toward Stevie. "Doll, I do believe you could make me go straight if I spent a little more time with you."

We all started laughing again.

"Oh, I'm just kidding," Bash continued. "But Stevie, you are something else. Where did you learn to belly dance?"

The rest of Brooke's birthday party group was returning to the table from doing their own dancing and as soon as they sat down, Stevie looked back at Bash and answered his question.

"My mom taught me."

"Seriously?"

I was just as surprised as Bash and was reminded that I still had so much to learn about Stevie.

"Seriously," she chuckled. "My mom took lessons when I was a teenager and whenever she practiced at home, I practiced with her. I still practice, too, because it's such great exercise."

"Did your mom ever perform anywhere?"

"Only for my dad and me. I don't know if you're aware of this but my dad, Steven Sinclair, is a Methodist pastor, so my mom was a closet belly dancer. She kept her wild side a secret because she—we all knew how church members would've frowned upon it had they found out."

Bash nodded in agreement. "So tell me this... Does your mom still belly dance?"

Stevie looked over at me and then turned her attention back to Bash.

"No. She passed away last year from breast cancer at the age of fifty-five."

"I-I am so sorry, Stevie. Damn."

Bash's facial expression had grown as serious as Brooke's, Ian's, and everyone else's sitting at our table. Then Brooke reached over and patted Stevie's arm.

"Guys, listen," Stevie said, waving off our concerns. "It's fine. I'm fine and my dad is fine. It's part of life. Besides, my mom is still with my dad and me. He and I get signs from her all the time. I don't know how any of you feel about that but I know it's real."

"It is real," Brooke added. "My mother visits me in my dreams and she also leaves pennies laying in the oddest places to be sure she gets my attention. And her name was Penny, so there you go."

"That's amazing!" Stevie said, and then she and Brooke hugged each other.

"Well, I haven't lost anyone close to me but I do believe spirits can visit us," Bash said, reaching across the table for Stevie's hand. She gave it to him and the two of them smiled—one friend to another. "So your dad is who you were named after?" Bash went on to ask.

"Yes. My dad and also Stevie Nicks."

"I knew it!" Bash said, pointing at my Stevie.

"You knew what?"

"That the queen of rock and roll had to be at least part of the reason behind your name."

"How long have you been wondering about that?"

"Since the day I met you."

"Then why didn't you just ask me?"

"I figured you get asked that a lot and probably get annoyed by it."

"Not at all. I'm honored to be named after my dad *and* Stevie Nicks."

Bash sat back in his chair and sighed. "Just so you know— I'm that witchy woman's biggest fan. Every time she tours with Fleetwood Mac or alone, I go see her."

"My mom and dad actually saw her during Fleetwood Mac's 'The Dance' tour in 1997—on Halloween night of all nights."

"Oh, I love that!"

"Then you'll also love this: I have my mom's concert t-shirt."

"Shut up!" Bash huffed out, acting jealous. It made all of us start laughing.

"I'll show it to you some time."

"Seriously?"

"Seriously."

"I just wanna hold it in my hands and smell it."

"No prob. You better give it back to me, though," Stevie said, raising an eyebrow at Bash.

"Maybe," he teased.

"Maybe's ass."

We all started laughing again. Then our waitress walked up and asked if everyone was ready for another round of drinks. We were, and as soon as she went to have our order filled, a song came on, but it was a slow one this time. I looked over at Stevie and she already had her eyes on me.

"You know this song too, don't you?" I asked her.

"Yes. It's another really good one."

"And my man and I are about to go dance to it," Brooke added. "I can handle this pace."

I grinned at her and Ian, then watched them along with the others who had a spouse/significant other with them start getting up from our table to go slow dance. It was just going to be Stevie, Bash and I left sitting here.

As soon as Brooke made it around the table, she walked up to me, leaned down, and whispered in my ear, "All your friends here tonight will think nothing of you dancing with Stevie one time, so go get her. I know you want to. I also know you're romantically involved with her and I'm okay with it. I understand. Now go make a memory with my Joan of Arc while you can."

Although I had already sensed that Brooke was aware of my affair with Stevie, it still shocked me to hear her affirm it. It also shocked me to hear her say that she was okay with it. I knew she was going to talk to me about it some more at a later time and I was actually looking forward to having that conversation with her because I wanted her to know everything about Stevie and me. I wanted to tell her about how innocently we began, how we fell in love, and also that we were committed to riding this thing out until a door opened for us to be together like a normal couple. I planned on telling Brooke that I would've already married her Joan of Arc if I could.

When she stood back up, she smiled at me and I thanked her. Like a mother, Brooke patted my face, and then she and Ian took off for the dance floor. As soon as they were gone, I looked across the table at Stevie. She was staring straight at me.

"What was that about?" she asked.

"Brooke knows about us."

"Oh shit!"

"Yes, oh shit!" Bash added.

I waved off their concern. "No, she's okay with it. She said she understands."

"How does she know about us?" Stevie asked.

"I don't know, but she told me to go dance with you. If it's just one time, no one will think anything of it. So would you please do me the honor of dancing with me?"

Stevie took a deep breath, nodded yes, and then we both got up from the table.

"Yes, go dance, you two! I can't wait to watch you," Bash said, pushing me on my arm. I didn't look at him, though. I kept my eyes on my lover.

She met me at the end of the table and I reached out my hand to hold hers, immediately feeling the tremble in it. I knew Stevie wasn't nervous about dancing with me. It was about Brooke knowing we were having an affair.

After leading Stevie to the middle of the dance floor, I turned around to face her and then pulled her to me, bringing her body closer to mine but leaving adequate space between us to keep any red flags from being raised. As I put my hands on Stevie's waist, she placed her hands on top of my shoulders, and then we began swaying back and forth, staring into each other's eyes. I could still see the concern in Stevie's, and decided to try reassuring her again that everything really was okay.

"Breathe. Brooke is good with you and me. I know she's gonna talk to me some more about everything later—in the next few days probably—and I can't wait to sit down with her and tell her how much I love you and all the reasons why I do."

Stevie took a deep breath and then nodded. "I would like to sit down with her too and tell her the same about you."

"I'm sure you'll get that chance. Who knows? Maybe Brooke will talk to us at the same time. But for now, please just try to relax and enjoy this moment with me."

"Okay. You're right."

"So you like this Hozier song too," I said, intentionally changing the subject.

"Yes. I have 'Movement' on that playlist of mine."

"I figured you did."

Stevie looked down at my mouth and then met my gaze again. "It's been such a struggle not touching you tonight. I know we're touching now but I need it to be so much more than this. It's like I'm having withdrawals from you."

I glanced around and didn't see any of our party group close by, so I took the opportunity to do something to Stevie while the two of us were camouflaged by the bodies of strangers surrounding us and the dim red glow of the chandelier hanging above us. I slid my hands down to Stevie's ass and pulled her all the way to me, leaving no space between us. She sighed against my face as soon as the front of her body touched mine and I was so tempted to kiss her since we were so close. I held back, though, because we were already pushing the limits.

"Do you know what I need?" I asked her.

"Tell me."

"To be inside you again."

"That's gonna happen when you come over to my house later tonight. Before it does though, I'm gonna taste you. I haven't done that yet and I want to."

"No, you haven't done that yet."

"But you've fantasized about me doing it, right?"

"Yes. And now that I've seen you belly dance, I've been fantasizing about you giving me a private show."

Stevie grinned. "I can do that. Back to me tasting you, though."

"What about it?"

"Since dancing with Bash, I've been fantasizing about you grabbing my hair and pushing me down to the floor like he did."

"What else?"

"Tasting you. Wrapping my lips around your Moby Dick and sucking you dry."

It was my turn to sigh and I did. "God, what you're doing to me, woman."

"I know. I feel it pressing against me."

Stevie glanced around us like I'd done, then moved her hand to my chest. After grinning at me again, she discreetly moved her hand down between our bodies and grabbed the front of my pants. When I felt her fingers touch my cock, I closed my eyes and sighed again because it felt so damn good. Stevie kept her hand on me for only a few seconds and then wrapped her arm back around my neck.

"I wanna ask you something," I said.

"Okay."

"Have you ever been dominated while having sex? Because that's what you're wanting me to do to you."

"No, I haven't been, but I've wanted to be. Have you ever been dominant while having sex?"

"No. But I've wanted to be."

"Well, you're gonna get a mild taste of it tonight while I get a big taste of you."

"What if I like dominating you and you like it too?"

"Then we'll keep playing out that fantasy in different ways."

I looked over Stevie's face, coming to rest on her beautiful deep blue eyes again. "I'll never hurt you."

"I know. And I'll never hurt you either when it's my turn to take charge."

I smiled. "I can so easily see you taking charge of me and taking exactly what you want."

"Same here."

The song was nearing its end and I wanted to seize one more opportunity with Stevie if possible. After glancing around and still not seeing any of our party group close by, I dipped Stevie back and held her body in mid-air while she kept her arms wrapped around my neck. Our mouths were even closer now and I couldn't resist kissing her any longer. I pressed my lips against hers. Then hers parted and our tongues entangled. It was brief, it was risky and it was worth it.

When I raised Stevie back up, she smiled and then nodded at my mouth. I knew it was covered in her sparkly lip gloss, so I quickly wiped it away even though I didn't want to. Then we started walking back to our table without holding hands.

Brooke and Ian, along with Jason, Ellie, Jennifer, David and their spouses and significant others, got back to the table at the same time. Bash was still sitting where we'd all left him and he was giving me another one of his sly grins. When I sat back down beside him, he leaned over to tell me something.

"I saw that kiss, Romeo," he quietly said.

"And?"

"I would've done the same damn thing to Juliet."

23
#drugofchoice

Stevie

I was the first person the limo driver took home after Brooke's birthday party. My boss hugged me goodbye before I got out of the limo, looked at me in a knowing way that we both understood, and then Zac and Bash walked me to my front door. They told me goodbye and also goodnight although my night was far from being over. I knew that as soon as the limo driver dropped off Zac at his house, he'd be in his car and making his way back to me. I'd be ready for him, too. Ready to do to him what I'd said I was going to do while we were slow-dancing at Candleroom.

I was standing in the kitchen when my cellphone chimed with a text message. Only one person would ever text me this late and it was Zac. He was almost to my house and needed me to open my garage door so that he could park there for the rest of the night and probably for most of the coming morning too.

As soon as he turned off his Blazer's engine, I lowered the garage door and watched him get out of his car. When he made it over to where I was standing in the open doorway that led into my house, he dropped his overnight bag onto the floor, grabbed my face, and then pulled me to him. Then he started kissing me and he kissed me really hard. It felt like an angry kiss. No, this was a hungry kiss that I was experiencing. A starving kiss. Although we'd just left each other's company less than an hour ago, we simply could not get enough of each other. I knew that I was his drug of choice and he was definitely mine. I wanted to shoot Zac straight into my veins and let him burn them up.

By the time he pulled his lips away from mine, we were both breathless. Then he said, "Let's go inside. Now."

I started backing up into the hallway as Zac kept walking toward me, closing the door behind him. Then he pulled me to him again but this time, he did more than that. He lifted me up underneath my arms, I wrapped them around his neck and my legs around his waist, and then we started kissing again. And while we were, Zac carried me all the way down the hallway to my bedroom.

After making it over to my bed, he fell forward onto it with me underneath him. Feeling his body on top of mine and also feeling his erection pressing into me through his pants and my dress, I couldn't help but moan because I wanted him so much. But not yet.

"First things first," I said.

Zac searched my eyes, then started grinning. "Okay."

"Give me just a minute to get things ready."

He sat on the edge of my bed as I walked over to close my bedroom door, then grabbed my portable speaker from my bathroom. After turning it on, I set it down on top of my dresser and synced my cellphone with it so that I could play a song from my playlist. It was the song by Hozier that Zac and I had slow danced to at Candleroom. I wanted to listen to it again while we did a different kind of dance. One that I knew my lover was going to greatly enjoy and so was I.

As soon as "Movement" began playing, Zac smiled at me, and then I lit the candle trio on my dresser and also the one on my nightstand. After that, I turned out all the lights and walked back over to Zac, whose blue eyes were flickering along with the candlelight.

"Take my dress off me...if you want to," I said.

"*If*? Come here to me."

Zac stood up and reached for the straps on my dress. After he'd lifted them off my shoulders, I pulled my arms out of them and Zac let go of the straps. The top half of my dress dropped down, completely uncovering my breasts, and I watched Zac's eyes gravitate to them. He reached out and touch me by holding my breasts in his hands, then he began rolling my nipples between his fingertips, sending a wave of arousal rushing through me. Moments later, he began sliding my dress down my body to my bare feet and as he was doing it, his mouth fell open.

"You didn't wear any panties tonight," he said, looking up at me.

"I told you that I never do."

Zac let out a groan that sounded more like a growl and hearing it made me do a quick all-over shiver because it was so carnal and animalistic. It was also a turn-on, along with what Zac did next. He leaned closer to me and softly bit the outside of my pussy as he was standing back up.

"Stevie, you just... Just you," he said, staring straight at me.

"What about me?"

"You're just so fucking sexy and bold and real. You drive me crazy and in all the right ways."

"I'm about to drive you really crazy. Get naked."

Zac kicked off his shoes, unbuttoned his fitted black shirt the rest of the way, and then flung it across my bedroom. But when he reached for the waistband on his pants, I stopped him from undressing any further.

"Allow me," I said, making the corners of his mouth curl up.

After getting his pants unbuttoned and unzipped, I jerked them down and as I was standing back up straight, I ran my tongue up the front of Zac's sports briefs. I didn't stop there, though. I continued making my way up his body, covering his muscular abs and chest, and when I got to his mouth, I tugged on his bottom lip with my teeth. Then I reached down into his sports briefs and took his hard cock into my hand. Zac let out another growling groan and then one more when I began playing with his tip. I played with it for a little longer, then let go of his cock and took his sports briefs off him.

Standing in front of Zac and looking straight at him, I said, "Put my mouth where you want it, Buchanan."

Seconds passed. Then he suddenly reached around to the back of my head and grabbed a handful of my hair just like Bash had while I was dancing with him at Candleroom. Then Zac pushed me down to the floor as Bash had done. He didn't push too hard, though. It was just enough force to let me know how serious he was about wanting to dominate me and also how serious he was about wanting me to taste him.

I was on my knees now and my mouth was only inches away from Zac's long, thick and erect cock. After wrapping my fingers around it, I ran my tongue up the full length of it while keeping my eyes on Zac's. His were full of fire and anticipation of me making him come undone in this way.

I licked my lips and then wrapped them around Zac's tip. As soon as my tongue touched it, I tasted the creamy saltiness that had already leaked from it and it tasted good to me. Zac tasted good to me. This part of his masculinity plus the fact that he still had me by my hair had just kicked my own arousal into high gear.

When I began swirling my tongue around Zac's tip, he tangled his fingers into my hair even tighter, which let me know how good I was making him feel. I wanted to make him feel even better, though, so I took in a few inches of him and then some more. I was moving my head, sliding my lips up and down Zac's cock, when I felt him move the hair that was still hanging around my face. He wanted to see every little thing that I was doing to him and I wasn't surprised. Men were such visual creatures and the more this one standing in front of me could see of this sex act, the more he was going to enjoy it.

I took my mouth off him and then started pumping his cock with my hand. When I looked up, Zac's eyes were half-closed, his lips were parted and he was taking even deeper breaths. I could tell that he was getting close to orgasming, but there was still more that I wanted to do to him first.

"Not yet, lover," I told him. "Hang on."

After he nodded at me, I leaned my head down and softly bit his sack. Then I started sucking on it while continuing to pump Zac's cock. About a minute had passed when I felt Zac's free hand stop mine from jacking him off, and I stopped sucking on him and looked up.

"Tell me what you want," I said.

"Take all of me into your mouth. Now."

I smiled and then did as I'd just been ordered to do. I relaxed my throat, took Zac's cock into my mouth again, and then began running my lips and tongue up and down every throbbing inch of it. Zac let go of my hair, placed both his hands on the sides of my head, and then started moving me in the exact way that he needed. It was slow and then it was fast. Slow again and then fast until the fast continued.

I kept my eyes closed and my throat expanded as Zac continued pushing himself into me but when I heard him letting out another growling groan, I opened my eyes and looked up at him. His dark eyebrows were pulled together, his blue eyes were closed and he was breathing hard through his clenched teeth. I loved watching his face whenever he orgasmed and I loved knowing I was the cause of him coming undone.

As soon as Zac's warmth began filling my mouth, I began swallowing it and didn't miss one drop. When my lover was done, I took my mouth off him at the same time that he opened his eyes. Then he startled me when he stumbled backward and quickly sat down on the edge of my bed.

"Are you okay?" I asked, grabbing onto the tops of his thighs.

"Yeah. I'm just a little dizzy," he breathed out while steadying himself. Then he started grinning at me.

I sat back on my heels and grinned back at him because I realized he was dizzy from the oral sex that I'd just performed on him and not from anything serious. It didn't take long for

Zac to completely level out and after he did, he reached out to me and ran his thumb across my bottom lip.

"What you just did to me felt incredible and you looked incredible doing it too," he said.

"Was it the best blowjob that you've ever had?"

"My God, yes!"

"Good. There's plenty more where that came from."

"And I'll take it any time you're willing to give it to me."

I stood up in front of Zac with plans to sit down beside him but before I could, he hugged me around the waist and rested his head against my breasts. While he was quiet and breathing his warm breath on my skin, I ran my fingers through his hair while thinking about our evening together. It was perfect in every way. It was adventurous, stylish, playful, sexy, risky, fun, arousing, gratifying—and also bonding. Every time that I thought I couldn't feel any closer to Zac than I already was, he proved me wrong, and he did it just by being himself. Just by loving me the way that he did.

"Which song is this one of Fleetwood Mac's?" he asked, keeping his head right where he had it.

The song had just started playing and the timing of it couldn't have been any better being that it came on during this tender moment with Zac.

"It's 'Sara.'"

"That's right."

"It was my mom's favorite and it's mine, too, out of all the songs that Stevie Nicks has written."

"Why is it your favorite?"

"Because of the first three lines."

"Refresh my memory. It's a little fuzzy at the moment because of what you did to me."

I chuckled. "Okay. They are: 'Wait a minute, baby. Stay with me a while. Said you'd give me light but you never told me about the fire.'"

"Yeah, I remember them now. They're really good."

"I've loved those lyrics for as long as I can remember and I've always tried imagining what it'd feel like to burn inside for someone. Now, because of you, I know what it feels like."

Zac lifted his head off my chest and looked up at me. "Same here," he whispered.

I held his face in my hands while running my thumbs across his stubbled jawline. "My mom loved that song because of those three lines too, and also because it reminded her of my dad. She even painted the lyrics onto a big canvas with a crescent moon and stars sprinkled around them and hung that painting in her and my dad's bedroom. It's still there."

"I wish I could've met your mom," Zac said.

"So do I. She would've loved you."

"I know I would've loved her too. She and her daughter seem to be just alike."

I smiled. "My dad often reminds me of that."

"You also look like your mom. Everything except for your eye color. I saw the picture of her and your dad in your living room."

"Yeah, her eyes were aqua-blue and mine are identical to my dad's. They're gray-blue or whatever you wanna call it."

"They're what I call *moody blue*. Your eyes say so much, Stevie. Whichever emotion that you happen to be feeling speaks directly through them. I've seen tranquil waters in them, soft waves, and I've also seen a tempest."

"And I get that from my mom."

Zac grew quiet and just kept staring at me.

"I love you," he finally said.

"I love you."

"I think it's time for me to take care of your needs now. If you still want me to. You may be too tired, though," he said.

"Give me your hand." Zac did as I said, and then I placed his hand between my legs. "Do you feel that?"

He smiled. "Yes."

"That's all you. That's what you do to me. You make me get so wet and no, I'm not too tired for you to take care of my needs. I would very much appreciate it if you tasted me like I did you."

"If you give me a minute, I can give you my Moby Dick instead of my tongue."

"I love your Moby Dick but I really want your tongue tonight."

Zac stood up and scooped me into his arms, then he laid me down on my bed. After moving his body down to the foot of it, he pushed my legs apart and crawled up me until his face was right above my pussy. Then with two fingers, he spread me apart and licked my clit with his hot tongue.

"Are you ready," he asked, looking up at me.

"Yes."

"I'm about to make you scream my name, Sinclair."

I grinned, and then Zac wrapped his lips around my clit and started sucking on it while fucking me with two of his fingers. What he was doing felt so good but then he started sucking on my clit even harder, which intensified everything I was feeling. He kept sucking harder and harder on it, making it rise up like a tower. I started trembling all over again as the sensation between my legs began nearing the point of no return, then reached it—and I screamed Zac's name.

24
#exception

Stevie

Zac and I woke up this morning to the sound of both our cell-phones notifying us that someone had sent us a text message. He grabbed them off my nightstand and then handed mine to me.

"It's Brooke," we said at the same time, looking back at each other. Then we read the messages in a group text between her, Zac and me.

"What do you wanna do?" Zac asked.

"Accept her invitation. Let's go have this talk. I'm ready."

"So am I."

Zac was supposed to pick up Malcolm from his parents' house at eleven but I knew he wasn't going to be able to do that now since Brooke was inviting the two of us to have brunch with her at her house at the same time. So he called his mother to let her know about the change in his schedule, but he didn't tell her the truth about why it had changed. He just said he'd had an issue come up with one of his clients and he needed to go meet with them at his office at eleven.

After getting off the phone with his mother, Zac told me that she wasn't concerned in the least about him having to pick up Malcolm later than planned and to go take care of business. He felt bad about lying to her, but I told him that was something that he and I were both going to have to get used to when it came to keeping our relationship under wraps. He agreed.

Now that Zac had Malcolm taken care of, we each texted Brooke back to accept her invitation. Then the two of us went outside onto my back patio and sat at the table while sipping on our cups of coffee. Zac kept watching me.

"I can see how much you're stressing about going over to Brooke's, and it's gonna be okay," he finally said. "Just breathe and have faith."

"That's easy for you to say—you know Brooke so much better than I do, plus you don't work for her. Big differences."

"That's true, but because I do know Brooke as well as I do, I'm not concerned about her lowering the boom on you or me when we get over to her house. She could've already done that, but she hasn't. And remember what she told me last night. She's okay about you and me being involved with each other. She understands."

"Zac, how do you think she found out about us?"

"I think she saw us kissing in the hallway at Mystic Bar on Monday night. I think she got up to use the restroom right after you did and there we were doing what we were doing. Brooke probably just turned around and went back to the table. Did she act any differently toward you when you got back? She didn't act any differently toward me."

"No, she was the same. The only thing that she did was ask me if I was okay because I'd taken so long. I told her that you and I saw each other in the hallway and talked about our Scottish heritage some more."

Zac dropped his head and sighed, then looked back up at me. "That's when Brooke found out about us. She saw us kissing in the hallway. I have no doubt about it now."

"I just thought of something else that she said."

"What?"

"When she was taking me back to pick up my car at her office, she brought up my case against you. She pointed out how friendly you and I have become, then basically wanted to know if I was going to be able to keep the personal and professional separate between you and me. Of course, I told her that I would. Doing my job has never been a problem for me."

"Don't I know it."

"Brooke knows it now too."

Zac slowly looked me up and down, then said, "Since we still have plenty of time before we go to Brooke's, I would like for you and me to do something. I think it would help you with how you're feeling."

"Yeah, you fucking me would probably help me a lot."

Zac smiled that big, dimpled smile of his that I loved so much. "That's actually my backup plan," he chuckled.

"What's your first plan then?"

After setting down his cup of coffee on the table and standing up, Zac motioned for me to come over to him. So I did.

"What now?" I went on to ask, staring up into his sparkling sky-blue eyes.

He was still smiling and before I knew it, he'd picked me up and thrown me over his shoulder and he was running toward the swimming pool. There wasn't enough time for me to break free from him before we both plunged down into the deep end— me only wearing my robe and Zac only wearing his sports briefs.

He hugged me to him while we were beneath the surface of the water. He was right: being in the water did help with all the anxiety that I was feeling about going to talk with Brooke. Zac hugging me helped too, but it was when he kissed me again, underwater, that I felt all the anxiety leave my body and peace take its place.

As Zac and I walked into my garage, we looked over at each other. The one thing that we hadn't talked about this morning was whether we were driving one or two vehicles over to Brooke's house.

"As much as I'd love to ride together, it's not wise," I said.

"No, it's not."

"Maybe on some other occasion. To somewhere else. I don't know what kind of occasion that would ever be, but maybe that door will open for us one day."

Zac stared at me, then leaned closer and kissed me. "Follow me to Brooke's, babe."

"Babe?"

"Um, yeah. That just came out and I don't know why. I've never called anyone that."

"I've never been called that...but I like it. It's a term of endearment."

Zac grinned. "You are my babe."

"And you're mine."

"I sure am."

Zac kissed me again. Then we got into our individual vehicles and headed to Brooke's.

As we were pulling into her driveway, I was happy to see that it was a long one. It curved around to the back of Brooke's house, and that's where Zac and I parked—where no one could see our cars. We were walking toward Brooke's back door when she opened it and then walked down the steps with the biggest smile on her face.

"Good morning, Joan of Arc and Buchanan!"

"Good morning," he and I said at the same time.

Zac hugged Brooke then she hugged me.

"Ian has already gone home, so it's just us and that's what I wanted. Are you two hungry?"

Zac and I both said, "Starving."

"Are you in the mood for a mimosa or three?"

"Absolutely," we said, also at the same time. I looked over at Zac and he already had his eyes on me. The corners of his mouth were also curled up. Our in-sync timing was humorous. Brooke apparently thought so too because she started laughing.

"Come on," she said. "Let's get this Sunday party started."

The moment I walked into her house, I liked the vibe that I felt going on inside. It was a peaceful place. It was a beautiful place, too, from what I could see so far. Brooke and I had like tastes in décor. She seemed to love the ocean as much as I did.

Inside the back door, there was a painting of rolling ocean waves with the sun high in the sky above them hanging on the wall, and in the breakfast room there was a lit Yankee candle sitting in the middle of the round table. The name of the candle was "Coconut Beach" and beside it were a big starfish and a sand dollar.

Beyond Brooke's breakfast room was an expansive kitchen and I immediately noticed all the white-washed cabinets. They were like the ones in my kitchen. Big, clean and crisp-looking. I also noticed the seashell-themed valances hanging above all the windows, as well as the seafoam-green canisters sitting on the counter. Their color matched the valances.

"Did I wake up you two this morning, when I texted you?" Brooke asked while getting the champagne and orange juice out of her fridge.

"You did, but it's no problem," Zac said, answering for both of us.

Brooke set down the mimosa mix on top of the island in the center of her kitchen and looked over at me and then at Zac. And she was smiling again.

"Whose bed were you sleeping in, Buchanan?"

I cut my eyes at him but he kept his focus on Brooke.

"Stevie's," he said, now smiling too.

"I thought so. And Stevie?" Brooke continued, turning her attention to me. "This is how Zac and I are when we're not around the others on the team. We talk openly and candidly about our lives. Are you okay with that?"

"I'm great with that."

"I was hoping so." Brooke walked over to a cabinet and pulled out three champagne glasses. Then she started making our mimosas and while she was, she continued with her candidness. "Last night, I told Zac that I knew about his romantic involvement with you and I also told him I'm okay with it, and that I understand it, as well."

"Yes, he shared that with me."

"I knew he would and I'm glad that he did. I just wanted to tell you the same thing in person. I'm truly good with every bit of this that's happening between you and Zac." Brooke looked over at him with adoring eyes and then looked back at me. "I know his story and I also know yours, Stevie. You two falling for each other is so easy to understand. I had a strong feeling that it was gonna happen because I saw sparks fly between you and Zac when you met at Mystic Bar. Literally, as soon as he turned around and saw you and you saw him—and it just continued from that point on."

"I tried so hard to hide how I was feeling that evening," I said.

"So did this one," Brooke said, poking Zac in the arm. "But I saw right through it—also when we all went back to Mystic Bar on Monday."

"Okay, I've gotta ask," Zac interjected. "How did you figure out Stevie and I were seeing each other?"

"I saw you kissing."

"In the hallway at Mystic Bar! I knew it!"

Brooke shook her head no. "Not there. Did you really kiss Stevie at the bar?"

"Yes."

"Oh my God. You did not," Brooke chuckled.

"Okay, wait. Where... Damn. You saw us in the parking lot by your office."

"I did. I was on my way out to my car and saw the two of you in that sweet embrace, kissing like lovers do—and my heart melted for you. I watched you for a few seconds then turned around and went back up to my office. What I needed to get out of my car could wait."

Zac and I looked at each other and both our faces were so red. Then we started laughing.

"You two are something else," Brooke said, handing us our drinks. Then she raised her glass toward Zac and me. "Here's to being in love. Cheers, my friends."

We clinked our three glasses together and took sips of our mimosas. Then Brooke led us into her dining room. The table was already set with brunch ready to eat. We sat down—Brooke at the head of the table and Zac and me to her left—then we began filling our plates. Brooke had baked a breakfast quiche, made waffles, and also prepared three fruit bowls full of blueberries, sliced strawberries, bananas, grapes and kiwifruit with yogurt drizzled on top.

While eating, we talked about Brooke's birthday party the night before and how much fun everyone had. Brooke loved her cake and gifts and thanked Zac again for the gift certificate he'd gotten for her, from the nail spa she went to. Then she thanked me again for my gift: a bottle of Wayfarer Chardonnay. It was Brooke's favorite.

She brought up my case against Zac and teased him about my win. He took it while grinning, and then Brooke told us something that neither of us had been aware of. She'd watched Zac and I go rounds that day. She'd come quietly into the courtroom, sat on the back row, and then left right before court was adjourned.

"You've met your match in more ways than one, Buchanan," she said.

"Yes, I know."

"About that case—your client fucked you over and he did it last minute."

"He did. I really thought he'd gotten his life back on track but I was wrong. I dropped him as a client that day."

"As you should have. He's a piece of shit. He not only has a major drug problem but a violence problem too. It was clear to me that he would've gotten ahold of you, Stevie, if he could have," Brooke said, looking over at me. "Thank God Zac was right there to keep him away from you."

"I know. No doubt, Mr. Ferguson could've hurt me had Zac not gotten to him in time, but I was never scared of him. If he had been able to reach me, I would've gone down fighting."

Brooke nodded. "We all know that. I spoke with Judge Smith later that day and he told me that he was impressed by your 'in-your-face assertiveness,' as he put it, and also how prepared you were with the case. He also said he was glad that you're part of my team now."

"I'm glad to be part of it too."

"Next week, you'll get to assert yourself again when Mrs. Ferguson has her day in court."

"If she doesn't mess up before then."

"There's no telling with people like her and her husband. Anyway... Enough of that. Now that we're done eating, I'm gonna shift gears on both of you by going back to talking about your relationship."

"Okay," Zac and I said in unison but this time, we didn't look over at each other and laugh. We kept our eyes on Brooke.

"When I told you that I understood your relationship, I meant it in a very personal way. I'm about to share something that neither of you know about but I think you'll appreciate hearing it. I was in your exact position at one time. I had an affair. My marriage to my kids' father was a miserable joke just like yours is to Avery, Zac. My ex-husband and I were living separate lives even though we lived under the same roof. We slept in separate bedrooms, we didn't eat meals together—nothing. He was a drunk jerk who barely worked because he was employed by his mommy and daddy. I worked all the time and also took care of the kids. I shut down emotionally and went through my days and nights like a robot...until I met 'the exception', as I will always call him. He was the only man that I ever broke all the rules for and I'm telling you—I broke them, willfully and unapologetically. He and I both did."

Brooke stopped talking long enough to take a big gulp of her mimosa, then continued telling Zac and me this all-too-familiar story.

"Like you, Stevie, he was divorced with no kids. And I was like you, Zac—unhappily married with... Well, more than one kid. Our affair began two weeks after we met, but our falling in love with each other began happening on the day we met. Our affair was so passionate. It was on fire and it consumed both of us."

Brooke stopped talking again and took a deep breath. There were tears in her eyes now and Zac reached out to hold her hand. It was trembling as she reached for his.

"We can take a break," Zac said.

Brooke shook her head no and smiled through her tears. "I need to finish telling you everything. I'll be all right."

"Okay."

"The exception and I wanted to build a life together. We talked about it so much but when it came down to making that leap, I pulled back. I couldn't do it. As pathetic as my ex-husband was, I didn't wanna split up my family by divorcing him. I didn't want my kids to have to uproot from the only home that they'd ever known. They were happy there, even with their father being who and how he was."

"They were happy with *you* being there, Brooke," Zac told her. "And they would've been happy living anywhere as long as you were there."

"I realized that too late." She pulled her hand away from Zac's to wipe her eyes and nose with her napkin, then took another drink of her mimosa. "One year to the day of when my affair with the exception began, it ended. It ended after I told him that I wouldn't get a divorce even as much as I wanted to. When we told each other goodbye, I felt my soul rip apart. I watched the one man who I loved with every ounce of my being walk away from me, crying just as hard as I was. He was my soul mate and I was his. We both knew it, too."

Zac looked at me and then wrapped his arm around my shoulders, pulling me closer to him. Then he hugged me with both his arms while resting his head on top of mine. All three of us sitting here at this table had tears flowing from our eyes now. We took a moment to collect ourselves and then Brooke started talking again. Going by what she'd last said, I'd thought her story ended there, but I was wrong.

"The exception and I never spoke to or saw each other again—not until I received a phone call from him three years later to tell me that he was dying of prostate cancer. He'd had it for several months and it was in its last stage. He asked me to come to see him because he didn't wanna leave this earth without seeing or touching me one last time, so I went to him. I went to the hospice that he was at and as soon as I walked into his room, I went straight to him in his bed. We hugged, we kissed each other and we cried. I stayed with him until he took his last breath four days later. I was holding him in my arms when he died. Zac Buchanan and Stevie Sinclair..."

"Yes?" we both choked out.

"I wanted to share all of this with you to teach you a lesson that I wish I'd learned a long time ago, and that's to be true to yourself. Listen to what your heart and soul are telling you and don't waste precious time hanging on to anything that keeps you from truly living *and* loving. If I could go back in time, I would've gotten divorced and made a life with my one and only exception."

I buried my face in the crook of Zac's neck, closed my eyes and continued to quietly cry. He was my one and only exception and I knew that I was his too. I also knew that I was never letting go of him, no matter how difficult things got.

"Brooke, I-I..." Zac stammered, then took a deep breath. "I'm sorry. I am so sorry that you went through all of that—that you lost him. And I am so sorry that he lost you. I've heard every single word that you've said and lesson already learned."

I raised up my head and looked at Brooke. "Same here."

"Stevie and I have already talked about building a life together," Zac went on to say. "We have no idea when we're gonna get that chance, but she and I have agreed to ride out this thing until a door opens for us to have our forever. She believes it won't happen until Malcolm is grown—when I'll no longer be concerned about being a part-time father to him. For some reason though, I sense a door opening so much sooner than that. It's anybody's guess as to what the circumstances that allow us to move forward into building a life together are gonna be, but they're gonna appear. That door is gonna open and when it does, I'm marrying this woman right here," Zac said, looking back at me. "She is my soul mate and I am hers. We both know it too."

Zac leaned his head down and kissed me. When we looked back at Brooke, she was smiling at us.

"Buchanan, I hope you're right. I'm gonna pray for that door to open sooner than later and also pray that no one gets hurt in the process. Situations like this are always such a gamble."

"We both know that."

"Okay," Brooke breathed out. "Switching gears on you again... Here's how it's gonna go with me being in the position that I am as the district attorney, Stevie working for me, and you two being romantically involved with each other. Should someone somehow figure out or *think* they've figured out you're involved and bring their concern to me about the obvious conflict of interest, I'm gonna play dumb. I don't know a thing. Got it?"

"Got it," Zac said and I nodded. "We're gonna be more careful when in the public eye, so no one should come to you about anything that has to do with Stevie and me."

Brooke grinned. "No more stealing kisses, huh?"

"No. Not even as tempting as I know it's gonna be."

"You two look really good in love. It's a fast and furious love just like mine was with the exception. I can tell that it's the real deal too. It isn't infatuation. It's not a fling."

"It is the real deal," Zac said. The expression on his face was as serious as Brooke's was now. "I would lay down my life for your Joan of Arc."

"I have no doubt that she would do the same for you."

25
#intuition

Zac

"Hey, I wanted to let you know I'm not gonna be able to meet you at the running trail after work. Malcolm has a fever and I'm actually on my way to my parents' house now to go pick him up," I told Stevie.

"No problem at all. Does Malcolm have any other symptoms?"

"My mom said he's congested, like he's getting a cold."

"Summer colds are the worst. I wish there was something I could do to help."

"You are helping, just by being understanding about me not being able to see you today."

"Of course I understand, Zac."

"Are you still gonna take a run?"

"I need to. It's been days since I've exercised, thanks to you," she chuckled.

"It's been worth it, hasn't it?"

"It absolutely has."

"No regrets here. But maybe we can meet at the trail in the next couple of days. I'll just have to see how my boy does."

"Do you have children's Tylenol or anything for colds for little ones?"

"Yes. I am well stocked up on all of the above."

259

"Good. Hey, hang on for just a sec."

"Okay."

I could hear muffled voices and realized that someone had walked into Stevie's office. As soon as she got back on the phone with me, she said it was David. He had a question about a case.

"I'm almost at my parents' house, so I'll let you go, but I'll call you later this evening," I said.

"Please do. I wanna know how Malcolm is doing."

"Of course. Oh, and you never said for sure if you're gonna go take a run."

"I am."

"Please be careful. Okay?"

"I will. I'll take my pepper spray with me, but I'm really not worried about anything happening out there. It's a great running trail."

"I know it is. It's just..."

"It's just what?"

"I'm protective of you, Stevie, and nothing can ever happen to you."

"Nothing's gonna happen to me...and I'm protective of you too. You and Malcolm both."

Hearing her say that made me smile. I knew how much Stevie cared for me and also my mini-me.

"I love you."

"I love you too."

"Talk to you later, babe."

"Can't wait."

I was pulling into my parents' driveway when Stevie and I hung up. My dad was mowing the front yard and when he saw me, he waved and I waved back. I'd just made it to the front door when my mom opened it and smiled.

"Malcolm is asleep on the couch. The cold meds knocked him out but they made his running nose dry up and his fever go away," she said.

"Good deal."

I stepped through the doorway, hugged my mom, and then walked into the living room to check on Malcolm. And he was out. Drool was running out of the corner of his mouth too, and I just grinned at the sight of him.

"Come on," my mom whispered to me. "I'll fix you something to eat."

"Mom, thanks, but I'm really not hungry right now. I am thirsty, though."

"Lucky for you, I just made a fresh pitcher of sweet tea."

"Sounds great."

I sat down at the bar in my parents' kitchen while my mom poured a glass of iced tea for me. It was Tetley tea. Not Lipton or any other brand. My mom had used it for years and swore it tasted the best. I agreed but had always felt that it had more to do with the way my mom brewed the tea, the pure cane sugar that she used, and the pinch of baking soda she stirred in rather than the brand.

"Here you go," she said, handing me the glass, then sat down on the barstool next to me.

"Thanks." I gulped down half of it then sighed. "That is so good."

"Of course it is."

"Because you made it."

"It's the brand."

"I know better."

"Okay, son. I'm not gonna argue with you about this again."

"Because you know you'll lose?"

"Zachariah, I'm gonna get my belt after you."

"You'd have to catch me first and you haven't been able to do that since I was twelve."

My mom side-eyed me and then started grinning. Our playful banter had always been there between us. She was my mom but she was also my friend. My dad was too, but my mom and I had an extra special bond. She'd always understood me so well and on too many occasions to count, I didn't have to say a word about what I was thinking or feeling before she already knew and knew exactly what to say to me. She also knew whenever I was hiding something.

"So how was your day?" she asked.

"Productive."

"How many cases do you have going now?"

"Too many. I could really use a mental vacation from all of them."

"I know they've always been mentally *and* emotionally taxing on you."

"Just comes with the territory, but I still enjoy what I do."

"That's a good thing. So have you heard anything from Avery?"

"No, and I don't expect to. She can stay in Lubbock from now on as far as I'm concerned."

"Your dad and I feel the same way. I am curious, though, how long she's gonna be gone this time."

"Your guess is as good as mine."

My mom canted her head to the side and looked over my face.

"What's the no shaving about that you've got going on now?"

"I just felt like letting my facial hair grow. It's nice not having to shave every day."

"But I can tell that you're keeping your beard groomed or it'd be all scraggly. It's short and neat-looking."

"Well, I am keeping it groomed."

"Daily, right?"

"Yes."

"So what's the difference in doing that versus shaving every day? About a minute?"

"A minute gained instead of wasted."

My mom looked over my face again then started searching my eyes—and I wanted to close them. I knew that she knew there was more to me having a scruffy face than what I'd just told her. My eyes had always given me away with her.

"My God, you've met someone," she said. "That's why you're looking different. And I haven't mentioned it to you, but I've noticed the pep in your step lately and wondered what it was about."

I opened my mouth to say something but then closed it.

"Zac, you've gotta tell me," she said, touching my arm.

"I can't."

"Yes, you can. It's me. Remember?"

I stared at her for a long moment, then sighed. "I don't want Dad to know. At least not yet."

"So you have met someone?"

"I have."

"Where did you meet her?"

"I saw her on the running trail first. We didn't speak to each other, but then a week later we did, at Mystic Bar. She was there with Brooke and her team. She's part of that team now."

"She's an assistant D.A.?"

"Yes. She handles all the C.P.S. cases."

"Holy shit, son."

"I know."

My mom shook her head back and forth like she couldn't believe all that I'd just told her, but then she smiled. "What I'm about to say may be wrong in every way, but I'm really happy for you. You deserve to have a little sunshine in your life."

"She's a lot of sunshine, Mom."

"So are you two really seeing each other? Or are you just friends?"

I grinned and looked down. Then my mom put her hand under my chin and made me look at her.

"We're really seeing each other," I said.

"Romantically? Like you've kissed her and *everything*?"

"Yes."

"Okay. Does she know you're married?"

"Yes."

"Does she know the circumstances of your marriage?"

"She knows everything about me."

"Please don't tell me that she's in the same kind of sad situation that you are."

"She was but she's divorced now."

"Does she have any children?"

"She lost her only child to SIDS four years ago. His name was Malcolm."

My mom's mouth fell open. Then she leaned back on her barstool and blew out a heavy breath. "I cannot imagine losing you, Zac. And I don't know what to think about her little boy's name being the same as your little boy's. Nothing other than *wow*."

"I was blown away too when I found out."

"How old is your sunshine-woman?"

"She's thirty."

"Seven years difference between you and her."

"It's just a number."

"You're right. It is." My mom looked over my face again. "What's her name?"

"Stevie."

"Stevie?"

"Yes."

"Like Stevie Nicks?"

"Yes, and Steven—her father. She was named after both."

"Okay. How serious are you and Stevie?"

"Very serious."

"And how long have you been seeing her?"

"Long enough to fall in love with her."

My mom slowly nodded, then asked, "Is she in love with you?"

"Yes."

"Okay. Do you happen to have a picture of Stevie?"

"I do."

"May I see it?"

I reached for my cellphone in my pants pocket and then pulled up one of the selfies that Stevie and I had taken together on Sunday morning before we went to Brooke's.

"Here you go," I said, handing my phone to my mom.

I watched her look at the picture of Stevie and me, then enlarge it with her fingertips.

"She's beautiful," my mom said, glancing up at me. "And she has really kind eyes."

"She is really kind and I know she's beautiful."

"This may be wrong for me to say, too, but you and Stevie go together with the way you look. You match. I never have thought you and Avery go together and I'm not just saying that because of how awful she is."

"I know you're not."

"Your features and Stevie's are so similar, and your coloring."

I smiled. "We've talked about that. I think it all has to do with our ancestry. She's of Scottish descent like we are. As a matter of fact, Stevie took a DNA test like you, Dad and I did through ancestry.com and coincidentally, her results are the exact same as mine, percentage-wise, on our Scottish heritage."

"What's her last name? Maiden name?"

"Sinclair, and she goes by it. She took it back when she divorced."

"Yeah, she's Scottish."

"We've talked about comparing our family tree records to see if there's an ancestral link between us somewhere down the line."

"It'd be something if there is."

"In the records that I have, I did find a Buchanan/Sinclair marriage back in the fifteen-hundreds."

"During the Renaissance."

"Yes. When Mary Queen of Scots sat on the throne."

My mom smiled again "I just got chills. I really do hope you and Stevie compare your records."

"I'm sure we will. That one marriage that I found may not be anything, though."

"But it could be. It could be your and Stevie's ancestors who fell in love all those centuries ago and here's another Buchanan man sitting in front of me who's fallen in love with a Sinclair woman."

"And he's fallen hard, too."

"I can see it in your eyes, son."

"I know you can. It's so hard to hide it."

"Well, you don't have to do that with me anymore."

My mom patted my cheek and then asked me if I had any more pictures of Stevie and me.

"Swipe to the left," I said.

I watched her examine the three other pictures of my babe and me. It was the last one, though, that she took the longest on, and I knew why. Stevie and I were kissing. There wasn't any tongue involved. It was just a sweet kiss with our lips pressed together and our eyes closed. I was breathing in Stevie when I captured that moment.

"This picture speaks volumes," my mom said, holding up my phone. "There's no mistaking what's between you and Stevie. Both of you have that gentle, peaceful, grateful, I have found the one whom my soul loves kind of look."

"Song of Solomon 3:4."

"The lovers book in the bible."

"My soul does love Stevie and somehow, it already knew her. Not to sound weird, but she's familiar to me in every way."

"You don't sound weird at all."

"Mom, I've never felt like this about anyone in my life."

"I know you haven't."

I looked up at the ceiling and took a deep breath. Then I met my mom's caring gaze again. "This feeling is so euphoric... and it's also scary."

"Why is it scary to you?"

"I keep thinking I'm gonna wake up and realize I've been dreaming this whole time. Stevie isn't real."

"True love is always scary, son. I felt just like you when I met your dad. Our circumstances were different from yours though, and I can imagine that yours magnify your fear. And with that said, I have to ask you where you see things going with Stevie, because your life with Avery is set until Malcolm is grown and we all know it."

"I don't believe it is set anymore."

"And why is that?"

"I'll put it to you this way: Stevie and I have both thrown our wishes to the stars about wanting to be together. We wanna build a life together and we've agreed to ride things out until we can, but it's not gonna take fourteen years for that to happen. I believe a door is gonna open for us in the near future that's gonna allow me to put a ring on Stevie's finger and also continue being a full-time father to my son. I don't know what the circumstances are gonna be that allow it and I'm not gonna worry about it. I feel it coming, though. My second chance at having a happy life is on the horizon."

My mom took both my hands into hers and stared at me.

"What's wrong?" I asked.

"Do you know what my fear is for you?"

"No."

"That you're gonna get badly hurt in all of this and you've hurt enough in your lifetime."

"What makes you think I'm gonna get hurt?"

"What you're wanting Stevie to do with riding things out with no real foreseeable change in your future is a lot to ask of her. I'm not trying to be mean by saying that, Zac."

"I know you're not. I also know I'm asking a lot of Stevie, but I'm telling you that she's in this with me. We've talked about it so much and she's trusting just like I am that the stars are gonna align and open a door to our forever. We want that more than anything and Mom, I've prayed about it. You know I've had zero faith about my life ever getting better too."

"Yes, I do know."

"Well, that beautiful Scottish woman has restored my faith. She's not gonna hurt me by throwing in the towel on this wonderful thing that we have together, and I'll never hurt her."

I could see the tears in my mom's eyes and she, without a doubt, could also see mine. She reached over and hugged my neck then I stood up with her in my arms, lifting her feet off the floor. She started giggling and so did I but that stopped as soon as we heard the back door open. My dad was coming into the house—either taking a break from mowing or he'd finished the job.

My mom and I quickly sat back down on our barstools and when I looked over at her, she smiled and winked at me. It was her way of telling me that everything we'd just talked about was between us. She was leaving it up to me to tell my dad about Stevie when I felt the time was right to do so. Now I just had to find the right time to tell Stevie that my mom knew we were having an affair.

26
#butterflies

Stevie

My heart was pounding as I was walking up the sidewalk to Zac's beautiful home. I glanced around and didn't see any of his neighbors outside but then again, it was after dark. That was the only way that I felt comfortable coming here. I needed the camouflage of the night.

After making it to Zac's front door, I texted him. Our plan was for me to *not* knock on the front door or ring the doorbell. We had to keep things as quiet as possible.

Me: I'm here.

Zac: Be there in ten seconds.

And he was. He was also smiling when he opened the door.

"Hey, you," he said quietly.

"Hey, *you*."

"Come on in."

Zac stepped back from the doorway and held out his arm for me to cross the threshold of his home. As I did, I recognized the scent in the air and was surprised to smell it.

"You're burning patchouli incense," I said, turning back around to look at Zac.

269

"How'd you know?"

"My mom used to burn it all the time. It was her favorite."

"It's my mom's favorite and she still burns it. I love the scent. I've tried others but keep coming back to this one," he said, pointing up into the air. Then he closed his front door.

"Patchouli is earthy, so it doesn't surprise me that you, Mr. Taurus, are drawn to it. Did you know that it's also an aphrodisiac?"

"I didn't know that. No wonder I love it so much," he chuckled.

"Of course you do."

Zac leaned down and kissed me. "I'm really happy you're here. You surprised me wanting to come over."

"I wanna see Malcolm. I've been concerned about him being sick."

"He's doing all right. The meds are helping."

"How long has he been asleep?""A couple of hours, and he's out."

"Good. He's resting."

Zac reached for my hand. "Let's go take a peek at him."

"Are you sure he won't wake up?"

"Yes, I'm sure."

"And you're sure there's no chance of Avery showing up?"

"Yes. Don't worry."

I took a deep breath. Then Zac started leading me to Malcolm's bedroom. On our way, I glanced around and got a peek of Zac's dining room, kitchen and living room. Everything was clean and neat. It was comfortable here, and peaceful. At least it was right now. I could imagine all the peace flying out the door as soon as Avery stepped through it.

Walking down the hallway, I noticed pictures of Malcolm on the wall and tugged at Zac's hand to give me a minute to look at them. The main one that caught my eye was the one of Zac holding a newborn Malcolm at the hospital. It was precious—Malcolm was, and so was the way that Zac was looking at his son. Zac was smiling but I could also see that he'd been crying tears of joy. I did too when my Malcolm was born.

I looked up at Zac and he already had his eyes on me.

"I love this picture," I whispered.

"Same here. My life completely changed on that day and for the better."

"I know. Children have a way of doing that."

"So do some people—like you, Sinclair. When I met you, my life got even better."

"Same here. Now take me to see your mini-me."

Zac cracked open Malcolm's bedroom door and peeked around it.

"He's still out," he whispered, looking back at me. Then he opened the door and the two of us tiptoed into the room.

Malcolm looked like a little sleeping angel with his blond hair, long lashes resting against the tops of his cheeks, button nose and cupid bow lips. I leaned down closer to him to listen to his breathing and could tell that he definitely had a cold. He sounded stuffy, but not too badly. The meds that Zac had given to him were doing their job.

I wanted to touch Malcolm but didn't know if it'd wake him. I watched him sleeping for about another minute and then couldn't help myself. I reached out and lightly ran my fingertips across the top of his hair and briefly touched his cheek. When I looked up at Zac, he had the most serene look on his face. Then he nodded as if he'd just acknowledged something to himself. I had a good idea of what it was, too. What we were doing felt right in every way. Being together did. The two of us standing here in Malcolm's bedroom did. Everything single thing did and it was something that I had no explanation for.

"We can go now," I whispered to Zac, and we tiptoed back into the hallway. After he closed Malcolm's door, I asked him who'd decorated his room.

"I did," he said.

"I love the train theme in there."

"So do I. My grandfather on my mother's side of the family was a train engineer. I can't tell you how many times it was that he snuck me onto his train when I was a kid."

"Did he really?"

"Yes. It wasn't ever for very long, though. My parents would meet him at one of the small towns that he went through outside of Dallas, then drive ahead to the next town where my grandfather would stop his train and let me get off."

"That's amazing. I can't imagine what it'd be like to ride on a train."

"I always enjoyed the scenery. The engineer and conductor see terrain that most people never do."

"Okay, I'm gonna have to add riding on a train to my bucket list."

"I'll see what I can do to make it happen for you. My parents and I still know a lot of people employed by Union Pacific."

"Really?"

Zac grinned. "Really. Come on. I wanna show you something."

"Okay."

We continued down the hallway, but not in the direction of the living room. We were heading toward Zac's bedroom—a place that I'd never thought I'd see. But I was standing in the middle of it now, with Zac beside me.

He had a gorgeous king-size canopy bed. The wood of the headboard, footboard and four posters was thick, heavy, and stained dark brown. I walked over to the bed to touch one of the posters because I wanted to feel the carved ivy on it. Then I ran my fingers across Zac's comforter. It was made of dark blue velvet on the top side and gray underneath. The four pillows were the same colors and just as plush. I could so easily imagine Zac sleeping in this bed without a stitch of clothing on his body. I'd seen him do that in my bed, but there was something about seeing his private chamber of rest that greatly appealed to me. This space had a king-like feeling to it: fitting for the kind of man that Zac was.

I glanced around the rest of his bedroom and noted that the two nightstands and dresser were made of the same heavy wood as the bed. So was the table in the corner of the room beside a gray chaise lounge chair. It had a lamp on it, as well as a stack of books.

When I turned around, Zac had his eyes on me.

"Are you okay with being at my house, Stevie?"

"Yes. I never thought I'd come here and I certainly never thought I'd be standing inside your bedroom."

"I never thought you would be either."

"Did you decorate your bedroom too?"

Zac nodded. "Do you like it?"

"I love it. It suits you."

"Thanks."

"Were you in here when you watched the Fifty Shades of Grey movies? You've got a flatscreen on the wall," I said, pointing at it.

"Yes, I was in here and I was alone."

I grinned at Zac.

"What is it?" he asked.

"I'm just imagining you watching one of the movies and touching yourself."

Zac grinned then. "And?"

"The thought of it turns me on."

"The thought of you touching yourself does that to me too."

"It's been three days since we've had sex. I don't know about you but I'm about to..." I sighed.

"Me too."

"I would love for it to happen here but it can't."

"Well, it could."

"No, it can't, Buchanan," I chuckled.

"I'm coming back to your house as soon as I can. It's all gonna depend on that little boy down the hallway."

"I understand every bit of that. And when you do come back to my house, I expect you to drop your pants as soon as you walk through the door."

"And I expect you to be naked."

"You know I will be."

"And we've gotta stop talking like this."

"Yeah, I see what it's doing to you," I said, glancing down at the front of Zac's running shorts.

"There is no hiding what you do to me."

"Same here. You can't see it but if you put your hand between my legs right now, you'd feel it."

Zac ran his hands over his face. "Really—we can't keep talking like this."

I giggled. "Okay."

"Listen, I brought you in here because I wanna give something to you. I planned to give it to you at the running trail today but obviously, I didn't make it there."

Zac walked over to his dresser, opened the top drawer, and handed me a small, gift-wrapped box.

"What is this?" I asked, looking back up at him. He was smiling that great big smile of his now and his dimple was showing.

"Open it and you'll find out."

I carefully took off the wrapping and as soon as I saw what was inside the box, I gasped.

"Zac, where did you find these?"

"You can find anything online if you look hard enough."

He'd bought me a pair of silver butterfly earrings. They were identical to the pair that my parents had bought for me on the day I graduated from law school.

"Thank you so much, but you didn't have to do this."

"I wanted to. When we were in the courtroom on that day you lost one, I could see how much those earrings meant to you."

I stared up at Zac, feeling so touched by what he'd done. "I love you."

"I love you and I want you to be happy."

"I am happy. And I wanna put on these earrings."

"Right over there," Zac said, pointing toward his bathroom.

He followed me into it and then watched me as I put on his gift.

"How do they look?" I asked, holding back my hair from my ears.

"They look good because they're on you."

"Thank you again."

"You're welcome, babe."

The look in Zac's eyes was serious now. I stepped toward him, wrapped my arms around his neck, and pressed my lips against his. He hugged my body and started kissing me with everything that he'd been holding back since we walked into his bedroom. Feeling the heat of his tongue, the heat of his breath, his warm hands on me, and his erection pressing against me, I wanted him to take me right here and now on his bathroom counter. Only a few minutes ago, I hadn't thought having sex with Zac at his house was something that needed to happen but he'd just changed my mind.

He grabbed my ass and lifted me up at the same time that I started wrapping my legs around his waist, then carried me back into his bedroom while continuing to kiss me. After walking us over to his door, he closed and locked it and then headed toward his bed. As soon as he sat me down on the edge, he began pulling my clothes off, and Zac's hit the floor next.

The two of us were already breathless with anticipation of what we were about to do, but I could tell by the fiercely passionate look in Zac's eyes now that he was going to be in charge. He was going to dominate me again and take exactly what he wanted. I could hardly wait.

I moved backward across the bed at the same time that Zac crawled forward, holding up his body over mine. As soon as I laid my head down on his velvet comforter, he reached between my legs and stuck two of his fingers inside my pussy, then started sliding them back and forth. I moaned from feeling him touching me like this again, then felt him pull his fingers out of me. While staring straight into my eyes, Zac stuck those two fingers into his mouth and then slowly removed them.

"God, I love the way you taste. It brings out the animal in me," he breathed against my face. Then he grabbed his ready cock and thrust it into my pussy. He kept thrusting it into me too, harder and harder and harder.

There was no pause from Zac this time. There was no tenderness and I liked it. A lot. There was a time for tenderness between us but it wasn't at this moment. The king was taking what he wanted from me how he wanted to take it because I was his. He could put me in a tower and keep me from now on and I'd be happy. Happy to be in his home and happy whenever he unlocked my door and rushed into my chamber to do whatever he wanted to me.

Minutes passed as our bodies continued moving together. We were all breath and sweat and hunger and raw emotion and I could feel myself on the edge of coming undone. Then Zac raised up and looked at me.

"Cum for me," he growled, thrusting even harder into my pussy. "Cum for me, now."

And right on cue, it began.

As the sensation started rushing through my body, I stayed as quiet as I could and it was so hard doing it. I wanted to moan, I wanted to scream because of the intensity of what I was feeling. Zac knew how to fuck so well, he knew how to move me, he knew exactly what I liked.

I kept watching him while I orgasmed and saw the satisfaction in his eyes about being able to make me feel this way. The sex that Graham and I used to have was something that I enjoyed, but never like this. I'd never experienced sex this good.

Zac was still pushing hard into me, but moving his body faster, and I knew he was about to cum. I reached up and held his face in my hands, then felt his warmth begin filling me. He usually closed his eyes whenever he orgasmed but not this time. He kept them open and I watched the fire inside them blaze even more. He quietly moaned like I had, and after coming down from his sexual high, he continued holding himself up with his arms on either side of me. We just kept looking at each other and after catching our breaths, Zac leaned his head down and softly kissed me.

"For what it's worth, Stevie Grace Sinclair, I would marry you tonight if I could. I love you so much. You have made me whole and you've made my life worth living."

I could feel the sting in my eyes, as well as the lump in my throat. "Same here," I whispered.

"I hate being apart from you but even when I am, I can still feel your presence. You're always with me."

"You're always with me too. I feel you all the time and sometimes, I think I hear your voice."

"I've had that same thing happen and I've looked around only to realize it was just my imagination."

"Or maybe we are that connected and are hearing each other's thoughts."

Zac smiled. "Maybe so. Either way, hearing your voice comforts me."

"Same here."

Zac looked over my face and I sensed there was something else that he wanted to say but was holding back.

"What is it?" I asked him.

"I'm about to tell you something and I'll preface it by saying there's no need for you to be concerned.

"Okay."

"I told my mom about us."

"You did what?"

"Shhh," Zac said, grinning and bringing his face closer to mine. My response had been louder than I meant it to be.

"Why did you tell her?"

"Let's get dressed and I'll fill you in with all the details."

By the time an hour had passed, Zac had told me all about telling his mother that we were having an affair. I realized her intuition was just as strong as my mother's had been. Mrs. Buchanan knew her son inside and out and she could also read him like a book.

I asked Zac what he was going to do when his mother asked him to introduce us. I knew it was coming—it was a natural thing for her to want to meet me. Zac said he'd leave that decision up to me when the time came.

I also asked Zac about his father. I wanted to know if he was planning to tell him about us too. His reply was, "Yes, when the time is right." It wasn't at the moment, though, and that wasn't a matter of Mr. Buchanan not being as understanding as his wife. Zac said he just wanted to hang on a little longer to it being only his mother, Bash and Brooke who knew about us. Thinking about those three, I recognized their shared intuition, as well as their ability to read people. Especially Zac and me.

Before I left Zac's house to go to mine, we checked on Malcolm again and he was still sleeping like an angel. Zac also showed me the rest of his house except for the bedroom that Avery slept in. He said it was a wreck, and I didn't want to see it anyway.

I also got to see Zac's swimming pool and loved it. It had a waterfall and the sound of the rushing water was so soothing. Before leaving the backyard, Zac pulled me aside and kissed me goodbye. Then he walked me out to my car. He stood in his driveway and watched me leave, and it wasn't a minute later that my cellphone started ringing. It was Zac. He told me to have sweet dreams, and I knew I would.

27
#reality
Zac

When I called my mom to check on Malcolm at lunchtime, she asked me if she and my dad could keep him overnight. He was feeling a lot better and my parents wanted to take him to the zoo tomorrow—Saturday. Of course, I was good with that, and as soon as I got off the phone with my mom, I sent a text to Stevie to let her know we could get together after work. I hadn't seen her since she'd come over to my house on Wednesday night and I was missing her so much. We'd talked on the phone and texted back and forth several times since Wednesday but it just wasn't the same as seeing her, touching her, and smelling her hair and skin.

Stevie called me from her office after she received my text and she was so excited. My plan was to stop by my house after work and pack an overnight bag, then I'd go to Stevie's house. That plan fell apart, though, when I checked my phone right before I left work. Avery was on her way back to Dallas from Lubbock. I knew that because of the tracker that I put on her car months ago. It was linked to an app on my cellphone. Taking that step was something that had to be done. It was all part of building my case against Avery should she ever decide to file for divorce and also custody of Malcolm.

I called Stevie back to let her know we couldn't get together because Avery was on her way back. I didn't tell her how I knew and she didn't ask. All she did was get quiet. After a long moment, she told me that she loved me and for me to call or text her whenever I could. She also told me that if I found an opportunity to come over to her house then to let her know.

After we hung up, I tossed my phone onto my desk and sat back in my chair. This was our first taste of what it was going to be like whenever Avery was around and it was bitter as hell. I knew Stevie hated it just as much as I did, but there was nothing I could do about it.

Avery was about an hour away from home when I got home from work. I changed into my swimsuit and then jumped into the pool to swim some laps. I knew it'd help get rid of some of the tension that I could feel in my body. I'd thought Avery was going to be gone for a lot longer than this. There was no telling why she decided to come back so soon. Maybe she'd gotten into it with Justin. Maybe he'd kicked her to the curb again.

I was sitting in the living room, watching the news on TV, when I heard the garage door—and I braced myself.

Avery came into the house, walking down the hallway toward me, and as soon as we made eye contact, she smiled. Then she said hello.

"What happened?" I asked.

"What do you mean?"

"You weren't gone for weeks this time."

"I was just ready to come home. Where's Malcolm?"

"He's with my parents. They're keeping him tonight and taking him to the zoo tomorrow if he's still feeling good."

"So he's been sick?"

"Yes. He's had a cold since Wednesday."

"Okay. So it's just us this evening then."

"Yes. Why?"

Avery sat down beside me on the couch.

"I thought it'd be nice to spend some time together. I've been thinking about everything that's happened between us," she said.

I felt nauseous. This wasn't happening. Not now. Avery could not be serious about wanting to work out things with me. She hadn't said that, exactly, but what she did say was code for wanting to do exactly that. I knew it because I'd been here with her before and on too many occasions to count.

It was too late for us to work out things, though. I'd given up on our marriage years before. Not only that, I wasn't in love with Avery anymore. She'd killed it. Even so, I knew I was going to have to play along with what she was doing if I expected any kind of peace around our home while she was here. I'd play along, but for only so long, and I'd allow Avery to go only so far with me. I'd be surprised if the peace between us lasted for a week. By then, her real motive behind acting this way toward me was sure to show itself. She wanted something, and I knew deep down in my heart that it wasn't me.

"What about everything that's happened?" I asked.

"I'm just so sorry, Zac. I know I'm the problem."

"Avery, I really don't wanna get into talking about all of this with you. We've done this so many times."

"I know we have and I don't wanna get into it with you either. What I would like to do is cook a meal together then sit down at our dining room table and share that meal. Have some drinks but not too many, and maybe go swimming."

I stared at Avery for a long moment, then asked, "What kind of meal are you thinking about?"

She smiled. "Homemade tacos with refried beans and rice. Does that sound good to you?"

"Yes, but we're gonna have to go to Whole Foods to get all of that."

"That's fine. Let me put my suitcases up and I'll be ready to go."

Avery and I took my car to the grocery store. As I pulled out of our driveway, I turned on the radio and then turned my face away from Avery because I was trying not to smile. There was a Norah Jones song playing. Stevie was in my car with me and Avery didn't have a fucking clue.

At the store, she and I checked off everything on the grocery list except for the produce. We were in that section and I'd just put two tomatoes into a plastic bag when I looked up and did a double take at the same time my breath caught in my throat. Stevie was here at Whole Foods, and she was pushing her buggy in my direction. She kept her eyes on me for only a few seconds. Then they went right to Avery, and if looks could've killed...

I stayed where I was, acting like I was getting some more tomatoes while randomly looking up at Stevie and then at Avery over by lettuce. We were all yards apart but Stevie was quickly closing the distance between herself and me.

"Zac, do you want jalapeno peppers to put into the ground beef?" Avery asked, looking over her shoulder at me.

"Sure," I said, and she walked over to the pepper section.

I looked back at Stevie and she had her tempest blue eyes on me again. She was also still coming toward me and I was wondering what kind of scene was about to happen here, but there wasn't one. Seconds before Stevie reached me, she glanced over at Avery, who had her back to us, met my worried gaze and quickly ran her fingertips across my stomach, making it quiver like before. She never made a sound, she didn't speak one word, but her presence was so loud.

I watched her from the corner of my eye as she left the produce section and then tossed a couple more tomatoes into the plastic bag I was still holding. Avery walked back up right after that with the jalapeno peppers, and as we headed toward the checkout, I wondered if Stevie and I were going to cross paths again inside this huge place. I hoped so. I also hoped she somehow knew I was simply going through the motions with Avery, all in an effort to keep the peace.

I got what I'd hoped for as soon as Avery and I made it to the checkout lines. Stevie was on the fourth one and I pushed my buggy to the fifth. While Avery was placing our groceries on the counter and talking to the cashier, I kept glancing over at Stevie. Her body language said so much. She was pissed off but I knew it wasn't at me because on one of the occasions that

I glanced at her, she just so happened to glance over at me at the same moment and she winked. It was exactly what I needed from her. It was a confirmation that we were okay despite Avery being back in Dallas.

Stevie left Whole Foods before Avery and I did, but I still looked around the parking lot for her as soon as I exited the store. I didn't see her anywhere—but then I did. The timing of it and where I saw her, sitting in her car, had me hiding my smile from Avery again. Stevie was stopped at the crosswalk that Avery and I were currently crossing. I cut my eyes over at her and quickly patted my chest twice, above my heart. I hoped Stevie knew it was my way of telling her that I loved her. When I stole one last glance at her, she patted her heart twice and I stopped hiding my smile.

"That was delicious," Avery said, wiping her mouth with her napkin. "You've always been such a good cook, Zac."

We were sitting at our dining room table and had just finished our homemade tacos, refried beans, and rice. Avery's help in cooking the meal had consisted of dicing up the tomatoes.

"Well, I've had a lot of practice."

"I know you have, and I appreciate every meal that you've cooked for me and for Malcolm."

"You're welcome."

"So what would you like to do now?"

"I'm gonna have a Hendricks and tonic."

"I'll have one too if you don't mind making it for me."

"But you don't like gin."

"I'm willing to try it again."

I sighed. "Okay."

I got up from the table and started picking up our plates but Avery stopped me by putting her hand on my arm.

"I'll clean up all of this, and the kitchen, if you'll get our gin and tonics ready."

I searched her brown eyes, then handed the plates to her. "Thanks."

While I was making our drinks and Avery was doing what she said she was going to do this time, I kept thinking about how I could not continue going through these motions with her. I didn't like the look in her eyes and I didn't like her touching me. I already knew where she was going to try to take things tonight and it wasn't happening. I would never fuck her again.

I took a shot of Hendricks while Avery was loading the dishwasher, then poured two more into my glass of tonic water and lime. I needed to numb myself but not so much that I didn't still have my wits about me. I was going to have to continue watching Avery's moves as closely as I'd been doing since she got home.

When she finished cleaning up the kitchen, she grabbed her drink off the counter then walked up to me. I was leaning against the refrigerator and had already drunk half of mine but Avery still wanted to make a toast.

"Here's to a good meal, a good drink, and even better company. Cheers, Zac," she said. Then she clinked her glass against mine. I didn't say anything in response to her toast. I just watched for her reaction after she took a sip of her gin and tonic. "That tastes good to me this time. It's refreshing," she went on to say.

"Really?"

"Yeah. I guess my tastebuds have changed."

"Okay then."

I knew Avery suddenly liking gin was a lie because I'd seen her slight wince when she took the first sip of it. She was putting on a good act though, and I was just going to let her continue running with it while I sat back and watched the ridiculous show.

"Do you feel like sitting out by the pool?" she asked, looking down at my mouth and then my jawline.

"Sure. But I'm gonna refill my glass first."

"Before you do that, do you mind telling me why you stopped shaving? I'm so used to seeing your smooth skin."

"I got tired of shaving every day."

"Don't get me wrong. I like it. I'm just gonna have to get used to it."

Avery reached up to touch my face and I jerked my head back.

"Don't do that," I spat.

"I just wanted to touch you is all, Zac."

"One step at a time."

Avery stared at me then nodded. "Okay. I'll meet you by the pool."

I watched her walk to the back door and as soon as she closed it behind her, I grabbed my cellphone out of my shorts pocket and opened up my text log with Stevie.

Me: Hey, you! Just wanted to let you know I'm thinking about you.

I waited for that little bubble with three dots in it to appear, letting me know that she was texting me back, but in the time that it took me to get another drink I never saw it. I wondered what Stevie was doing. Was she floating in her pool? Did she decide to take a late run at the trail? Or was she intentionally not texting me back because she decided she couldn't continue on with our relationship after seeing me with Avery at Whole Foods and also seeing me act like I didn't know her? I checked one last time before joining Avery outside and there still wasn't any reply from Stevie. My stomach was in knots and my heart would not stop jumping around inside my chest.

When I first walked outside, I didn't see Avery anywhere but I did see her glass sitting on the pool deck beside one of the lounge chairs. Then she popped her head up above the water in the deep end and smiled at me. I was walking toward her when I realized she was completely naked and I shook my head to myself.

So much for taking it one fake step at a time.

"Come take a swim with me," she said.

"I'm gonna relax right here, Avery."

I sat down on one of the other lounge chairs and continued sipping on my Hendricks and tonic while Avery swam around in the water. After only a couple of minutes, she came over to the edge of the pool, right in front of me.

"Are you relaxed now?" she asked.

"Getting there."

"Zac, I don't expect you to welcome how I'm feeling about us and how I'm being toward you overnight. I know this is gonna take time."

"What's gonna take time?"

"You and I working things out."

"Avery, you haven't once asked me how I feel about all of this. You haven't asked me if I want us to work out. You're assuming that I do."

"I got the impression that you do since you were willing to talk to me when I got home, then go grocery shopping with me, cook a meal with me, share that meal, make me a drink and come out here."

"It's better if you and I communicate and do it peacefully. We also have to eat and it's better if we do that in peace too, as well as drink in peace, swim in peace—just live in peace. All I want is a peaceful life and it hasn't been that way with you," I said, instantly realizing that I might have said too much.

I was expecting Avery to come back at me with an onslaught of four-letter words and for things to escalate from there, but they didn't. She got quiet, and it reminded me of how Stevie got quiet on the phone when I let her know I couldn't see her tonight like we'd planned.

"I know that's all you've wanted, Zac, and you've tried really hard to have that kind of life with me. Again, I'm sorry. I've fucked everything up."

"Where is all of this coming from? Why the sudden change of heart?" I asked.

Avery shrugged. "I told you that I've just been thinking about us."

"Yeah, but what prompted it?"

"A dream that I had while I was at my mom and dad's."

"A dream?"

"Yes."

"And when did you have this dream?"

"Last night."

"So that's why you came home today?"

"Yes."

"What was the dream about?"

"You."

"What about me?"

"You fell in love with someone and ended us."

"Avery, there hasn't been an 'us' since before Malcolm was born and you know it. We've been nothing more than roommates who hate each other most of the time, but I'm the roommate who's been footing all the expenses. Financial *and* emotional expenses."

"I know. It's just that my dream was so real, and when I saw you with the other woman, and how happy you were, it did something to me. I woke up crying. I realized what a fool I've been for not being a good wife to you all these years."

"What about for not being a good mother to Malcolm?"

"Well, that too."

I took a deep breath and then downed my drink. "Our son has never been anything to you but a fucking afterthought. I'm going to bed, Avery," I said, getting up from my chair.

"Zac, wait!"

I pointed at her and stared hard. "No! Don't say another word to me tonight. Swim, drink some more, do whatever you want. I don't care. Just leave me the hell alone."

Avery nodded and then I went back into the house, going straight to my bedroom and closing the door behind me. I locked it, walked over and collapsed on my bed, then pulled my cellphone out of my shorts pocket to see if Stevie had texted me back.

Stevie: Hey, you! I was outside doing yard work when you texted me and didn't have my cellphone on me. I thought I did. Sorry. And FYI, I've been thinking about you too. Is everything okay?

Me: Sorry I'm just now replying to your text. We keep missing each other. I just came back into my house from being outside in the backyard with Avery and no, everything isn't okay.

Stevie: What happened?

Me: Avery told me that she wants to work out things with me but I know it's a lie. She wants something from me and it's probably nothing more than for me to continue financing her fucked up lifestyle.

That little bubble with the three dots in it popped up but then it went away. I waited a little longer to see if Stevie was going to reply but she didn't.

Me: May I call you?

Stevie: Yes.

"What if Avery really does want to work out things with you, Zac?" Stevie asked. That was how she answered her phone.

"I'm telling you that it's a lie and even if she wasn't lying to me, I would never reconcile with her. I don't love her and haven't in years and I damn sure don't trust her. You know I'm with Avery only because of Malcolm. We are married on paper and that is it."

Stevie sighed. "I just needed to hear you say that again.

"But do you believe it?"

"Yes. It's just so hard knowing you're there with her. I want you here with me."

"And I wanna be there with you. So badly."

"Zac, I don't understand Avery's sudden turnaround about her feelings toward you."

"Yeah... I asked her about that. She told me that she had a dream about me last night. I'd fallen in love with another woman and ended things with her."

"Wow."

"Why the 'wow'?"

"A woman's intuition. That's why I said that. Women know things, they sense them. Even women like Avery—and it appears that she's somehow sensing us."

"Stevie, it was a dream that she had, and it was her guilty conscience that prompted it—if she really did have the dream. She's probably lying about it just to get some sympathy from me, which she hasn't and won't."

"Where are you right now?"

"In my bedroom with the door locked."

"Jesus, you're like a prisoner in your own home."

That was hard to hear Stevie say, but she was right. "In some ways I am, and it's just how it is."

"What if Avery hears you talking through the door? It wouldn't surprise me if she's listened in on you before and is maybe listening now."

"It'd only be my side of the conversation that she'd hear."

"Still—how would you explain it away? A lot can be deciphered from just hearing one side."

"I wouldn't explain anything. What I do and who I talk to is none of her business."

"Do me a favor."

"Okay."

"Please go into your bathroom and close the door."

"Stevie, I'm not worried about Avery hearing me talk to you."

"But I am. My biggest fear is all of this blowing up in your face."

"I'm walking into my bathroom now."

"Thank you."

"Okay, I just laid down on the floor and I'm about to share something with you that will hopefully put you at ease about this whole situation. As you know, I've been documenting incidents with Avery whenever they happen. I've also taken pictures of the marks that she's left on me. I've videoed her too whenever she's been in one of her rages and comes at me or tears up things around here. There's more that I've done, though, and am still doing."

"What?"

"I put a tracker on her car months ago and I also hired a private investigator. He's provided me with photos and video footage of Avery with that guy she met in college and was engaged to. The two of them are currently having an affair."

Stevie grew quiet and remained that way.

"Are you still there?" I asked.

"Yes. Just processing what you told me."

"I understand."

"What is the guy's name?"

"Justin Edwards."

"Is he from Lubbock?"

"Yes, and he still lives there. He's the reason why Avery goes to west Texas so often and stays gone like she does. It's not just to see her family and friends as she's always claimed."

"What kind of photos and videos do you have of her and Justin?"

"Them holding hands, hugging and kissing in public, and also her leaving his house early in the morning after spending the night with him."

"That doesn't prove they've slept together."

"Well, I have evidence of that too."

"Are you serious?"

"Yes. The private investigator I hired is really good at what he does. Listen, I'm covering all the bases should Avery ever decide to take me to court. I don't know if the evidence that I have on her would amount to much in a judge's eyes, but I have to have something."

"You already have so much, Zac."

"But I still don't think it's enough. Not for the courts to strip Avery of her mother's rights to Malcolm."

"You're both in a catch-22."

"You're right. We are."

"How did it make you feel when you found out about Avery's involvement with Justin?"

"I didn't get angry if that's what you mean."

"It is."

"I just felt indifferent and still do, because I don't care about their affair. The evidence that I have simply affirmed what I'd been suspecting for some time."

"Do you know where Avery is at the moment?"

"No, but I left her outside in the swimming pool before I came into my bedroom and texted you."

"You went swimming with her?"

"Hell no. She asked me to, but there was no way that I was getting into the water with her. She tried to lure me in by taking off all her clothes."

"Wow."

"Another wow, huh?"

"She just boggles my mind. She left you and Malcolm like she did a week and a half ago, you have proof that she's having an affair with Justin, then she suddenly comes back home and tells you that she wants to work out things with you. Avery obviously wanted you to fuck her too or she wouldn't have taken off her clothes. To me, it sounds like something happened between her and Justin."

"I thought the same thing but then again, Avery likes to try buttering me up so that my financing of her lifestyle doesn't stop."

"How do you know that's her motive?"

"I overheard her talking on the phone about it with her sister before. That's how. What she doesn't realize is that I wouldn't stop the money flow if she didn't try buttering me up. Keeping it going equates to peace. Well, it does most of the time."

"Going to the grocery store with Avery must equate to peace too," Stevie said.

"It did. She wanted homemade tacos for dinner."

"I sound jealous, don't I?"

"No. You sound concerned about the game that you see Avery playing with me."

"I'm not jealous of her because there is absolutely nothing to be jealous of. I am concerned about the bullshit that she's pulling and I'm also territorial about you, Zac."

"I feel the same way about you because you're mine."

"That I am."

"I hope you can find some humor in what I'm about to say. I nearly shit myself when I saw you walking into the produce section. The possibility of you being at Whole Foods hadn't even crossed my mind."

"I didn't expect to see you there with Avery. I was caught completely off guard, but Zac, I would never just walk up to Avery and make a scene. I know the possibility of me doing that very thing ran through your mind."

"Yeah, it did and I can understand you wanting to walk up to her and give her a piece of your mind."

"The only time that I would ever do that is if she made a scene that involved you or Malcolm and I was a witness to it."

"I hope you never have to witness how she really is. It's ugly."

"Yeah, it is. I've seen the evidence of her ugliness on your body."

I sighed. "And speaking of bodies... I wish I could see yours. I wish I could see your face."

"Then Face-Time me."

"You don't mind?"

"No. Why would I?"

"We've just never done that before."

"There's a lot that we haven't done before and we're just gonna keep marking off that list."

"Sounds good to me."

We hung up and I got up off the bathroom floor, then leaned against the counter and Face-Timed Stevie. As soon as I saw her on my phone screen, I smiled.

"Look at you, my beautiful lover," I said.

"And look at you, Mr. Moby Dick."

We both started laughing and it felt so damn good.

"Thank you for doing this with me, Stevie. I already feel better just from getting to see you."

"Would you like to see more of me?"

I grinned. "You know the answer to that."

"Well, I'll show you mine if you show me yours."

"You're serious?"

"Absolutely.

"Okay—but I wanna see *all* of you."

"Take off all your clothes first and let me watch you do it."

I chuckled and shook my head. We were really about to do this. "Okay. Hang on."

I positioned my phone on my bathroom counter so that Stevie had a clear view of me, then started taking off my clothes. When I was done, I told her that it was her turn.

"I'll take off mine in just a minute. I'm enjoying looking at you right now. You're already getting hard, Buchanan."

"I can't help it. I'm thinking about you."

"Touch yourself for me."

"You really want me to?"

"I do."

"Okay."

Staring straight at Stevie on my phone screen, I took my cock into my hand and began stroking it while imagining it was inside Stevie's body. I was fully erect within seconds.

"Do you want me to keep going?" I asked her.

"Yes. And while you are, I'm gonna get naked and you're gonna watch."

I kept pumping myself as she stripped down to nothing. Then she moved closer to her phone on her nightstand and acted like she was licking the screen.

"I wish you were in my mouth," she said.

"I wish my mouth was on you. Show me yours up close, Sinclair."

She smiled and did as I said, and I groaned as she spread herself apart and I saw her swollen clit.

"Goddamn," I breathed out. "You are driving me crazy."

"I intended to. I'm gonna lay down on my bed now and I'm taking you with me."

"You better."

After stretching out across the top of her comforter and propping up her head on two pillows, Stevie held her phone down by her pussy. I could see it but I could also still see Stevie's toned abdomen, round breasts, and smiling face, and she was still watching me play with my cock. Then she started playing with herself. When she touched her clit she sucked in a deep breath, then licked those pouty lips of hers.

"What are you imagining?" I asked.

"You making my clit raise up like a tower again."

"You liked that, huh?"

"I loved it and you know it."

"Yeah, I do know it. You screamed my name like I said you were gonna do."

"Move closer to your screen, Buchanan. I wanna see more of your Moby Dick."

I stepped closer to my phone but was still able to watch what Stevie was doing. She had stopped playing with her clit and started fingering herself.

"Tell me what you're imagining now," I said.

"You fucking me slow and easy."

"Watching you do that to yourself is gonna make me cum," I told her.

"That was the plan."

"I want you to cum first, though."

"Then slow down what you're doing to yourself."

I did exactly that, then stopped altogether for about thirty seconds while continuing to watch Stevie masturbate."

"I'm almost there," she whispered.

I grabbed my cock and started pumping it again, keeping the same rhythm as Stevie's fingers going into and out of her pussy.

"Here I cum, lover," she breathed out.

Then I heard her start moaning and that was all it took to make me lose control too. I started shooting off while keeping my hand on my cock and my eyes on Stevie as she continued finger-fucking herself. I joined in on the moaning that she was still doing and when our orgasms ended, we both took a deep breath, then smiled satisfied smiles at each other.

"I've gotta sit down," I said, grabbing my cellphone off the bathroom counter and sitting on the edge of the bathtub.

"Dizzy again, I see."

"Yeah. You make me that way. It doesn't matter if we're together having sex or doing it like this."

"Well, I hope *this* has relieved some of your stress."

"It has. I'm relaxed now."

"Me too."

"Can I tell you something?"

"You can tell me anything."

"I really like that I can be so open with you. I've never experienced this level of intimacy and vulnerability with anyone. Our intimacy isn't just physical, either."

Stevie nodded. "I know. It's emotional and spiritual too."

"Yes, it is. Every time we've been together—whether we've had sex or not—I feel like I've been to church. I've been renewed just like I feel now."

"Zac, you're not gonna believe this, but I wrote those same words about you and me in my journal."

"I didn't know you kept a journal. But I believe you wrote those same words in it. Our minds are linked together just like our hearts and our souls."

"Yes, they are."

"I'm so grateful to have crossed paths with you, Stevie. You have lit up my entire world."

"Same here."

We wiped our eyes, and then Stevie said, "I've never told you this but one of many things that I love and admire about you is that you aren't afraid to show your emotions. Men generally hide what they're really feeling and won't allow themselves to cry in front of others because they think it makes them look weak. It doesn't, though. It shows strength and courage. And you, my sexy-as-fuck kinsman, have it in spades."

I wanted to crawl through my phone screen and go straight to Stevie so I could wrap my arms around her and kiss her.

"That's it," I said, standing up.

"What's it?"

"I'm coming over to your house."

"When."

"Now."

"But what about Avery?"

"I don't give a fuck."

"But what about keeping the peace with her?"

"I don't give a fuck."

"Zac..."

"What?"

"Now think about this."

"There's nothing to think about."

"But there is. If you come over here and then go back home, Avery is gonna ask you where you went?"

"I'll tell her that I went for a run. I've gotta get out of here. I've gotta see you, Stevie, even if it's only for five minutes."

She started chewing on her fingernail but she was also smiling. "Okay," she finally said. "Text me when you're almost here."

28
#pounce

Stevie

Since Avery camE back into town two weeks ago, Zac and I had seen each other only a handful of times. Some of those occasions happened while I was at the courthouse, taking care of one of the many cases that I'd been assigned. I saw Zac in the security line again then he saw me in it on three different days and waited for me to clear it. We walked to the elevators together and made certain to keep adequate space between us, as well as a serious professional expression on our faces. That was until we got onto the elevator and the doors closed.

On those three occasions, the stars aligned again for Zac and me by allowing us to be completely alone on our ride up. We kissed during those private seconds but the three kisses that we shared weren't soft like before. They were hungry kisses because we were starving for each other.

Afterward, Zac wiped my lip gloss off his mouth and I tidied up what was left on mine. Our lips were redder than usual and so was the skin around them. Zac's redness didn't show as much as mine did because of his short beard. I wasn't concerned, though. Like Brooke said she was going to do should anyone come to her with their suspicion of Zac and me having an affair, I was prepared to play dumb—or whichever role was necessary.

The other occasions that I'd seen Zac in the past two weeks happened at the Starbucks that was around the corner from the D.A.'s office and also at the running trail. I met him in the parking lot of Starbucks where he came over to my car and handed me a large coffee with a splash of whole milk. Then he leaned through my driver's side window and stole a quick kiss—both of us mischievously grinning afterward.

During the two times that we'd met at the running trail, we did take our separate runs but then met in the woods where I'd overheard Zac arguing with Avery on his cellphone on that Sunday morning. We were secluded from anyone seeing us then and we were also secluded during the two times that we walked into the camouflage of the trees after taking our runs.

As soon as we were alone on both those days, Zac was all over me as much as I was him. The first time, I'd thought all we were going to do was kiss each other but when Zac started pulling down my shorts, I realized what he had in mind—and I didn't mind. Not at all. On the first day, we fucked each other on top of the soft grass, and then on the second day, Zac took me from behind while I held onto one of the trees to keep myself steady. We were like animals taking what we wanted and also needed from each other...and it felt so good.

Zac hadn't been able to break away from his house to come over again since the night that Avery had come back into town. He'd had Malcolm with him on each night and I understood him having to stay home to take care of his precious mini-me. Something was going to have to give, though, for both of us. We needed more time together than the periodic brief moments that we'd been able to steal from time.

On the Avery front, Zac said she hadn't wavered from her calm demeanor toward him and she also hadn't backed off from trying to work out things with him. She'd told him again, on three other occasions, that it was what she wanted more than anything in the world. Zac still didn't believe her, still didn't love her, and still didn't want a thing to do with her. He was just biding his time and doing what needed to be done to keep the peace within his home while waiting for Avery's true colors to reappear.

I heard a knock on my office door and Brooke peeked her head around it.

"Hey, Stevie," she said.

"Hey. What's going on?"

"Everyone up here wants to go to Mystic Bar after work because of the week it's been."

"Yeah, it's been a doozy. It's like the moon is stuck on full."

"It certainly feels that way. So do you wanna join us?"

"Um..."

"I've already texted Buchanan and he's in if you are," she said quietly, grinning. I didn't grin, though. I smiled all over.

"I'm in."

"Thought you would be. Do you wanna ride with me?"

"I'm just gonna take my car this time but I appreciate your offer."

"No prob."

"Change of subject. I have an update for you on the Ferguson case."

"Okay." Brooke walked into my office and sat down in one of the chairs in front of my desk.

"Mr. Ferguson was arrested for domestic violence two days ago. He beat the hell out of his wife."

"Do you know what prompted it?"

"The police report that I read stated that the two were strung out on some kind of drug or drugs. They were acting crazy but especially ol' Billy boy."

"That doesn't surprise me at all. How's his son doing with his foster family?"

"He's doing great. That family has asked about adopting him and now they can since the Fergusons have no legal rights to their son. It was all finalized."

"Good."

"Anyway...I just wanted to let you know about the latest."

Brooke nodded, then started clicking her tongue. She was looking at me but through me, lost in her own thoughts. Then she said, "I get such a thrill whenever I find out someone like Mr. Ferguson has reaped what they've sown, and he has by losing all rights to his little boy. It's not over yet, though. There's more karma coming for a violent man like him."

"I agree. I'm sure we'll hear more about him in the weeks and months to come. If I get any more news, you'll be the first to know."

I heard another knock on my door and Brooke and I looked up to see David looking around it.

"Brooke, I need you for a minute if you don't mind," he said.

"Okay. I'll be right there."

"Thanks."

As David walked off, Brooke got up but didn't move from where she was standing. She just kept her eyes on me.

"What is it?" I asked.

"Are you happy, Stevie?"

"With my exception?"

"Yes."

"Very much so."

"But the circumstances keeping you two apart is tough isn't it?"

"Yes."

"Hang in there. I feel like your exception does—a door's gonna open for you and him. I don't know how or when, but it's gonna happen. Just don't give up."

"I'll never give up on my exception. Not under any circumstances. I couldn't let him go if I tried, Brooke."

"I understand."

"I know you do. Thank you for being a friend to me in all of this."

"Thank you for being my friend, as well. Yes, I'm old enough to be your mother, but age doesn't matter in this. We're two women and you're walking down a pathway that I've already traveled down. If I can spare you some heartache by sharing some of my life lessons with you then what I've been through won't be for nothing."

I got up from my desk and walked over to Brooke to hug her. We hugged each other tightly too then smiled at each other.

"See you in about..." Brooke glanced at her watch. "An hour."

"I'm looking forward to all of us getting together again. We're all due a breather."

I was the last one to arrive at Mystic Bar because my dad called me at 4:50 p.m. to tell me that he was going to have some tests run on his heart next week. It'd been fluttering on and off "for a while," as he put it. I asked him why he hadn't said anything to me about it before now. His reasoning was that he didn't want to worry me.

I offered to drive to Austin to go with him to get the tests done but he told me that he'd be fine. I didn't like the thought of him going alone, though. Not for something like that. I was planning to talk to Brooke about taking off work for a couple of days so I could go with my dad but I didn't say anything to him about it because I wanted to clear it with Brooke first.

I was walking toward the table where Zac, Bash, Brooke, and my comrades were all sitting with their drinks in hand, as well as a variety of appetizers spread out in front of them, when Brooke nodded in my direction. Zac looked over his shoulder, then immediately smiled at me and stood up.

"Hey, Sinclair," he said as I made it to the table.

"Hey, Buchanan. Sorry I'm late, everyone. I got a call from my dad as I was getting ready to leave work."

"Is he okay?" Brooke asked.

"Yeah. He's just gotta have some tests run on his heart next week. I had no clue that it's been fluttering. He didn't tell me about it."

"Because he didn't wanna worry you."

I chuckled. "That's exactly what he told me."

"He's the parent, you're his daughter."

"Yeah, but I'm all he's got," I said, sitting down beside Brooke.

"Why don't you go with him?"

"I was gonna ask you about doing that very thing."

"We'll hold the fort down while you're gone."

"Are you sure?"

"Absolutely."

I stared at Brooke, then looked around the table at the rest of my team.

"We've got you covered," Jason said. "Don't worry. Even Joan of Arc has to leave the battlefield every now and then."

"But I don't like leaving it."

"But you're going to," Brooke insisted.

I blew out a long sigh. "Thank you for understanding."

"Are you ready for a Hendricks and tonic?" Zac asked me.

I looked at him, sitting in his usual spot across the table from me where we could be close to each other but not too close. Still close enough for me to feel his foot nudging mine underneath the table. And the private flirtations between us had just begun.

"I would love one. Actually, two shots of gin this time, please."

Zac waved at our waitress and while he was giving her my drink order, Bash started talking to me.

"Doll, everything is gonna be okay with your dad. I can tell that you're really worried about it."

"It's just that my dad has always been so healthy. Not one thing has ever been wrong with him. He eats really well, he's active, he gets adequate sleep."

"Sometimes genetics take the upper hand despite our efforts to live a healthy lifestyle. But with all the advances in medicine, I'd just take a deep breath if I were you and tell yourself that your dad is gonna be fine. Have faith."

I reached for Bash's hand and he gave mine a squeeze. After that, we all fell right back into a mix of conversations while drinking and eating and laughing. This was the exact kind of decompression that I needed—plus seeing my handsome blue-eyed lover again.

His foot was resting against mine now and we kept stealing glances at each other—and grinning. I could feel the heat rising up through my body not only because of the gin flowing through my veins but also because of the sexual tension between Zac and me. It was so thick and sultry and begging for release. There was a chance of that happening later this evening at my house. Zac had texted me earlier to let me know that his parents were keeping Malcolm tonight with plans to take him to the zoo again tomorrow. I just didn't know how Zac was going to handle matters with Avery. I'd know soon enough, though.

I noticed Zac checking his cellphone. It was the third time that he'd done it while we'd all been sitting here. Someone was texting him, apparently, and while reading each text Zac's eyebrows pulled into a knot. He appeared irritated and I couldn't help but wonder if it was Avery who'd texted him, but he hadn't replied, just slipped his phone back into his pants pocket.

I was listening to David and Jennifer's conversation about one of the cases that David was working on when Brooke grabbed my hand underneath the table and squeezed it. Then she said, "Zac, Avery is here and coming this way."

He looked over his shoulder and sighed, then turned back around and glanced at everyone sitting here.

"Please excuse me," he said.

We all nodded, and Zac stood up and started walking in Avery's direction. I kept my eyes on him as he made it over to her, then saw her reach out to touch his arm. I couldn't see Zac's face because his back was to me but his rigid posture said it all. He didn't want Avery touching him and he certainly didn't want her to be here at Mystic Bar.

He and Avery kept talking to each other, and then the two of them started walking toward the table. Zac stared straight at me the whole time too. This was about to get interesting.

"Hi, Brooke, Bash, and all you other attorneys," Avery said while fake smiling at us.

Everyone told her hello but me and now, she was looking at me.

"I don't believe I know you," she said, canting her head to the side.

I fake smiled then, got up from my chair, walked around the table and came to a stop directly in front of Avery.

"No, you don't know me. I'm Stevie Sinclair," I said, extending my hand to shake hers.

She slowly took hold of my hand while looking me up and down. "I'm Avery Buchanan—Zac's wife."

"It's so nice to meet you, Avery."

"Are you part of Brooke's group or just a friend?"

I kept fake smiling and I also kept shaking her hand as tightly as I could. "I'm part of Brooke's group and we're all good friends."

"Oh, so you're an assistant D.A. then?" Avery pulled her hand out of mine and stretched out her fingers.

"Correct. I handle C.P.S. cases."

"Well, that's great. I feel so bad for abused kids."

"So do I. I also feel bad for adults who get abused. I legally help them too," I said, glancing at Zac standing next to her.

The expression on his face wasn't an "oh shit" one like it was when I'd run into him and Avery at Whole Foods. Right now, he had a resolved look, as if he'd accepted this tense situation for exactly what it was. There was nothing that he could do about this situation *or* the way that I'd chosen to handle his joke of a wife. Zac was simply standing here: watching, listening, and waiting to see what happened next.

I was staring hard at Avery now and could feel my heart pounding. So much, I wanted to punch her in her bitch-face because she deserved it. I laughed to myself because my mother's genetics were showing in me at the moment—and I was proud. Proud to have made who I was very clear to Avery and also proud to still be fake smiling at her despite my anger. She was so damn uncomfortable.

She looked away from me and turned her attention to everyone sitting at the table. "I guess I'll go and let you get back to your Friday night fun. I only stopped by because I wondered if my husband was here and sure enough, he is," she said, cutting her eyes up at Zac. "I've been texting him and he's been ignoring my texts."

"Come on. You're leaving now, Avery," Zac said. Then he grabbed her arm but she jerked it away and gave him a go-to-hell look.

"I'll walk myself out. I don't need you."

Avery looked at me again and I was still staring hard at her.

"I just thought of something. Your first name—*Stevie*," she said.

"What about it?"

"It's unusual. I've heard of only two other people with your name: Stevie Nicks and a woman employed by the Dallas Zoo who hangs out at the aquarium, calls herself a mermaid but doesn't have a tail, and confuses the hell out of children."

"My first name is more common than you realize. And about that mermaid at the zoo? Maybe she was just taking a break from swimming in the aquarium while still entertaining the children there. It sounds like loads of fun to me."

Avery scoffed and then pushed by Zac. We all watched her leave and as soon as she was out of sight, Zac turned to me and our table of friends and apologized for Avery's rude behavior. Every one of us immediately waved off his apology.

"No need to apologize, Buchanan," Brooke said. "Sit back down and join us. Order yourself another gin and tonic. You too, Joan of Arc. Let the bullshit go."

Zac and I looked at each other and nodded in silence. After we took our seats again, Bash started chuckling.

"I have to say something here and I hope all of you take it in the right way—but especially you and you," Bash said, pointing at Zac and me. "Stevie, I really thought you were gonna pounce on Avery. Holy shit."

As soon as he said that, everyone at our table busted out laughing, including me, and then started chiming in with their mutual agreement on the matter. Everyone except for Zac. He didn't laugh or agree with anything. He didn't have to, though. His smiling blue eyes did.

"Listen," I said, looking at Zac and then at everyone else sitting around the table. "All of you know me and I have no tolerance for behavior like what we all just witnessed. I don't care who it is."

"Oh, I'm the same way," Bash added. "I started to say something but you had it under control."

I looked at Zac again and he still had his eyes on me. "I'm really sorry that you were just put in that position by your wife, Buchanan."

"It is what it is. I'll say one more thing about it and then I want all of us to move on. Okay?" he said, taking the time to look directly at everyone in our group, and we all nodded in agreement. "Every one of you is aware to varying degrees of what my life with Avery has been like. We haven't all talked about it but we don't have to. I know how quickly word gets around in our legal community. I don't want one of you to feel sorry for me. All I ask is that you try to understand my position. I do what I do *only* because of my son."

I was shocked by Zac's transparency with everyone but then again, after Avery acted in the way she did, Zac addressing it was something that I should've expected. He was embarrassed by Avery but he was also making a stand for himself by stating his position on the matter.

"Buchanan, we do understand and we respect you," Brooke said, speaking for all of us.

"Thank you. Now let's get on with our merriment. Shall we?"

We all said "Yes" at the same time, but I had to do more than that. I got up from the table, walked around to Zac, and then leaned over and hugged his neck. He hugged me like a friend would've done and even patted my arm. When I stood back up and looked at him, he smiled at me. Yes, we were lovers, but we were friends first. Our friendship was a caring foundation for us and it was going to be what carried Zac and me through whatever lay ahead. Undoubtedly, there were going to be rough waters that we'd eventually have to sail through, but I knew that as long as we hung on to each other, we'd survive any storm that came our way.

29
#embrace

Zac

"Stevie, just hold me. Please," I said, and she wrapped her arms around me.

It was after eleven when I texted her that I was on my way to her house and that I'd explain everything after I arrived. As soon as I got out of my Blazer in her garage, Stevie's mouth fell open. Then she covered it with her hands and started screaming out her anger. She screamed because of the cuts that she saw on the left side of my face.

After I'd arrived home from Mystic Bar, Avery and I got into an argument. I bitched her out about the way she'd acted when she showed up at the bar and then she started coming after me. She tried hitting me but I just kept dodging her punches and pushing her away from me. She finally tired out and I walked off from her, but before I made it out of the kitchen, Avery called me a weak-ass man.

When I turned my head to look over my shoulder at her, she'd already grabbed her empty vodka glass off the counter and thrown it at me. It hit the left side of my face and shattered into pieces. The cuts that some of those pieces made started bleeding but I paid no attention to them. Instead, I ran after Avery, who was running away from me. I had enough.

I caught up with her in the hallway, heading toward the guest bedroom, and grabbed her from behind by wrapping my arms around her upper torso. Then I dragged her, kicking and screaming and trying to hit me again, into the living room and threw her down on the couch. She acted shocked that I'd done that—that I'd actually fought back. I didn't hit her but I damn sure got her attention, then I said what I wanted to say.

I told Avery that her violence toward me was going to stop right then, and if it didn't then I was going to call the police and press charges against her. I wouldn't hold back.

She took in what I said but didn't say anything in response. Instead, she got up from the couch and stormed off to her bedroom. I followed her and watched her throw her clothes into her suitcases. Then she flipped me off, got into her car and left. She was going back to Lubbock. I tracked her on my cellphone.

After getting the cuts on my face to stop bleeding, I cleaned up the glass on the kitchen floor, as well as the spots of blood on the carpet in the living room and in the hallway. Then I packed an overnight bag, because there was no way that I was staying at my house tonight. I wanted to stay at Stevie's.

Now that I was here, now that Stevie had seen what happened to me and now that she was holding me in her arms, we both started crying. Not hard. Quietly. We were both so angry and hurt and frustrated about everything.

A couple of minutes later, Stevie led me by the hand into her bathroom, where she proceeded to doctor my face. Using some tweezers, she was able to pull out the little pieces of glass that were still in my skin. Then she gently dabbed hydrogen peroxide onto all the cuts. Neosporin came next, followed by Stevie's soft kiss on my lips. It wasn't until after she kissed me that we spoke to each other again.

As I began telling Stevie about everything that happened after I got home from Mystic Bar, she listened and asked questions. When I was done catching her up, we stared at each other in silence again. The only thing I could hear were the breaths we were taking.

"Let me take you to bed. It's what you need," Stevie whispered.

That surprised me. Having sex was the last thing on my mind and I thought it would've been the last thing on hers too—but she was right. I needed this. I needed *her*. As soon as I nodded yes, she again led me by the hand to where she wanted me.

Standing in the middle of her bedroom, we undressed each other, and then Stevie told me to lie down on her bed on my back. After I did, she lit all the candles in her room, turned off all the lights, and then got on top of me. Not on my cock because it wasn't hard yet. She stretched out and rested her body on top of mine, and then I wrapped my arms around her. Feeling the warmth of her skin and the warmth of her breath blowing against my neck was all it took for me to be ready for this beautiful woman to love me.

She took it slow and was so gentle as she moved her body up and down on top of mine. I kept expecting Stevie to start moving faster and harder but she didn't. She just stayed steady and completely focused on me. Our bodies were moving in sync and the breaths we were taking matched. Several minutes passed and finally, I came. When I was done, Stevie took a deep breath and smiled at me.

"Better now?" she asked.

"So much better. Whenever I'm with you, everything disappears. The chaos in my life, the disorder—all of it."

"Same here."

"I love you."

"And I love you. Let's just go to sleep now, okay? It's so late."

"But what about you? I wanna take care of your needs."

"You already have, Zac. You're here with me and I get to fall asleep in your arms tonight."

"Really, I don't mind."

"Shhh," she said, placing her finger against my lips. "Please just hold me. I need to cry again."

Stevie and I slept in until almost ten o'clock and neither of us could believe it. It went without saying that we needed the rest.

"You stay here in bed," she said, getting up out of it.

"And where are you going?"

"To make us some coffee. Sound good to you?"

"Yes, it does."

After opening her curtains, Stevie walked out of her bedroom completely naked and I just smiled. Waking up like this with her was something that I could do every day for the rest of my life.

While listening to Stevie down the hallway, I took the time to really look around her bedroom in the morning sunlight. There was ocean and beach décor on top of her dresser and the nightstands and also on the walls. Nothing gaudy. It was all tasteful and had Stevie written all over it. Some way and somehow, I was going to get that mermaid back to the ocean. I wanted to take her on a trip that neither of us would ever forget but I just had to figure out how to make that getaway happen.

I looked over at the nightstand closest to me and thought about picking up the tiny urn sitting on top of it so that I could take a closer look. I'd seen it before but hadn't mentioned it to Stevie. I already knew, though, that her son's ashes were inside it.

I could still hear Stevie in the kitchen, so I decided to take a closer look at the urn. It appeared to be made of heavy aluminum and had a Celtic design inscribed on it, front and back. It was unique, and I could see Stevie choosing it because of her reverence for her Scottish ancestry. She wanted the remains of her son to be protected by ancient symbolism. I would have wanted that too.

"It's pretty, isn't it?" she asked, startling me as she was walking back into her bedroom.

"Yes. I hope you don't mind me looking at it."

"I don't mind. Feel free to ask me anything you want about my Malcolm, too."

I carefully set down his urn and then moved over so his mother could sit beside me while we drank our coffee in bed.

"I do have a question for you," I told Stevie.

"What is it?"

"Have you had any more dreams about your Malcolm?"

"Yes. Two."

"Was he an infant?"

"No. He appeared to be around four years old again—and he looked so much like your Malcolm," Stevie said, smiling up at me.

"How does that make you feel?"

"It doesn't weird me out if that's what you mean."

"Yeah, that's what I mean."

"Does it weird you out?"

"Not at all."

"I don't understand why my Malcolm is coming through looking like that but I love it."

"Maybe it's our genetics. You and I do have the same coloring and similar features, so it makes sense that our children would resemble one another. Even in the spirit world."

"I agree. I just wish I knew why my son was coming through to me at the same age as your son and not as an infant."

"I wish I knew why too. But did your Malcolm talk to you again in your dreams?"

"No, but he did keep smiling at me and nodding his head. I sensed it was his way of telling me that everything is gonna be okay."

"What's gonna be okay?"

"My life with you. I've been praying about it. Is it wrong for me to do that? Praying for us to be blessed when we're committing such sin?"

I searched Stevie's eyes. "I think God understands."

Stevie kept staring at me, then looked down at the cuts on my face. "He should. At least for you."

"You too." I glanced over at her Malcolm's urn and then met Stevie's gaze again.

"I hope you're right."

"I am."

We both grew quiet for about a minute, taking sips of our coffee. Then Stevie asked me how I was feeling about what happened with Avery last night.

"I'm numb about it. I knew it was just a matter of time before her true colors came back out," I said.

"And all because you didn't text her back."

"Yes."

"Why didn't you?"

"Because I didn't wanna deal with her. She wanted to know where I was and she wanted me to come home. She texted that she was missing me. The thing is—I'm not accountable to Avery. Whenever she goes to Lubbock, I don't hear a word from her, so she can't expect me to report to her. Even when she's been at home, she goes and does as she pleases and doesn't tell me a thing. I felt all of this coming to a head, especially over the past few days."

"What do you mean?"

I sighed. I really didn't want to talk about it but could tell that Stevie needed me to.

"Avery started pouring her attention onto me. She started touching me more which I didn't want, and I pushed her away several times. I told her to stop. I also told her that I didn't wanna hear any more from her about us working out. She acted hurt, and like she couldn't understand why I feel the way I do. Hell, I have a list that's a mile long as to why, and she knows that. Anyway... The side of her you saw at the bar last night was a tiny glimpse of who she really is. You got a peek of how she is when she doesn't get her way."

"Do you really believe she was acting about her wanting to work out things with you?"

"I have no doubt about it."

"How can you be sure? Maybe she finally woke up and realized what she has with you."

"*Had* with me."

"Okay...had."

"If Avery had been sincere about everything that she said to me about wanting us to work out, or sincere in the way she's acted toward me after coming back home, then she wouldn't have been in constant contact with Justin all this time."

"You looked up your phone records."

"Sure did. It's so easy to do, too. The thought of me doing that hasn't crossed Avery's mind—or it has and she just doesn't care."

"So all of that acting she did was for what purpose?"

"I've already told you. It's about the money. She must have gotten worried again about me cutting it off for some reason and decided to play nice for a while. I've never once threatened her with that, though. And again, like I've said, paying for her lifestyle equates to peace for Malcolm and me...most of the time."

Stevie sighed. "What a selfish and dangerous game she plays, toying with people and their emotions. You know you're not the only one she does that with."

"Yes, I do know that. She manipulates everyone around her for her own benefit."

"Zac, tell me how Avery's parents are toward you."

"When Avery and I were dating and then first married, they were great. But when Avery turned on me during our first year of marriage, her parents did too, as well as her brother and sister. They all blamed me for our issues. Never Avery. Not for one damn thing."

"They all sound like enablers."

"That's exactly what they are and they're also users like Avery. I haven't seen her family in years."

"Years?"

"Since Malcolm's birth."

"You're serious?"

"I am."

"So you're telling me that Avery's family has seen Malcolm only one time since he was born?"

"That's right."

"How do they do that? How can they not care about Malcolm and want to see him? He's their flesh and blood."

"I think it's all a matter of them appeasing Avery. They go along with anything she wants or doesn't want—and she never wanted to have children, as you know. Malcolm is too much responsibility for her and gets in the way of what she wants to do."

"I haven't asked you this yet, because I felt like I'd get upset by your answer, but I have to know. How was Avery with Malcolm while she was at home this time?"

"She acted interested in him and spent a little time with him, playing games and such, but I watched her closely like I always do and saw right through her performance. The funny thing is Malcolm ended up seeing through it too. He walked away from Avery several times and came over to me, especially during this past week."

"Malcolm is so perceptive of others."

"He always has been. He was really perceptive of you as soon as you two met."

Stevie smiled. "He was, and I'm so glad that he likes me."

"Likes? My boy loves you. You and Malcolm are kindred spirits."

"We are kindreds. I feel that connection with him and I also feel it with you. I know we've talked about it before but I really do feel like I've known you for so much longer than this. Sure, there are little things that we've yet to learn about each other and will learn, but it's just..." Stevie stopped talking to take a deep breath. "It's just a knowing that I feel deep inside. I *know* you, Zac Buchanan."

I stared at Stevie, understanding every word that she'd just said to me. I understood them to my core.

"I've known you for lifetimes, Stevie Sinclair, and no one could convince me otherwise. Now let me do for you what you wouldn't let me do last night."

"Bed me?"

"Pleasure you."

Stevie's eyes were shining as they danced across my face. "Are you sure you're up to it?" she asked.

"Yes, I'm sure. I'm already getting hard just talking about it."

"Then come on. Pleasure me, lover."

I stayed at Stevie's house until my mom texted me that she, my dad and Malcolm were back from the zoo. I needed to go pick up my boy, take him home and let him get settled back into being there again without his mother. Even though he hadn't had a whole lot to do with Avery over the past two weeks, he knew she was in the house and he was noticeably on guard. He'd learned to be that way around her just like I had.

Before I drove over to my parents' house, I called my mom and told her what happened with Avery last night, then asked her to pass it on to my dad. I also told her about the cuts on my face and to not be alarmed when she saw me. She asked me what I was going to tell Malcolm because she knew, just like I did, that he was going to ask me what happened. I'd decided to tell him that I was on a ladder in our backyard, cleaning out the house gutters, and lost my footing and fell off the ladder. I hated lying to him but there was no way that I was going to tell him what his mother had done. He wouldn't understand it.

Before I left Stevie's house, she doctored my face again then groomed my beard for me. She trimmed it, cleaned up the edges, and even shaved the back of my neck like my barber did. While she was doing all that, I watched her movements with her hands and her eyes. She was so caring and gentle and I just wanted to pick her up into my arms and take her home with me.

Stevie and I agreed to try to get together sometime during the upcoming week before she went to Austin to go with her dad to get his heart tests done. That was scheduled for Thursday. I already knew my parents wouldn't mind watching Malcolm for me after I got off work so I could take a run at the trail, aka see Stevie. They wouldn't care if it was one day or Monday through Wednesday and I was grateful. I was also grateful that I was going to get to see Stevie again and soon. I had to see her, I had to touch her and hear her voice in person. I didn't care if we had sex again in the woods or if it happened at her house. I just needed to be near my soulmate and breathe her in. She was my lifeline and the only thing keeping me afloat.

While driving over to my mom and dad's house, I made the decision to tell my dad about Stevie. It was time. I knew he was going to be angry about what Avery did to me but I also felt like he'd be happy for me knowing that I'd met someone like Stevie.

After arriving at my parents' house, I quietly told my mom what my plan was and she took Malcolm outside to play so I could have some one-on-one time with my dad. He and I talked about everything for about half an hour. He said he understood my position and then asked me if I was in love with Stevie. Of course, I told him that I was, and also showed him the same pictures of her that I'd shown to my mom. He made the same comments that she made about Stevie being so beautiful and also how he'd never seen me look so happy. Then my dad asked me about meeting Stevie. My mom hadn't done that yet even though I knew she'd been wanting to.

I told my dad that I would talk to Stevie about meeting him and my mom. I also told him that I felt like she'd be all for it. He smiled and then hugged me—and it was just what I needed. Acceptance. Acceptance for who I was, how I was, whom I loved, and why I wanted to spend the rest of my life with her. I could hardly wait for my mom and dad to meet Stevie Sinclair—the love of my life.

30
#tides

Zac

"That fucking bitch," Bash said under his breath as he was walking into my house.

I'd texted him earlier this morning—Sunday—to ask him if he had time to come by to talk to me in person. I also let him know that Avery was back in Lubbock. Bash rang my doorbell thirty minutes later, and he'd just seen the cuts on my face.

"Yeah, Avery threw a glass at me again."

"When?"

"After I got home on Friday night."

Bash shook his head and sighed. "This can't keep happening, Zac."

"I don't think it will happen again. I put my hands on Avery this time."

"You didn't hit her, did you?"

"No, but I did drag her into the living room and threw her down on the couch. Then I threatened her with calling the police and pressing charges against her. And I would have if she'd started coming at me again, hitting me and all that."

"You don't know how much I'd love to see her goddamn mugshot."

"Yeah, I do."

"Uncle Bash!" Malcolm said, running up to him. We were standing in the entryway while Malcolm had been in his room playing.

"Hey, little buddy! How are you?" Bash asked, picking him up and hugging him.

"Will you go swimming with Daddy and me?"

"Oh, I wish I could but I didn't bring my swimsuit. I didn't know you were going swimming."

"Daddy said we had to wait one hour because we just ate breakfast."

"Yeah, you need to let your food settle in your tummy before you go swimming because if you don't, then your tummy might cramp up and that wouldn't be good."

Malcolm nodded his head in agreement.

"Here, I brought you something," Bash said, reaching into his shorts pocket. Then he presented Malcolm with a package of sour gummy worms.

"Thank you, Uncle Bash!"

"You're welcome, buddy. Save those until after you've gone swimming. Okay?"

"Okay."

Bash put Malcolm down and we watched him take off running toward his room, smiling.

"Is it too early to have a drink?" Bash asked me.

"You know it's not. What do you want?"

"Do you still have some Jose Cuervo?"

"Yep."

"Triple Sec?"

"Yep."

"Limes?"

"Always."

"I'm about to go fix myself a margarita then."

"Let's go. I'll have a Hendricks and tonic. Fuck it."

Bash patted my arm as the two of us walked into the kitchen. He knew the layout of my entire house as well as I knew his and began making himself at home. While he was gathering the ingredients for a margarita, I got what I needed for my drink.

"Aw, look," he said, pointing at Avery's bottle of vodka in the cabinet. "I don't think this needs to be here when the bitch gets back. You can tell her that I got rid of it. If she has a problem with that then she can take it up with me."

Bash grabbed the bottle, emptied its contents into my kitchen sink, then tossed it into the trash can. When he looked back at me, we both started chuckling, and it felt good doing it, too. After making our drinks, the two of us sat down on the living room couch and Bash held up his glass toward me.

"Here's to you, Zac—my best friend. You are a saint and I don't know how you do what you do, living like this with Avery. But as always, my hat's off to you and you have all my respect. Cheers."

"Thank you for that," I said, clinking my glass against his. Then we both took a big gulp.

"Does Stevie know what happened to you?" Bash asked.

I held up my finger to my mouth. "Call her Joan because of..." I nodded toward Malcolm's bedroom.

"Will do."

"And yes, she knows. I spent Friday night with her."

"What was her reaction when she saw you?"

"She screamed in anger, then cried."

"Whew. Yeah," Bash said, taking another gulp of his margarita. "I bet she did."

"Then she picked the shards of glass out of my skin and doctored my face."

"Ste... Joan is a saint too."

"Yes, she is."

Bash half-laughed. "The vision just ran through my mind of her *handling* Avery. I'd sit ringside with a bucket of popcorn while enjoying watching Avery getting her sorry ass handed to her."

"Joan could do it."

"She's really tough, Zac, but do you think she's tough enough to continue handling all of this with you?"

I studied Bash's eyes, seeing his concern in them. "I do. It's not to say there won't be days when we both get tired of these shit circumstances and falter, because there will be days like that. I expect them and I know Joan does too."

"So she's really on board with riding this out with you until who knows when?"

"Until we can be together in the open like a normal couple? Yes, she is on board. I know it's so much to ask of her."

"It is a lot, but I get it. I get why you had to ask that of her and I get why she's willing to go along with it. You two are so in love with each other. I saw right through your friendship façade at the bar on Friday night. I know the others didn't but I know you and I know Ste... *Joan*. She feels like a little sister to me."

I nodded. "Yeah, I can see that. She thinks the world of you."

"As I do her. I'd do anything for her and you."

"I appreciate it."

Bash finished his drink and set it down on the coffee table. "About your face," he said, pointing at the left side of it. "The cuts show but not too badly. Your beard helps camouflage it."

"Joan said the same thing."

"Did Malcolm ask you what happened?"

"Of course he did."

"And you told him?"

"I fell off my ladder while cleaning out the gutters back there," I said, pointing out the window into my backyard.

"Hopefully, you'll never have to lie to him again about his mother."

"I really don't think I will. If you'd seen Avery's face after I threw her down onto this couch, you'd understand why I feel like she won't put her hands on me again or throw anything at me."

"I'm so happy that you finally came back at her."

"When that glass hit my face and I started bleeding, that was it. I guess the look on my face told Avery that it was because she took off running to get away from me and she's never done that. I know she thought I was gonna do more than drag her into here. It still got her attention, though."

"I hope it keeps it. Time will tell how seriously Avery really took you."

"I'm not worried about it. I'm just glad she's gone again."

"Yeah, well, maybe something will happen that'll keep her out west and you won't ever have to be concerned about her darkening the doorway of this house again."

"Like what?"

Bash shrugged. "I don't know. I'm just wishing out loud. Hey, um, I'm thinking about having a party at my house in a couple of weeks and if I do, I want you and Joan to come."

"What kind of party?"

"A private, invitation-only kind."

"So Brooke, Ian, and the others won't be attending."

"That's right. My *other* group of friends will be there."

"You haven't had a party like that in quite a while."

"I know. I'm ready to cut loose like we've done before."

"Are costumes required again?"

"Yes."

"Which kind this time?"

"You know the movie Moulin Rouge, right?"

"Who doesn't?"

"Well, the costumes that the women and men wore in the movie are what you and Ste...dammit—*Joan* would have to wear."

"So lingerie and high heels for her and a suit with a tailcoat, tie, hat and all for me?"

"That's right," Bash said, grinning. "Think you can handle that?"

I finished off my Hendricks and tonic then blew out a hard breath. "Yeah, it's just that..."

"Just that what?"

"I'm already imagining Joan in costume."

Bash started chuckling. "Me too. She'll be gorgeous, but I'm really hoping she goes with the style of costume that Christina

Aguilera, Pink and the others wore in the Moulin Rouge music video. They're sexier."

"Sounds like you're no longer *thinking* about having a party. You've decided to have one."

"Yeah, I am gonna have one. And it's gonna be great getting to watch you and your Joan of Arc together without having to hold back from each other. You'll be free to do whatever you wanna do. And remember I have four bedrooms."

I shook my finger at Bash and smiled. "That won't happen in any of them. We'll go back to her house."

"After an evening like what you're gonna experience at mine, you're not gonna want to wait to take your Moulin Rouge girl to bed anywhere other than right where you are. I'll bet you a hundred bucks."

Bash held out his hand toward me but I pushed it away. "I'm not betting you—because you're right. I just hope Joan is up to doing all of this."

"I can already tell you that she will be. She likes a good party and she obviously likes to dance."

"I can't wait to see her do that again."

"Me either. My friends are gonna love her. They already love you, but Stevie," he whispered, "is extra special."

"She most certainly is. So when are you sending out your invitations?"

"All I've gotta do is print them. As a matter of fact, I'm gonna do that when I get home, then I'll run back over and give you yours and Joan's."

"I'm gonna try to see her tomorrow and if I do, then I'll give hers to her. We'll talk on the phone tonight, though, after Malcolm goes to sleep, and I'm gonna go ahead and let her know about the party. She and I are gonna have to get busy finding costumes."

"I already have a website for you."

Bash grabbed his cellphone out of his pocket and texted the link to me. I browsed through the website and saw the costume that I hoped Stevie would wanna get. Mine was on there too and I also hoped it met Stevie's approval.

"Zac, there's one more thing that I wanna say to you about Avery before I go home," Bash said and his voice was serious.

"Okay."

"If she happens to be back in town on the night of my party, your ass is still coming."

"Nothing could stop me. The tides are turning, man. I feel it."

"So do I."

I held up my left hand and looked at the gold band still on my finger. It had no meaning to it whatsoever, so I took it off and looked back at Bash.

"What are you gonna do with that thing?" he asked.

"After you leave, I'm flushing it down the toilet. I can't look at it anymore. I'm done trying to present an image of a happily married man to the people with whom we work and socialize. Most of them know better anyway."

Bash nodded in agreement.

"One thing that I forgot to tell you is Avery flipped me off before she left here on Friday night. Me taking off this gold band is my way of telling her to go to hell."

"A-fucking-men to that."

31
#justbreathe

Stevie

"**M**y parents would like to meet you this coming weekend if you're good with that," Zac said.

"I'm great with that, but I won't be back from Austin until Sunday afternoon."

"I thought you were coming back on Friday."

"That was my plan, but my dad called me just a little while ago and asked me to stay until Sunday. He wants me to go to church with him. I'll get to listen to him preach again."

"I understand. I'm excited for you."

"But I hear the disappointment in your voice."

"I just hate being apart from you, Stevie, and I was really hoping my parents could meet you this weekend."

"If it's not too late for them when I get back on Sunday, then I'm happy to go over to their house."

"You don't think you'll be too tired after the drive?"

"No, not at all. Road trips are relaxing to me. I listen to my favorite music the whole time."

"Okay. I've already talked to Bash about him coming over to watch Malcolm whenever it worked out for us to go to my parents'. I'm just to let him know when and he said he'll be here."

"Great! All I need is your mom and dad's address and I'll meet you there on Sunday."

"No, I want you to ride with me."

"Zac, this is no different from us going to Brooke's."

"I don't care anymore. I'm coming to your house to pick you up and you're riding with me. And not only that. You're gonna hold my hand and we're gonna listen to the radio and talk and do whatever else you want."

I giggled. "You talked me into it."

"Well, there's one more thing that I hope I can talk you into doing."

"What?"

"Go to Bash's party with me."

"I didn't know he was having one."

"He let me know about it earlier today and now I'm letting you know. I actually have your invitation lying next to mine on top of my dresser."

"Bash is that official about a party?"

"This is a private, invitation-only one. Brooke, the rest of your team, and Ian aren't on the guest list because this party is gonna be rather risqué."

"How so?"

"Because of the costumes that Bash is requiring all of us to wear. Well, not the men, but the women. However, I wouldn't be surprised if some of the male guests wear women's costumes and some of the female guests wear men's costumes. Bash has a wide variety of friends who attend his private parties. I've met several of them over the years and they're all great."

"We'll get to Bash's friends in a minute. Right now, I wanna know what kind of costume I'm expected to wear."

"I'm gonna text you a link to a website to answer that question. Hang on."

"Okay." I was putting Zac on speaker when his text came through, and then I opened the link. When I saw what was on the website, my jaw dropped. "Oh my God, Bash is having a Moulin Rouge party!"

"I know. You sound excited about it."

"I am! I love it! I'm gonna keep scrolling through all these costumes while we're talking."

"Okay."

"Have you ever seen the movie?"

"I did, years ago."

"It was so good!"

"Bash did mention to me that he hoped you went more with the style of costumes in the Moulin Rouge music video rather than the ones in the movie."

"Oh yeah! That video has Mya, Lil' Kim, Pink, and Christina Aguilera in it and it is so sexy-hot. 'Lady Marmalade' is the title of the song and now I'm gonna have to listen to it. You do know what it's about, right?"

"Ladies of the evening down in the French Quarter of New Orleans."

"Correct. But do you know what they're saying in the song when they speak French during the chorus?"

"I do not but I know you're gonna tell me."

"Yes, I am! *Voulez-vous coucher avec moi ce soir* translates into: Do you wanna sleep with me tonight?"

"You must've taken French in high school because those words just rolled off your tongue like it was nothing."

I chuckled. "No, I've never taken French, but I've sung along with that song so many times."

"So is your excitement about all of this a yes to going to Bash's party?"

"You couldn't stop me."

"He said you'd wanna go because you love a good party and you love to dance."

"Yes, and I also love to dress up. Especially for you."

"I can't wait to see you in your costume *and* dance. I know Bash is gonna want to dirty dance with you again. He met his match in you when it comes to doing that."

I chuckled again. "What I can't wait to do is see you in *your* costume and also dance with *you* again. The way we moved together at Candleroom was just..."

"Intense."

"Yes. It was so sexy and sultry."

"You made it that way."

"So did you, Buchanan. You've got superior rhythm in more ways than one."

"Well, I try."

I could hear him smiling.

"About your costume... You're gonna have to get a top hat, tail coat, dress pants—everything."

"I'm planning on it. I'll bet you already know the exact costume that you want, don't you?"

"Yes," I giggled.

"Which one is it?"

"I'm not telling you. I want it to be a total surprise when you see me."

"Then I'm not telling you which costume I'm getting."

"That's fine. We'll both be in suspense until then."

"That's one way to put it."

"Zac, this is gonna be so much fun. It's gonna be so nice not having to be secretive about us. We can be in the open. Well, in the openness of Bash's house and mixed company."

"He has a large house and I already know you're gonna love its design and how Bash has it decorated."

"I'm sure I will."

"As you know, he goes all out when it comes to parties, so you can expect the same with this one. He told me that he's gonna have a full bar with a bartender, lots of catered food, and he's also hiring a D.J."

"Oh wow! Yeah, this occasion is gonna be another one that we'll never forget."

"You're right. I won't ever forget it because you'll be there with me," Zac said.

"I love you."

"I love you. Thank you for being willing to go to this party."

"Of course. Have you been to any other private parties of Bash's before?"

"Just one."

"Was it a costume party?"

"Yes. A Pirates of The Caribbean theme. Bash is a big Johnny Depp fan."

"So am I! He made for the best Captain Jack Sparrow."

"And that's who Bash dressed up as that night."

"Did you go alone?"

"No, Avery went with me."

"What did you two dress up as?"

"I was Orlando Bloom's character, Will Turner, and Avery was um... I can't remember her name."

"Elizabeth Swann?"

"Yes."

"Keira Knightley played her and she did a great job of doing it too."

"Yes she did."

"So I have to ask you how it went with Avery that night."

"It was a disaster."

"What made it a disaster?"

"Avery, of course."

"What'd she do?"

"Besides getting drunk off her ass, she also got pissed off."

"About what?"

"Two things. She didn't win best female character costume and she also got jealous of the way I was looking at the woman who did win. I swear to God, I was looking at her costume. It was great! Hell, I looked at the men's costumes too, comparing them to mine."

"You've never been able to win with Avery. You can't do anything right in her petty mind."

"Nope, I can't and I never wanted to be in an embarrassing situation like that with her again. That's why I've never attended another one of Bash's private parties."

"Like—was she just standing next to you and looking pissed off or what?"

"That and she also got mouthy with the woman who won the best female character costume. She was dressed like Elizabeth Swann, too, but she put a whole lot more effort into her costume, makeup, hair and everything. Avery half-assed getting into character-slash-costume just like she does with everything else."

"I'm so sorry, Zac. You don't ever have to worry about me getting drunk off my ass or being jealous about the way you happen to be looking at someone, and you also don't have to worry about me getting mouthy with someone who did something better than I did. I'd only ever get mouthy for one reason and it all has to do with someone being mistreated."

"I know. I've witnessed you doing that very thing during court and also when Avery showed up at Mystic Bar. Your mouthiness was controlled, though. You were precise with those arrows that you shot. You knew exactly what you were doing."

"I just do what I do."

"And it comes naturally to you, Joan of Arc."

"I suppose it does. I like to think I got it from my mom. She was so sweet-spirited but she was also fierce when it came to not only protecting others but also drawing a line in the sand about her boundaries."

"I have no doubt that you got it from your mom and probably several other of your fighter ancestors."

I smiled thinking about what Zac had just said, then decided to go deeper into a subject that he and I had covered before.

"Slight change of subject. I wanna ask you a *spiritual* question."

"Okay."

"Do you really believe we're soul mates?"

Zac chuckled. "Yes. Why?"

"I've just been thinking about the whole theory. The romantic in me embraces it a hundred percent, but there's the other side of me that feels like it just can't be possible. That two souls travel together through time to be together again. That's reincarnation, Zac."

"I know it is."

"When did you become a believer in all of this?"

"After meeting you. I had never put much thought into the validity of soul mates or reincarnation until then. The familiarity of you and the way you make me feel are things I've never experienced with anyone before, and it got me wondering what it was about, so I read up on it. What I found in all the articles that I combed through were countless other people who believe in soul mates and reincarnation—and they believe in it without an ounce of scientific proof. One after another said the validity is in what you feel. It's a *knowing* that you feel so strongly in the center of your being. I immediately felt that with you. I didn't know what to make of it at first but figured it out pretty quickly."

"What you just said about scientific proof is the same thing my dad said to me in a conversation that he and I had about the souls of our passed-on loved ones visiting us. He said science can't prove or disprove it. Once you've experienced a loved one visiting you like my mom has done with my dad and me, you know it's real. The same as my Malcolm visiting me."

"Why do you believe in that but question the soul mate and reincarnation theory?"

"Because you seem too good to be true, Zac."

"So do you—but I still know we're soul mates. I'm not letting a logical world steal that away from me. I *choose* to believe in the magic of us."

"We are magical, aren't we?"

"Yes. And we're really good at making magic."

I sighed out a smile. "Indeed, we are."

"Stevie, whenever your belief in soul mates wavers, I want you to do something that has kept me in check."

"What?"

"Stop whatever you're doing, close your eyes, place your hand over your heart and allow yourself to sense the truth about us. Shut out the world and listen to what your soul is telling you."

"Okay...I'll do that," I said, wiping my eyes. Zac's words were so beautiful and rang of complete truth.

"Tell me something now."

"What?"

"Do you believe you and I are soul mates? At this very second?"

"Yes."

"Good. That makes me really happy to hear. If you start questioning it again, then please do what I suggested. I also want you to lean on me and let my belief and faith in us carry you."

"I will."

Zac and I both paused. I heard him take a deep breath and I knew he heard me when I took one too. We'd just covered a lot of ground that I'd needed him to lead me through.

"Stevie, I'm amazed by what you told me about your dad and his belief in passed-on loved ones visiting us. He's not the typical man of the cloth."

"Because of my mom. My dad told me that she set his soul on fire the moment they met. That was when he became a believer in soul mates."

"The same as when I met you."

"Yes."

"I see another cycle here," Zac chuckled.

"So do I."

"And speaking of parents... I appreciate your willingness to meet mine."

"I'm excited about it but I'm also nervous."

"There's no reason to be nervous."

"They're meeting the woman their son is having an affair with."

"They don't view you like that. They see you as the woman their son loves and also the woman who has made their son so very happy."

"Was there ever a time when they liked Avery?"

"They seemed to, while she and I were dating and during the early part of our first year of marriage. When things started falling apart between Avery and me during that first year, though—when she told me that she really didn't want to have children—my mom and dad both told me that there was something about her that didn't settle with them from the start. They kept hoping they were wrong about their negative gut feelings about her but they obviously weren't wrong. They were on-target."

"Please do me a favor."

"Anything."

"If your mom and dad share their gut feelings about me with you, then tell me. I'd really like to know what they are," I said.

"Of course. But I can already tell you that they're gonna love you. They're gonna see how beautiful you are, inside and out. They're also gonna see how authentic and caring you are. There's not a fake bone in your body, Stevie Sinclair."

"I am who I am. I just hope it's enough for your parents."

"You're more than enough, so stop worrying. Don't be nervous. I'm gonna be right there with you, holding your hand."

"Okay."

"So when do I get to see you again?"

"I was hoping we could meet at the running trail after work tomorrow."

"That's what I was hoping—and also on Tuesday and Wednesday. I've gotta see you as much as I can before you go to Austin."

I could hear the *want* so thickly in Zac's deep voice and all it did was increase my desire for him.

"On one of those evenings, you're gonna have to come over to my house. I need to go swimming with you."

"Is that code for you wanting me to run you like a river again?"

"Yes, it is."

"Happy to do it. We may not go to the trail at all this week. I may just go swimming with you Monday through Wednesday."

"And I'm happy to do that."

"Hang on. My mini-me just walked in," Zac whispered into the phone.

"Okay."

"What are you doing up, buddy?" he asked Malcolm. I loved that I was getting to hear another conversation between them.

"Is that mermaid Stevie?" Malcolm asked.

Zac didn't answer him right away and I knew why. He was shocked again by Malcolm automatically thinking it was me that his daddy was talking to. Then I was shocked by what Zac ended up telling his precious son. He told him the truth. He told him that it was me on the phone—and then Malcolm said he wanted to talk to me.

"Let me ask her if she has time, okay?" Zac told him. Then he got back on the phone. "Um..."

"Yes, I'll talk to him. I've wanted to," I said.

"I know you have. Here he is."

For the next few minutes, Malcolm and I talked about how he was doing and all the fun things that he'd been doing. I got to tell him how much I loved the two pictures he'd drawn for me and that I'd taped them to the front of my refrigerator. Then he said he was going back to bed because he was sleepy. Before he got off the phone, though, he told me that he loved me. I was so taken aback by him doing that and also so touched. After I told him that I loved him too, Zac got back on the phone with me.

"Hey, hang on just a sec," he said, then asked Malcolm if he was going to sleep again. Malcolm must've nodded yes because Zac told him he loved him and to have sweet dreams.

"Well, that was something else, wasn't it?" he asked me, then I heard him sniffle.

"Yes, it was. You sound as choked up as I am."

"I'm just..."

"I know, Zac. Me too. I loved being able to talk to Malcolm. Although it may not have been the wisest thing for you and me to let happen, I feel like you do now. I don't care anymore about playing it safe so much. Getting to hear your angel boy's voice just filled my soul."

"Him getting to hear yours filled his soul too. You should've seen his face, Stevie."

"I wish I could have."

"Once again, I'm blown away by Malcolm automatically thinking I was talking to you. I can't tell you how many times Malcolm has heard me on the phone with Bash or another colleague during the evening. Not only that, but I haven't mentioned your name since telling him that you loved the second drawing that he did for you."

"I believe it all has to do with how in tune he is with you. I have no doubt that he can read your body language and also notices the change of tone in your voice depending on whom you're talking to. I believe Malcolm senses what you're feeling too. Whatever he's picking up on at a time such as you and I being on the phone together may be some kind of flashback for him like when we were at the zoo, Baskin-Robbins, or here at my house. I know my body language and also the energy that I give off is very different whenever we're on the phone like this or around each other. I'm just happy."

"That's it. That has to be it. Malcolm can tell I'm happy now. He's equated my happiness to you and he couldn't be more right."

32
#returntosender

Stevie

"Here's your mail," Jason said, handing it to me.

"Thanks."

"No prob."

He closed my office door behind him as I started going through the stack of envelopes. The fourth one appeared strange. It wasn't the envelope itself as much as the way that it was addressed, as well as the handwriting. My full name—middle name included—was on the front along with the D.A.'s office address, but there was no return address. And the handwriting? I didn't recognize it, but it appeared to be a woman's.

There was a single sheet of white letter-size paper inside and when I unfolded and read what was written on it, I didn't know what to think. All it said was "I'M WATCHING YOU" in all caps. Black ink. No signature.

I picked up my office phone and buzzed Brooke.

"Hey, Stevie," she said.

"Would you mind coming to my office for a minute? I need to show you something I just got in the mail."

"Be right there."

Less than a minute later, Brooke was standing in front of me. I handed her the envelope and anonymous letter. She looked them over, then looked back at me, and I could see the concern on her face.

"What?" I asked her.

"You appear to have a stalker."

"What? Why?"

"Stevie, we piss people off on the daily through our work in the legal system and it seems someone you pissed off is trying to get back at you. They're taunting you," she said, holding up the letter.

"So someone is really watching me then?"

Brooke shrugged. "They may be—or this may be nothing."

"I've never dealt with anything like this before."

"I have, plenty of times. Unfortunately, it just goes with our jobs."

"So what in the hell am I supposed to do, Brooke? Look over my shoulder all the time now for someone that I've pissed off to come up to me all because I was doing my fucking job?"

"I'm always looking over my shoulder. That's why I carry pepper spray with me and that's also why I have a gun locked in the console of my car. I've had officers walk me out to and from my car plenty of times."

"I don't wanna have to do that bullshit."

"You have no choice now, Stevie, and I'm sorry."

As we were staring at each other, Brooke's eyes filled with sympathy for me while mine filled with even more anger. When my cellphone chimed, we both jumped. Zac was texting me. Brooke looked over at my phone and then met my gaze.

"You need to tell him what's happened. You'll feel better if you do and he's probably gonna want to start escorting you to and from this building and also the courthouse."

"He can't do that, Brooke."

"Sure he can. I can too. We'll get some police officers to help as well, and I already know Bash is gonna want to jump in on this."

"And how long is all of this bullshit gonna have to go on?"

"For a while. We're just gonna play it safe and see how things go. If nothing else comes up—say after a month—then we can start backing off a little at a time."

I grabbed the letter out of Brooke's hand and held it up in front of her. "This is a woman's writing."

"Yes, it appears to be."

"I don't remember pissing off any woman in court to this degree."

"Maybe you didn't realize you did."

I threw the letter down onto my desk and fumed. I wished whoever had done this was standing in front of me now because I'd shove their threat up their ass.

"Joan of Arc, you're gonna stroke out on me if you don't breathe and try to relax. I understand how angry you are. The first time I received a letter like that, I was enraged. I couldn't believe someone had the gall to send it—and by the way, I never found out who it was. Nothing else ever came of it, and that's probably gonna be what happens with this."

I blew out a heavy breath and shook my head back and forth, still fuming.

"I'm gonna leave your office now and you're gonna call Buchanan. You need to talk to him and I'm gonna go let the rest of the team know what the postman delivered to you today. Okay?"

"Okay."

As soon as Brooke closed my door, I opened Zac's text and my jaw dropped.

Zac: Hey, you. My stomach just knotted up for no reason, and then I saw you in my mind. What's wrong?

Me: May I call you?

Zac replied by immediately calling me and I answered his call by sighing.

"Stevie, what happened?"

"Some asshole sent an anonymous letter to me here at the D.A.'s office."

"What did it say?"

"I'm watching you."

"Did they write anything else?"

"Nope. It was short and sweet."

"Was the letter typed?"

"Handwritten, and it looks like a woman's writing because of the swirls and loops. Brooke thinks the letter came from someone involved in one of the cases that I was on. I've apparently pissed someone off."

"That just goes with the territory."

"Brooke said that too, and I know it's true. It's just that I've never dealt with anything like this. I am so angry right now and wish whoever sent this letter to me was standing here in front of me. I'd..."

"And I know you would. It's gonna be okay though, Stevie, and here's what I'm gonna start doing."

"Escorting me to and from the D.A.'s office and the courthouse?"

"Yes."

"Brooke said you were gonna want to do that. I appreciate it, but Zac, you can't escort me every day. You've got your own work to do. Besides, I carry pepper spray with me and I'll be fine. I'm just gonna be more watchful for a while."

"Babe?"

"Yeah?"

"I'm doing this. Rearranging my schedule is no problem. You are my priority."

"But I..."

"It's non-negotiable."

I leaned my head back against my chair and closed my eyes. "I don't like having to do this."

"I know you don't, but you're gonna do it and keep doing it until some time has passed. This may be nothing at all but we're not gonna take a chance. We're gonna be proactive. It's a crazy world out there and you know that as well as I do."

"Listen, Brooke has already talked to me about getting some of the police officers up here to walk me to and from my car. She even thinks Bash will want in on doing this, so you won't have to do it all."

"Bash will definitely want in on this but for now, I'm handling it. Yes, I'm gonna tell him about what's happened and I'm also gonna call Brooke to talk to her about it. The three of us will make all the safety arrangements for you."

I got quiet, trying to process what was happening.

"Are you still there?" Zac asked.

"Yes," I mumbled.

"It's three-fifty. I'm gonna call Brooke and Bash. I want you to go walk around inside that big building that you're in. Take a break. Go get a snack out of the vending machines. Grab a Gatorade. Just don't keep sitting around and fretting about all of this. Okay?"

"Okay."

"I'll meet you at five, right there in your office."

"Zac, I can meet you downstairs at the front door of the building."

"Stevie?"

"What?"

"It's non-negotiable."

Zac *and* Brooke peeked their heads around my office door at 4:55 p.m. and grinned at me.

"Okay, you two," I said, unable to keep from grinning back at them.

"You better now?" Zac asked me as they walked into my office.

"Yeah, I'm better."

Brooke started chuckling. "I can tell you're better because your face isn't beet-red anymore."

"No, it's not. I accepted that this is just how things are gonna be for now."

"Well, one benefit of it is having Buchanan protecting you."

I looked over at him and he was still grinning at me.

"That's the best benefit."

"I'll let you two be," Brooke said, looking back and forth at us. "And I'll see you tomorrow, Joan of Arc."

"Okay. And Brooke?"

"Yeah?"

"Thank you. For everything."

"You're welcome."

After she closed my office door behind her, Zac walked around my desk, then pulled me up from my chair by my hands. Without hesitation, he wrapped his arms around me and I melted into him, resting my head on his shoulder.

"I'm so happy to see you and hold you again," he whispered, then softly kissed my forehead.

"Same here. I love you."

"I love you too. Everything is gonna be all right."

"I know it is."

"Are you about ready to leave? No rush. Just wondering."

I raised my head and looked up at Zac. His blue eyes were sparkling. "Yeah. I've just gotta grab my purse and briefcase is all."

"One more question. Do you know how to shoot a gun?"

"Yes. Graham is a deer hunter and used to take me hunting with him. I've done lots of target practice."

"Do you own a gun?"

"No."

"I didn't think so. I have one that I wanna give to you. It's in my car."

"You don't have to do that."

"I'm going to do that and you're going to take it."

"But Zac..."

Before I could say another word, he pressed his warm lips against mine and held them there. I closed my eyes and just breathed him in. When he pulled away and looked at me again, I nodded because I already knew what was on the tip of his tongue.

"I know. It's non-negotiable," I said.

He smiled that big, dimpled smile of his. Then I grabbed my purse and briefcase, and he escorted me to my car. We both looked around on our way to the parking lot and nothing unusual stood out. We didn't see any strange people lurking anywhere.

After I got into my car, Zac stepped over to his. It was parked next to mine and when he came back over to me, he handed me a gun case. I opened it to see a sleek black Glock. I didn't know which model it was but what I did know was what this brand of gun was capable of doing because Graham had owned three of them.

"Do you know how to shoot it?" Zac asked.

"Yes."

"Good. Put it in your console but when you get home, take it out. I want you to keep it with you whenever you're there."

I'd never seen Zac look so serious except on the day we were together in this same parking lot and he'd thought I was ending our relationship because I wasn't willing to wait for our forever. I'd sensed his pain and urgency then just as strongly as I was sensing it now. He was pained by these precautions having to be taken and he was urgent about my doing all I could to stay safe.

"I will. Thank you for watching out for me," I said.

"It's like I've told you before, Stevie... Nothing can ever happen to you. I can't lose you under any circumstances. It would shatter me."

33
#hearttrouble

Zac

It was Thursday evening, I was on the phone with Stevie and she'd just told me that her dad had a blockage in one of his heart arteries. She said his doctor was going to treat it with medicine since the blockage was less than 70%. Stevie and her dad felt positive about everything and I was relieved for both of them.

My lover still planned to stay with her dad until Sunday and it couldn't get here fast enough. I was having withdrawals from her again and the pain that I was feeling in my heart from not seeing her was real. It radiated out from the center of my chest, making me ache all over. They say people can die from a broken heart and now, I understood how that could really happen.

"Zac, there's something else that I need to tell you, but it has nothing to do with my dad," Stevie went on to say.

"What is it?"

"After we left the doctor's office, I stopped by the grocery store that's close to my dad's parsonage to grab a few items for him. I ran into Graham."

"Oh. Okay."

"Everything went fine. He was cordial and so was I. He asked me what I was doing back in Austin and I told him about my dad's heart issue."

"Stevie, I'm glad everything went well with him. You're lucky that it can be that way."

"There's no reason for there to be any animosity between Graham and me. Yes, we have a very long history with each other, but we've both moved on and we're not the same two people we used to be."

"I think you're exactly who you've always been and I love the person you are."

"Yes, I'm me, but yet I'm different with you than how I was with Graham."

"What do you mean?"

"Because I'm with you, I feel free to be *all* of who I am. Meeting you, becoming intimate with you and also falling in love with you has made me throw off every one of the self-imposed life restraints that caused me to be... Well, just not me all the way."

"What you did was throw off all your religious restraints."

"Yes. That's what I did," Stevie breathed out.

"And so did I."

"And it set us both free to be a hundred percent of who we are and to feel what we feel without guilt."

"I've never felt guilty for one thing that has to do with us. I know you did for a little while, and I understand because I know your background."

"But you grew up going to church too, so how have you not felt any kind of guilt about our affair?"

"Because in my heart, I'm not a married man. I'm as single as you are. Yes, I had to wrap my brain around the fact that technically, we are having an affair because I am married, even though it's only on paper."

"I've never asked you this, but I have wondered if you've ever been approached by a woman showing romantic interest in you since you've been married."

"I have been approached," I admitted.

"Several times, I bet."

"No, not several. Twice."

"Did you know the women?"

"I knew one of them. She's a defense attorney who's no longer living in Dallas or practicing law here."

"Were you two actually friends?"

"No. We knew each other distantly through the legal community."

"Still—she had to have known you were married."

"She did, and not just because of the wedding band that I wore at the time, but also because I told her I was married after she approached me with her romantic interest. She didn't care, though."

"She just wanted what she wanted and that was you."

"Apparently so."

"I can't say that I blame her," Stevie chuckled.

"I'm choosing to take that as a compliment."

"I intend it as one. Now tell me about the other woman."

"She was a total stranger who approached me at the mall when I was there alone. I immediately shut down her advances, too."

"I didn't make romantic advances toward you at first, but you did toward me."

"Yes I did. We've talked about this before and again, I have no explanation as to why I was willing to throw off all my religious restraints other than it was just you, Stevie. The first time I laid my eyes on you, something about you called to me and didn't let go. I never thought I was going to see you again but then I did and when I did, I just knew."

"Knew what?"

"That you were the one for me. That you were my exception."

"God, I miss you, Zac, even though it's only been one day since we've seen each other."

"I miss you more."

"I really appreciate your understanding about Graham and me running into each other."

"Sure, I understand. Again, you're lucky that things can be cordial between you and him. But I do have a question."

"What?"

"You haven't mentioned anyone being with Graham. So he was alone?"

"He was."

"Did he bring up your ex-best friend?"

"No, but I did. I asked Graham if he was still with Emma and he said no. They split up two months ago and he's not dating anybody."

"How'd parting ways with Graham go?"

"Fine. He told me to tell my dad hello and that he'd pray for him, and then we hugged each other goodbye. That was it."

"I really hope you don't mind me asking all of this, Stevie. I can't help but be territorial *and* protective of you."

"I've told you that I feel the same way toward you. It's normal, Zac."

"If I'm coming across as jealous, I don't mean to. I'm not jealous of Graham at all other than he got to see you today and I didn't."

"You're not coming across as jealous. If you were, though, I would've told you that there's nothing to be jealous of when it comes to Graham or any other man. You're all I see."

"Same here. Now get back home so I can take you to bed."

"I'll be there in three short days."

"Long days."

Stevie giggled. "Well, if you can't wait for me to get back, then you know we can always have FaceTime sex."

"I may just have to take you up on that."

"You just let me know when."

"Okay, tonight."

"Deal. I'll text you as soon as I know my dad is out for the night. I can always tell by his snoring."

"You know what talking about this is already doing to me, right?"

"Yes. It's doing it to me too but we're both gonna have to hang on for just a little longer. My dad usually goes to bed by nine."

"You know Malcolm will be asleep by then."

"Let's just hope he doesn't wake up like he did on Sunday night."

"You know what?"

"What?"

"I'm gonna take him for a late swim and really tire him out. I don't want any interruptions tonight when I see your face and the rest of your beautiful body on my phone screen," I said, already imagining *all* of Stevie.

"Sounds good to me. Go take that boy swimming and I'll let you know when my dad is asleep."

"Okay. I love you."

"I love you too."

Three days later

I woke up before sunrise with Stevie on my mind. I was so excited about her coming back home today and I was also excited about my parents getting to meet her. My mom had asked me if I wanted her to cook dinner for all of us but I suggested snacks instead. Chips, salsa, guacamole or a cold plate of cheese, olives, pickles with crackers. My mom's usual appetizers that were always filling.

I talked to Bash and he said he'd be waiting for my call for him to come over to watch Malcolm while Stevie and I were at my parents' house. I'd told Malcolm that his Uncle Bash was coming over to hang out with him because I had to go to my office to do some work and he didn't question anything other than how soon Bash was coming over. Malcolm loved him. They really were buddies.

To pass the time, I detail-cleaned the entire house, then took Malcolm swimming. Afterward, while he was napping, I checked on Avery's status and was relieved to see that she was still in Lubbock, at Justin's residence. The last thing I wanted was for her to show up here while Bash was watching Malcolm. Avery wouldn't have cared but I knew that things would be tense between her and Bash. He wouldn't say anything off-color to her because of Malcolm. Regardless, I didn't want him to be in that tempting position.

Stevie called me when she was an hour away from her house, and then I let Bash know it was time for him to come over to mine. He, Malcolm and I lounged in my living room—Malcolm munching on some more candy that Bash brought him and watching some cartoons on T.V. while stretched out on the floor. As Bash and I sat on the couch discussing one of his cases, I looked at the clock on my wall probably a hundred times because I was so anxious to see Stevie again.

After she'd texted me that she'd made it back safe and sound, I sped all the way to her house and as soon as I saw her standing in her garage, smiling, waiting for me to park my Blazer, I felt the biggest sense of relief. She was the one and only remedy for all that ailed me.

"You are a sight for sore eyes, Sinclair," I told her as I was getting out of my car. Then I caught the scent of that lotion from Bath & Body Works that she liked to rub onto her skin after showering. "And you smell like a warm sugar cookie again—and I'm about to take a big bite of you!"

She giggled-screamed, then took off running back into her house as I ran after her. I caught up with her in her living room and the two of us went round and round her coffee table until I finally jumped across it, pulled Stevie into my arms and started kissing her. We were all over each other but couldn't seem to get close enough.

"Do we have time?" she asked, pulling her lips away from mine.

"Yes, we have time."

"Then take me to bed, Buchanan."

I picked her up underneath her arms as she wrapped her legs around my waist and her arms around my neck. We kissed all the way down the hallway and into her bedroom until we made it over to her bed. Then we took off our clothes as quickly as we could. At the moment that Stevie and I became one again, we both sighed, and as we began moving in our easy rhythm, I watched Stevie's moody blue eyes. They were happy today and they were also full of desire for me...and I was home.

34
#welcome

Stevie

I looked down at Zac's hand holding mine on the console of his Blazer then looked back up at his handsome, smiling face. We were on our way to his mom and dad's house, but I still had about ten more minutes to enjoy what Zac and I were doing now.

This was the first time that we'd ever ridden together somewhere. We'd never risked it before because we didn't want to take a chance on someone seeing us together. With every passing day, though, we were both caring less and less about if that happened. Riding alongside him like this felt right. It felt good. It was a small thing yet so big.

Zac brought my hand up to his mouth and kissed it, then said, "We're about a mile away. You still feeling okay about this?"

"Yes, I feel fine about it. I wanna know your family, Zac."

"And I hope to meet your dad one day."

His eyes went back to watching the road, but I kept watching him while imagining my dad meeting him. I would love for that to happen. In a perfect world, it would. But the truth was, because of the status of my relationship with Zac, my dad would probably never want to meet him. I didn't think he'd ever accept the man that I'd given my heart to because no matter how I framed our relationship, Zac and I were still having an affair.

As he was pulling into his parents' driveway, I immediately noticed the big porch across the front of their brick home and also the swing. I loved seeing them. To me, they were a throwback to simpler and better times when the world wasn't so busy and families gathered.

Hanging along the front porch were several Boston ferns and there were also manicured flowerbeds in front of it. Either Zac's mom, dad, or both of them had green thumbs and enjoyed being outdoors with their hands in the earth—just like my mom and dad.

Zac came around to my side of his car and opened the door for me again, then he took my hand and helped me to my feet.

"Breathe, Stevie," he chuckled. "It's all good here at this house."

"I just got nervous all of a sudden."

"I think the reality of what we're about to do just hit you."

"It's a big deal."

"I know it is."

"Zac, I hope they like me."

"They're gonna love you. Now let's go."

Just as Zac and I reached the front door, it opened and I looked up to see his mom and dad's smiling faces. In both of them, I recognized physical traits of Zac's. He was a perfect blend of his parents.

"Hello and welcome!" his mom said, reaching out and hugging me. Then she pulled back and looked over my face. "Stevie, it's so nice to meet you."

"It's nice to meet you too, Mrs. Buchanan."

"Oh please, just call me Beth."

I smiled. "Okay—Beth."

"This is my husband, Gregg," she said, turning to him, and he held out his arms to hug me too.

"I'm really happy to meet you, Stevie," he said.

"You too."

"We're an affectionate family. Hope you don't mind."

"Not at all. Mine is the same way."

"You two come on in," Beth said as she and Gregg stepped aside.

"I guess I'm just chopped liver now since you've met Stevie. I don't even get a hug," Zac teased.

"Oh come here, you spoiled thing!" Beth said.

She and Gregg hugged their only son, and then the four of us walked into the living room of this cozy home. I already loved the vibe inside and I also loved the positive energy of Zac's parents.

"I can give you a tour of this place now or we can do it later," Beth said, looking at me. Then she cut her eyes over at Zac. "I have snacks ready and I don't know about either of you, but I could use an afternoon drink."

"I think we all could," Zac chuckled.

"Then let's go."

As we were leaving the living room, I glanced around and noticed the big collage of pictures on the wall behind the couch. I saw a whole lot of pictures of Malcolm and a whole lot of Zac at different ages and I could hardly wait to get a closer look at them.

The kitchen reminded me of something from a children's witch's tale. It had a cottage-like feeling to it with its earth tones and an archway of bricks stretching across the stovetop area in a beautiful, old-world-looking pattern that pulled at me. There were more pictures of Malcolm and Zac on the walls along with a wrought iron Celtic cross over by the dining room table. Beth had votive candles burning here and there and a little speaker on the kitchen counter playing some country music. I could tell that her home was her sanctuary.

Gregg looked at me and said, "I know what Zac wants to drink but what would you like, Stevie? We have red, white, and rosé wine, some Bud Lite, gin, tequila... Pretty much anything you want."

"I'm a gin girl."

"We have Hendricks."

"And that one is my favorite. I have a bottle of the original at home and also a tiny bit of Neptunia left. It's one of Hendricks' limited-release gins. They make some others too that are really good."

Gregg grinned at Zac. "She knows her gin."

"Yes, she does, and she likes her gin and tonic the same way that I do."

"Then two gin and tonics with extra lime it is."

After Gregg made Zac's drink and mine, he poured a large glass of rosé for Beth, then opened a Bud Lite for himself and poured it into a frosty mug. As the four of us stood together in the middle of the kitchen, holding our drinks, Gregg and Beth held up theirs toward Zac and me.

"Here's to happiness," Gregg said. He was smiling and so was Beth. "Cheers!"

"Cheers," Zac and I said together. Then our glasses met his parents' and we each took a big sip.

Beth then started pulling prepared snack trays out of the refrigerator and set them on the kitchen counter. She also had a basket of tortilla chips with salsa and some delicious looking guacamole.

"Zac and Stevie, you two go ahead and fix your plates, and we'll join you in the dining room."

Zac held out his hand for me to go first but before I grabbed a plate, I looked up at him. His eyes were shining so brightly. I didn't say anything. I just nodded to let him know this meeting with his parents was good. Really good. It was peaceful and wrapped in his mom and dad's unconditional love.

While we were all enjoying the food and drinks, our conversation stayed light. We covered subjects ranging from Malcolm to Zac's job and mine to the new set of golf clubs that Gregg had bought for himself the week before. Nothing too serious. I didn't know if it was going to stay this way or if Zac's parents had some serious questions they wanted to ask me—or some serious statements to make. Then Beth made a statement to me.

"Stevie, Zac told Gregg and me about your family, where you grew up and everything, and I just want you to know I am so sorry about your mother's passing," she said.

I cleared my throat. "I appreciate it."

"I'm sorry about it too, Stevie," Gregg added. "I'm glad you still have your father."

"Me too. We're very close."

"Zac mentioned that he was having some heart issues and you went to Austin to go to the doctor with him."

"Yes. He has some blockage in one of his arteries but it's not a lot, so his doctor is gonna treat it with medication."

"That's great news. I'll bet he's relieved."

"He really is. So am I. I told my dad that nothing can happen to him because he's all I've got left. No grandparents or anything on either side of my family, plus I'm an only child like Zac," I said, grinning at him sitting next to me. "I'm a little spoiled too."

Zac and his parents laughed, and Gregg reached across the table and extended his hand toward me. After I took it, he looked straight into my eyes with his blue ones that were identical to Zac's, gave my hand a gentle squeeze, and then smiled at me.

"I speak for my family and I want you to know that you're accepted here, Stevie. There is no judgment of your and my son's relationship. The way that Beth and I view Zac's marriage to Avery is that they're married only on paper, and it's been that way for over four years. I'm sure I'm not telling you anything that you don't already know but I just felt a need to be transparent with you about my feelings on all of this. Because your father is a pastor and because of your church upbringing, I have no doubt that you've grappled with the circumstances of your relationship with Zac," Gregg said, glancing over at him.

"Yes, sir, I have."

"It's understandable, sweetheart, but you're gonna learn that when it comes to matters of the heart, certain manmade rules and laws will never apply."

"This that Zac and I share has been a big lesson in that very thing."

Gregg gave my hand another squeeze, then let go of it and took a sip of his beer.

"Stevie, in the short amount of time that you've been here in my home, I've already witnessed enough between you and Zac to know you two are very much in love. Now, I have no idea what the future holds for you or my son, but I do know that I hope you're in his future. I've never seen him like this," Gregg said, pointing at Zac and smiling. Then he looked back at me. "You can't fake what I see showing in his eyes and also yours, young lady."

I had already started getting choked up from listening to everything that Gregg was saying, but it was his last sentence that really got to me.

"No, you can't fake it," I said, smiling through my tears.

I glanced at Beth and she was in the same boat as me, then I looked up at Zac to see him wiping his eyes. His dad was right there with him, doing the same thing.

"Thank you for coming here, Stevie," Gregg went on to say. "You're a true delight, just like Zac said you were."

I thanked him for his kind words, and then Beth asked all of us if we'd like to go relax in the living room.

"I know you wanna check out that picture collage in there," Zac said, nudging me. "I saw you looking at it earlier."

"Yes, I do wanna check it out. Especially those pictures of you when you were younger."

"That's fine. You can check them out and then you can get your jabs out of the way."

I held up my hands, acting innocent. "Who said I was gonna do that?" I teased.

"No one—but I know you, Sinclair. This one here likes to give me a hard time, Mom and Dad," Zac said, looking across the table at them.

"Sounds like she's just keeping you on your toes, son," Gregg chuckled. "I know someone who's good at doing that to me."

He looked at Beth sitting beside him. They smiled at each other, and then Gregg leaned over and kissed her. In that brief moment, watching them, I saw Zac and myself. The sweet affection was the same and so was the friendship.

By the time another hour had passed, Zac, his parents and I had sat down in the living room to relax and talk some more, but not before Beth gave me a quick tour of her home and also showed me all the pictures of Zac in the collage on the wall behind her couch. There were ones from when he was a baby all the way through his elementary, junior high and high school years; one of him on the day that he graduated from law school; one of him rocking Malcolm when he was a baby; and also a recent one of Zac. I knew it was recent because he looked just like he did now with the short beard that he grew just for me.

When I asked Beth when it was taken, she smiled and said, "I took it on the day that Zac told me about you. I wanted to take a picture of my son because his happiness about having you in his life was so obvious. He was glowing all over just like he is now." Beth glanced over at him sitting in the chair next to his dad, who was chatting with him, then turned her attention back to me.

"I love this picture of Zac so much," I said, looking at it again.

"I'm gonna go print a copy for you right now. Which size would you like?"

"Same as yours, please."

"One five-by-seven picture of Zachariah Dalton Buchanan in love coming up," she said, then flitted off. I smiled at hearing her call Zac by his full name because I'd done that too.

When I turned around, Zac smiled at me and then patted his leg for me to come over to him and sit down. As soon as I was in his lap, he wrapped his arms around my waist and hugged me to him, and he kept holding on to me while he and his dad continued their conversation.

Beth was gone for only a few minutes, and when she returned to the living room, she walked up to me and handed me a manila envelope.

"The picture is in there, sweetheart, so it won't get bent up or anything," she said.

"Thank you so much."

"You've very welcome."

Beth kept staring into my eyes, then reached out and cupped my face in her hand. It was what my mom used to do and I missed it. There was something about Zac's mom doing it, though, that filled the emptiness inside me for the moment, and I cherished it more than she knew.

When it came time for Zac and me to leave, his parents walked us to their front door, said they'd love for the four of us to get together again soon, and then hugged us goodbye. On the drive back to my house, Zac held my hand again while the radio played and the two of us kept smiling. It had been such a wonderful day.

"It's so strange seeing you without your wedding band," I told Zac.

We were standing in my kitchen now, stealing a few more minutes together before he went home to relieve Bash of uncle duty.

"It feels right to me."

"Whenever Avery comes back, what are you gonna tell her if she asks you about it?"

"The truth. That I can't look at it anymore because it's a joke. She and I are a joke and I'm not gonna fake anything about my relationship with her any longer."

"She still wears her wedding ring."

"Only because she likes to show it off."

"It's a pretty ring."

"Yeah, it is. I bought it for a different person, though."

"I know you did."

"Stevie, thank you for going to meet my parents."

"They're amazing. I had so much fun with them, getting to know them and all. They're both free spirits and they're so cute together. I love how they still flirt with each other and show their affection."

"They've always been just like you saw them."

"You had a fun and peaceful childhood with good role models, then."

"I did."

"Me too."

"I want what's left of my son's childhood to be that way."

"Malcolm already has a good role model in you and you make his life fun and peaceful. I've seen it.'"

"Yeah, but there's a huge puzzle piece missing and that's you."

I took a deep breath and stared up at Zac.

"I'm sorry," he continued. "I shouldn't have gone there. I'm bringing down all the good of this day."

"No, it's fine. I have the same thoughts you do."

"Are you getting tired of waiting for that door to open to our forever?"

"Yes, I'm tired of waiting, just like you are, but that doesn't mean I'm going anywhere. Do you doubt that?"

He shrugged. "I don't wanna doubt it, but honestly, I do wonder if one day you're just gonna get enough of waiting and throw in the towel. You're human, Stevie, and I know that what I've asked of you is so damn much."

"I signed up for this, Zac. I agreed to journey down this pathway with you knowing full well that it was going to be hard. You and I have already had to deal with things that we've never had to deal with before and so far, we've done a good job of handling them. But I know there are gonna be days when we do a shit job of handling matters because we're human. That doesn't mean we quit, though. It means we pull ourselves up off the floor and keep fighting for what we want. Besides, I love a good fight. You should know that."

Zac smiled. "I do know that, Joan of Arc—and I love you."

"I love you, heart and soul. Now tell me goodbye and go home to your sweet Malcolm. I've got a picture of you that I wanna frame and put on my nightstand," I said, pointing at the manila envelope sitting on my kitchen counter.

"Okay, I'll go, but where's your gun?"

"In my nightstand drawer."

"I know you have a security system, but it's just that..."

"You're territorial and protective of me."

"Yes."

"I feel completely safe because of you."

"Good. That's what I want. I'll call you after Malcolm goes to sleep."

"And I'll be waiting."

I walked Zac out to the garage, but before I raised the door, he held me in his arms for longer than I expected. He was quiet the whole time, too, and afterward, he didn't give me a passionate kiss goodbye. He just pressed his lips against mine while breathing me in. Yes, saying goodbye to him like this was getting old, even though he and I were so new. I was tired of having to do it, but there was still nothing in this world that could ever make me walk away from what this incredible man and I shared.

35
#guarded

Stevie

"I'm gonna go to the mall to see if I can find a pair of high heels I like. I already have a pair that would work but they're not exactly what I envisioned wearing with my Moulin Rouge costume," I told Zac.

"What color high heels?"

"I'm not telling you, because if I do you'll know the color of my costume. Well, one of the colors."

He sighed but I could also hear his smile over the phone. "Fine."

"I've already told you that I want it to be a total surprise."

"I know. I just keep hoping you might give me a hint. I can hardly wait to see you looking like you stepped out of the 'Lady Marmalade' music video. I'll bet you went with a costume that's similar to Christina Aguilera's."

"What makes you think I did?"

"Her costume is one that I can easily imagine on you and I can also imagine your makeup and hair done the same as Christina's in the video."

"You can keep betting and imagining all day long about that and keep wondering about it too. I'm not telling you a thing. You're just gonna have to wait and see, Buchanan," I chuckled.

He sighed again. "Okay, well, I'm planning to take Malcolm over to my mom and dad's at six, and then I'll come over to your house and get dressed."

"I changed my mind about you getting dressed here."

"What?"

"I want to meet you at Bash's."

"But why?"

"I really want it to be a total surprise when you see the costume that I got. I wanna walk into Bash's house and see your face. It's all about anticipation."

"You're torturing me, Stevie."

"I don't mean to. Will you please do this for me?"

"You know I will. Anything you want, Creole Lady Marmalade."

I laughed at hearing him say that. "I am your Creole Lady Marmalade and thank you for agreeing to change up our 'getting ready' plans."

"You're welcome."

"I'm gonna go on over to the mall so I can get back home before dark."

"Okay. Let me know when you make it back home.

"I will, and then I'll see you tomorrow at Bash's party. I'm so excited."

The Galleria mall was busy when I got here, but I should've expected that on a Friday evening. I wasn't familiar with this place so I spent about twenty minutes walking around, making mental notes of the different stores and their locations. Then I saw a shoe store with a display of vampy high heels in assorted colors and walked right in.

The third pair I tried on was the one that I decided to buy. Not only were the shoes a comfortable fit, but their color and bling matched my costume. I'd be able to walk around in them all evening at Bash's party without killing my feet and they would also look sexy as hell. I knew Zac was going to love them as much as he'd loved the black heels I'd worn to Brooke's birthday party.

I spent more time inside the mall than I realized and when I left it to go back to my car, it was dark outside. The parking lot was well lit but I still kept a sharp eye on my surroundings and carried my pepper spray in my hand. The anonymous letter that I'd received at work still had me on edge, as well as pissed off.

I was about twenty yards away from my car when that feeling of someone watching me came over me. I stopped walking and looked around the parking lot but didn't see anyone acting unusual. There were people walking toward the mall and coming out of it, but their behavior was as normal as mine.

By the time that I made it to my car, I'd already unlocked it with my key fob and had just grabbed the door handle when chills crawled up my spine. I sensed someone standing behind me and spun around—but there was no one. I hurried into my car and locked it, grabbed the gun that Zac had given me out of the console, and then looked around the parking lot again through my windows. I hated feeling like this. I was unnerved and paranoid and shouldn't have to feel this way.

I called Zac as I was backing out of my parking space because I knew that just hearing his voice would calm my nerves. I realized Malcolm might not be asleep yet but it didn't matter. I had to talk to his daddy.

"Hey, you!" he said, answering his phone on the first ring.

"Can you talk or is Malcolm still awake?"

"He's already in bed. He's really tired today for some reason. Probably the moon cycle," Zac chuckled.

"Please just talk to me."

"What's wrong, Stevie."

"I'm driving out of the Galleria parking lot right now and just had something really weird happen."

"What?"

"You know that feeling when you sense someone is watching you?"

"Yes."

"Well, I felt it while I was walking out to my car but I didn't see anyone acting unusual. No one was staring at me or anything. Then when I got to my car, I sensed someone standing behind me and spun around to see who it was but again—there wasn't anyone near me. I'm just kinda freaked out at the moment and need to talk to you."

"I'm right here, Stevie, and you call me anytime you need to. It doesn't matter if it's before Malcolm's bedtime.

"Thank you so much, Zac."

"My God, of course. Have you made it out of the parking lot yet?"

"Almost."

"Okay. Keep talking to me. You're staying on the phone with me until you get home."

"I was hoping to. I already feel better just hearing your voice."

"I'm so sorry all that just happened to you."

"I'm obviously imagining things, and I know it's because I'm a little paranoid after receiving that damn letter at work."

"It's understandable that you'd feel that way."

"The good news is I found the perfect pair of high heels to go with my costume."

"That is good news. Care to tell me what color they are?"

"Because you're helping me to chill the hell out right now? Is this a trade-off or something?" I chuckled.

"Look at it however you want."

"I'm still not telling you, Buchanan."

He sighed but I could tell that he was smiling on the other end of the line.

"So tell me how you're feeling at the moment," he said.

"Calm, thanks to you. And I just pulled out of the parking lot."

"Do you want me to come over? I know my parents would watch Malcolm for me."

"No, you're not waking him up. I'm fine. Really, Zac. Just talking to you like this is what I needed."

Zac and I didn't hang up until after I'd gone into my house and reset my alarm to "On." I'd planned to try on my costume again along with my new pair of high heels but I wanted to have a Hendricks and tonic while I was getting vamped up, so I went into the kitchen and made one. Then I walked into my bedroom, turned on my portable speaker, pulled up "Lady Marmalade" on my Pandora app and pushed play.

Looking at myself now in the full-length mirror in my bedroom, I smiled. I knew that when Zac saw me tomorrow evening at Bash's, he was going to smile that huge, dimpled smile of his and he was also going to get an instant hard-on. Then he was going to want to take me to bed. That was going to have to wait until after the party was over, though. Then I was going to play the role of one of New Orleans' ladies of the evening just for Zac.

I knew him well enough to know how much he'd already been imagining that very thing happening—just like I had. This sexual playground of ours was so much fun, but I wanted to push the limits of it even more. There was a lot more that I wanted to do for and to my lover and there was a lot more that I wanted him to do for and to me.

36
#monamour

Zac

It was almost 8:30 p.m. and Stevie hadn't made it to Bash's party yet. It had started an hour ago, so I texted her to see if she was okay and she sent back a thumbs-up emoji plus "I'll be there soon." If I had to guess, it was taking Stevie longer to get in costume than she'd planned. No doubt, she was meticulous about dressing herself and wanted everything to be perfect.

I walked over to the bar and ordered another Hendricks and tonic. Like Bash had said he was going to do, he'd provided a full bar and hired a bartender, had a long buffet table of delicious-looking catered food, and hired a D.J. to play a mix of music. All the guests were mingling and enjoying this high-energy setting.

Bash's back doors were French and he had them wide open, allowing the festivities to spill outside onto his back patio which was expansive. It was lit up with strings of white lights that stretched high across the perimeter, as well as red candles on the black tablecloths of all the tables that Bash had set up out there.

When I first arrived, I'd talked with some friends of his whom I'd met before and also met several women and men with whom I wasn't acquainted. Everyone was in a great mood and happy to be here having a great time. Some of the women were wearing costumes I recognized from the 'Lady Marmalade' music video while some had gone with styles from the Moulin Rouge movie. There were also a few women dressed similarly to me, as well as some men in feminine attire, and they were all pulling off their looks like pros.

I was so anxious to see Stevie's costume. She had kept it a big mystery all this time but I knew that whatever she'd picked out was going to be gorgeous on her because of her. My own costume was one Stevie had seen online, but she didn't know I'd finally decided to go with it. I was really hoping she liked it on me.

My dress pants were light gray with thin black crisscrosses on them, my shoes were black, my shirt was white, my tie was black, my vest was crimson red, my tailcoat was black and also my gloves, and my top hat was light gray with a black band. I was even carrying a black cane and had on glasses with round crimson lenses in them. Surprisingly, my costume was very comfortable.

The bartender handed my drink to me and when I turned around, I did a doubletake and my breath caught in my throat. Stevie had just walked through Bash's front door and was taking off her black cloak, revealing what she had on underneath. I lowered my glasses to get a better look at her, then saw Bash quickly end a conversation with one of his friends so he could run to greet Stevie, which he did with his arms flailing in pure excitement.

"Doll! Look at you!" he said as the two of them hugged.

Stevie handed Bash a gift bag which I knew contained a bottle of Clase Azul Reposado tequila. It was Bash's favorite, which he indulged in only on special occasions, and I already knew that he'd be opening the bottle sometime tonight.

When Bash saw Stevie's gift, he hugged her again, and just like when he'd seen what Stevie was wearing on the night of Brooke's birthday party, he slowly spun her around so he could look at *all* of her. Stevie was giggling at Bash and the two of them had huge smiles on their faces.

I started walking toward them while my heart pounded inside my chest. Stevie was breathtaking and so damn sexy in her costume. She had on a crimson and black striped bodice that pushed up her breasts, making them appear even fuller than they already were. She was also wearing crimson satin short-shorts with black fishnet stockings underneath. There was a black-sequined garter on each thigh, and the black high heels she'd bought for this night couldn't have been a better match for her costume.

Stevie was also wearing long black lace gloves that reached well beyond her elbows. On each of her wrists was a diamond bracelet that matched the diamond chain draped around her hips, the wide choker around her neck and her hoop earrings.

Stevie's makeup was dark and dramatic and artistically done. Her pouty lips were crimson, her high cheekbones were contoured and her moody blue eyes appeared catlike with the black liner she'd applied. There were even little diamonds placed here and there around her eyes that she must've glued onto her skin.

I smiled when I saw how classily she'd styled her hair. It was parted on one side and finger-waved in the front. Those front strands of hair were loosely pulled into the back where the rest of Stevie's long blond hair was secured in a low bun with black netting over it. But that wasn't all. Stevie was also wearing long crimson and black feathers in her hair. She looked so exotic—and now, she was looking straight at me as I came to a standstill in front of her.

"Hey, you," I said, taking off my top hat.

"Hey, you...and look at you, Buchanan."

"Look at you, Sinclair. Once again, you rendered me speechless when I first saw you. You're stunning."

"Thank you, and so are you. You remind me of Gary Oldman in the movie 'Dracula.' You're mysterious looking and so handsome."

"I didn't intentionally go for the Dracula look but if you like it, then I'm good with that. I may just have to sink my teeth into you later."

"I expect you to."

Bash sighed. "Okay... Here the three of us are again, and *again*, I'm the one on the sideline listening to the two of you drip the lusty words and eye-fuck each other."

Stevie and I busted out laughing. Then I said, "Thanks for not minding, buddy. I know you really don't."

"No, I don't. You, Dracula, and Creole Lady Marmalade here are entertaining. Now take your lady by the hand and go join the party."

Bash kissed Stevie on the cheek, patted me on the shoulder, and then walked off, leaving Stevie and me alone in the wide foyer of his home.

"Put your top hat back on," she said, so I did.

"Anything else?"

"Yes."

"What?"

"Kiss me."

I leaned in and gently kissed Stevie, careful not to mess up her crimson lips. When I pulled back, she looked down at my mouth, grinned, and then wiped off my lips with one of her black lace gloves.

"Thank you for taking care of me," I told her.

"I'm happy to. Now would you mind taking me to get a drink?"

"I'm happy to."

"Bash has everything looking like the movie set of Moulin Rouge," Stevie said, glancing over my shoulder. "It's gorgeous and seductive at the same time."

"Does it arouse you?"

"Yes—but you especially do."

Stevie glanced over my shoulder again, and then I felt her hand on my crotch. I didn't flinch, though, because I'd expected her to do that.

"You're also aroused, sir," she said, coming even closer to me and staring straight into my eyes.

"Yes, I am. But what's with calling me 'sir?'"

"Ladies of the evening are always respectful of the gentlemen who come to see them."

Stevie had just stepped into role-playing and it was my turn to do the same, so I held out my arm for her to take.

"Now if you'll please join me at the bar. I'd like to order a Hendricks and tonic with extra lime for you, beautiful lady."

The hours flew by as alcohol and the buffet of catered food continued to be consumed by all of Bash's guests, including Stevie and me. Everyone was feeling good, laughing and having so much fun. It was obvious that as the night grew later and the higher everyone became, the more free they were about expressing themselves. Not only through dancing, but also through physical affection.

Couples who came here together were currently all over each other and strangers who'd just met tonight were doing the same. Stevie and I were no exception. I'd kissed her several times since she'd arrived at this party and not in a manner that was mindful of her crimson lips. I was ready to devour her, but then a song came on that made her start dancing again. I knew there'd be no stopping her, nor Bash, nor his animated friends who'd taken center stage all evening on the dance floor that Bash set up in his large, cleared-out living room. He was there now and had just hollered, "Come on, doll!" to Stevie. She smiled at me and then started heading in his direction.

By the time she made it over, Simone, Macie, Jackson, Audrey, and Adam were back on the dance floor alongside Bash and they were all moving in rhythm with the song "Lady Marmalade." Not Patti LaBelle's version. It was the one sung by Mya, Pink, Lil' Kim and Christina Aguilera.

I kept my eyes on Stevie while sipping on my eighth Hendricks and tonic. She was like poetry in motion as she moved her tall, slender body along with the beat of the song that exuded sex in its rawest form. Bash was on her right in his dapper suit and top hat and Simone was on her left in a costume that was identical to Lil' Kim's in the music video, and the three of them kept looking back and forth at each other while doing the same music video movements, singing along with the song and laughing their asses off. The rest of the group moved closer to them and then some of the other partygoers, who hadn't been dancing, joined the dance orgy. It was one big mashup of gyrating Moulin Rouge bodies and sweat.

When the song reached the chorus for the second time, Stevie looked across the room at me and then started strutting over in my direction. When she reached me, she took my bottom lip between her teeth, tugged at it, let it go, and then turned around and shook her fine ass in front of me. After that, she backed up her body against mine and started slithering up and down it. I grabbed her around her waist and pulled her even harder against me, and then she looked over her shoulder and smiled.

"You wanna fuck me right now, don't you?" she gin-breathed against my face.

"You know I do."

"Just a couple more minutes and then you can. And when you do, I want you to fuck me harder than you ever have, Buchanan. I know you've been wanting to up that level and I wanna experience all of the hungry wolf inside you."

Stevie quickly kissed me and then took off toward Bash and the others, rejoining them on the dance floor while keeping her eyes on me. All I could do was stare at my lover while thinking about what she'd just said to me. Since we began our affair, I'd made myself hold back from doing to her what I desired to do—and that was exactly what she just described. I was about to take Stevie into my wolf's den and sink my goddamn teeth into her in every way.

I watched her as she kept dancing to the seductive song, and then she and the others grabbed their breasts in unison, what was between their legs, dropped down to the floor, spread their legs, and then stood back up. I was hard as a rock too from watching my personal Creole Lady Marmalade.

As soon as the song ended, she strutted back over to me and asked me where we could be alone. I knew exactly where to take her. One of Bash's guest bedrooms—the one furthest away from the party.

After we'd made it inside, I locked the door behind us, threw off my top hat and glasses, and then went up to Stevie, grabbed her around her head, pulled her closer to me and started kissing her. Our tongues entangled and our teeth gnashed against each other's. We were breathing hard and it just kept building. Then I pulled away from Stevie and pushed her backward toward the king-size bed in the room.

She was still facing me and said, "Fucking do it! Take me like you've been wanting to."

I started pulling her costume off her and I didn't do it gently either. I heard the fabric rip several times but I didn't care. I was going to get exactly what I'd been wanting and needing from this woman and in the manner that I'd been imagining.

She was standing completely naked in front of me now and I shoved her backward onto the bed, then jerked down my pants and sports briefs. I watched Stevie look down at my hard cock and lick her lips, and then she met my gaze again. Her eyes were smoldering and I could tell that she was as hungry as I was for what was about to happen here.

I moved to get on top of her and as soon as I did, I thrust my cock into her. Her mouth fell open and her eyebrows pulled together as if I'd hurt her, but then she closed her eyes and moaned.

"More," she breathed out, then I began fucking her without any restraint.

Little by little, I pushed Stevie across the bed with my body until her head was hanging off the other side. I held it in my hands and stared into Stevie's half-closed eyes as I kept pounding into her. When I started to cum, I buried my face in the crook of her neck and then bit the top of her shoulder. I didn't know why I did that other than I just felt the urge. Stevie winced but then she relaxed and kept moving her body beneath mine until I leaked everything from my body that I could into hers. When I was done, I collapsed beside her on the bed and we held each other while we caught our breaths.

"Are you okay?" I asked her.

"Yes."

"How do you feel?"

"Happy for you. You got exactly what you'd been needing."

"Yeah, I did. It's your turn now, though. What do you need me to do for you? Because you didn't cum."

Stevie reached up and took my face into her hands. "I need you to not fuck me."

"What do you need then? My mouth between your legs? My hand?"

"No. I need you to make love to me, Zac. I need you to take things slower than you ever have. I wanna breathe you in. I wanna feel your warm skin all over mine. I want your soul to take mine on a journey."

I looked over Stevie's face but didn't say anything. What I did do was lean closer and start kissing her, and I kept kissing her just like she needed me to. Then I moved into the next stage and the next of loving her body with mine.

Time escaped me, but by the time I made Stevie lose control, we were both breathless again and covered in sweat. Watching her arch her back and listening to all the sounds she was making sent me over the top again and while it was happening, we stared into each other's eyes. Stevie's soul and mine had just journeyed to a place that I wanted us to go to again. Half an hour later, we did.

Stevie and I didn't leave Bash's guest bedroom until this morning, after the sun had already come up. We both put back on most of the pieces of our costumes and then quietly walked down the hallway toward Bash's living room and dining area. The Moulin Rouge décor was still in place but all the empty trays that had catered food on them had been cleaned up, as well as the bar. I walked into the kitchen to see it in the same orderly state. Then Stevie and I went over to take a look at the back patio.

The red candles on the black-cloth tables had been blown out, the strings of white lights had been unplugged and there wasn't one empty bottle, can, or glass laying around anywhere. I was relieved that Bash's house hadn't been left in a mess by all the party guests. As wild as things had gotten by the time Stevie and I escaped to that guest bedroom to be alone, I thought for certain Bash's house was going to look like the movie set of "Animal House" this morning.

"Told you that you'd take Stevie to bed while you were here," Bash said, walking up behind us.

He was wearing a pair of pajama pants and no shirt. His hair was disheveled and his eyes looked tired, but he was smiling.

"Yeah, you did. Glad I didn't take your bet," I said and Stevie started laughing.

"You're such guys," she added. "Great party, though, Bash. I had a blast."

"A good time was had by all and that makes me happy. My God, you have a love bite on you." Bash reached out and lightly touched the top of Stevie's shoulder. "Damn, Buchanan. You turned into a vampire last night," he chuckled.

"I prefer wolf. Surprised you didn't hear me howling while I had this one in my den." I glanced over at Stevie and she shoved me on my arm.

"Oh, that was you?" Bash winked, then he waved me off. "How about I cook us some breakfast?"

"I appreciate it, man, but don't go to all that trouble. We're about to leave and I'm gonna stop by Whataburger for some taquitos, and then I'm gonna hang out at Stevie's until noon. Gotta pick up Malcolm then and take him home."

"I gotcha."

"Is everyone gone? I didn't look in the other guest bed-rooms."

"Yeah, everyone went home except for... Well, there's still one party guest here. He's passed out in my bed," Bash said, grinning.

"I don't need to know who he is."

"I wouldn't tell you anyway. I just needed him for last night because I needed a good fuck like you two did." Bash patted my cheek, kissed Stevie's, and then started walking toward his kitchen. "I've gotta get some coffee. Enjoy the day, my friends."

He wiggled his fingers over his shoulder at us to tell us goodbye, and then Stevie and I left Bash's house. On our way back to hers, she asked me about my best friend's past. She wanted to know if he'd ever had a serious partner.

"Yes, he did. They were together for five years, then they split up," I said.

"What caused it?"

"Bash's partner, Logan, was seeing someone else and Bash found out."

Stevie sighed. "That breaks my heart for him. He's such a great person."

"I know."

"Has he tried dating anyone since then?"

"Nothing serious. Just like what you saw back there at his house. He'll occasionally hook up with someone."

"Please tell me that he's careful about doing that."

"Careful in which way?"

"Two ways. Does he know the people he hooks up with and does he use protection?"

"Yes and yes."

"Good. It is a crazy world and I'd hate for something to happen to Bash."

"Really, don't worry. He takes all precautions when it comes to his lifestyle."

"I wish he could find someone worth loving and spending his life with."

"He does too, but he's not worried about it. He has the attitude that if it happens, then it happens. In the meantime, he's hellbent on enjoying life to the fullest."

"That's obvious. Bash is such an inspiration."

"And you're mine," I said, then kissed Stevie's hand. "I'll never forget last night with you. It was amazing."

She smiled. "Yeah, it was. We should get away like that more often. Well, we didn't really get away, but you know what I mean. We were able to be open about our relationship without worrying and it was so nice."

I looked over at Stevie again, grinned, and then looked back at the road.

"What?" she asked.

"Nothing. I just enjoy watching you is all."

That wasn't all, though. I was still trying to figure out a way to get this beautiful mermaid back to the ocean where she could be free with me again.

37
#time

Stevie

Zac left my house at 11:30 a.m. on Sunday to go pick up Malcolm from his parents. After the sweet boy went to bed that night, his daddy and I talked on the phone for almost an hour, going back over the highlights from Bash's party and also talking about us.

One of the things that Zac told me about us was that he didn't want to tell me goodbye anymore. He only wanted to tell me goodnight from now on, and to be able to do it with me lying next to him in bed. Not miles apart. We both knew that wasn't possible, though. At least not yet. But Zac and I were still clinging to our shared belief that a door was going to eventually open and give us our forever.

After making myself a cup of coffee on early Monday morning, I took a picture of it sitting beside Zac's empty cup on my kitchen counter. I was about to text him the picture to tell him that there was something very wrong with it when he texted me. It was a picture of him with his bottom lip stuck out like he was sad. The message that followed read: "Tha mi gad ionndrainn." I didn't know what it meant but as soon as I Googled it, I smiled at my handsome kinsman's message. In Scottish Gaelic, Zac was telling me that he missed me, and so much, I wanted to crawl through my phone and into his strong arms.

He and I didn't get to see each other on Monday or Tuesday but we did talk on the phone several times and sent dozens of texts back and forth during those two days. We even sent some sexy pics that we'd taken of ourselves for the other. My favorite selfie of Zac was the one of him facing his pool at night. All the underwater lights were on, and the angle gave me the perfect illuminated view of his blue eyes along with a view of his muscled chest, abs and the dark hair beneath his navel that trailed down to his big cock.

I'd been sitting at my desk at work, going over a case file, when Zac texted me that picture and I nearly dropped my phone when I saw it. It was the first completely nude one that he'd sent. It took me a minute to reply to him but when I did, I texted him a row of flaming red hearts—but that wasn't all. I'd been reserving a nude picture that I'd taken of myself while taking a bubble bath. The time was finally right to send it to Zac, and when I did, he responded by sending me a brief voice recording of himself saying "Fuck! You're torturing me, Sinclair!" and I just laughed. Turnabout was fair play.

On Wednesday, we were able to meet at the running trail after work. Zac got there before I did and was waiting for me in what we now called our "secret garden." It was a special place for both of us. We'd shared so much in the seclusion of those woods, and we did again on Wednesday when we had sex once more while laying on top of the soft grass. And like before, after Zac and I were done, he picked blades of grass out of my hair and brushed off my clothes, and then I did the same to him while we grinned at each other like two mischievous kids.

Thursday passed by in a flash but it didn't include seeing Zac again. Only taking care of my cases at the D.A.'s office, cleaning and treating my swimming pool after I got home from work, and then mowing my yard. It was while I was mowing the front yard that I had that feeling come over me again—that someone was watching me. I looked around and didn't see anyone at first, then spotted a car slowly making its way up my street, heading in my direction.

I didn't recognize it and didn't think anything else of it until it came to a complete stop in front of my house. I stopped mowing, took out my earbuds, and stared at the dark-tinted windows of the sporty red Audi. I kept thinking that surely the driver was going to roll down the window and ask for directions because they seemed to be lost, but they didn't. On my riding mower, I strained to see the face of the driver but I couldn't make out any detail because of those dark windows. The only visible thing was a partial silhouette and I could tell it was of a woman.

After a few more seconds of sitting on my mower, I got off and started walking toward the car. I wanted to find out what the driver's problem was, but before I could make it over to them, they sped off. I looked for the license plate but strangely, there wasn't one.

When the car turned the corner at the end of my street and then disappeared from my sight, I looked all around me and everything seemed normal in my neighborhood, as it had since I moved here. It was peaceful, and my neighbors on either side of my house and also across the street from me were all so friendly. I knew I'd eventually see them again, standing in their driveways or mowing their yards like I'd been doing, and I planned to ask them if they knew a woman who drove a red Audi with dark tinted windows. If one of them did then I was going to ask them to speak to their friend about their driving behavior, because it was cause for concern.

I was expecting Zac to call me around 9:00 p.m. but he called at 8:25 and it surprised me.

"Hey, you," I said. "You're calling me early."

"Yeah, Malcolm was extra tired this evening, so I got him fed, bathed, and was reading him a bedtime story, but he didn't make it halfway through it before he fell asleep. My mom got him outside in her flowerbeds with her today and worked him, and then my dad showed him the fine art of mowing a lawn." Zac chuckled and so did I.

"That's great that they're teaching him how to do all of that even at his young age."

"They started teaching me at the same age and it has served me well."

"Yes, it has. I've seen how manicured your yard and flowerbeds are. You really do have an artistic eye and a green thumb, Buchanan."

"So do you. I've checked out your yard and flowerbeds too."

"That's not all you've checked out."

Zac chuckled again. "You're right about that. I really like the way you keep certain parts of you landscaped."

"You do, huh?"

"Yes, I do."

"I'm happy to keep up the maintenance as long as you do. I know I've already told you this a dozen times but I really do love your beard. Of course, you look so handsome with or without it but there's something about you looking rugged that really gets to me. Plus, I love the way your beard feels."

"Between your legs?"

"I was gonna say when you kiss me but yes, between my legs too."

"Okay, we've gotta change the subject or I'm gonna have to ask you to have FaceTime sex with me again."

"I can do that."

"I know you can, and I may just take you up on that in a little while, but tell me about your evening first. Are you worn out from all the pool maintenance and mowing?"

"Not too badly."

"I hate that you have to do all that by yourself. I'd do every bit of it for you if I were there."

"No you wouldn't, because I'd be right beside you helping. We'd make a great team."

"We already do."

I smiled. "Yeah, we do. Hey, I wanna tell you about something that happened while I was mowing."

"Okay."

"I was in the front yard when a sporty red Audi stopped on the street directly in front of my house. The windows were tinted so I couldn't see who it was. Only a silhouette of a woman. I thought she might be lost and was gonna ask me for directions but she just kept sitting there, so I got off my mower to see what the problem was but the woman sped off before I could reach her. It was really strange. And I wanted to get the license plate number on the car, but there wasn't one. Anyway—I felt like I should tell you about what happened."

"May I call you back in a minute?"

"Sure."

"Okay, thanks."

While I was waiting, I pictured Malcolm walking into his daddy's room again and seeing him on the phone. If that was what had just happened, I guessed he hadn't asked Zac if he was talking to me again or asked to talk to me himself. I wished he would have. I hadn't talked to Malcolm on the phone since that one evening. He'd asked Zac about me a few times since then but that was it.

"Hey, you," I said, answering Zac's call. "Everything okay? Did Malcolm wake up?"

"No, he's still asleep."

The change in Zac's tone of voice was very apparent and it concerned me.

"What's wrong?"

"After you described that car and how the driver was acting, I checked to see where Avery was."

"Why?"

"Because she drives a sporty red Audi with tinted windows."

I gasped. "What the hell, Zac?"

"Don't worry. She's still in Lubbock. I just checked the app."

"Are you a hundred percent certain she's still in Lubbock?"

"Yes. And I apologize for getting off the phone a few minutes ago. What you told me about that car in front of your house threw me for a loop."

I sighed. "It did for me too, and so has finding out that Avery has the same kind of car. What are the odds?"

"Stevie, it's only a coincidence."

"Thank God that's all it is."

"How the driver of that car was acting still concerns me, though."

"It does me too and I plan to ask my neighbors if they know anyone who drives a red Audi. Whether they do or not, I'm gonna stay watchful. I swear, what happened at the Galleria parking lot and then this today has just..."

"Unnerved you to the max?"

"It's pissed me off more than anything and now, thinking about if that'd actually been Avery who stopped in front of my house earlier—well, I wouldn't have had a problem handling anything she dished out."

"I know you wouldn't have."

"My concerns, though, would've been how she knew where I lived, why she was at my house and what her next crazy move was gonna be."

"I thought you were gonna say you'd be worried that she'd found out about us."

"That's a given in all of this and the last thing that I want to happen because if she did find out, then I have no doubt she'd make things even more hellish on you—even though she has no right to cast one stone."

"She can't make it any worse than it already is."

"Oh, but she could, by deciding to file for divorce from you and also custody of Malcolm because of our affair."

"The way I feel about that is this: I dare her to go there. If she were to, then she'd have a legal war on her hands because I'd bring out not only all the evidence that I have of her volatile and adulterous behavior, but I'd also have Justin, Avery's immediate family, and her closest friends subpoenaed to court. Even though I still don't believe doing all of that would sway a judge to award me full custody of Malcolm, I would still fight until there was nothing left of me."

"I know you would fight until there was nothing left of you, Zac, but I don't want you to ever have to do that and the only way to keep it from happening is for Avery to not find out about you and me. I believe if she did, then she would file for divorce from you and custody of Malcolm. She'd do it to punish you because you fell out of love with her and in love with someone else who loves you unlike she ever could. She'd punish both of us but it'd ultimately be you and Malcolm who pay the price and I couldn't live with that. It would devastate me."

"Stevie, listen to me. Avery isn't gonna find out about us. She is caught up in her own world out there in west Texas and doesn't give a shit about mine and Malcolm's here in Dallas. Are you listening to me?"

I cleared my throat. "Yes, I'm listening."

"But do you hear me?"

"I do. I really do. I just wish Avery would go away for good. Don't misunderstand me. I don't wish her dead. Okay?"

"I know you don't. You're not that kind of person."

"I just want her to get on with living her fucked up life somewhere else and with someone else. Justin or whichever poor soul she can sucker into putting up with her bullshit. I don't care. I just want her to move on so that you and Malcolm can move on with your lives and live in peace. No more back and forth wondering if and when Avery is gonna come back home and start another war so she can run off to Lubbock yet again. It's such a messed up cycle."

"That has benefitted her and also allowed me to remain a full-time father to Malcolm. It's just the price that I have to pay for marrying Avery and also having a child with her."

"It's not the only price that's being paid."

"What do you mean?"

"I'm paying a high price for getting involved with you."

"For falling in love with me? Isn't that what you meant to say or did you forget that part?"

Zac's tone of voice had just gone to a stern level that I'd only heard him use once, and that was when he and I opposed each other on the Ferguson case in court. He wasn't standing in front of me where I could see his face but I already knew what his expression was like right now. His dark eyebrows were knotted up, his blue eyes were angry and his nostrils were flaring. And the expression on my face? It matched his, and not because of Zac's tone of voice. It was due to the last thing he'd asked me.

"I didn't forget anything," I said, biting back my anger.

"Well, to me, there's a big difference between saying you're involved with someone and saying you're in love with them. It's the difference between fucking them and making love to them."

"I'm well aware of that."

"Then tell me that you're in love with me and not just involved with me."

"No, I'm not telling you a damn thing because of how you're being about this. It's ridiculous and you knew exactly what I meant a minute ago."

I spat the words to Zac because I felt like he was backing me into a corner and trying to force me to say something that he already knew was true. I wasn't into this kind of dominance from him and would never tolerate it.

"So now you won't tell me that you're in love with me, now I'm ridiculous to you, and the price that you're paying for getting involved with me is high. Apparently too high for you."

"Zac..."

"Don't say another word to me, Stevie. I'm gonna end our phone call by telling you this: You're not the only one in this boat who's paying a high price for our involvement with each other *and* for falling in love. But if you feel the price that you're paying really is too costly, then all you gotta do is tell me. I'll jump overboard, babe, and let you sail on to a better life—a life that you certainly deserve."

I heard Zac hang up and all I could do was stare at my phone.

Maybe I should've seen it coming. Maybe I should've seen all of this between us escalating to the point that it just had, but

I didn't. Our conversation fell apart so fast. *We* fell apart so fast, and the pain that I was feeling in my chest hurt so much.

I didn't know what to do now. Zac and I wouldn't be talking to each other on the phone again tonight. I wasn't going to hear him say, "I love you, sweet dreams, goodnight, and goodbye," before I went to bed and he wasn't going to hear me say those words to him either. The only thing that we were going to sleep with was silence. Our shared silence stemming from our insecurities revisiting us along with our pain and anger. That was why we'd reacted to each other in such a defensive manner on the phone. Would we be able to work through this? I didn't know because we'd never been to this place of hurt with each other before. I hoped we could work through it but I knew myself well enough to know that I was going to need some time to myself first. Time to cool off and also reexamine my life.

38
#goingunder

Zac

Stevie was walking toward Bash and me at the Dallas court-house. We were all on the third floor; Bash and I had just left two different hearings and it appeared that Stevie was on her way to one. I didn't know for certain because I hadn't talked to her since I hung up on her last night. Our conversation got out of hand so quickly, and I never intended for things to take the negative turn that they did. Although I was more than ready to apologize to Stevie, I could tell by the tempest in her moody blue eyes right now that she wasn't ready to hear anything come from my mouth, so I would just wait until she lowered her sword.

"Hey, doll," Bash said to her as she approached.

"Hey, Bash. How are you?" Stevie's voice was flat and unemotional.

"I'm good. How about yourself?"

She looked straight at me.

"I'm fucking great," she said, keeping her eyes glued to mine until she'd walked past.

We stopped walking, turned around, and looked at Stevie, and then Bash pushed me on the arm.

"What the hell did you do?" he asked.

I sighed and shook my head. "It's too much to go into now."

"Whatever it is, you better fix it, Zac."

"I will."

"Now I understand why you've been such an edgy dick today. I just wish you'd told me what the deal was when I asked you what your problem was earlier."

"I wasn't ready to talk about it then and I'm still not."

"That's fine—but I'm here for you whenever you decide you are."

"I know and I appreciate it."

Bash stared hard at me. "Zac?"

"What?"

"Just take Joan of Arc to bed. Fight her there. It's what she wants and it's what you both need to make everything right. You've gotta get physically close again. Doing that will help heal the pain I see you two trying to hide."

I half-laughed. "First I've gotta get her to talk to me again. I need to apologize for some things that I said and did last night."

"Text her that apology and make it heartfelt."

"That won't be a problem."

"It'll open the door to the rest of what needs to happen."

I searched Bash's eyes, thinking about a door opening for Stevie and me. Yes, I wanted the one that Bash was talking about to open, but I was so ready for that one door to open that would let Stevie and me move beyond the baggage of my past and my present. The baggage of Avery.

My conversation with Stevie last night let me know exactly how tired she really was of the unfavorable circumstances surrounding our love affair. I didn't know if she intended to reveal that to me or if it just slipped out. Whatever the case, I hoped she still had it in her to keep holding on to us. I didn't want to jump out of the boat that we were in together but I would do it if that was what she believed was best for her. All I wanted was for Stevie to be happy and if it meant letting her go, then I would, even though I knew I'd drown without her.

I'd just left my last hearing of the day when I spotted Stevie ahead of me, standing to the side of the hallway. Her back was mostly to me but I could still see that she was looking over a file she was holding. Just like when I'd seen her earlier, I didn't know if she was about to go to a hearing or had just left one because we hadn't talked to each other. Either way, I was happy just getting to see her again.

I'd texted Stevie earlier and apologized for what I said to her during the last part of our conversation last night, as well as how I ended it. I also told her that if she wanted to talk more in-depth about everything then I was ready to do it. I didn't include an emoji of any kind at the end of my text although I'd been tempted to add a red heart. I just typed out the words while choking back my emotions and then waited for Stevie to reply, but she never did.

I'd almost reached her when she dropped her pen and I hurried to pick it up for her. When she turned around and saw me kneeling down on the floor with the pen in my hand, looking up at her, the expression on her face was one of total surprise. I didn't move and neither did she. We just kept staring at each other, and then I slowly stood back up and held out the pen toward her.

"Thank you," she whispered. As she was taking it from me, I noticed her hand was trembling.

"You're welcome."

We again stared at each other without saying anything but Stevie's eyes were speaking volumes to me. It wasn't just the "I'm happy to see you" look in them but also the tears brimming in them. They matched mine.

"I love you and I wanna tell you in person that I'm sorry for last night," I continued.

Stevie glanced around us like she was worried that some-one might've heard me but I wasn't worried about it. I didn't give a damn. I wouldn't care if every person in this building had heard what I just said to this beautiful woman standing in front of me.

"Same here," she breathed.

"Are you going to or leaving a hearing?"

"Leaving. I'm done for the day."

"Me too. Will you meet me at my office?"

Stevie paused, then slowly nodded yes.

"It's time you saw it," I went on to say.

"I agree."

"Text me a couple of minutes before you pull into the parking garage. I'll meet you there."

"Okay."

"Do you have someone meeting you here to walk you out to your car?"

"Yes, Jason is."

"If you don't mind, let him know that I'm here and will handle it."

Stevie sent a quick text to Jason and then looked back up at me. "He told me to tell you thanks. We can go now."

On our way to the elevators, Stevie and I walked closer to each other than we ever had while here at the courthouse. We didn't say anything, though. We just kept stealing glances at one another. After our elevator arrived, we got on and stood at the back behind all the other occupants. Stevie and I were side by side, only inches apart, and I could now smell the vanilla scent on her skin.

I closed my eyes and took a deep breath just to inhale her again, then felt her head on my shoulder. I glanced down at her to see a soft smile on her sparkly lips and then I smiled too. Moments later, I felt Stevie's fingertips lightly touch my hand and I seized that opportunity to hold hers. I didn't let go until after we'd reached the first floor.

As Stevie and I were walking to her car, I kept a close eye on our surroundings and made mental notes of everyone I saw but none of the people gave me cause for concern. Their behavior was normal and the people that we passed by were all polite.

After Stevie got into her car, I closed the driver's side door then she lowered the window and looked up at me.

"Thank you for keeping me safe," she said.

"I'm happy to."

"Come here for just a sec."

Stevie waved me over to her and when I leaned down to see what she needed, she surprised me by grabbing me by my tie and pulling me the rest of the way to her. Then she kissed me. It was slow, soft and so warm, and when she stopped, I leaned my forehead against hers.

"I needed that," I whispered.

"Same here. I'll meet you at your office, Buchanan."

My office was on the twenty-first floor of one of the high-rise buildings in downtown Dallas. Stevie met me in the underground parking garage, parking next to my Blazer, and the two of us walked to the elevator. As we were getting on, Stevie asked me about my secretary and paralegal. She wanted to know if they were still at work since it was only a little after four.

"No, I told them to go on home. They're on salary so it's all good," I said.

"Okay then."

Stevie and I were alone on this elevator ride but we held back from even holding hands. Without talking about it, she knew as well as I did what would get started if we touched each other again right now. And that didn't need to happen until we were behind secure closed doors.

On my floor, I unlocked the office door and then locked it behind Stevie and me. She began walking around the front area, looking at everything, and I just kept looking at her.

"This is a really nice workspace for your employees. Lots of room. Where is *your* office, though?" she asked and I nodded in its direction.

"Are you sure you wanna see it?"

Stevie's gaze trickled down to my mouth. "I'm sure."

"Then come with me."

After walking into my personal workspace, I stood back again and watched Stevie check out everything inside the room. She went over to my desk first and ran her fingertips across the top, then lightly touched the paperwork that I had sitting there. My high-back executive chair came next and then my library of law books. Stevie also took the time to look at the pictures of Malcolm and me that were displayed on my walls. She didn't say a word—but her smile did.

After that, she walked over to my round bar cart, which had a bottle of Hendricks gin sitting on top of it and also a set of Copa gin glasses, then opened my mini fridge, where I had tonic water, limes, and ice. Stevie smiled again then headed toward my couch and coffee table. While she was checking them out, my pride continued surging because of her obvious interest in where I worked and also her respect for the job I did.

The one and only time that Avery had come here, she gave my office a quick once-over, shrugged her shoulders at me, and was then ready to leave. She didn't care about anything other than the fruits of all my labor.

I was still standing by my door watching Stevie when she stopped and looked at me from across the room. She was in front of my picture window and the sunlight streaming in through it was illuminating everything about her but especially her deep blue eyes with those little gold flecks in them.

"Zac, I love it here," she said, smiling once more.

"Thank you."

"This space is so you. It even smells like you."

"I hope that's a good thing."

"It is. You decorated your entire office space, didn't you?"

"Yes."

"Well, if you ever get tired of practicing law then you'd make one hell of an interior decorator."

We both laughed, and then I asked Stevie if she'd like to have a Hendricks and tonic with extra lime.

"Only if you're having one," she said.

"I am. I need it."

"Why do you need it?"

"My nerves."

"Why are you nervous?"

"Because you're here with me like this. Stevie, I again wanna tell you..."

"Stop right there. Don't say anything else about last night because there's no need to. You and I both know why we took our conversation where we did. We both know the hurtful things of our past that plague our present. We also know what we need to do to keep those things from affecting our relationship again. I'm not like anyone in your past, nor are you like anyone in mine. We need to remind ourselves of that every day but especially when we feel those tentacles of our past trying to pull us down *and* apart."

I nodded in agreement. "If you ever get tired of practicing law, you'd make one hell of a therapist."

Stevie laughed again but I kept a straight face and she noticed.

"What is it?" she then asked.

"I need to make love to you."

"What if I need you to just fuck me right now? What if I want it hard and fast?"

"You know I can do that and do it well, but do you know... Do you *really* know what you mean to me? Do you *really* know how deeply in love with you that I am?"

"Yes. Do you *really* know that I feel the exact same way about you?"

"I do."

"Then come over here and fuck me, Buchanan."

I reached for my tie to loosen it at the same time that Stevie began unbuttoning her blouse. I helped her finish taking off her clothes while she helped me finish taking off mine. My tie, suit coat, shirt, belt, pants, sports briefs, dress shoes and socks were scattered across my office floor along with Stevie's blouse, bra, pencil skirt and high heels. We were completely naked and she had her arms wrapped around my neck, her legs around my waist, her lips on mine, my hands grabbing her ass, her back pressed against the picture window—and I was fucking her hard and fast.

Stevie pulled her lips away from mine, leaned her head against the glass and closed her eyes while I kept thrusting myself into her. About a minute later, I carried her over to my desk and pushed every piece of paperwork off it and also my lamp. As soon as it all hit the floor, I laid Stevie down on top of my desk and continued giving her what she'd requested from me.

"I'm about to cum, Zac. Oh my God," she breathed against my face.

Then I felt Stevie's pussy tighten around my cock, saw her arch her back and heard her start moaning. And like all the other times, that was all it took to send me over the top along with her. We came together and after it was over, I relaxed my body on top of Stevie's while she kept her arms and legs wrapped around me.

"Make-up sex with you is the best," she whispered in my ear and I started laughing. So did Stevie.

"I'm glad you enjoyed it."

"Did you?"

I raised my head and looked at my lover. "You know I did."

"I wish we could stay here all night."

"We could—but we could also stay at your house if you want."

"Your mom and dad are keeping Malcolm tonight?"

"Yes."

"And there's another open door for us to be together."

"I know."

"Then you need to go pack an overnight bag and get your fine ass over to my house."

"What are you gonna do with me when I get there?"

"It's what *you're* gonna do with me."

I grinned. "Okay. What do you want me to do with you?"

"You're gonna have a Hendricks and tonic with me since we never got around to having one here at your office. You're also gonna eat dinner with me and it's gonna be pizza tonight. Then you're gonna slow dance with me on my back patio while we listen to Norah Jones."

"Can we listen to Hozier too?"

"We sure can and after that, you're going swimming with me."

"Anything else?"

"There is one more thing, but it's something that I'm gonna do *to* you."

I side-eyed Stevie, unsure of where she was going with this conversation. "Should I be concerned?"

"No. Not at all."

"Then what are you gonna do *to* me?"

"You just gave me what I needed and later this evening, I'm gonna do the same for you. I'm gonna make love to you while we're in my pool. I needed you hard and fast this time and you still need me slow and easy. And you know I can do that well."

"Yes, I do know."

"This mermaid is gonna pull you under to her bed again and give you her treasure trove."

"And I can hardly wait."

39
#firsttime

Stevie

"Do you know what today is?" Zac asked me. It was Saturday morning, we'd been awake for about five minutes and we were still tangled up with each other in my bed.

"September twenty-second, the first day of autumn. Time to put out all my Halloween decorations, plant some mums and buy some candy corn to munch on."

"Besides that," Zac chuckled.

"Um, there's not anything else."

"Sure there is. It was eight weeks ago today that I saw you for the first time."

I smiled. "And I saw you for the first time."

"But there's more that I've kept up with. Wanna hear it?"

"Yes."

"It was fifty days ago that we officially met, forty-one days since our first kiss, forty days since we had sex the first time, forty days since we fell asleep in each other's arms the first time, and thirty-eight days since we said I love you to each other the first time. And I did not mean to make you cry, Stevie," Zac said, hugging me even tighter.

I buried my face in his chest for a few seconds then looked back up and smiled at him again through tears. Happy and grateful tears.

"You are so sentimental," I said.

"About some things, and you are definitely one of them."

"Has it really only been eight weeks since we saw each other on the running trail that first time?"

"Yes."

"It feels like it's been so much longer than that, and I mean it in such a wonderful way because our little bit of time together has been so wonderful."

Zac and I kept staring into each other's eyes, and the longer that I stared into his, the fuller my heart was becoming and I didn't think it could get any fuller. I just kept falling more and more in love with this man beside me. This man whose soul, I knew, had traveled through time with mine so we could love each other again here on earth. That was what my mom used to say about my dad. I never really understood the full scale of what she meant and why she felt so strongly about it but now, I did. Now, I whole-heartedly believed in past lives, all because Zac and I had crossed paths.

He reached up and ran his thumb across my bottom lip, then leaned his head down and kissed me. "*Wonderful* doesn't quite cover what our time together has been like. I'm adding amazing, extraordinary, blissful, heavenly. I could go on and on."

"So could I."

After that sweet moment, Zac and I got up out of bed to have coffee together on my back patio. The mornings were noticeably cooler now and this morning, in particular, was a lot cooler. When Zac saw my arms and legs covered in goosebumps, he grabbed two beach towels out of the storage bench, wrapped one of them around my shoulders and back, and draped the other one over my legs.

"Better?" he asked, grinning at me.

"A lot better. Thanks."

"You're welcome. The mermaid in you is gonna freeze by the time November gets here."

"That's what the heater in my swimming pool is for. It'll get me by until summer comes back around. And how are you not the least bit chilly right now?" I asked Zac, looking him over.

He'd just sat back down in the chair across from me and was only wearing a pair of cargo shorts and his sports briefs underneath them. I'd never seen him in any kind of shorts other than running ones but I really liked the ones he had on now. The tan color went so well with his tan skin.

"I'm just not. It feels great out here to me," he said, shrugging his shoulders.

"It's the Scotsman in you."

"You have just as much Scottish blood running through your veins, so what's the deal, Sinclair?"

"Warm weather preference is what my deal is."

Zac chuckled, then grabbed his cellphone off the table. I watched him scroll his fingertip across the screen.

"Do you mind if I play a song for you?" he asked, looking back up at me.

"So that's what you were doing. You were searching for a song. And no, I don't mind. Are you about to romance me with some Hozier again?"

"Not this time. I've got another song in mind, but it's an older one. A lot older. I'm curious if you know it."

"Then push play."

"Okay. Here we go."

Only a few seconds into the song's intro and I recognized it.

"Two Tickets to Paradise by Eddie Money! Another classic rock goodie."

"Yes, it is. And how do you know this song?"

I smiled. "My mom, of course."

Zac and I got quiet and just kept looking at each other while listening to the song, but after the chorus had played one time, Zac turned off the music.

"What are you doing?" I asked.

He didn't answer me. But the corners of his mouth were curled up and his eyes had mischief in them now.

"I wanna give something to you," he finally said, reaching into the pocket of his cargo shorts. Then he held up an envelope.

"A letter?"

"Not yet, but it's coming."

"I'm confused."

"Here. Just open *this* envelope first."

Zac handed it to me, and I looked at the front of it but didn't see any kind of writing. Then I flipped it over and still, there was nothing to clue me in about what was inside the envelope. I looked back over at Zac and sighed.

"Okay, you've got me feeling nervous about this."

"There's no reason to be. Just open it—and I hope you say yes."

I kept my eyes on him while thinking about the now obvious set-up here that I recognized. Whatever this was about, Zac had planned it step by step and it included those cargo shorts of his because of the pockets, the song by Eddie Money and whatever was inside this envelope that I was still holding. As soon as I opened it, took out its contents and read what was printed on them, my jaw dropped.

"Oh my God, you did not," I said, looking back up at Zac.

"Yeah, I did."

He was smiling that big, dimpled smile of his while I sat in stunned silence. When I finally opened my mouth to speak, I closed it again because I still didn't know what to say about the two airline tickets that I was holding in my hand. Two tickets to the paradise of Destin, Florida.

"Stevie, will you go with me?" Zac asked.

"I-I... You know I want to but I can't take off from work next week. That's not enough notice for Brooke. Wait. The date?" I said, looking at the tickets again. "Shit! Our flight to Destin is today!"

"I know it is."

"Zac!"

"Stevie."

"There's no way that I can go. I'm gonna cry—I've dreamed of going to that beach with you."

"No, no, no. Don't cry," he said, holding up his hands. Then he walked over and kneeled down in front of me. "Here you go."

He was holding another envelope, and then he gave it to me. This one had a letter in it, and it was handwritten, short, sweet, to the point...and it was from Brooke. She told me to have fun in Destin with my exception and to not worry about my cases. My team had them covered.

I dropped my head when I finished reading what Brooke had written and started crying happy and grateful tears again. Zac cupped my face in his hands, then raised it up and looked straight at me.

"Beautiful mermaid of mine, will you let me take you to the ocean for a week?"

I took a deep breath, then choked out, "Yes."

Tears were still rolling down my cheeks, my bottom lip was quivering and my body was trembling. Zac saw and felt it all, then pulled me into his arms. After a couple of minutes, I'd composed myself and sat back in my chair while Zac kneeled back down in front of me.

"I had no idea all of this would have such an effect on you, Stevie."

"Well, it's a dream come true. You and I get to be together. Just us for a whole week, and we get to be open about it too. We can walk up and down the beach while holding hands, we can go swimming in the ocean and kiss each other. We can sit in a restaurant, order two Hendricks and tonics with extra lime, share a delicious meal or go do anything that we wanna do without any restrictions or worry. So yes, I'm greatly affected by this gift from you. Thank you so much for doing this, Zac. I still can't believe it."

He smiled while wiping off my face. "I was determined to make it happen because I knew you needed this as much as I did."

"But what about your court cases?"

"I rescheduled the hearings."

"What are you gonna do about sweet Malcolm?"

"I talked to my parents days ago about watching him so that you and I could get away together and they were immediately on board."

"You've never been away from Malcolm for a week."

"He'll be fine. My mom and dad love and spoil him just like I do."

"You are something else, Buchanan."

"So are you."

"When did you talk to Brooke about all of this? And when did you buy these tickets?"

"Wednesday, for both. I'd already planned to surprise you like this but after our conversation on Thursday night, I was really worried that this was all gonna be for nothing. But then it worked out. *We* worked out. Another door opened."

"Yeah, it did."

"So go pack your bags, your suitcase, or whatever you need to take with you, Sinclair. We've gotta be at the airport in two hours."

"What?"

"Two hours."

"Wait!" I said, looking at our tickets again. "Shit! I cannot see or think straight right now!"

"You better get moving."

"What about your bags?"

"They're already in the back of my Blazer."

I sighed out a smile, then Zac stood up in front of me and held out his hand for me to take. I set the airline tickets and Brooke's letter on the table, got up from my chair, wrapped my arms around Zac's neck and kissed him.

"Before you start packing, I've got one more surprise for you," he said, grinning at me again. "I was gonna wait until after we got to Destin to give it to you but something told me that I should give it to you before we leave."

Zac pulled out another envelope from one of the pockets on his cargo shorts and handed it to me. My reaction upon opening was the same as when I saw the two airline tickets. Zac was taking me to see Norah Jones in concert while we were in paradise.

40
#wavesofblue

Zac

Stevie and I took my car to the Dallas/Fort Worth International Airport but after parking and unloading our luggage, we began acting like we didn't know each other. While riding the shuttle over to our gate, we sat at opposite ends. After reaching our gate, we got off the shuttle at different times, and then Stevie walked ahead of me into the airport.

At the baggage check-in, I stood in line several yards away from her and did the same while we went through security. We had to take precautions like this in case we ran into someone we knew. I wasn't concerned about it but Stevie was and insisted we continue playing it safe while in the Dallas public eye. This charade of ours would continue until we boarded our plane. Then we'd be free to be *us*.

We were in the waiting area now, along with all the other passengers who were on our flight. Stevie was sitting in one of the chairs, looking at a magazine, and I was standing by the window, watching planes take off and land. We kept randomly looking over at each other and neither of us could keep from grinning. There was something about acting like we didn't know each other that was intriguing and also fun.

When passengers began boarding the plane, I went ahead of Stevie this time and then waited for her to join me in first class. Almost ten minutes had passed and she still hadn't shown up. I wondered what the deal was—if Stevie had actually run into someone she knew or if something else had happened. I'd just stood up from my seat to go check on her when she stepped onto the plane. I sighed in relief and smiled at her but her smile was a nervous one now. Extremely nervous. So were her eyes. When she reached me, I asked her if she was okay.

"I just need to sit down," she said.

I stepped aside so she could take her seat by the window, then sat down beside her.

"Stevie, what's wrong? Your whole demeanor has changed."

"You're gonna think I'm silly."

"Silly about what?"

"Flying makes me so fucking nervous," she whispered, glancing around the cabin.

"I didn't know that. Why didn't you say something to me about it before now?"

"Because I thought I could handle it this time."

"So you get nervous like this every time you fly somewhere?"

"Yes."

"Come here," I chuckled, then hugged Stevie to me. "You're gonna be fine.

"I really wish I could have a gin and tonic."

"I really wish you could too, but there's not enough time before our departure. As soon as we're in the air though, I'll order one for you *and* me."

"Sounds great."

"You know, there is something else we could do to help you relax. There's still enough time for that."

Stevie leaned back in her seat, looked up at the ceiling, and then shook her head at herself. "I can't believe I let you talk me into putting this thing inside me."

I chuckled again. "I didn't talk you into doing anything, Sinclair. You were all for having some pre-flight fun until you got onto the plane."

"I know, I know. Jesus."

"What'd you do to ease your nerves when you traveled before?"

"Had a gin and tonic. One before the plane took off and then a couple more while in the air."

"Well, again, you having one before we take off isn't an option, so let me take care of you in the other way. I know it'll relax you."

I searched Stevie's still-nervous eyes and then finally, she nodded yes. I grabbed my cellphone from out of my shorts pocket and opened the wireless vibrator app so I could turn on the vibrator that was currently inside Stevie's pussy. It was one of a few sex toys that we'd gotten and really enjoyed playing with. I especially liked this one because even when Stevie and I were miles apart, I could still make her cum and I could also watch her do it via FaceTime. We'd done that on several occasions while lying in our beds. I'd also gotten her off while I sat behind my office desk and she sat behind hers—both with our office doors locked, of course.

Through the app, I was able to create my own vibration patterns by moving my fingertip across my phone screen, up and down, or in a circle that rotated all the different speeds. I knew the pattern that would make Stevie cum the quickest and was about to implement it because we didn't have much time before one of the flight attendants told everyone they needed to turn off their cellphones.

As soon as Stevie closed her eyes, I began drawing circles in slow motion on my phone screen and continued doing that for about a minute while listening to Stevie's breathing deepen. Then I moved my fingertip to medium speed and held it there. When Stevie pushed her hands against the tops of her thighs, I put the vibrator speed on high and watched Stevie's legs start to tremble. I knew she was about to come undone but she was going to have to do it without making a sound.

When I saw her lips part and the slight jerks of her body, I knew she was orgasming. It went on for several seconds and after it ended, I turned off the vibrator, Stevie relaxed against her seat and took a deep breath. She still had her eyes closed when a flight attendant walked up and looked across me at Stevie. Then she leaned down and quietly asked me if she was okay.

"Yes, she just gets really nervous before takeoff. She'll be fine as soon as we get in the air," I said, trying hard to keep a straight face.

The flight attendant nodded at me, patting my shoulder, then walked off. I looked over at Stevie to see her grinning at me. We leaned into each other and shared a quiet laugh because of what we'd just gotten away with doing and could've so easily been caught doing. It was another one of those shared rushes between us that we couldn't seem to get enough of.

"Better now?" I asked her.

"So much better. Thank you."

"Any time."

"We're crazy," she chuckled.

"I love our kind of crazy."

"So do I."

"You need to use the restroom now, don't you?"

"Yes. I wanna take this thing out of me and also get cleaned up."

"A little wet, huh?"

"Like you need to ask?"

I smiled at Stevie and then leaned in for a quick kiss. "No, I don't need to ask. I know your body inside and out."

"Like I know yours."

"Yes, you do."

Stevie glanced around the cabin. "I don't think there's enough time."

"There is if you hurry."

"Okay."

I stood up to move out of Stevie's way and while she was stepping past me, she brushed the back of her hand across the front of my shorts. It was her way of letting me know that she'd seen how aroused I was from getting her off. My erection was going away but I still had a good-size bulge that I knew Stevie's eyes wouldn't miss.

As soon as she sat back down beside me, we both buckled up. Although I'd given Stevie quite a bit of nerve relief, I wasn't sure if it was enough to get her through takeoff. But as the plane lifted into the air, she was calm as ever. She was smiling at me, too, while holding my hand. We were finally on our way to paradise. We were really doing this.

On the flight, Stevie asked me where we were staying in Destin, but I wouldn't tell her. I wanted it to be a total surprise and knew she was going to love the private beach house that I'd rented. It was really nice and spacious and sat so close to the ocean that I knew if Stevie and I slept with the patio doors open in the master bedroom we'd be able to smell the salty air and feel the breeze.

After landing at the Destin-Fort Walton Beach Airport, we picked up our luggage and then our rental car and headed to the beach house. As I was pulling into the driveway, Stevie gasped.

"Oh—my—God. Zac! This beach house is huge!"

"I know. I wanted lots of room for you and me and also lots of privacy. We can do anything we want within the walls of this place and also outside of them."

After lowering the garage door, we walked into the rental. I was already familiar with the layout from all the online pictures I'd studied, so I led Stevie into the open living and dining area first. Like the rest of this beach house, the color palette here was aqua, white, and a soft sandy color. Perfect for the beautiful mermaid that I was currently watching walk around while looking at everything in complete silence.

When she made it over to the back patio doors, she pushed them open and went outside, then she gazed out at the ocean. I walked up behind her, wrapped my arms around her waist and kissed her cheek.

"Are you home now?" I asked.

"Yes, I am. Thank you so much for doing all of this, Zac."

"It's my pleasure. I want you to be happy."

"I would be happy if we stayed in a tent on the beach all week because I would be with you."

"Same here. But I wanted you to have the best for this first trip of ours. I wanted it to be one for the books—one that you'll never forget."

Stevie looked over her shoulder at me. "I will never forget this trip with you or anything else that we've done together. I love you so much."

"I love you too. Now, are you ready to see the rest of this place?"

"This amazing place? Yes."

After covering the beach level and then the second level, we began unpacking our luggage. While hanging up our clothes together in the closet, placing our shoes side by side, putting our undergarments and swimsuits together in the dresser drawers, and organizing our toiletries in the bathroom, Stevie and I kept glancing at each other and smiling. What we were doing felt so right. It felt natural like we were supposed to be doing this and should've been doing this a long time ago in a home that we shared.

When we were done with all the unpacking, I asked Stevie what she wanted to do next.

"Go swim in the ocean with you," she said, looking straight at me and never more serious.

Although this property included a swimming pool and also a hot tub, I wasn't surprised that Stevie had paid no attention to them. She would later, when nighttime arrived, but for now she needed to be in the warm, salty water of the Gulf of Mexico, and she wanted me with her too.

We changed into our swimsuits and then started making our way to the shoreline, which was only about fifty yards away from our beach house. When Stevie took off running, I just watched her go. I'd never seen her come more alive than she was being here. The ocean really was her home.

When she reached the water, she waded in up to her knees and lifted her arms toward the sky, then leaned her head back. Moments later, she turned around and looked at me. I'd just made it to the shoreline and was still videoing my lover with my cellphone.

"Come on," she said, smiling from cheek to cheek.

I tossed our two towels and my phone onto the sand and then met Stevie where she was. After grabbing hands, the two of us walked further out into the water and then dove in. It was clear and as blue as the sky above us.

I didn't know how far we swam but when we stopped, I tried to stand up and was still able to. My shoulders were above the water and my feet were anchored in the sand while Stevie treaded water in front of me.

"Doesn't this feel so good?" she asked.

"Yes."

"I can't believe we're really here. This feels like a dream, Zac."

"Come here to me."

I pulled Stevie into my arms and started kissing her. She wrapped herself all around me and I just held onto her that much tighter as soft wave after soft wave met us. We weren't only breathless from the swimming but also from what we were doing now. Our kiss kept getting more heated and my cock kept getting harder with every passing second. Then Stevie pulled away and looked at me.

"What is it?" I asked, searching her eyes.

"Take me right here and right now."

"I can do that."

"Then do that, Buchanan."

I smiled, Stevie smiled, and then we both took off our swimsuits but kept them in our tight grasps. The last thing that needed to happen was for a wave to sweep them away from us and then leave us with no choice but to run back to our beach house only wearing our skin.

As soon as Stevie wrapped her legs around my waist again, I grabbed onto hers and then pushed her body down on top of my cock at the same time that I thrust myself into her. She didn't close her eyes or lean her head back while moaning this time. She just kept watching what I was doing. She watched me as I fucked her in this warm, salty water—looking back and forth from my face to my cock sliding in and out of her pussy.

"The look in your eyes and the way you move your body when we're having sex is the biggest turn-on," she breathed out.

"Same goes to you."

"How good are you feeling at this very moment?"

"So damn good. How about you?"

"So damn good."

"I'm gonna start fucking you harder *and* faster now."

"And you're gonna make me cum when you do."

"That was the plan, babe."

I grabbed onto her waist even tighter and started doing exactly what I'd said I was going to do. Less than a minute later, I watched this mermaid that I'd captured and was in love with lose complete control of herself while she watched me do the same. When it was over, I held her in my arms while breathing in the paradise of her and never wanting to let her go.

41
#ink

Zac

"How painful was it to get your tattoo?" Stevie asked me.
"It wasn't too bad. After a while, I couldn't feel anything. It was like my skin grew numb to the needle."

Stevie brushed her fingertips across my chest where my tattoo of Malcolm's footprints and his birthdate were.

"Have you ever thought about getting another one?"

"No. If I ever did, though, it'd have to be as meaningful as this one that I already have—or close to it."

Stevie chewed at her bottom lip while looking at the ink on my chest again. "Would you take me to get a tattoo today?" she asked, surprising the hell out of me.

"Are you serious?"

"Yes."

"I'd be happy to take you. I'm sure there are plenty of tattoo parlors here in Destin but Stevie... You're *really* serious about getting one?"

"I am."

"What made you want to?"

"You. Me. Being here. I want something symbolic of us on my skin."

I looked at Stevie's naked body lying next to mine. It was Sunday morning and we were still in bed inside the master bedroom of our beach house. The sun was shining and the ocean breeze was blowing in through the open patio doors.

"Do you know where you want it?"

"Here," she said, touching just below her left collarbone.

"Okay. That shouldn't be too painful."

"I'm not worried about the pain."

I searched Stevie's sleepy blue eyes and then shook my head at her. "I can't believe you really wanna do this."

"Well, believe it."

"You already know what you want, don't you?"

"I do."

"What?"

"Scottish thistle."

As soon as those two words left her mouth, I knew what I was going to have to do.

"If you're gonna get our motherland's emblem inked onto your skin, then I'm getting it inked onto mine too."

"No, Zac, you don't have to do that. If Scottish thistle doesn't mean as much to you as Malcolm's tattoo, then please don't get it. Don't do it just because I am."

"But it does mean as much now that I think about it. You said you want something symbolic of us, and there's no better choice than Scottish thistle," I said, sitting up in bed. I was getting more and more excited with every passing second.

"Okay, but..."

"Stevie, I wanna do this with you. It means a lot that you asked me to take you to get your first tattoo and it means a lot that we'd both have one that reminds us of us every time we look at it."

"I don't think you're gonna want the one that I found online last night while you were sleeping. It's really feminine looking."

I reached for Stevie's cellphone on the nightstand and handed it to her. "Show me what you found."

She was right about the tattoo design being feminine looking. The dainty sprig of thistle had a green stem, a delicate purple flower, and appeared to be about three inches in length. It would look amazing on Stevie but not on me.

"That one is perfect for you. I'm about to start looking for a Scottish thistle tattoo that would fit me."

"Can I help you look for it?"

"Of course you can! I want your input. We're doing this together, babe."

"Zac, this is gonna be so much fun."

"I know."

"I'm gonna go make us some coffee and you start looking for a tattoo. I'll be right back."

"Okay."

I leaned over and kissed Stevie. Then she got up out of bed and just like she'd done so many times before at her house when I was there—she walked out of the bedroom naked as the day she was born. I couldn't keep from smiling either.

"What do you think?" Stevie asked me.

"I love it! It is *you*. It's beautiful."

"Ma'am, I need to get you bandaged up," Eddie told her.

He was the owner of the tattoo parlor where Stevie and I had been for hours and had tattooed Stevie's Scottish thistle below her left collar bone.

"You did such a great job. Thank you," she told him.

"I aim to please. Now come on and have a seat."

Stevie sat back down in his chair and I stayed where I was. We'd been side by side all this time while Eddie worked on Stevie and his brother, Tyler, worked on me. He was still working on me, too, because my tattoo was large.

As soon as Stevie and I had seen the online picture of an all-black Scottish thistle overlaid with a Celtic design, we both knew that was the tattoo for me, and Tyler had about an hour to go before he finished it. The same as when I got Malcolm's tattoo, I couldn't feel the needle going into my skin any longer. My right bicep was numb.

I took a picture of Stevie's new ink before Eddie bandaged it and after Tyler finished mine, Stevie returned the favor. Then she texted Bash the two pictures from my cellphone along with, "Look at what we did!"

Bash didn't text back. He called, and when Stevie answered my phone, she started laughing. I could only imagine what Bash was saying to her. I knew he would love what Stevie and I had done. I also knew it was going to make him want to get another tattoo.

"You do know we can't go swimming in the ocean or the pool now. We have to keep our thistles bandaged and clean for three days," I told Stevie.

"Um, we can get in the water a little. Like up to here." She held her hand in front of her chest.

"We'll have to be really careful, though."

"We will be."

I was right about my estimation of when Tyler would be done with me and after Stevie and I got back into our rental car, we looked at each other and smiled.

"We really just did this," I said.

"I know. It's permanent too."

"I want it to be. I want you to be permanent."

"Same here."

"What would you like to go do now?"

"Get something to eat. I'm surprised you didn't hear my stomach growling in there," Stevie said, looking back at the tattoo parlor.

"Well, they had music playing, so..."

"Are you hungry?"

"I can always eat. What sounds good to you?"

"Seafood."

"You mean you wanna eat your brethren, Miss Mermaid?"

Her mouth fell open like she was so offended but then she started laughing. "You're damn straight I'll eat them!"

"Then let's go feast."

I took Stevie to a restaurant called The Back Porch. It was on the beach and the atmosphere and service were great. The smorgasbord of seafood that Stevie and I ordered was too. We had everything: Mahi, shrimp, scallops, crab cakes. And our drinks? Two Hendricks and tonic with extra lime.

Stevie and I had just finished eating when my mom texted me to see how we were doing. I told Stevie what she'd said, then motioned for our waitress to come over to our table.

"Would you mind taking a picture of us?" I asked her.

"Not at all, sir."

I handed her my cellphone with the camera app ready to go, and she snapped several pictures of Stevie and me sitting at the table with the sunny Destin, Florida beach in the background. I texted my mom the photos and let her know that Stevie and I were having a blast. While waiting for her reply, I asked Stevie if she minded me sending her the pictures of our tattoos.

"You may as well. She's gonna see them when we get back. Of course, she'll see yours first and hopefully mine in the near future. Do you think she'll like them, though?"

"She'll love them. So will my dad."

"Then send the pictures. I can't wait to hear what her response is."

My mom texted back three smiley face emojis after she received the pictures the waitress had taken, and sent a row of Scottish flags and red hearts after seeing our Scottish thistle tattoos. My mom also texted that she and my dad were proud of our new ink and that they loved it.

I asked my mom how Malcolm was doing and she let me know what I already knew: he was doing great. I'd briefly talked to him on the phone last night, before his bedtime, and I planned to do the same tonight and also on the rest of the nights that Stevie and I were here in Destin. I'd told Malcolm that I was out of town working and he didn't question it. I worked all the time, so that was nothing new to him. Just being apart from me during the morning and evening was. I missed my mini-me but I was also at peace knowing what good hands he was in with my parents.

After Stevie and I left the restaurant, we agreed it would be good to take a nap as soon as we got back to our beach house since the Norah Jones concert didn't start until 9:00 p.m. The venue was a smaller one with an intimate setting and limited seats. I'd lucked out by being able to purchase front-row tickets and could hardly wait to make this memory with Stevie.

She and I woke up totally refreshed after an hour's nap and were ready to take on the night. While we were getting ready for the concert, Stevie played a variety of Norah Jones' songs on her cellphone. She kept smiling too while randomly dancing around in the bathroom and bedroom. I loved watching her move her body. It really was like poetry in motion.

I wore a pair of tan chino pants with a white t-shirt and a denim button-down shirt over it that I left unbuttoned, and my shoes were a pair of comfortable white sneakers. Stevie wore a light blue spaghetti-strap dress that reached the tops of her knees and her shoes were some blingy light blue sandals. When she came walking out of the bathroom, dressed and ready to go, all I could do was stare at the vision of her. She was breathtaking as always.

When we got to our seats at the concert, Stevie looked all around us and just kept smiling and shaking her head.

"Is something wrong?" I asked her, even though I knew nothing was wrong.

"I cannot believe we're really here, Zac. This is another dream come true for me."

"Same here."

"We're at a freakin' Norah Jones concert!" she squealed, and I laughed. Stevie was so excited, and seeing her this way brought me so much joy.

A few minutes later, the lights inside the venue dimmed and the musicians started walking onto the stage. Their warm-up got the crowd going and then Norah appeared, immediately prompting everyone, including Stevie and me, to jump to our feet, clap and cheer. When Norah made it over to her microphone stand centerstage, she smiled and then greeted all her fans.

"Good evening and thank you for joining me tonight here in Destin, Florida! How's everyone doing?" she asked.

The crowd began clapping and cheering again, and then the musicians began playing the first song: "What Am I To You?" When I looked over at Stevie, she was smiling and swaying her body back and forth. I pulled her closer, moving her so she was standing directly in front of me, and then I wrapped my arms around her waist. She leaned her head back onto my shoulder and after I kissed her, the two of us began moving together in rhythm with the music while watching Norah Jones perform.

Toward the end of the song, she looked at Stevie and me, then motioned for us to come over to her. As soon as the security guard walked us up to the stage, Norah shook Stevie's hand and mine while singing in that smooth, sultry voice of hers. When the song ended, my mermaid and I received yet another surprise when Norah made a statement directly to me.

"Tell me what this beautiful woman is to you," she said, glancing down at Stevie, who was standing in front of me with my arms wrapped around her waist again.

"She's my everything. My heart, my soul, and I can't imagine my life without her."

Norah smiled. "Good answer, my man! Good answer!"

Stevie, me, and everyone inside the place started laughing, and then the band began playing the next song.

An hour and a half later, the concert ended. On our way back to our beach house, Stevie asked me if I wouldn't mind walking down to the shoreline after we got back.

"I wouldn't mind at all. It's a great idea," I said.

"I think it'd be the perfect way to bring this perfect evening to a close."

"It has been a perfect evening, hasn't it?"

"So much! I still cannot believe we got to shake Norah Jones' hand, plus she sang to us and then talked to you."

"I know. I was so surprised by all of it. She puts on one hell of a show."

"Yes, she does. I wouldn't mind seeing her in concert again sometime."

"And I'll keep that in mind."

After Stevie and I changed into t-shirts and shorts, we began making our way down to the water, holding hands. The full moon was high above us, illuminating everything within view, but especially Stevie's flowing blond hair and still-smiling face.

"Zac, let's just sit here and relax," she said, looking down at the white sand and then back up at me. We were still several yards away from where the waves were rolling in.

"Whatever you wanna do, babe."

She down and I nestled in behind her with my legs stretched out alongside hers. As she leaned back against my chest, I wrapped my arms around her shoulders and rested my face against hers. We stayed right where we were for over an hour, looking out at the ocean, talking and laughing.

"I know it's late, but do you mind if we stay out here for a little while longer?" Stevie asked, looking over her shoulder at me.

"We can stay for as long as you want."

"I enjoy hearing the waves and all, but I really enjoy seeing that." She pointed up at the sky.

"The moon?"

"Yes—but mainly all the stars. It looks like an ocean of them up there.

"I've never heard it put that way, but you're right."

"That music playlist of mine is titled 'Ocean of Stars.'"

"Really?"

"Yes. The first song that I added to it was "Nightingale" by Norah Jones, and I did it sitting on this Destin beach one night. I flew here alone after my Malcolm died and grieved while letting the ocean, moon and stars heal me—and also the music. Not just Norah Jones, though. Several other artists. Over the years, I've continued adding to my playlist and whenever I listen to it, I can hear my process of healing. I can also hear when I found true happiness again, and that was when you and I found each other. It is so evident in all the songs that I've added to my playlist since you and I met."

Stevie looked over her shoulder at me again and I kissed her, thinking about how much I loved her and also about all the loss that she had endured. Then I asked her why she'd flown to Destin alone.

"I didn't want anyone with me. Not even Graham. He got angry about that trip but I didn't care. I knew what I needed to do for myself, and that was to come to this place alone where I could think clearly and begin processing everything I was feeling," Stevie said.

"I'm glad you did that for yourself. I can see this beach always being a place of solace for you."

"So can I."

42

#truth

Stevie

Monday, Tuesday and Wednesday flew by. Zac and I had spent those three days at the beach, going out to eat, driving around Destin, sightseeing, and we also took a few dips in the swimming pool and hot tub at our beach house. Each evening, Zac talked to Malcolm then checked the tracker app to see what Avery's status was. It was Thursday evening now and Zac was checking the app again. Then he looked up at me with dread in his eyes.

"Avery is on her way back to Dallas or she's already there at your house, isn't she?" I asked.

"She's at the house. When I checked the app earlier, she was still in Lubbock."

"And I know you have no idea why she decided to come back now."

"I don't. Nothing other than she may be thinking she needs to play nice with me again."

"So you'll continue financing her fucked lifestyle. Yes, I know."

"Stevie, please don't let this taint things. We have two days left in Destin and I want them to be as wonderful as all the other days."

"I do too. You and I both knew, though, that it was only a matter of time before Avery came back and we'd be forced out of this make-believe world that we've been living in since she's been gone."

Zac's eyebrows pulled together. "Make-believe world? Are you kidding me?"

"No, I'm not kidding you."

"Everything about us is real. There is no make-believe."

I sighed. "It's times like what's happening right now that make me feel like we've just been playing house with each other. Playing husband and wife. Whatever."

"I cannot believe you're saying this."

"Well, believe it."

"Stevie, listen... I know you're upset about Avery being back and so am I. I don't wanna go home. I don't wanna see her face or hear her voice—but I have to."

"I'm well aware of that."

"I feel like you and I are back to where we were last Thursday night when our conversation began falling apart because our emotions got out of hand. They talked for us instead of our logic, and we cannot let that happen again. You said that yourself."

"My emotions aren't out of hand this time, Zac. I've just stated facts."

"But Stevie, we haven't been *playing* anything. This between us is the most real thing that I've ever experienced in my life and you've also said that yourself."

I shrugged my shoulders and got up from the couch.

"Where are you going?" Zac asked but I didn't answer him. "Stevie, where are you going?" he asked again, but I still didn't answer. I just kept walking toward the back patio. Before I made it outside, though, Zac grabbed my arm and spun me around to face him.

"Don't ever grab me like that again," I said, jerking my arm away from him and then pointing in his face.

"I'm sorry. Just please—please stop. Don't do this, Stevie."

"Don't do what?"

"Don't shut down. Don't run away from you and me just because Avery is back. I know it's gonna be challenging trying to navigate around everything again but we can do it. We've done it."

"I'm gonna walk outside now, Zac, and I do not want you to follow me. I need to be alone for a little while."

I could see frustration and hurt in his eyes, but I was frustrated and hurting too and just needed some damn space. As soon as Zac nodded at me, I turned around and walked outside, but I didn't stay on the patio. I didn't go near the swimming pool or hot tub either. I walked down to the ocean.

I had no idea how long I'd been sitting on the beach when I felt a gentle nudge on my back and looked up to see Zac. He had two glasses of Hendricks gin and tonic in his hands. He'd bought the mix and limes for us after we got to Destin and we'd enjoyed sharing a drink together every night.

"Here," Zac said, handing me a glass. Then he sat down beside me in the sand. He didn't say anything else and I remained quiet. We just sipped on our drinks while looking out at the ocean. Because the moon was still mostly full and there wasn't a cloud in the sky, the waves rolling in to the shoreline sparkled like they had diamonds sprinkled across them.

"It's mesmerizing, isn't it?" I asked, pointing at the water.

"Yes, it is."

The words between Zac and me stopped again, but after about a minute, I turned and looked straight at him so I could tell him what was on my mind *and* my heart.

"I-I'm sorry," I choked out. "I didn't mean what I said about us playing make-believe. It's just..."

"I know, Stevie—and I'm sorry that things are the way they are with my home life. Please don't give up on us."

"Just because I get upset, say things I shouldn't, and need time alone doesn't mean I'm giving up on us."

"I really do fear you will one day, though. Your growing tired of waiting for our forever and then moving on scares me to death."

"I love you too much to ever do that."

"You are the love of my life, and I want you to know I'm never letting go of you—even if you were to let me go."

We smiled at each other through the tears in our eyes, and then Zac leaned over and kissed me. I crawled into his lap and rested my head against his chest while he rocked me back and forth underneath this starry September night sky.

"What would you like to do today, Sinclair?" Zac asked.

"Since it's our last full day in Destin, I'd like to do all we can."

"Such as?"

"Go to the beach, play in the ocean, day-drink, boil the shrimp you bought, and then watch a movie in the entertainment room here at this gorgeous beach house that I still can't believe you rented for us. I'd also like to take another dip in the swimming pool, fuck each other in it, relax in the hot tub again and then fall asleep in your arms in our comfy king-size bed with the ocean breeze blowing through the open patio doors all night. Sound good to you?"

"Sounds heavenly to me."

"Then it's a date."

"Deal. But you left out one thing."

"What?"

"Eating dinner somewhere. I'd like to take you someplace nice."

I reached up and ran my fingertips across Zac's lips and then along his bearded jawline. "You've already taken me to so many nice places to eat and I appreciate it so much."

"I know you do."

"If you don't mind though, let's just stay here this evening and not drive anywhere."

"I don't mind doing that at all. We can always have something delivered for dinner."

Zac leaned over and kissed my forehead at the same time my cellphone chimed on the nightstand. As soon as I read the text message, I smiled.

"My dad is checking to see how I'm doing," I said, looking back over at Zac. "I need to call him later and catch up on everything. We haven't actually talked on the phone in over a week."

"Call him now if you want to."

"No, first things first. Let's go to the beach and then we can start working on the rest of our to-do list."

For a quick and easy breakfast, Zac and I ate some leftover raspberry kolaches from the day before. Then we put on our swimsuits, grabbed two towels and two bottles of water, and headed to the shoreline.

"Do you wanna take a walk this morning or are you ready to go jump in the water?" Zac asked.

"Let's take a walk. I wanna find some more seashells."

We took our time making our way along the water's edge and I didn't realize how far we'd gone until I turned around to look behind us.

"This is the furthest we've ever walked down this beach," I said.

Zac glanced over his shoulder. "Wanna keep going?"

"Why not?"

My handsome lover smiled and then leaned over, stealing a quick kiss from me. A couple of minutes later, I noticed a family ahead of us that was coming our way: a man and woman with two young children who appeared to be the same age based on their height. One of them was a little boy with red hair, and the little girl had a headful of black curls that cascaded down her back.

As the family got closer, the little girl and boy took off running towards a cluster of seashells on the shoreline. They both jumped up and down and squealed with excitement, then started picking up the different treasures the tide had brought in.

Zac and I both waved at the parents as we neared them and their little shell hunters, and they waved back.

"Good morning," Zac and I said at the same time.

"Good morning," the man said while the woman just smiled at us. Their children weren't concerned about greeting anybody, though. They just wanted the seashells.

"I'm Zac Buchanan and this is my girlfriend, Stevie Sinclair," he said, reaching out to shake the man's hand.

"Nice to meet you, Zac and Stevie. I'm Sam Hunter and this is my wife, London."

All four of us took turns shaking each other's hand, then London told us the names of her and Sam's children. They were Lilly and Skylar.

"They're so adorable," I said, glancing over at them still looking at the treasures in the sand.

"Thank you."

"They look to be the same age."

"They're twins."

"Oh my goodness! How old are they?"

"Four."

"It's so cute how Skylar looks like you, London, and Lilly looks like you, Sam."

"We think so too," Sam said, smiling at London.

It was easy to see how in love they were and also how happy. They were the perfect little family.

"Are you on vacation?" Zac asked them.

"Yes, and also spending some time with my grandparents. As a matter of fact, that's their beach house," Sam said, pointing at it behind him.

"This is a vacation for us too. It's nice coming here this time of year when the beach isn't so crowded."

"That's exactly why we're here now. Where are you two from?"

"Stevie is originally from Austin, Texas, and moved to Dallas a few months ago. That's where I'm from."

"And how nice it is to meet some of my people," London said. "I'm originally from Houston."

"I wondered if you were from Texas because of your accent," I said.

"Oh, I know. Sam still teases me about my drawl." London cut her eyes at him and winked. "He's from Colorado. That's where I call home now."

"Which part of Colorado?" I asked, turning my attention to him.

"Aspen Heights. It's a small town about forty-five minutes west of Denver."

"I hope neither of you mind me asking, but how did you meet, being from different states?"

"I went to Aspen Heights for a work vacation and on my second day there, Sam and I met at the one and only grocery store in town," London said. "As a matter of fact, he saved me from dropping all the groceries I was holding. I didn't bother to get a basket or a buggy before I went shopping because I didn't plan on getting that much stuff, but I was hungry."

"I have done that so many times and have had to walk back up to the front of the store to grab a basket. You'd think I would learn my lesson."

We all laughed and then London asked Zac and me how we'd met.

"We first saw each other at a running trail but we didn't talk then. We did a lot of staring, though. Then a mutual friend of ours introduced us a week later when we all happened to meet up at the same bar after work," Zac said.

"And everything blossomed very quickly after that," I added.

Sam shook his head. "Yeah, it was the same way for London and me. You know when they're the one. There is no mistaking it."

I looked back over at Zac and he was smiling that dimpled smile of his.

"Here," Lilly said, walking up and surprising me.

I squatted down and took the shiny blue and white seashell out of her hand. "This is so pretty! Thank you, Lilly."

She stared into my eyes and then hugged me, surprising me again. I looked up at London and Sam to see them both grinning, and after their daughter walked off to continue looking through the loot of seashells with her twin brother, I stood back up.

"That was the sweetest thing," I said.

"Lilly is our little social butterfly and never meets a stranger, while Skylar is the shy one—until he gets to know you. Then he'll talk your ear off," London chuckled.

"Well, all of this has made my day and we won't take up any more of yours," I told London and Sam. "It was so nice meeting and talking with you."

"Same to you," they said at the same time, reminding me of how Zac and I did that very thing.

We shook their hands again, wished them a great vacation, and then continued making our way down the beach. After finding a few more keepsake seashells, we turned around and started heading back to our beach house. Before we went back inside, though, Zac and I dropped everything we were holding onto the sand and took a short swim in the ocean. The water felt so good and so did the warm sun. After about fifteen minutes of soaking up both, I asked Zac if he was ready to leave.

"Whenever you are. I'm just along for the journey, babe" he said, smiling at me.

"Then let's journey into our beach house and boil some shrimp for lunch."

"Sounds good to me."

After stuffing ourselves, Zac said he wanted to take a shower. I told him to go ahead, and also that while he was getting all the sand and salty water off him, I'd call my dad. Not from the master bedroom, though, where Zac could possibly hear the conversation. My dad still didn't know about my relationship with Zac and I knew that if Zac happened to overhear my conversation with my dad, he'd figure that out. Me not mentioning that I was in Destin would be the first clue.

Zac had never asked me if I'd let my dad know about us. I could tell that he'd assumed I had, because he'd told his mom and dad about our relationship. It was a different scenario for me, though, because of who my dad was. Because he was a Methodist pastor.

I'd just hung up from talking to him when Zac walked into the living room wearing only a white towel around his waist and drying off his hair with another one.

"Hey, you," I said, smiling at him.

"How's your dad doing?"

"He's fine. He asked me when I was gonna come to see him again or when he could come to see me."

"What'd you tell him?"

"That I would try to figure out a time."

"I'd like to meet him if he comes to Dallas."

"Okay," I said, smiling again, but Zac's quick squint let me know he wasn't buying it. Not my agreement nor my smile.

"Explain to me why you haven't told your dad about us, Stevie."

"What makes you think I haven't?"

"Because I just overheard enough of your side of your conversation with him while I was walking down that hallway," Zac said, pointing at it, "to *know* you haven't. You didn't mention my name, where we are—nothing. You pretended like you were at work."

I sighed and then slowly nodded at Zac. "You're right. I haven't told my dad about us."

"Why?"

"Because he's a pastor."

"Yes, I know. But going by what you told me about him, he doesn't adhere to religious dogma a hundred percent, so he shouldn't have a problem with us. The way that he and your mom began their relationship is no different than how we did."

"But there is a difference. My parents didn't kiss each other until *after* my dad was legally divorced and they didn't have sex until *after* they were married."

"And I respect that. You seem to have forgotten, though, what else you told me about your mom and dad."

"And what is that?"

"They sinned with their eyes by the way they looked at each other while your dad was still married to his first wife. That came straight out of your dad's mouth, according to you, and to me, it sounds like his first marriage was nothing more than piece of paper. The same as mine."

Zac was standing in front of me now, looking down at me sitting on the couch and I didn't know what else to say to him.

"Are you ashamed of us, Stevie?" he asked.

"No. It's just...my dad."

"What are you afraid of?"

"Disappointing him."

"Don't you think I was afraid of disappointing my parents when I told them about us? They had me in church every Sunday when I was growing up."

I looked down at the floor.

"Stevie? Stevie?"

"What?" I asked, staring up at Zac again.

"Here's what I'm gonna do about this situation between you and your dad. I'm leaving it where it is. I won't bring it up again. But you need to realize there's gonna come a day when you're gonna have to tell your pastor dad about our relationship and when you finally do tell him, I think it's gonna feel so good to stand in your truth. Not only about who you are now at this stage in your life but also about who we are as a couple. I say that from my own experience."

43
#home

Zac

Stevie and I had a good flight back to Dallas and it had nothing to do with the flight itself. Our plane actually ran into quite a bit of turbulence not long after we left Destin, but as far as my tattooed mermaid and I were concerned—we were great. Despite the turbulence and what we both knew was waiting for me when I got back home, we were still connected in every way. We held hands and never stopped talking. We laughed, too, while reliving several of the memories we'd made in paradise.

After driving us back to Stevie's house from the D.F.W. airport, I decided to stay for a little while. I wouldn't be picking up Malcolm from my parents until tomorrow morning—Sunday—so I was in no rush to go home. When I got ready to leave Stevie's, though, I was full of dread—but then I had a realization come to me: I didn't have to go anywhere. Because I'd become so programmed from being married to Avery all these years, I automatically felt like I needed to go home to keep an eye on everything, but I didn't need to do that anymore. I didn't have to. Avery could burn down my fucking house. It didn't matter to me.

When I told Stevie that I was spending the night with her, the look on her face was priceless. She smiled that beautiful smile of hers and then jumped into my arms. We left not long after that to get some Tex-Mex from a nearby taqueria. After eating at one of the picnic tables out front, we rode around the outskirts of Dallas while streaming Stevie's music playlist through my Blazer's speakers.

As we were listening to some of the first songs, I began to realize how deeply traumatic it had been for Stevie to lose her son. When she saw me choking back my tears, she switched to playing all the songs that she'd begun adding to her playlist on the day we met. One that I wasn't familiar with was "Deep Water" by Haley Reinhart.

While listening, I smiled over at Stevie at least a dozen times, mentally capturing the moments of her swaying back and forth in my passenger seat with her hands in the air like she was praising God. She also sang along with the lyrics of the song and I was blown away by how well she harmonized with the singer. She could've sung "Deep Water" all by herself.

After it ended, I commented on the illicit romantic relationship versus religious dogma scenario described in the song. Stevie told me that was why she loved the song so much. She related to it because of her initial back-and-forth struggle about becoming romantically involved with me. She also said the song came full circle for her after she and I had sex for the first time. She knew she was in deep water with me.

"I'm so happy you were able to spend last night with me," Stevie said. We were standing next to my Blazer in her garage and I hugged her to me even tighter.

"Me too. It did me a world of good. I'm ready to take on whatever Avery decides to dish out today."

"Hopefully, she won't dish out anything."

"Yeah, hopefully. If she does, though, I'll handle it—even if it means calling the police."

"Zac, I'm so sorry that you even have to think like that."

"It's just how it is, but being with you makes it easier for me to deal with all the nonsense. You are the spark that keeps me going."

"I love you."

"I love you too, babe."

I kissed her goodbye and then got into my car and left her house. As I was pulling into my garage, I looked down at the license plate on the rear of Avery's Audi and shook my head at myself. I knew it wasn't Avery who'd stopped in front of Stevie's house when she was mowing. The tracker app didn't lie. But on that day, I was still unnerved by the fleeting thought that it actually could have been Avery parked in front of Stevie's house.

My concern had nothing to do with me so much as it did Stevie. I didn't want her to have to deal with Avery's crazy behavior again. She'd already dealt with some of it when she met Avery at Mystic Bar. As far as the real driver of that red Audi in front of Stevie's house was concerned? I still wondered who it was, why they'd acted so strangely, and also why their license plate was missing.

I walked into the living room and then the kitchen but didn't see Avery anywhere. When I turned around to leave the kitchen, she rounded the corner and came to an immediate stop.

"Why are you back?" I asked her.

"Nice to see you too."

"Don't even try that with me. Why are you back? What do you need?"

"I just wanted to come home."

I half-laughed. "Right."

I walked off to go get my suitcase out of my Blazer and came back inside to find Avery waiting for me in the hallway. I immediately turned away from her and headed into my bedroom. I didn't think she was following me, but when I looked over my shoulder I saw her leaning against my doorframe.

"What the hell do you want?" I spat. I was in no mood for her games and she was already playing them.

"Where'd you go to need your suitcase?"

"None of your business."

"Yes, it is."

"No, it's not. You don't tell me anything about where you go or what you do."

"Do you want me to tell you?"

"I used to but I don't give a damn anymore."

Avery crossed her arms and sighed. "Well, wherever you went, I hope you had fun. You obviously worked on your tan while you were there."

I shook my head in disgust at her and then unzipped my suitcase on top of my bed. Avery kept standing where she was while I unpacked it and after I was done, I walked past her to go make myself a Hendricks and tonic. When I opened the kitchen cabinet to get my gin, I noticed Avery had replaced the bottle of vodka that Bash had poured out and a third of it was gone. I pushed it aside, grabbed the Hendricks, and then set it down on top of the counter next to my glass of ice. I'd just finished pouring in two shots and was about to squeeze in some lime when Avery came walking into the kitchen, stopping a few yards away from me.

"I like your new tattoo, but I don't like it that you're not wearing your wedding band. Why aren't you?" she asked, ignoring what I'd just told her about my life being none of her business.

I finished making my drink and took a big gulp of it while staring straight at Avery. I'd almost started to walk away again, but I was curious about something.

"What is my tattoo?" I asked.

"A flower with some kind of masculine-looking design around it."

"What kind of flower?"

"I don't know."

"You really don't recognize it?"

"No."

"Or the design?"

"No, Zac."

"Of course you don't. Not even after seeing all the pictures that I've shown to you of Scottish thistle and Celtic knots."

Avery sighed. "I just forgot is all. I remember now, though."

"Bullshit."

I shook my head in disgust again, then started walking back to my bedroom.

"Why aren't you wearing your wedding band, Zac?" Avery asked again, but this time, she did it by yelling her question down the hallway at me.

Although I could've answered her and also added daggers to my words, I didn't do either. I wanted Avery to wrestle with the truth that she already knew deep down about my reason for having a bare ring finger on my left hand now. She knew exactly what she'd done to destroy our marriage and I knew her only concern behind my wedding band being history was what it was going to make her look like to others who knew us. Most of them already knew the truth about her anyway.

After locking my bedroom door behind me, I quietly laughed because I was thinking about what Stevie had said about me being a prisoner in my own home. She was so right, and it was just going to have to be this way until... I didn't know for how long. But as long as I had Stevie in my life, I could deal with it.

I texted my mom to let her know how things had been going with Avery since I got home, and she asked me if I was concerned about it enough to want her and my dad to keep Malcolm for another night or two. I said no because I was ready to see my boy. I was ready to get him back home with me where he belonged.

As soon as I got off the phone with my mom, I stretched out across my bed to relax for a few minutes and ended up falling asleep. An hour and a half later, I woke up and couldn't believe I had knocked out like that. I didn't think I needed the rest because I slept so soundly at Stevie's last night, but then I realized my fatigue had to do with Avery being back and having to be on guard again. It had always been taxing but not to this degree. Everything was magnified for some reason.

While smoothing out my bedspread, I noticed a long strand of blond hair on it and smiled. Then I picked up Stevie's hair to get a closer look at it. It was so pretty and shiny and I liked that there was a trace of Stevie here at my house. It came from the night she'd come over to check on Malcolm because he had a cold. Neither of us had planned to have sex while she was here, but with Malcolm being sound asleep in his room, plus Stevie and I being near each other again... Well, she and I couldn't keep our hands off each other. I carried her to my bed and then we gave each other what we'd both been wanting and needing.

After placing Stevie's strand of hair underneath my pillow, I headed toward the garage. As I was walking down the hallway, Avery came out of the guest bedroom and stared at me.

"I'm going to pick up Malcolm from my parents," I said, coming to a standstill in front of her.

"Good. I look forward to seeing him."

"Funny, that's the first time you've mentioned him to me since I got here. He's always an afterthought for you, isn't he? No real concern because I'm covering all the concerns and responsibilities of having a child. I'll always do that for my son, too."

"He's also my son."

I shook my finger at Avery. "No, he was a mistake according to you and you didn't want him."

"Zac..."

"I'm leaving now and I suggest you be on your best behavior when I get back here with Malcolm. There better not be any drama coming from you, no drunken rages or anything. It's gonna be peaceful around here for my son. If you don't think you can conduct yourself in a peaceful manner, then pack your shit and go back to Lubbock. Stay there from now on. I do not care."

Avery's eyes were brimming with tears now. I didn't trust her display of emotion or her meek countenance. I'd witnessed her turning on her tears before only to quickly turn them off like a water faucet. I had also witnessed her demure body language only to see it turn into a raging inferno too many times to count.

I walked off but before I could make it to the garage, she called out my name.

"What do you want now?" I asked her.

"To tell you that I'm staying here and it will be peaceful. I promise."

44
#safety

Stevie

"Tell me the highlights from your Destin trip with Buchanan," Brooke said.

"The whole trip was one giant highlight."

"I'll bet."

"We spent so much time at the beach, ate out at some wonderful restaurants, and Zac took me to a Norah Jones concert that was amazing. And we did something else."

"What?"

"It's something really special that will always stand out from all the other stuff we did on the trip, but you won't get to see Zac's part until you see him again. Here's mine, though."

I pulled back the collar of my blouse to show Brooke my tattoo and her jaw dropped.

"Stevie! That is beautiful and so delicate-looking," she said.

"I think it is too. I'm really pleased with the job that the tattoo artist did."

"What flower is that?"

"It's Scottish thistle."

"You better not tell me that Zac's tattoo matches yours or I'm gonna give him so much shit."

I chuckled. "No, ours don't match. His is all black with a Celtic theme to it."

"Where'd he get his?"

"On his right bicep. It's quite large, too, and I just love it on him."

"Is this your first tattoo?"

"Yes."

"It's Zac's second one. I'll never forget when he showed me Malcolm's footprints and birthdate on his chest. Both of his tattoos and yours are very symbolic."

"They certainly are."

"And seeing your Scottish thistle made me think of your and Zac's ancestry. Did you ever get around to comparing your records?"

"Not yet. While we were in Destin, we talked about doing that after we got back to Dallas. It's gonna take hours and hours to get it all done."

"Do it while you have time because you never know when it's gonna run out," Brooke said, smiling at me in a motherly way that I remembered my mother doing.

I searched her eyes and then hugged her. "Thank you for helping me get away with Zac."

"Of course. My exception and I were able to do that a few times and it was wonderful being in the open with our relationship instead of hiding it."

"I know exactly what you mean. Oh, by the way—Avery is back."

"When did that happen?"

"Saturday."

"How is Zac?"

"So far, so good. Malcolm too."

"Good. I haven't thought to ask you this, but have you seen a picture of that precious little boy yet? Surely you have."

"Yes, I have. I've also met him, Brooke."

Her jaw dropped again. "When?"

"I happened to run into Zac and him at the zoo before Zac and I became involved."

"On that weekend when your dad was here."

"Yes. Well, I went to the zoo after he left to go back to Austin."

"I remember you telling me that you went and I understand now why you didn't tell me the whole story at the time."

I grinned. "Yeah, I thought it was best that I not say anything."

"I'm glad you did now, though. And about Malcolm... Isn't he the most adorable kid ever?"

"He is. I call him Zac's mini-me."

"You are right about that. Zac showed me pictures of himself as a newborn and also when he was one, two, three, and four years old. He and Malcolm are identical."

"I know. I saw those pictures plus a whole bunch of other ones of Malcolm and Zac at his mom and dad's house."

And there went jaw-drop #3. This time, Brooke grabbed my arm in surprise and I just laughed. Then she asked me how it had come to be that I'd gone over to the Buchanans' home. After telling her about the chain of events that led up to it and also explaining how my meeting with Zac's parents was arranged, she asked me what my impression was of the Buchanans.

"They're such wonderful people," I said.

"They are—and they raised a wonderful son whom they've wanted to see happy for so long. Now they have, because of you."

There was a knock at my office door and I told whoever it was to come in. It was David.

"Hey, ladies. Sorry to interrupt."

"No prob. What's up?" Brooke asked him.

"I've got some questions about a case and I'd like to go over them with you."

"Sure. Give Stevie and me just a few more minutes and I'll come to your office."

"Thanks."

After David left, I asked Brooke about lightening up my security. As a matter of fact, I wanted all of it to stop. No longer did I feel like I needed to be escorted to and from my work or the courthouse: I hadn't received any more anonymous letters or anything along those strange lines.

"I don't know about that, Stevie. I'd feel better if we continued keeping an eye on you for a while longer," Brooke said.

"I appreciate your concern so much, but everything is fine now. I feel good about it. I'm also tired of being babysat."

"I know you are, but we want our Joan of Arc safe."

"Brooke... I'm safe."

She let out a heavy sigh. "Okay then. Have it your way. I'll let everybody know."

"Thank you. And I'll let Zac know."

I was walking down the crowded hallway on the sixth floor of the Dallas courthouse when I saw Zac and Bash coming in my direction. I smiled and waved at them and they returned the gesture.

"Good afternoon, guys," I said as the three of us met and stepped aside, out of everyone else's way, to talk.

"Hey, doll," Bash then said. And like always, he hugged me, and while he was, I looked over his shoulder at Zac. His sky-blue eyes were sparkling and staring straight at me.

As soon as Bash and I let go of each other, Zac held out his hand to shake mine. Professional mode was back in full effect.

"How are you doing, Sinclair?" he asked, giving my hand a gentle squeeze.

"I'm great. How are you?"

"I'm great too. How'd you feel coming here alone?"

"Fine. Really, I'm not worried about anything crazy happening to me anymore."

Zac glanced down at my lips. "If you change your mind about that then let me know. I'm happy to resume my position as your main bodyguard."

"And I'm here for you in any way that I can help," Bash added.

"I appreciate you both so much."

"How'd your hearing go?" Zac then asked me.

"Smoothly. How do you feel about Brooke assigning me to another one of your cases?"

"I feel good about it but this next time, my gloves are coming off."

"They did last time."

"No, they didn't. Not all the way. I held back."

"You held back?"

"Yes—because I told Brooke that I'd take it easy on you the first time. I let you win the case."

"You did not," I chuckled. "I won it because of your client's last-minute illegal drug indiscretion that you knew nothing about because you didn't do your homework as thoroughly as I did mine."

"But I did know about it."

"Your reaction to my revelation of Mr. Ferguson's stunt made it very clear to everyone in the courtroom that you didn't know."

"I swear, I did. I was ready to be rid of Mr. Ferguson as a client."

I shook my head no because I didn't believe Zac and he just kept grinning at me.

"I'm not buying it, so you can stop messing with me now," I said.

"I'm not messing with you."

"Bash, is there any truth to what your best friend here just said?"

"He is telling you the truth, Stevie. He already knew what Mr. Ferguson did and Zac did take it easy on you. When you're back in court with him, you'll see the difference."

I kept looking back and forth at Bash and Zac, and finally rolled my eyes at them. "I'm still not convinced about any of this. And as far as gloves coming off all the way goes? What you don't realize, Buchanan, is that I held back in court on that day too."

"You did, huh?"

"Yes. You got a small taste of what I'm capable of, as well."

The corners of Zac's mouth curled up even more. "I'm looking forward to getting a full taste of it and then a full taste of you afterward."

And there went Zac's professional mode flying out the door.

"I'm gonna go ahead and leave on that note. It's been fun, guys," I chuckled.

"See you later, doll," Bash said, but Zac didn't say anything else. He just kept staring at me and grinning.

After walking a few yards down the hallway, I looked over my shoulder to see Zac's eyes still on me. Then he quickly patted his chest above his heart. Without anyone around us knowing it, he had just told me that he loved me. I smiled and nodded at him, then rounded the corner to go to the elevators.

"I have a surprise for you," I told Zac.

"You're my surprise. Always."

"Well, another one then."

"Okay," he said, walking up to me in my kitchen.

"Close your eyes."

"Done."

"Hold out your hands."

"Done."

I reached into the cabinet beside me, pulled out Zac's surprise and placed it in his hands.

"May I open my eyes now?"

"Yes."

As soon as he saw the bottle of Hendrick's Neptunia gin, he smiled that big, dimpled smile of his, making his eyes squint and crinkle around the corners.

"You found some!" he cheered.

"I did. Two bottles, actually. One for you and one for me."

He held up his and studied the label. "Of course this has a mermaid on it."

"I know. Every time you see it, I hope you think of me."

"I'm always thinking of you, Sinclair. Come here." Zac set the bottle down on the kitchen counter and pulled me into his arms, hugging me tightly. "Thank you for my gift," he whispered into my ear.

"You're welcome. Would you like to try some of that limited-release gin?"

"I would love to, but only if you're having some."

"Oh, I am."

Zac kissed me. Then I started making our drinks.

"When did you find the Neptunia?" he asked.

"Today. On my way home from work, I stopped by Specs just to see if they'd restocked it and I was so excited to see two bottles sitting on the shelf."

"That's all they had?"

"Yes, and I snagged them. Proudly." I chuckled and so did Zac.

"This has me thinking about our ancestry. We really do need to compare our records soon."

"I know. When would you like to do that?"

"Maybe this weekend if my parents don't mind keeping Malcolm for me. I mean, I know they won't but I just don't want to seem like I'm taking advantage of their generosity. They already do so much to help me with Malcolm."

"Comparing our records this weekend would be a problem."

"Why is that?"

"I talked to my dad earlier and he wants to see me this weekend."

"Okay. Are you going to Austin or is he coming here?"

"He asked to come here."

"I understand. Um, it's great that you get to see him."

Zac had been sincere about what he'd just said to me. I could see it showing in his eyes. But there was something else showing in them: sadness. I knew he wasn't sad about this weekend not working out to compare our ancestry records. It had to do with the fact that I still hadn't told my dad about my relationship with Zac. I'd been thinking about doing it though and now, because of the conversation that Zac and I were in the middle of having, I'd just made up my mind to do it.

"I'm gonna tell my dad about you and me this weekend," I said.

Zac swallowed hard. "Stevie, you don't have to if you're really not ready. Don't do it for me because that's the wrong reason. Yes, I want your dad to know about us and I really would like to meet him, but only when it's right for you."

"I'm ready to let him in on our wonderful little secret. Whatever happens, happens."

"Are you really worried about him reacting negatively?"

I shook my head no. "Not so much anymore. I've been thinking about everything you said to me about my dad and us while we were in Destin. I think things will be fine. I want my dad to know all about you. I wanna tell him how in love with you I am and how happy you make me. Depending on how it all goes, you may be meeting him this weekend."

Zac smiled. "That'd be great. You just let me know when."

Zac left my house not long after finishing his Neptunia gin and tonic with extra lime. He loved how it tasted and thanked me again for his surprise. I was so excited that he'd been able to stop by my house after work. I hadn't been sure that he was going to have time, because he needed to pick up Malcolm from his parents and then go home, where Avery was still hanging out.

According to Zac, she was sticking to what she told him she was gonna do and that was to stay at their home and keep it peaceful. I knew as well as Zac did that it was only a matter of time until it wouldn't be that way, and I'd be waiting with open arms for him to come home to me.

45
#toolate

Zac

"Thanks for not minding me being in Malcolm's room when you read him that bedtime story," Avery said.

"He enjoyed you being there."

"Do you mind sitting outside by the pool with me for a little while now?"

"Why do you wanna do that?"

"To relax and to just visit with you."

I stared at Avery standing in the hallway with me, outside Malcolm's bedroom. He was sound asleep, but I could tell that I wasn't going to be sleeping any time soon. I wanted to find out the real motive behind Avery's request.

"That's fine. Let's go," I said.

She smiled at me. Before we left the house though, I grabbed a bottle of water out of the refrigerator.

"Do you want one? I asked Avery, holding up mine.

"No, I'm good. Thank you, though."

"What about your usual?"

"I'm not drinking vodka tonight."

"I saw your new bottle in the cabinet."

"Yeah, I got it while I was in Lubbock."

"You haven't touched it since you've been back here. I saw where the line was and it hasn't moved."

Avery shrugged. "It just doesn't sound good to me right now."

After opening the back door, I motioned for Avery to walk ahead of me and followed her to the lounge chairs on the pool deck. I flipped on the pool lights to give the backyard a little more light since it was nighttime. When I sat down next to Avery, she smiled at me again.

"I've always loved our pool. The lights and waterfall are so pretty," she said.

"I think they are too."

"Would you be up to going for a swim with me?"

"No, I wouldn't. We can sit right here. You told me that you wanted to visit so talk."

"Zac, I don't even know where to begin other than to tell you that I'm so sorry for the hell that I've put you through all these years."

I jerked my head back in surprise. "Where is all of this coming from?"

"I've been thinking about life and how short it is. I've lost out on so much with you and Malcolm."

"Especially Malcolm."

"I want nothing more than a fresh start with you and him. I want us to be a family."

"That's not gonna happen with me. It's too late. It isn't with Malcolm, though."

Avery nodded and then choked out, "D-do you hate me?"

Her eyes were filled with tears now and it was going to be interesting to see how long they lasted this time.

"What I hate is all you've done that killed our marriage, but the thing that I hate even more than that is you didn't want Malcolm. He's an innocent child and he's also the best kid."

"I know—and you're the best husband. I don't deserve you, but it doesn't change the fact that I love you. I always have."

"That's a lie. You could not have possibly loved me all this time and treated me as you have."

"I hated myself and took it out on you, Zac."

"So you don't hate yourself anymore?"

"I'll put it to you this way: I'm learning to love myself and forgive myself for all the wrongs that I've done."

"Sounds like you've been in counseling."

"No counseling. Just lots of deep reflection."

I sighed and then looked off from Avery at the pool. "I cannot trust anything that you tell me. You've played me so many times."

"I know I have, but I'm not that person anymore. Please give me one last chance, Zac. Let me earn back your trust *and* your love. You'll see that I'm telling you the truth. That I'm for real this time."

"No. The only thing that I'll give you a chance to do is be a mother to Malcolm."

"I want him and you both. I love you both."

I looked back over at Avery. "Just tell me what happened in Lubbock. Something must have for you to have done this complete turnaround."

"Nothing happened."

"Something did for you to come home acting like this. The person you're being now is the one that I fell in love with ten years ago. You're being kind and attentive, you've been smiling and I've even heard you laughing a few times while playing with Malcolm. You've cooked some meals this week and cleaned the house and washed Malcolm's laundry and mine."

"I know, Zac. I know. I should've been doing that all along. You do so much for me."

Avery covered her face with her hands and started crying hard. I looked up at the sky until I couldn't listen to her any longer and got up from my chair.

"Where are you going?" Avery asked.

"Inside. I can't do this with you. This is all a huge déjà vu for me and the feelings that it's stirred up inside me are something that I don't wanna feel because it feels bad. It's toxic. You're toxic, Avery, and I don't believe one word that you just said to me."

She hurried up from her chair and walked over to me. "I'll do anything it takes to prove to you that I'm telling you the truth. I've changed, Zac. I promise."

"No—you haven't."

I turned to leave, but before I could, Avery threw her arms around my neck and started kissing me. I was caught off guard and in the couple of seconds that she had her lips on mine, all I could think about was Stevie. All I could see was Stevie.

"Stop!" I yelled at Avery, pushing her away from me. "This isn't happening."

"I just wanna be with you."

"You just wanna fuck me?"

"I wanna be close to you again, Zac. We used to be so good together."

I scoffed at Avery and then went back inside expecting her to follow me but she didn't. I wanted to talk to Stevie, but before I called her, I fixed myself a strong gin and tonic with the bottle of Neptunia that she bought for me. As soon as I was back inside my bedroom with the door locked, I sat down on the edge of my bed and called my lover whom I hoped was going to be understanding of what just happened between Avery and me.

"Hey, you," she said, answering her phone.

"Hey."

"I was getting worried because I hadn't heard from you this evening. I thought Avery might've pulled something."

"Well, she did pull something."

"God, she didn't hit, scratch or throw something at you again, did she?"

"No. Not that."

"Then what?"

"Well, I've already told you how she's kept things peaceful this week and also how she's been doing things around here like cooking, cleaning, and all."

"Right."

"Tonight, she asked me about joining in on Malcolm's bedtime story. Thinking of it benefitting him, I told Avery yes and it went well."

"Where was she in his room?"

"She sat on the floor beside his bed while I lay in it with him and read him the story."

Stevie sighed. "Okay."

"Malcolm fell asleep before I finished, then Avery and I left his room. While we were in the hallway, she asked me if I'd go sit by the pool with her because she wanted to relax and just visit with me. I didn't wanna go but decided to because I wanted to see if I could find out what her real motive was for asking me outside."

"And did you?"

"Yes. After apologizing to me for all the hell that she's brought to our marriage, she begged me for a second chance. She promised me that she's changed."

"What did you say, Zac?"

"I told her that it was too late for us and also that I didn't believe a word she said, then she started crying. I stood up to leave and Avery threw herself at me."

"Threw herself at you?"

"Yes, she kissed me but I pushed her away. Then she told me that she wanted to be close to me because we used to be so good together."

"You mean, you and Avery used to fuck *so good* together."

I blew out a hard breath. "Yes—in the beginning, but it didn't last long because Avery changed. Listen, Stevie, I hate telling you all of this. I can tell that it's upset you and rightfully so, but I figured you'd wanna know what happened."

"I do wanna know and yes, I'm upset—but not at you. I'm pissed off at Avery. She is desperately trying to manipulate you into rekindling your marriage and I wanna know why."

"So do I. I asked her what happened in Lubbock that prompted the big turnaround in her behavior and she said nothing happened. She's just been thinking about how short life is and how much she's missed out on with me *and* Malcolm."

"She doesn't have a fucking clue of how much she's missed out on."

"She never will, either."

"Zac, do you really think something happened while she was in Lubbock that's making her behave this way?"

"Yes."

"What?"

"She either got crossways with her parents or Justin. Hell, maybe all three. Maybe they all got enough of her bullshit and told her to leave. I'm her last resort."

Stevie grew quiet again and I just listened to her breathe over the phone. I knew there was more that she wanted to say, but I wasn't going to pressure her.

"I don't like Avery sitting close to you in Malcolm's bedroom," she finally said.

"I know you don't."

"I don't like her standing close to you in the hallway in your house or anywhere. I don't like her talking to you. I don't like her touching you. I don't like her kissing you for even one second and I damn sure don't like the thought of you fucking her. It makes me feel sick."

"It does me too."

"I know you're stuck in your living situation and I understand all the reasons why, but I need you to understand that it's infuriating to me *for* you and Malcolm. All of this tonight makes me feel like driving over to your house, packing up you and Malcolm, slapping Avery on our way out the door, and then bringing you and your precious little boy home with me for good. Fuck it."

"Oh, my sweet lover," I breathed out. "If you only knew how many times I've dreamed of Malcolm, you and me being together under one roof and calling it 'home.'"

"I've dreamed the same thing, Zac. More than you know."

"I wish I could see you."

"Same here."

"Do you wanna FaceTime?"

"Yes."

"Do you wanna..."

"Not tonight. I need you in person. I need to feel you all over me, so let's wait."

"Okay. I'm happy just getting to see your beautiful face again. And Stevie?"

"Yeah."

"Thank you for listening to all I had to say and also for understanding."

"I love you. Now FaceTime me, Buchanan."

46
#nightmare

Zac

Brooke: So are you holding my Joan of Arc hostage or something?

Me: I wish. Why?

Brooke: Before she left my office earlier, she told me that she planned to be back here no later than 2:00 p.m. Well, it's almost 3:00 p.m. and I've texted her twice but she hasn't replied. I just thought you two might've taken a quick rendezvous somewhere.

Me: Where did Stevie go?

Brooke: The courthouse. She had a hearing and was gonna run over to the records division afterward.

Me: Let me get back to you. I'm gonna try calling her.

Brooke: Okay.

I called Stevie twice but she didn't answer, so I texted her. She still didn't reply so I left my office to drive over to the Dallas courthouse to see if she was still there, caught up in some legal matter. I was about five minutes away when my cellphone rang. It wasn't Stevie calling me back, though. It was Bash.

"Where are you, Zac?"

"On my way to the courthouse to find Stevie."

"I want you to listen to me and I want you to listen closely."

"What's wrong?"

"There's a situation at the courthouse that's happening right now."

"What are you talking about?"

"The news is reporting that a man is there in the parking lot and he's taken a hostage at gunpoint. It's Stevie, Zac. The son of a bitch has Stevie. I saw her in the video online."

And all at once everything began closing in on me as I was driving down the interstate. Then I heard a car bear down on its horn, honking at me. It jarred me back into the reality of where I was and what was happening, and I pulled back into my lane. Then I pushed down on the gas even harder.

"I'm gonna fucking kill him," I said through my gritted teeth.

"No, Zac! Don't go up there!"

"I see the scene ahead of me now. The police are everywhere and there are helicopters in the air."

I hung up on Bash before he could say anything else and less than thirty seconds later, I was exiting off the interstate. I already knew I wasn't going to be able to park my car anywhere near the courthouse, so I pulled up to a gas station and parked in their lot. Then I took off running.

As I was approaching a line of Dallas police officers and their barricades, they held up their hands and ordered me to stop but I didn't. I kept running, but they stopped me by grabbing my arms and pulling me back.

"Let me go!" I screamed. "That's my girlfriend that the man is holding hostage! Stevie Sinclair! That's her name!"

"Sir! You can't go over there!" one of the officers said. "I'm sorry but you can't!"

"No! I've gotta save her!"

"We're on the situation and trying to talk the man into letting your girlfriend go."

My chest was hurting so badly and I could hardly breathe.

"Sir, what is your name?" another officer asked.

"Zac. Zac Buchanan."

"Mr. Buchanan, you've gotta try to calm down."

I grabbed my head. "I-I've gotta... She can't..."

The officer standing closest to me looked at the other one, and then they nodded at each other. Right after that, I was led over to a S.W.A.T. vehicle that was closer to the scene. I was standing behind it along with several police officers and we all had our eyes on Stevie and the man who had her down on the ground in the parking lot, backed up against a car with his gun held to her head—and I recognized the man. It was Mr. Ferguson, the man whom I'd represented in the C.P.S. court case that Stevie had won. The case that she'd won on her own because she did her homework and I didn't. I was only teasing her on that day in the hallway on the sixth floor of the courthouse.

I told one of the police officers everything I knew about Mr. Ferguson, and he radioed in all the information. As I listened to him, I kept watching Stevie and could see the tempest raging in her eyes. She wasn't scared of Mr. Ferguson. She was furious about what he was doing to her. We all were.

I had no idea how much time had passed when I heard Bash calling my name from behind me and as I was turning around, he grabbed me and hugged me. A Dallas police officer was standing next to him and nodded at me when I looked at him. He allowed my best friend to be here with me while my heart was breaking in two.

"It's gonna be all right, Zac," Bash said, patting my back. "Stevie is gonna survive this."

I didn't say anything. I just kept looking straight ahead at what was happening and could see Mr. Ferguson saying something to Stevie. Then she threw her head back and hit him in the nose. His gun went off right after that and I jumped and gasped at the same time, and then an officer yelled that Mr. Ferguson shot his gun into the air.

I slowly stepped away from the S.W.A.T. vehicle a few feet and then took a couple of steps forward while keeping my eyes on Stevie. That was when she saw me and as soon as she did, she lifted her right hand to her chest and patted it to tell me that she loved me. I patted my chest too, then felt the tears that I'd been holding back start falling.

Mr. Ferguson was holding his gun to Stevie's head again and I could see fear in her eyes now. She wasn't afraid of dying; we'd talked about that subject before. She was afraid of losing our chance to have a forever together just like I was.

"Mr. Buchanan, I need you to step back," an officer said.

As I was easing toward the S.W.A.T vehicle, I saw Stevie throw her head back again, hitting Mr. Ferguson in his nose for a second time. Then she started fighting him with all she had. His gun went off again and my stomach dropped—and then I heard another gunshot. I quickly realized it didn't come from Mr. Ferguson. A police officer had just shot him with a well-aimed bullet. He was slumped over and no longer moving."

With my adrenaline higher than it had ever been, I took off running toward Stevie, breaking through all law enforcement lines. As I was closing the space between us as fast as I could, I watched her crab-crawl away from the limp body of Mr. Ferguson and then rise up to her feet, turn around and take off running in my direction. When I saw the front of her, my stomach dropped again: Mr. Ferguson's blood was splattered across Stevie's face, her hair and her white blouse.

Only yards apart now, she held out her arms at the same time that I did and we collided into each other. I felt her body start giving way and picked her up as she was passing out, then watched her eyes close. Dozens of officers surrounded us within seconds and helped lead me to an ambulance nearby. I carried Stevie into it, laid her on the stretcher, and then rode with her to the hospital. She never regained consciousness during that time but one of the paramedics told me that her vitals were good.

As the ambulance was pulling up to the emergency room, I saw Bash, Brooke and her team standing out front. They gathered around the back of the ambulance as the paramedics were unloading Stevie and we all went into the hospital. As soon as Stevie was taken back to be assessed, Brooke came up to me.

"Come here, Buchanan," she said, pulling me into her arms. I rested my head against hers and breathed for a long minute, then looked at her and shook my head in disbelief.

"I-I don't know what to think about all of this. Or what to do."

"The only thing to do is to be there for Stevie."

"You know I will be."

"So will I."

"We all will be," Bash added.

I looked over at him and all of Brooke's team, then nodded my thanks to them.

"Brooke, that man was my client, Mr. Ferguson," I said.

"I know."

"I feel like this is all my fault."

"It's no one's fault other than Mr. Ferguson's. He was crazy and volatile. I just wish I'd continued Stevie's security detail and maybe this wouldn't have happened."

"A man like Mr. Ferguson would've found a way to get to Stevie. It was only a matter of time," Jason interjected.

I looked over at the doors that led to wherever Stevie had been taken and wanted to run through them to find her. I needed to see her again. I needed to touch her.

Brooke had just given me another hug when three Dallas police officers walked into the emergency room waiting area and I recognized them. I'd stood next to them by the S.W.A.T. vehicle.

"Mr. Buchanan, these are Ms. Sinclair's," one of them said, handing me her purse and briefcase. "She dropped them in the parking lot. I believe all the contents are there. They were scattered but I picked them up."

"Okay, thank you."

"I hope you don't mind my asking but we're all wondering how your girlfriend is doing after going through such a traumatic event."

I didn't blink at the officer calling Stevie my girlfriend in front of Brooke's team. I didn't care if they heard what he said or what they thought about it.

"She was still unconscious when we arrived here but her vitals were good," I said.

"That's a relief. I hope everything turns out well. We'll be praying for her and for you."

I stared into the officer's eyes, thinking about him or anyone praying for Stevie and me. Because of this nightmare, I was back at square one with my trust and faith in God, but I thanked the officer for his kindness anyway.

"Investigators will be up here later. They're gonna want to talk to your girlfriend about everything," he went on to tell me.

"Okay."

"I also wanted to let you know that Mr. Ferguson did not survive his injuries."

"Good."

The police officer nodded in agreement with me. "Take care, Mr. Buchanan."

We shook hands, and as soon as he and the other officers left, Brooke asked me about contacting Stevie's father to let him know what happened.

"I hope Stevie's phone is in here because that's the only way I know how to contact him," I said, looking inside her purse. I saw her phone and grabbed it. Then I looked up at Brooke.

"I'll do it," she said, holding out her hand for me to give her Stevie's phone, as well as her purse and briefcase.

She knew me so well—like a mother. Like my mother. I didn't have to say a word because she already knew what I was thinking and it was that it would be best if Brooke contacted Mr. Sinclair instead of me.

As she was walking outside to make that phone call, I turned around and walked down the hallway to call my parents to let them know what happened and where Stevie and I were. Of course they were shocked and saddened when I told them but so grateful that Stevie had survived the ordeal. My mom told me not to worry about Malcolm and also to let her know if there was anything that she or my dad could do to help Stevie in any way.

Brooke and I met back in the waiting area and she told me that Mr. Sinclair was on his way to Dallas. She also said, "After I found his number on Stevie's phone, I called him from mine so I will be his go-to in all of this."

"Okay. I wonder how soon he's gonna get here."

"Three or four hours, depending on the traffic."

"I'm gonna wait here for him to arrive. As a matter of fact, I'm not leaving this hospital. I know they're keeping Stevie overnight and I'm gonna be right beside her."

"So am I."

"And so am I," Bash then said, walking up to Brooke and me. "We're Stevie's family here."

And he was right. We were.

Brooke told Jason, Ellie, David and Jennifer that they could all go home and she'd keep them posted about Stevie. It wasn't long after they left that a doctor walked up and asked which one of us was Zac Buchanan.

"I am," I said.

"Ms. Sinclair is awake now and she's doing well. She also wants to see you."

"Please take me to her."

"Can we see her too? I'm her mother and this is her brother, Bash," Brooke told the doctor.

"Ms. Murphy—district attorney of Dallas—I know better than that but yes, you can see Ms. Sinclair too. You *and* her brother."

When we walked into Stevie's room, she was sitting up in her hospital bed, alert and looking strong as ever. She smiled when she saw us and then covered her mouth because she had started crying. I walked straight to her, then leaned down and kissed her. She wrapped her arms around my neck and held her forehead against mine for a long moment, then looked over at Brooke and Bash.

"Please hold my hands," she told them.

They moved closer to her and took her trembling hands into theirs while I continued standing beside Stevie and stroking her hair. Hospital personnel had cleaned Mr. Ferguson's blood out of it and had also washed it off her face, neck and chest.

"All I know to say is thank you and I love all of you," she choked out.

"We love you too," Brooke said, and Bash nodded in agreement. He couldn't talk because he was more choked up than Stevie.

"Can I get you anything?" I asked her.

"A Hendricks and tonic with extra lime would be wonderful right about now." We all laughed and then Stevie's expression grew serious. "I know all of you are worried about me, but I'm okay. Really. I'm just happy that son of a bitch, Mr. Billy Ferguson, was shot by the police."

"Before we came in here to see you, we found out that he died from his injuries," I then said.

Stevie stared at me for a long moment. "That makes me even happier. This world is a much better place without a man like that."

"Yes, it is," Brooke and I said at the same time. Bash just shook his head again.

"Um, I need to call my dad to let him know about everything that's happened."

"I've already called him, Stevie, and he's on his way here," Brooke said. "Oh, and I put your briefcase and purse over there." She pointed at them sitting on the table next to the door. "One of the police officers brought them to the E.R. He thinks all the contents are in them. He said they were scattered on the parking lot and he picked up everything he could find."

"Yeah, my purse is how Mr. Ferguson pulled me backward when I was walking to my car. He came up behind me and grabbed the strap on my shoulder. It happened so fast. I even had my pepper spray in my hand but it was useless. It is a crazy fucking world."

"And only getting crazier."

"It really is." Stevie took a deep breath. Then she told us that her doctor had insisted on keeping her at the hospital tonight despite her objection. "Brooke and Bash—and you, my protector," she said, looking up at me, "can go home. I'll have my dad here with me."

"None of us mind staying here with you, Stevie," Brooke said.

"I know you don't, and I appreciate it so much, but really, I'm fine."

"They can go but I'm staying with you, Sinclair," I told her.

She looked back up at me and searched my eyes. "Then you're gonna get to meet the pastor."

47
#itsallintheeyes

Stevie

By the time my dad made it to the hospital, two investigators had interviewed me and I told them everything I knew. I told them about my case against Mr. Ferguson and his behavior toward me on that day in court, and then I detailed what happened in the parking lot, beginning at the moment he pulled me backward by my purse strap up until I ran into Zac's arms and passed out.

My dad and Zac's introduction went well. I told my dad that Zac was a colleague and friend of mine but nothing more. I didn't mention our romantic involvement because I felt the hospital wasn't the place for that to happen. I wanted to wait until I got home to not only tell my dad that I was having an affair with Zac but also that we were in love.

In between my doctor checking on me again and a nurse doing the same several times, my dad asked me questions about what had happened to me. He was careful with his word choices because he didn't want to upset me, I knew. He wouldn't have upset me, though, if he hadn't been careful. I had no problem taking the most direct questions about Mr. Billy Ferguson and what he'd done to me, as well as his son and his wife. Regardless, I still appreciated my sweet dad being my sweet dad.

After I answered his questions, he turned his attention to Zac, sitting in the chair next to him. They had already been chit-chatting but had kept their conversation light. I hoped it stayed that way too. At least on Zac's part. He was going to have to continue being careful with the details he revealed about himself or it was going to give away too much. My dad was sharp-minded and also keen about reading people. It wouldn't take much for him to clue in on the fact that Zac was not only married but was also my lover.

At some point, while my dad and Zac were talking, I fell asleep. I woke around three in the morning and I lay here in my hospital bed wide awake and watching the two men that I loved more than life sleeping in their chairs. I thought about taking a picture of them with my cellphone but decided not to because I didn't want to risk waking them.

Looking at Zac, I wished the hospital had given him something to change into because his white-collared button-up shirt and tie had Mr. Ferguson's dried blood on them, transferred to him through me. As soon as I ran into Zac's arms, the red mess on me went onto him. Seeing it didn't bother me, but I wondered if it bothered Zac and he just hadn't said anything.

After I'd regained consciousness, a nurse had helped me change out of my work clothes and into a hospital gown. Then she washed off all the remnants of Mr. Ferguson on my body. Misty was her name and I would never forget her kindness, the crescent moon and star ring on her finger, or all the tattoos on her arms. While she was cleaning me up, she told me the stories behind every one of them and I thought to myself how much my mom would've enjoyed meeting her. Misty was a free spirit with a rebel heart just like my mom and me.

I was still awake and had my eyes on Zac when I realized my dad was awake and watching me. I smiled at him, and he quietly got up, took my hand into his, sat down on the edge of the mattress and leaned down to me.

"Having trouble sleeping?" he quietly asked.

"I am. My mind is in overdrive about everything."

"It's understandable. You went through so much yesterday. Would you like for me to check with a nurse about getting something for you to take that will help you sleep?"

"No, but thank you. I'd rather be awake and sharp-minded than fuzzy."

"Okay."

My dad looked over my face and then softly smiled.

"What is it?" I asked.

"There's something else that's keeping you from resting and it has nothing to do with what happened to you."

"What are you talking about?"

"I recognize that look in your eyes, daughter. I also recognize the look that I saw in Zac's eyes earlier. You two are in love with each other."

I slowly drew in a deep breath and then blew it out. "I have a lot to tell you, Dad."

"So tell me, but only if you're up to it. If you're not right now, then this conversation can certainly wait."

I looked over at Zac still sound asleep in his chair and readied myself to confess the truth that now lay within me.

"I am up to it," I said, meeting my dad's caring gaze. "I *need* to tell you what has been going on with me."

"Whenever you're ready."

"You're right about Zac and me. We are in love. Deeply in love. But there's one problem with our relationship that I don't think you're gonna like. In fact, you may wanna disown me after I tell you what it is."

"I know he's married, Stevie, and I would never disown you over anything."

"But... How did... Did Zac tell you?"

"No. I just know, though."

Of course you do, I thought to myself.

"Dad, neither of us was looking for this to happen. We just fell into it and we fell so fast."

"I know that too."

"At first, I really struggled with our affair because of how you and mom raised me, and also because of Graham's affair with Emma. I not only knew better than to let myself do this but I struggled with being a hypocrite. I don't care about any of that now."

"Because now you understand the full meaning behind the saying: things aren't always black and white. Like me with your mom, it took you falling in love with someone that society says you shouldn't fall in love with because they view that love as being wrong due to the circumstances surrounding it. Also like your mom and me, you see the ridiculousness in some of the manmade rules and laws that we're expected to live by. When it comes to love, they don't apply and never will."

"N-no, they won't," I choked out.

My dad looked over my face again and then squeezed my hand. "How did you and Zac meet?"

"Through Brooke. At the end of my first week of working for her, she invited me to join her and my team at a local bar that they all frequent. Zac and his best friend, Sebastian, or *Bash* as we all call him, showed up there which I learned is a normal thing. Brooke considers Zac and Bash to be bonus sons. They're all very close."

"So it started that night for you and Zac?"

"No. It started six days earlier at the running trail. I saw him there, but we didn't do anything other than stare at each other. Zac was running toward me and as soon as I saw his eyes, something began pulling me to him. It was a deep, burning ache that I felt inside my body, and in those few seconds that Zac and I held eye contact, that tie from me to him felt tangible. Like I could've felt it had I reached out and touched the space between us. Do I sound like I've gone crazy?"

My dad quietly chuckled. "No. Not at all."

"At the time, I didn't know what to make of everything that I was feeling, but after Zac and I met that night at the bar, I did. At least I began to understand it. Zac was and still is so familiar to me in a way that I can't explain, and the more we've gotten to know each other, he just—just feels like home to me. A home that I've never been to before but somehow know."

"What you experienced when you made eye contact with Zac is identical to what happened to me when I looked into your mom's eyes the first time. I was immediately drawn to her and I also felt a deep, burning ache inside my body. I didn't know what was happening to me at the time either but soon realized what it was. Your mom did too. Our souls picked each other's to love and we were finally *home*."

My dad and I smiled at each other through our tears, then both took a deep breath.

"I have never felt anything so real in all my life as what Zac and I share," I whispered while stealing a glance at him. I loved watching him sleep and had done it every time he spent the night with me. He slept so peacefully and seeing it brought me peace.

"It shows, daughter. What I've already seen between you and Zac in the short amount of time that I've been at this hospital leaves no doubt in my mind that you two really are deeply in love. It is very clear to me that you've found a home within his heart and he's done the same with yours."

"We have."

A few more tears, another deep breath and a shared tired smile between my dad and me, and then he asked about Zac's marriage. I told him everything that I knew about it as quickly as I could; I was worried about Zac waking up. I also told my dad about Zac's Malcolm and when I said his name, he nodded and then kissed my hand. I'd just finished telling him about all the likenesses between Zac and me when a nurse came in. She said she needed to check my vitals, so my dad went back over to his chair.

My blood pressure was a little higher than the last time it was checked, but the nurse expressed no concern about it. I knew it was higher due to the conversation my dad and I had and it was also due to my noticing the slightly curled-up corners of Zac's mouth right after the nurse came into my room.

His eyes were still closed and he still appeared to be very much asleep, although I knew better. Now, I couldn't help but wonder how long he'd been awake and how much he'd heard of the conversation between my dad and me. Going by those curled-up corners of his mouth, I could tell my lover liked what he heard.

My doctor released me from the hospital at ten this morning, but not before talking with me at length about the trauma I'd experienced yesterday—especially its lingering effects. I assured him that I was doing well. Then he asked me if I'd consider talking with a counselor. I said no. I didn't need to. I just needed to go home. The last thing my doctor asked me to do was to contact him if I began feeling *off* in the slightest and I told him that I would.

As Zac was walking my dad and me out to my dad's car, he mentioned mine.

"We need to get it back to your house so if you don't mind, I'm gonna go get your car, leave mine in the courthouse parking lot and drive yours," he said.

"I appreciate it. After you get to my house, I'll drive you back over to your car."

"Or I can," my dad said, smiling at Zac and me. I was in between them.

"Sure, Dad. Whatever is easiest for you guys."

And here we all were with things growing more awkward by the second— because Zac knew that my dad knew about our relationship, but my dad wasn't aware of that fact. He had no idea that Zac had overheard the majority of last night's conversation, beginning with me admitting to Zac and I being in love.

Earlier this morning, when my dad had gone to the hospital cafeteria to get some coffee, Zac got up and gave me a good morning kiss, and then I asked him at which point he'd woken up and begun listening to the conversation with my dad. After he told me, he said he was touched by what he heard. He was also relieved about my dad's acceptance of our relationship.

Zac and I both knew the time was coming for him and my dad to have their own little chat about matters and if I had to guess, it was going to happen after Zac brought my car back to my house. But my dad decided to talk to him as soon as the three of us made it to his car.

"I wanna clear the air with you," he began, looking straight at Zac. "I know you overheard the conversation that Stevie and I had in the middle of the night about the affair that you two are having and I appreciate you acting like you were still asleep so we could have it. I know you could tell how difficult it was for my daughter to admit to her relationship with you."

"Yes, sir, I could."

"There was a time when I found myself in the very position that you've found yourself in, being in an unhappy marriage and then meeting someone whom your soul immediately recognizes, loves, and longs to be with. For me, that was Stevie's mother. There's much more to that story, and that's something that you and I can talk more about at a later time. For now, I just wanted to let you know I'm not casting any stones at you or Stevie. She knows I'm not that kind of person and I want you to know it too. I always seek understanding in any situation, and in this case, I understand it well. I accept it too, Zac. I accept you. You're a really good man. You're just in a catch-22 like I was. But have faith, son. If this that you have with Stevie is meant to be, then a door will open for you two to be together."

Zac looked over at me and his eyes were filled with tears like mine and my dad's. When he turned back to face my dad, Zac thanked him for the words that he'd spoken and then held out his hand. My dad didn't shake it, though. He hugged Zac instead. While he was embracing him, I saw the pastor side of my dad but also the father—and Zac received his heartfelt affection with open arms.

My dad and I left to go to my house as Zac headed to the Dallas Courthouse parking lot to get my car. Before we parted ways though, Zac stepped up to me and pulled me into his arms. It felt so good to be in them again and feel Zac's warm and secure strength. I wondered if he was going to kiss me goodbye since my dad was sitting in his driver's seat by that point. He did kiss me but it was on my forehead, and I smiled to myself when he did it. Zac was being respectful of my dad in his own way and I appreciated it more than he knew.

On the way to my house, I asked my dad how he'd figured out Zac was married.

"The base of his left ring finger is smaller than the rest of it, and also slightly lighter than his entire hand," he said, glancing over at me.

"I hadn't even noticed that, but I should've known you would."

"I didn't notice it right away. What made me take a closer look at Zac was when he began sharing more detail about his family with me, after you fell asleep. He told me all about his son and also his parents. He never mentioned a wife, but he did pause mid-sentence a few times while he was talking to me and then changed the subject. It was as if he caught himself on the verge of saying something that he didn't want me to know. By then, I sensed there was a wife in the picture so I took a good look at Zac's left hand on one of the many occasions when he looked over at you in your hospital bed."

"You're not only a Jesus expert. You're a *people* expert."

"I don't think I'm either. I've just lived a long time and read the bible inside and out too many times to count. At my church, I've also counseled many married couples, as well as individuals in the same situation as you and Zac."

"I have no doubt that you've seen and heard it all."

"About the time that I think I have, I always hear something new that shocks me. The latest is what you told me about Zac's wife and how she treats Zac and also their son. I can't imagine living like that. I do understand Zac's reasoning, though, and I respect him for it."

"So do I."

"I'm gonna keep Zac and Malcolm in my prayers."

"Thank you, Dad."

He smiled at me, then reached over and gave my hand a gentle squeeze. "I wanna tell you again how thankful I am that you survived yesterday. What happened still doesn't feel real to me."

"It does to me."

"Yet you seem so indifferent about it. I can't get over how composed you are."

I shrugged my shoulders. "I'm just jaded about certain things in life is all. The cruelty of people is one of them. I have witnessed so much cruelty in my cases at work that nothing surprises me anymore. It just makes me angry. I don't know if being this way is a good thing or a bad thing."

"I think it's a survival thing, and a good thing in your line of work. That tough outer shell of yours helps you to help others."

I gazed out the window at the autumn sky, contemplating whether or not to tell my dad about something that occurred while Mr. Ferguson was holding his gun to my head. Then I decided to.

"As you know, I'm not afraid of dying," I said.

"Yes, Stevie, I do know that about you."

"Well, I really believed I was gonna die yesterday. I felt myself surrendering to it. While sitting there on the ground in Mr. Ferguson's clutches, my whole life flashed by in front of me, and what stood out was everything I've lost: Malcolm, Mom, and a marriage that was supposed to last forever. Then I pictured you and Zac. I was gonna be losing you and him by not being here on this earth any longer. The last of my happiness was about to be stripped away from me—and I was furious. I was also ready to die because I wanted the pain in my heart to end."

I stopped talking so I could get control over the tears that I was crying again and also catch my breath.

"Do you want me to pull over somewhere? Get a Dr. Pepper or something for you to drink?" my dad asked, rubbing my shoulder.

I shook my head no, took another minute just to be still, and then began telling my dad the rest of what had occurred yesterday while I was being held hostage by Mr. Ferguson.

"Right after I pictured you and Zac, I saw Mom. She came to me, Dad, but it obviously wasn't in a dream like before. I saw her standing in front of me in that parking lot and she told me to keep fighting. She said she knew I was tired but that I couldn't give up since *he* traveled through time to find me again. She was talking about Zac—his name was the next thing she said to me. I really have found the one whom my soul loves and also knows. I just hope life doesn't tear us apart."

48
#newsflash

Zac

On the way to my house from Stevie's, I called my mom with another update on the love of my life. I let her know that Stevie was doing great and also that Mr. Sinclair and I had talked about my relationship with his daughter. After telling my mom all the kind and supportive things he'd said, I heard her breathe a sigh of relief, and then she asked me if she and my dad could keep Malcolm overnight again.

Because I hadn't let Avery know where Malcolm nor I had spent the night, my mom was worried about a storm brewing at my house and she especially didn't want her grandson to witness it blowing up into a hurricane as it'd done before. Although what I personally did and also chose to do with my son was none of Avery's business, I understood my mom's concern. It was a valid one given not only Avery's history but also the way she'd been acting toward me all week. She still very much wanted us to work on our marriage—making my life her business again—and that wasn't going to happen.

I told my mom yes to keeping Malcolm again and told her that I'd check in with her later to see how he was doing and to also let her and my dad know how things were at my house. Hopefully, Avery would still be as calm and peaceful as she'd been the rest of the week.

As soon as I got home, I went directly to my bathroom. I also took off my bloodstained tie and shirt. When I walked back into my bedroom, Avery was sitting on the edge of my bed.

"What are you doing in here?" I asked her.

"I saw you and your pretty woman-friend, Stevie Sinclair, on the news. I saw what happened to her in the courthouse parking lot. I saw you run past all the police to rescue her after that man was shot. I saw Stevie run into your arms and pass out. I saw you pick her up and carry her to the ambulance. I also saw something else: the streaks on your face from the tears that you'd been crying and the kiss you gave Stevie on the cheek when you turned around to carry her to that ambulance. She's the reason why you're not willing to give me another chance, isn't she?"

"No, Avery—you're the reason. You and only you."

"Because of the way that I've treated you for so long, I understand you turning to someone else."

I shook my head in disgust. "You don't understand a damn thing about me. Now get the hell out of my bedroom."

"No."

"Avery, I swear to God, you better leave me alone. Now!"

"No. I'm staying right here and am gonna prove to you how much I love you. I've changed, Zac. Please just give me one more chance to get things right. Let me make it up to you."

Avery stood up and pulled off her t-shirt. She wasn't wearing a bra and she didn't have on any panties underneath the shorts that she took off next. I picked up her clothes off my bedroom floor, grabbed Avery's shoulders, and then pushed her out into the hallway. As she was turning to look at me, I slammed my bedroom door in her face and locked it. I didn't hear Avery start crying. I only heard her close the guest bedroom door a few seconds later.

I started pacing around inside my room, furious about what Avery had just pulled with me. I didn't like her even mentioning Stevie's name and I damn sure didn't like seeing her naked. In the brief amount of time that she stood in front of me without her clothes on, I'd thought about two things. The first was all the photos and videos that I received in the past and was still receiving from the private investigator I'd hired. Photos and videos that he took of Avery and Justin holding hands, hugging, kissing, and fucking each other in different locations. The most recent batch had come in two weeks ago.

The second thing that I thought of was Malcolm. He came to my mind when I saw the stretch marks on Avery's body. Stretch marks that she didn't want and bitched about the whole time she was pregnant, but especially after she gave birth to Malcolm.

The photos and videos of Avery and Justin didn't anger me. I didn't care about them being involved with each other. I was angry about Avery trying to play me for a fool when she came into my bedroom and said what she said and then did what she did. Seeing the stretch marks on her body angered me too, but it had nothing to do with Malcolm. It was all about Avery and the fact that she didn't want him. She refused to see the gift of him and also the gift of what her body was able to do by carrying and then having a child. Avery's had been nothing more than an incubator for Malcolm.

When it came to Avery bringing up that she saw Stevie and me on the news, plus recognizing Stevie and I were more than friends—I was never going to discuss the matter with her because just like my life was none of Avery's business, neither was Stevie's.

"Yeah, my dad is asleep. I could hear him snoring through the bedroom door when I checked on him a few minutes ago," Stevie told me.

"Good, because I need to talk to you. First, tell me how you're feeling."

"About what?"

I half-laughed. "About what you went through yesterday."

"Zac, I feel fine. Really. I'm trying not to think about it too much because I just start getting pissed off again. And I know this may sound cold-hearted, but I feel nothing about Mr. Ferguson being dead other than I'm glad."

"It's not cold-hearted. It's understandable."

"He was an awful human being."

"Yes, he was."

"Anyway... What else do you wanna talk to me about?"

"Have you watched the Dallas news yet?"

"No, and that's intentional. I figured what happened to me was on it and I don't wanna see it."

"Stevie, there's one video that I want you to watch and I'm not trying to upset you in any way."

"Why do you want me to watch it?"

"Because of what it shows of you *and* me."

She let out a long sigh. "Okay."

"Thank you. I'm gonna text you a link, so hang on."

"I'm hanging."

I sent the link and waited for her to watch it. About a minute later, she got back on the phone.

"That was really hard to watch, yet I loved seeing you coming to rescue me. I'm so choked up right now," she said, and I could hear the emotion in her voice.

"Did you see when I kissed your cheek?"

"Yes. I could tell that you'd been crying too."

"Avery saw all of that on the news. When I got home, she confronted me about it."

"The thought of that hadn't even crossed my mind. Oh my God, Zac! That video clearly shows how close you and I are. Did you admit it to Avery?"

"No. I refused to discuss anything about you and me with her because it's none of her business."

"But she knows about us now."

"She knows very little, Stevie. What was on the news could easily be viewed as one friend running to help another and being thankful that she survived being taken hostage and nearly killed. The people who know you and know me in this community will see it as just that. Bash was in the video too, in the background, when I was carrying you to the ambulance. We're *all* close friends and that's the story that I'm sticking to because it's also true."

"I didn't notice Bash because I was so focused on you. Oh, Zac, I'm really worried."

"About what?"

"Avery knowing that you and I are romantically involved. You not admitting it to her is irrelevant."

"Stevie, you don't need to worry. I'm not. I have no idea how much she knows, but I don't care. If she's figured it out, I want her to wrestle with the reality of you and me, and also all she did that destroyed our marriage and pushed me completely away from her."

"And into the arms of another woman."

"Yes. A woman that I'm so in love with. I never thought I could feel this way about anyone. Not until I met you. The thing about this entire situation is Avery knows she can't cast one stone at me. She doesn't know that I'm aware of that fact because she has no clue that I know about her relationship with Justin. She also has no clue about all the evidence that I have that proves she's been having an affair for years."

"Yes, I know. Otherwise, she wouldn't still be carrying on with her big charade. And about evidence... She now has some on us that would prove our affair."

"I go back to what I just told you. You and I come across as good and caring friends in that video and Avery can't prove we're anything more than that."

Stevie sighed. "Okay, here's what I think about this whole fucked-up deal. I do believe something happened between Avery and Justin the last time she was in Lubbock and that's why she returned home suddenly so adamant about working things out with you. Justin is no longer an option and you've always been Avery's backup plan. Because you've tolerated her bullshit all this time, I believe she's always believed she could reel you back in if things ever went south out west. Now that they seemed to have done exactly that *and* now that Avery knows about you and me, you can expect her to dig in her heels about winning you back. Even if it takes her threatening to divorce you and file for joint custody of Malcolm to achieve it."

"Stevie, I don't believe she'll ever do it."

"But she will do it, because she's that desperate. I can see her following through with taking the legal route if you don't agree to reconcile with her. Avery really doesn't want you. She just wants the financial security that you provide, but things are two-fold now since she knows about us. She still doesn't want you. She just doesn't want anybody else to have you, and if she can't have you, then she'll still get a big payout since you've been married to her for ten years. She can still take your money and she can still take Malcolm away from you through split custody."

"What are you really saying by bringing up all of this?"

Stevie paused for several long seconds. I could hear her taking one deep breath after another, and then she cried, "Our relationship needs to end. Today."

"No!"

"Yes, Zac, it does."

"No! You told me that you'd wait for our forever!"

"I know I did. Foolish me for saying it. Foolish me for believing we'd ever get a forever. Foolish me for thinking Avery wouldn't find out about us. Foolish me for every goddamn thing."

"Stevie, don't do this! Please!"

"I have to because I know you won't. You told me in the beginning that you'd never be the one to end us, so I am. I'm doing it because I love you and Malcolm so much and this is the only way that I can protect you both. Now go save your marriage with Avery—even if you have to fake it. Do whatever you have to do. Just don't lose your son."

49
#never

Zac

I rang Stevie's doorbell and waited. After about thirty seconds I rang it again, but she still didn't come to the door. She hadn't replied to any of the texts I'd sent her last night after she hung up on me. She also hadn't called me back although I pleaded with her to call me in all the voicemails that I left.

I'd wanted to come over here last night but knew that Stevie's father was still at her house. His car wasn't in the driveway now, but he could still be in town—the two of them could very well be eating out somewhere, and that could be why Stevie wasn't answering her front door. I couldn't eat anything right now if tried because my stomach was so knotted up about Stevie saying we needed to end our relationship. If she really meant it, she was going to have to tell me in person. I wanted her to look me in the eyes.

I gave her doorbell one more ring, then stepped off the front porch and looked around the quiet neighborhood. Then I decided to go look in Stevie's backyard. I realized she could be in her pool and didn't know I was here.

I quietly opened the gate and when I looked over at the pool, I saw Stevie floating on her back, and my heart started beating even harder. Stevie's eyes were closed and they remained that way even after I walked up and stood on the pool deck, directly across from her. She continued floating and I kept watching her in her silent reverie. Then she unexpectedly opened her eyes and looked at me. She stayed where she was, in the deep end of the pool, and I stayed where I was as we both began falling apart in front of each other.

"Did you mean what you said to me last night? Are we over, Stevie?" I choked out.

She stopped floating on her back and began treading water. "Yes. It's best and we both know it."

"No, I don't know it."

"Yes, you do. It's not what we want but it is best for all involved. Especially Malcolm. You are his world and he needs to keep his full-time daddy."

I shook my head in frustration. "Stevie, don't worry about that. Avery is not gonna do anything, legally."

"Mark my word—if you don't reconcile with her, she will."

"It's not happening. The thought sickens me to no end."

"Then like I told you last night: fake it."

We both grew quiet. The silence between us was deafening and I listened to it until I couldn't anymore.

"If we're really over, then tell me to my face. Look me in the eyes and say it," I whispered.

Stevie glanced down at the water, then met my blurry gaze again. "We're really over, Zac, and it's killing me. It is the right thing to do, though. Actually, the right thing for us to have done was to have never gotten involved with each other."

"You cannot possibly mean that after all that we've shared."

"But I do mean it."

"Then say it again. Tell me that we're really over again too. Hell, go ahead and tell me that you never loved me because it sure feels that way."

"Zac..."

"Fuck it!"

I tossed my cellphone and keys into the grass, then dove into the water with all my clothes on. As soon as I swam up to Stevie, I wrapped my arms around her and held her tight against me.

"Stop it, Zac! Stop it!" she screamed while trying to break away. Then she got an arm free and started hitting me everywhere she could and also kicking me with her legs beneath the water.

"Hit and kick me all you want, Stevie! I'm never letting you go!"

We were both crying so hard and finally—Stevie stopped fighting me and wrapped her arms around my neck, holding me as tight as I was still holding her. I swam us over to the shallow end of the pool and then carried Stevie over to the steps where I sat down and just held her in my lap. After a couple of minutes, we'd calmed down and somewhat collected ourselves, then Stevie lifted her head off my shoulder and looked at me.

"Take me to bed. Please. I need you, Zac," she breathed out.

I didn't say a word. I just picked up Stevie and carried her into her bedroom. After I took off her bikini, she peeled all my wet clothes off my body and then we laid down together on her bed. For the next hour, we loved each other in every way we knew how. We did it while crying again, smiling through our tears.

It wasn't until after we'd worn ourselves completely out and Stevie was lying in my arms with her head on my chest that she told me that we still had to end us. I immediately sat up and stared at her in disbelief. Although we hadn't discussed our relationship again, to me, it seemed understood that we weren't over due to what we'd just done together in bed.

"What did we just do here, Stevie?" I asked, pointing down at the mattress.

"What we've always done so damn well. It was what we both needed."

"No. You just led me to believe you were still in this. That our relationship wasn't over."

Stevie got up out of her bed, put on her robe, and then turned around to look at me.

"Selfishly, I wanted to be with you one last time because I wanted the memory. I will always love you, Zac," she said, breaking down again. "Go save your marriage. Go save your son."

I got up out of Stevie's bed and put back on my wet clothes. I didn't say another word to her before leaving her house. I couldn't. All I could do was throw up—as soon as I reached her front yard. Then I drove around Dallas for a while and ended up heading east down Interstate-20 and didn't stop until I reached Bossier City, Louisiana.

I decided to go to the Margaritaville Resort Casino even though my running shoes were still wet and my t-shirt, shorts, and briefs were still a little damp. I didn't care and I knew that no one else would either.

As I was pulling into the parking lot, I laughed seeing all the tropical décor on the building. It reminded me of Stevie. I hadn't even considered it because my mind and my heart were so fucked up but I didn't feel like driving to a different casino so I stayed at this one.

I went straight to the blackjack tables, sat down at one, and placed my bet. When a cocktail waitress walked by, I ordered a gin and tonic with extra lime. After having four more, plus losing every bet I'd placed, I stepped away from the table and then walked outside to call Bash.

"Stevie ended our relationship," I said as soon as he answered his phone.

"What?"

"Stevie and I are over."

"When did that happen?"

"It started last night and carried over into this morning."

"Why did she end things?"

"Because she believes Avery figured out we were having an affair and Stevie is afraid that Avery is gonna file for divorce from me now and also joint custody of Malcolm. She told me to work things out with Avery, all to save my son."

"Holy fucking shit, Zac."

I sighed and looked up at the sky. "I'm in Bossier City at the Margaritaville Casino, I'm drunk, I've lost my ass gambling and I need you here. Will you drive over?"

"I'm on my way. Don't go anywhere."

50
#lettinggo
Stevie

It had been two weeks since I was held hostage by Mr. Ferguson and twelve days since I'd ended my relationship with Zac. I was at work, sitting at my desk, and it felt like the walls were closing in around me. I'd been handling everything rather well but could tell now that it was all catching up with me—and quickly. I wouldn't be able to hide the trauma of what Mr. Ferguson had done to me for much longer, nor the shattered state of my heart after bringing my love affair with Zac to a necessary close.

He and I had passed each other three times in the courthouse hallways last week and twice during the prior one. That first time, he tried to talk to me but I just kept walking, and it was so hard to do. The second time, he stared at me with tears in his eyes but that was it. After seeing him that way, I hurried down the hallway to the women's restroom and locked myself in one of the stalls while trying not to hyperventilate.

Last week, on the other three occasions, Zac just looked angry when I saw him. No more hurt. Just a storm raging in his beautiful blue eyes. He didn't try to say anything to me on those days, but if he only knew how close I'd come to saying something to him on the last one. I wanted to tell him again how sorry I was that things had to be this way. I also wanted to tell him again that I loved him, but I knew it'd only add fuel to the fire of his anger.

I took a deep breath, stood up from my desk, grabbed my purse and briefcase, and then left for the Dallas courthouse. The second C.P.S. case that I was opposing Zac on was set to start in an hour. I needed to get going not only due to the horrendous traffic in this congested city but also due to the fact that I needed the drive time to prepare myself for coming face-to-face with Zac again. But not only that. On this occasion, we were going to have to speak to each other. Several times.

As I was walking down the main hallway in the D.A.'s office, though, Brooke caught up with me.

"Will you come to talk to me for a minute?" she asked.

"Okay."

In her office, she closed the door behind us.

"Stevie, I know I've asked you this a hundred times in the past two weeks, but can you handle this with Zac today?"

I cleared my throat. "Yes."

"That doesn't sound like a true yes. It sounds like you're about to come unraveled. You're trembling all over."

"I'll be fine, Brooke. I just need to get this day over with. Once it's done, I won't have to have any more contact with Zac. I know we'll cross paths again at the courthouse but we won't be legally fighting each other. I don't have to say a word to him or even look at him."

"But you want to, don't you?"

I stared down at the floor. Then Brooke lifted my chin back up with her finger.

"Joan of Arc, you are so strong, but you're also deeply wounded from everything that's happened to you. You need to lay down your sword. It's not too late. Your case can be rescheduled and I can assign someone else to it."

"No. I've already told you that I finish what I start—just like with my relationship with Zac. He asked me to be his lover, but it didn't start until I told him yes. My mistake. Now I need to go."

Brooke stepped aside and I left her office, wanting to run down the rest of the hallway instead of walk. I didn't, though. I kept my professional composure intact.

While driving over to the courthouse, I wondered if Brooke was going to sneak into the back of the courtroom. I wouldn't be surprised if she did that again. I knew she was really worried about me, as well as Zac. She had talked to me several times about my ending my relationship with him and I had no doubt she'd talked to Zac about it too.

When I explained to Brooke why I'd called it quits with Zac, she sounded like he did, telling me that she didn't believe Avery was going to do a thing, legally. I still wasn't willing to take the gamble of remaining in the picture, and all because of sweet Malcolm Buchanan. I'd lost my son in the worst possible way and didn't want Zac to come remotely close to feeling the kind of pain that I still felt from missing my little boy.

I was on my way up to the sixth floor of the courthouse, standing at the back, behind everyone else, when the elevator stopped at the third. As soon as the doors opened, I saw Zac standing there and he looked straight at me. He sighed and then stepped on, but he stayed far away from me. It hurt, too. I wanted him to stand beside me again. I wanted him to steal another kiss from me and hold my hand like he'd done before. That was wasn't going to happen, though. Not ever again.

As some people were getting off the elevator at the sixth floor, I stood back and waited for Zac to go ahead of me. I knew he needed to get off here too. But he didn't move. When the doors started to close, I pushed the button to open them again and then waited for Zac once more. He still didn't move, so I finally looked over at him and he had his eyes on me. I didn't see anger in them this time. Only love.

When Zac motioned for me to walk ahead of him, I did, hurrying down the hallway. He kept up with me and when we reached the courtroom door, he placed his hand against it and then looked into my eyes. I watched him canvass my face, stop at my lips, and then meet my gaze again. I thought Zac was going to say something to me but he didn't. He opened the door and we walked into the courtroom.

After Judge Mike Smith's court was called into session, Zac and I began presenting our sides of the case. It was identical to the Ferguson case with its circumstances of repeated drug use by the parents, plus their neglect and abuse of their little boy. The parents had been given two prior chances to clean up their lives and blew it. Today, I was going to do all I could to make sure the mother didn't get a third one. She was on the stand now and it was my turn to question her.

"Mrs. Calbert, I'm Stevie Sinclair and I'm representing your son for the state of Texas," I said, walking over and coming a stop in front of her.

"Hello, Miss Sinclair."

"Ms."

"Ms."

"Do you understand why we're all here today?"

"Yes."

"Tell me why we're all here today."

"Objection, your honor. We've already covered this," Zac interjected.

I looked over my shoulder at him standing behind the defense table. Then I turned around and started walking toward him.

"I wanna hear it come from your client's mouth, Mr. Buchanan. I wanna hear this mother explain to me *how* she could ever speak a cruel word or lay a mean hand on her four-year-old son."

"She knows what she's done, Ms. Sinclair."

"She needs to say it aloud for all to hear."

Zac walked around from behind the defense table and came up to me. "I think you're the only one who wants to hear it. You wanna bully my client in this way."

"I'm holding her accountable, Mr. Buchanan, and this time, I want you to listen closely to what she has to say. And after you do, I want you to tell me if that pitiful-acting client of yours reminds you of your alcoholic and abusive wife. Then I want you to tell me if you've thought about your son while working this case."

"That's enough, counsel!" Judge Smith yelled as Zac quietly growled "How dare you" at me.

I stepped even closer to him. "No. How dare *you*. How dare you make me love you."

"I didn't make you do that. You chose to."

"And you broke my heart."

"You broke your own damn heart, Stevie, and you broke mine too. You promised me that you'd wait for our forever," he said through his gritted teeth.

"Well, plans change."

"And how easily you walked away from them too." Zac's eyes were filled with tears now just like mine were.

"Ms. Sinclair? Mr. Buchanan? I'm warning you. Stop what you're doing. This is a court of law, not a counselor's office," Judge Smith continued, but we still paid no attention to him.

"You think it was easy for me?" I asked Zac. "Nothing has been easy for me in my life. Nothing!"

Zac and I were nearly nose-to-nose and our tears were streaming down our cheeks now. When Judge Smith began pounding his gavel, we finally stepped away from each other—both of us hurting so much and fuming. And that was when Zac's client began throwing up.

He ran over to her and for the next couple of minutes, she emptied whatever was in her stomach into a trash can behind the stand. As I watched her, replaying in my mind what Zac and I had just so unprofessionally done, I knew what Judge Smith was about to do. Then he did it. He continued this case to be heard at another time.

I thought for certain that he was also going to order Zac and me into his chambers to find out what in the hell happened between us, but he didn't. Before leaving his bench, he just pointed at us, gave us a hard look, and then dismissed court. When I looked over at Zac, he had his eyes on me and he shook his head. Not a *no* but a *yes*. An acknowledging yes that I knew meant he'd just accepted that we really were over. There'd never be any turning back.

As I was walking toward the door, I saw Brooke standing by it. She opened it for me and then the two of us walked in silence down the hallway, got on an elevator, rode it down to the first floor and left the courthouse. After making it down the steps, Brooke grabbed my arm and stopped me from walking any further.

"Look at me," she said.

"What do you want from me, Brooke?"

"The first thing is to take a deep breath."

"I can't take enough of them."

We stared at each other. Then I went on to apologize for what happened in the courtroom with Zac.

"Your apology isn't necessary, Stevie. I'm not worried about what happened. As a matter of fact, I predicted it. You and Zac have been holding in so much emotion and there was bound to be an explosion of it like what I just witnessed up there in Judge Smith's courtroom."

"And he continued this case. I'm gonna have to go through all of this with Zac again. I won't lose my shit again. I'm just gonna have to face Zac and speak to him. I thought all of that would be behind me after today."

Brooke gave me a sympathetic smile and then her cellphone started ringing.

"I've gotta take this," she said. "It's Jennifer and she never calls me. She only texts, so this must be really important."

I nodded and Brooke answered her call.

"Yes, I'm with Stevie. Why?" she asked.

As soon as I heard Brooke say that, I knew something was wrong. Then I saw the change in her eyes. They were now filled with even more concern for me. Less than thirty seconds later, she hung up and put her hand on my shoulder.

"The assistant pastor at your dad's church has been trying to call you but your phone must be on silent. Your dad had a stroke, Stevie. He's in the hospital."

I turned around and took off running to my car while Brooke yelled for me to stop but I didn't. I just kept running—hoping and praying that I could make it to my dad before I lost him.

51
#pleasureandpain

Stevie

When I got to the hospital, my dad was in his bed with an IV needle stuck in his left hand and an oxygen mask on his face, and he was sleeping. His assistant pastor, Kyle, and his church secretary, Margie, were in the room and came over to me as soon as they saw me. Their greeting was heartfelt and so was mine. Then I walked over to my dad, held his hand, and watched him breathing. He didn't wake up at my touch and my guess was that he must be sedated.

I heard the door open and looked over to see a man in a white coat, kindly smiling while extending his hand to shake mine.

"Hi, I'm Doctor Richardson. You must be Mr. Sinclair's daughter, Stevie," he said.

"Yes, sir, I am."

"It's nice to meet you."

"It's nice to meet you too. Please tell me everything that's going on here with my dad."

"Are you aware that he had a stroke?"

"Yes."

"Okay. I currently have your dad on an IV drip with a medicine that will help break up the clot in his brain. As far as the full extent of damage that the clot has done to your dad's brain, plus the effect on his speech and physical abilities—I'm not sure yet. Right now, my concern is keeping him still and resting. We have him sedated and plan to keep him that way until tomorrow."

"I understand. What is the rehabilitation process for someone who's had a stroke?"

"It's typically a long road. It could take months or even years. It all depends on the extent of damage to your dad's brain. After he leaves here, he'll likely need to go to a nursing facility or an inpatient rehab center. If he hasn't been affected by the stroke too badly, then he could go home, but he'll still need help. Someone to look after him until he's capable of caring for himself again."

"I'll do whatever is necessary for him."

"Stevie, your dad is in good hands here and he also has a lot of people praying for him, including me."

"I appreciate it, Dr. Richardson."

As he continued talking to me in more detail about my dad's rehabilitation process, my mind had already moved ahead to what I knew I was going to have to do now: move back to Austin to take care of my dad. I was going to make sure he received all the medical care that he needed so he could recover from his stroke as much as possible.

Between being held hostage at gunpoint by Mr. Ferguson, ending my relationship with Zac, and now this with my dad, I could only shake my head at this perfect storm pouring down its poison rain on top of me—and I couldn't take another thing happening.

After Dr. Richardson left the room, I texted Brooke a brief update on my dad and also let her know that I'd keep her informed as things moved along here. I also let her know that I wouldn't be at work the rest of this week and then apologized. She told me not to worry about it and to do whatever I needed to do. I didn't bring up that I'd soon be resigning from my position at her office, but planned on doing it once I had a better hold on everything that was going on here.

Right after our text-chat ended, my old boss/friend and District Attorney of Austin peeked her head into the room.

"Melissa!" I said, rushing over to her.

We hugged each other and kept hanging on. I'd missed her so much.

"Stevie, it is so good to see you again. I hate that it's under these circumstances."

"So do I."

"How is your dad?" she asked, looking over at him.

"Sedated. His doctor is keeping him that way until tomorrow. We don't yet know the extent of damage the stroke did, but what we do know is my dad will have to go to rehab. My guess is he's gonna be in it for a good while too."

"Excuse me, Stevie," Kyle said, walking over. "Margie and I are gonna go now."

"Oh, okay. Um, this is my good friend, Melissa Landry. A little late for an introduction and I apologize."

"No worries at all, sweetheart."

Kyle and Melissa greeted each other, and then Margie came over and met her. After that, my dad's church family members quietly left, and Melissa and I sat down in the chairs next to my dad's bed. I continued sharing details with her about all that Dr. Richardson told me about stroke recovery but I'd barely got started before I saw the change in Melissa's eyes. There was a smile in them now and I knew why. She realized I was going to be moving back to Austin.

When I'd covered all the medical stuff, Melissa said, "Shall I start helping you house hunt?" and I couldn't help but chuckle.

"Yeah, I'm gonna need it. Hopefully, everything will fall into place with this move just like it did when I moved to Dallas."

"Yes, hopefully, it will. You sold your house here so quickly."

"I know. Melissa, how do you think Brooke is gonna take me resigning after only three and a half months?"

"I know she'll understand, but like me, she's gonna hate losing her Joan of Arc. She's kept me up to date on your cases *and* your fight. She thinks the world of you."

"I think the world of her too."

"She cares for you as an employee but also as a friend."

And the look in Melissa's eyes changed again. I knew what that change was about, too.

"Brooke told you about my dad having a stroke, didn't she? And that I was on my way to Austin? And also about Zac Buchanan and me?"

"Yes. And about you and Zac... I know your heart is completely broken and I am so very sorry."

I shrugged my shoulders. "You warned me about keeping the professional *and* personal boundary lines drawn with him."

"I was just looking out for my dear friend, but Stevie, I do understand why you and Zac fell for each other. I also understand why you ended the relationship."

I was getting choked up but needed to keep talking about all of this with Melissa. Even though it hurt, it also felt good to get the words out.

"When I think about my life, there is a definite *before* Zac mark and a definite *after* Zac mark. What I experienced with him between those marks is just—just so much. So much love and passion and laughter and magic. I'll never get over him."

Melissa was choked up now and reached out to hold my hand. "I wish you'd kept me in the loop about you and him. Why didn't you call me?"

"I started to so many times, but because Zac and I were having an affair, I decided to keep it all to myself."

"You would've never received any kind of judgment from me."

I nodded in agreement. "I judged myself."

"Well, stop doing that shit. It's a waste of your time and energy."

"I'll try."

Melissa looked me over and then waved her hand up and down in front of me.

"Stevie, how in the world are you holding up like this? Even with all you've been through, you look amazing."

"Thank you. But I don't think I look amazing with these big bags under my eyes."

"What damn bags?"

I chuckled. Melissa had always been so blunt and funny. "These damn bags," I said, pointing at them.

"I don't know what you're talking about."

I waved her off, chuckling again. Then she asked me again how I was holding up so well.

"Denial and lots of Hendricks gin. That's how. I just have to keep going. There isn't time for anything else."

"Stevie, you're gonna have to make time to process your trauma. A trifecta has hit you all at once with you being taken hostage, you and Zac being over, and now this with your dad. If you don't make time, then that deep wound inside you is gonna keep festering. It won't go away on its own."

"I hear what you're saying and I know that I need to let myself start grieving yet again. I'm gonna have to take it really slow, though."

"Of course. Grieving is not a fast process and it's never linear."

"No, it's up and down, back and forth."

"Have you thought about going to Destin like you did after Malcolm passed away? I remember how much good that trip did for you."

I shook my head no. "I'll never go back to Destin."

"Why?"

"Because Zac took me there a few weeks ago. That's why."

I heard a light knock on the door and got up to go see who it was. Before I could open the door though, the person standing on the other side of it did. It was Graham.

"Hey," I said, surprised to see him.

"Hey, Stevie. I heard about your dad and came to check on him. I hope you don't mind me being here."

"Um, no, it's fine. Come on in."

I stepped back and Graham walked into the room. Then he saw Melissa sitting in her chair.

"How are you?" he asked her.

"I'm doing well, Graham. How are you?"

"I'm doing well too. Thank you for asking."

Graham looked back at me and I motioned toward my dad.

"You can go on over. His doctor has him sedated, so..."

"Okay."

As Graham was walking over to my dad's bedside, I looked over at Melissa and she bugged out her eyes at me. It was her way of asking if I was really okay with my ex-husband being here and I was. I nodded and then Melissa did.

After giving Graham a minute to be with my dad, I walked over to the other side of his bed, held his hand again, and then looked up to see the stress on Graham's face. His eyebrows were knotted up and the sides of jaws were popping out from clenching his teeth.

"If this is too much for you to see, I understand," I told him.

"Your dad has always seemed invincible to me and something like this happening to him is just hard for me to register."

Graham looked up at me as he was saying that but didn't keep his eyes on mine They made their way down to my lips and then back up. It reminded me of the way that Zac used to look at me.

"I know. I feel the same way."

"What all has his doctor said?"

After I filled Graham in with all the medical details, he asked me if there was anything he could do to help.

"Nothing that I know of. I appreciate your offering, though," I said.

"My cellphone number hasn't changed. Do you still have it?"

"Yes."

"If you think of anything that I can do to help or anything you need, then call me. It doesn't matter if it's day or night. I'll be there."

Graham and I stared at each other, and I wondered if he was dating anyone. When I ran into Graham at the grocery store last month, he'd told me that he and Emma were no longer together and also that he wasn't seeing anybody. If he still wasn't, then I hoped that one day he would meet a woman who was perfect for him. I wanted Graham to be happy. He looked happy at this very moment. He was still so handsome, too, with his wavy dark brown hair, bright green eyes, and goatee. Allowing myself to look at him in this way again was easy to do since I'd let my hurtful past with him go, and also since I'd found myself walking in his shoes when Zac and I began our affair.

"Okay, I will. Thank you again," I said, smiling.

Graham and I stayed at my dad's bedside for another couple minutes going back over some of what the doctor had told me, and then he said something that I wasn't expecting.

"You're gonna have to move back to Austin to take care of your dad, aren't you?" he asked.

"Yes."

"How do you feel about that?"

"I'm fine with it."

"I'm not surprised to hear you say that, Stevie. I know you'll take the best care of Pastor Sinclair here." Graham looked down at my dad again and then met my gaze once more. "If I can do anything to help make your move back to Austin easier and faster, then let me know about that too. Your dad, your move—anything you need. Okay?"

He reached across my dad's hospital bed for my hand and I gave it to him. He ran his thumb across the top of my fingers but kept his eyes on mine. I found myself suddenly caught up in what had attracted me to Graham when we first met all those years ago in high school: his kind eyes, his kind words, his gentle spirit, his gentle touch. Just him.

"Okay," I finally whispered. "I'll let you know."

52
#goodbye

Zac

"I knew that was coming next," I told Brooke. "After you called me about Stevie's dad, my first thought was that she's gonna have to take care of him *if* he survives the stroke. She is the only family that he has. Her moving back to Austin is the logical step. She has to take it and I understand."

"But how do you feel about it?"

"I hate it. This is like a continuous heartbreak going on inside me. It never gets the chance to start healing because things keep coming up that shatter it all over again."

"I'm so sorry, Zac."

"You know, I really believed Stevie and I were gonna eventually get back together. I thought that given a little time, she'd see the big picture, and realize she could trust what I told her about Avery not doing anything, legally. Now that Stevie is moving to Austin, I'll never get a second chance with her."

"You don't know that."

"Yes, I do. It's too late, Brooke. Stevie has clearly let me go and she's got so much ahead of her that she's gotta tackle now."

"FYI... Before she and I hung up earlier, she asked me about you. She wanted to know how you were doing and also if you ever ask about her."

"What'd you tell her?"

"The truth. I told her that you were still so torn up about the two of you ending and that you mention her every time I talk to you."

"And what'd she say?"

"Well, first, she started crying. Then she told me that you were the love of her life and always would be. She also said she had no regrets and would go through everything all over again just to experience the love you gave to her."

I blew out a hard breath and kept pacing around in my and Stevie's secret spot in the woods at the running trail.

"Brooke, why would God allow me to meet someone like Stevie Sinclair and fall in love with her if He didn't intend for us to be together?"

"Maybe, just maybe, He's not done with you and her yet."

"Oh, He is. That's so damn obvious."

"It sounds like Stevie isn't the only one who needs a little time to see the big picture."

"I see it now," I said, then took a drink from my water bottle. "So when is Stevie's last day at your office?"

"She's already resigned."

"What?"

"She was adamant about giving me at least two weeks' notice, but I told her no because she needs to be with her dad full time as soon as possible."

"Okay, there's another blow to my heart. I was hoping to see her at the courthouse again before she resigned. There wouldn't have been anything said between us but..."

"I know, Zac. I know that longing just to take in the vision of her again. I was the same way about my exception. Hell, I still am."

"You got to tell him goodbye. I never did with Stevie because I've been too angry—and now she's moving away."

"Are you still angry? Because you don't sound like it."

"No, I'm not anymore."

"Then go tell your exception goodbye. She's at her house packing up as we speak—and she's there alone."

I was a few houses down the street from Stevie's when I saw her step outside onto her front porch and begin taking down the Halloween decorations. Seeing her do that made my chest tighten up even more. She really was leaving Dallas and I really wasn't going to get a second chance with her.

Her back was to me when I started pulling into her driveway, but she heard my car and turned around. As soon as she saw me, she dropped the witch hat in her hand onto the grass and didn't move again. Not even after I got out of my car and walked up to her.

Stevie's bottom lip was quivering and her beautiful deep blue eyes were brimming with tears just like mine were. Unable to hold myself back any longer, I pulled Stevie into my arms and held her trembling body against mine as tightly as I could. Then we both broke down and cried like we'd both been needing to do.

After the tidal wave of our emotions began to subside, Stevie lifted her head off my chest and looked up at me. I wiped off her cheeks and she wiped off mine. Then she asked me a question I'd known was coming. She wanted to know why I was here.

Before answering her, I looked over her face again and then said, "I didn't tell you goodbye. That's why I'm here. I know about your dad and I am so sorry. I know you've resigned from your position at the D.A.'s office and I also know you're moving back to Austin. I couldn't let you leave without seeing you one last time, telling you how I feel, and telling you goodbye."

Stevie searched my eyes and then nodded at me. "Tell me how you feel right now."

"Brokenhearted because you and I are over, but I'm happy for you that you can go help your dad."

"I'm brokenhearted too—and I miss you so much. I dream about us, and in my dreams, I relive all the special times that we shared. I'll always carry them with me, Zac."

"I dream about you every night. Even Malcolm has been dreaming about you."

"What?"

"Yeah, he has, Stevie. It started last Saturday—a reoccurring dream that he's having every night. He sees you on a beach trying to get back to the ocean but you can't because your sparkly blue tail is stuck in the sand. Malcolm has cried every time he's told me about it, and he always says, over and over, 'Daddy, we have to help mermaid Stevie get back home.' When I told him the first time that it was just a dream and not real, he put his hands on my face, stared me straight in the eyes and said his dream was real. I've just gone along with it since then because I don't wanna upset him. I told him that I'm gonna figure out a way to help you get back home."

Stevie didn't say anything. She just searched my eyes again.

"Are you okay?" I finally asked.

"I don't know what I am anymore, Zac."

"I understand."

"I'm sorry that all of this between us has caused you so much pain."

"I'm sorry too. I never intended for you to get hurt in any way."

"I want you to know that I don't regret having an affair with you."

"I don't either. You changed my life. Now I know what it feels like to really be loved by someone."

"Same here."

"I will take my last breath loving you, Stevie."

She covered her face with her hands and started crying again. I did too and then pulled her back into my arms. We stood on her lawn for I don't know how long, just holding onto each other and swaying back and forth in the cool breeze of this October evening.

When it came time to say our last goodbye, I took Stevie's beautiful face into my hands, looked into her eyes, told her that I loved her again, and then we kissed. When that kiss ended, we stared at each other and we kept staring. It became apparent that neither of us wanted to say the word goodbye because of its biting finality. We weren't going to say it, so I made myself turn around and walk away from Stevie while feeling my soul rip apart.

As soon as I backed out of her driveway, I looked over at her one last time. She was sitting in the grass with her arms wrapped around herself, rocking back and forth, and she was still crying just like me. Then she did something that I was never going to forget. She patted her chest twice above her heart and then pointed at me.

53
#timepassages

Stevie

I watched Zac drive away and when I could no longer see the taillights of his Blazer down my street, I slowly got up out of the grass and went back inside.

I was done packing for my move back to Austin. Standing in the middle of my living room, I looked around at this house that I'd tried to make a home for myself and shook my head. Was I ever going to be settled and at peace again? Would I ever be happy again? Probably not.

As I was walking into my kitchen to get a paper towel to dry off my face, I heard my cellphone chime on the counter. When I saw 'Buchanan' on the text notification, I gasped, because I thought what had happened between us in my front yard only minutes ago was the last contact I was ever going to have with him. As soon as I opened his text and saw the link though, I knew this would be it. Zac couldn't say goodbye to me in person but he could do it through a song.

Before listening to it, I grabbed my bottle of Neptunia out of the cabinet. I didn't want any tonic water and lime mixed with it this time. I just wanted the taste of the gin on my tongue, and after taking two shots, I picked up my cellphone off the counter and then walked outside to sit down at the patio table.

499

I took a minute just to be still and breathe and ready myself for the next wave of emotions that I knew was about to hit me. I had the feeling, though, that this wave was going to take me under, and deeper than I'd ever gone before.

Looking at the link again, I realized I had never heard of the artist before. His name was Dylan Wheeler and the genre was a big mystery until about twenty seconds into the intro of "Tree Song." Dylan was a country music artist who had a whole lot of rock and roll in his rich and soulful voice, as well as an alternative sound that reminded me of the lead singers from Pearl Jam and Soundgarden.

As the song continued playing, I realized what Zac was trying to say to me through the haunting lyrics. It wasn't just goodbye. He wanted to tell me how hard he'd tried to stand tall for me and do right by me—and I knew he had. He also wondered if, as time went on, I'd view him in the same way, miss him, or forget him altogether. That part had me bawling, but especially the part of the song that talked about whether or not I'd find it hard to breathe when Zac was no longer around, here on earth. I was already struggling to breathe without him and always would.

After hearing the line "Remember me when it rains," I turned off my cellphone because it hurt too damn much to keep going. I wouldn't be adding "Tree Song" to my playlist. I'd never listen to it again and I'd also never forget Zachariah Dalton Buchanan—my exception, my soulmate, the love of my life.

Two weeks later

"I really hope my house sells fast. I'm ready to close that chapter in Dallas and just focus on this one here with my dad," I told Melissa.

"You feel good about the realtor you hired, so keep thinking positive thoughts."

"I'm trying to."

"So you're just gonna stay at your dad's house for now?"

"Yes, the church parsonage. The assistant pastor, Kyle, told me I can stay for as long as I need. In the meantime, I'm just gonna keep taking care of my dad, helping him in rehab and looking for a house here in Austin."

"Does it feel strange to be back?"

"I thought it would but it hasn't at all. It's really kinda nice seeing my old stomping ground again and people I've known my whole life. Hang on a sec. Someone just rang the doorbell."

"Okay."

When I looked through peephole, I smiled and then asked myself why I was happy to see Graham standing on the other side of the door. I didn't know why other than I just was. Maybe it was the familiarity of him, the comfort that he brought and just his easygoing company.

"Melissa, I'll call you back later if that's all right."

"Of course. Is everything okay, though?"

"Yeah."

"Who was at the door?"

"Um, Graham. He's still there. I haven't answered it yet."

"Should I be concerned?"

"About what?"

"You and him."

"What about us?"

"I didn't say anything to you at the time but I did notice a little flicker of attraction between you and Graham when he came to see your dad at the hospital."

"Melissa, there's nothing there. We are friends now and I'm thankful that we can be. We have a long history together."

"Okay then. You better call me later tonight with a full report."

I chuckled. "Yes, ma'am."

As soon as she hung up, I opened my dad's front door and Graham smiled at me.

"Hi," I said, smiling back.

"Hi."

"How are you?"

"I'm good. Just thought I'd stop by to see if you need any-thing."

"I don't believe I need a thing. I've been to the grocery store again, the pharmacy, and even stopped by Home Depot to pick up a mum."

"Yeah, I see it here on the front porch. The burgundy ones are still your favorite, huh?"

I smiled again. "Yes, they are."

"How are you holding up with everything?"

"I'm doing okay. Just so busy and really hoping my house in Dallas sells soon. Sorry, I'm being rude," I said, stepping back from the doorway. "Come on in."

"You don't mind?"

"Not at all. I know you."

Graham glanced down at my lips and then nodded. "I know you too."

After coming inside the parsonage, I offered him some-thing to drink and he asked me what I had. As we were walking into the kitchen, I rambled off the list.

"There's orange juice, milk, Dr. Pepper, and a bottle of Pi-not Grigio in the fridge. Oh, and I have some Hendricks in the cabinet. Would any of that interest you?"

Graham's green eyes danced across my face. "So you're still a fan of gin."

"Always. How about you?"

"Always."

"It's after five o'clock, so would you like to enjoy some now? I have tonic water and limes too."

"Of course you do. And sure, I'll have a Hendricks and tonic with extra lime—with you. I'm happy to, but please allow me to make our drinks. It'll be like old times."

"Fun times."

"Yes. Very fun times."

While Graham was making our drinks, we continued catching up about all that'd been going on in his life and mine.

Our conversation carried over into my dad's living room and after having two more gin and tonics with me, the expression on Graham's face grew serious. Then he took my hand into his. I looked down at what he was doing and then met his gaze again.

"Are you okay with me doing this?" he asked.

I paused and then nodded yes. "It feels really nice."

"I appreciate you keeping me up-to-date on how your dad is doing."

"You're welcome. I know you've always cared about him just like he's always cared about you."

"I do care about him. I care about you too. I've never stopped caring about you, Stevie."

"I've never stopped caring about you either. We've known each other for so long and have been through so much."

"Yes, we have."

"Time is a funny thing."

"How so?"

"How it changes your perspective."

"In general or are you talking about something specific?"

"Specific."

"Okay."

I looked down at my hand still in Graham's, took a deep breath, and then said, "My perspective on extramarital affairs has changed. I don't view them as black and white anymore."

"Are you sure you wanna talk about this with me? I don't want you to get upset."

"I'm sure. I need to talk to you about it."

"Then I'm right here for you."

"It may be the Hendricks I've had that's giving me the courage to go here with you, but oh well."

"I've never known you to be short on courage, Stevie."

"I was short on it when it came to the topic of adultery because I didn't fully understand it. Not until I found myself walking in your shoes in Dallas."

Graham jerked his head back in surprise. "You-you had an affair?"

"Yes."

"Okay. A coworker?"

"No, a defense attorney."

Graham paused and stared at me. I could tell the wheels in his mind were spinning.

"Did you fall in love with him?" he finally asked.

"Yes."

"Are you still in love with him?"

"Yes."

"Who ended the affair?"

"I did."

"Was he good to you?"

"Yes."

"So why did you end it?"

I blew out a hard breath. "It was just time."

"And are you okay?"

"I'm up and down—about everything that's going on in my life."

Graham took another sip of his gin and tonic. "Why did you wanna tell me about all of this?"

"So I could tell you this: I'm sorry for not being the wife and friend that you needed the last four years of our marriage and I'm sorry for making you feel like you had to turn to someone else."

"Stevie, you did the best you could after we lost Malcolm. I should've been more of a man and not given in to my loneliness."

The words between us stopped and we just looked at each other. Graham was still holding my hand and gently rubbing his thumb across the top of it.

"How about you and I make a deal," I finally said.

"What kind of deal?"

"From this day forward, let's not beat up ourselves over the mistakes of our pasts. Let's just embrace the lessons."

Graham nodded "Sounds good to me. May I tell you the main lesson that I learned from all that we went through?"

"Yes."

"I don't know if you'd categorized it as a lesson. It's more of a realization."

"Okay."

"I realized how much I love you, Stevie. I'm still in love with you, and I told you those same words on the day I drove away from our house for the last time."

"I remember."

"Is there any part of you that still loves me?"

I looked over Graham's handsome face, appreciating everything that I saw. In him, I could see my youth, my innocence, my faith, and so many years of happiness before we lost Malcolm. We faltered then and turned away from everything good when there was still so much good in life. So much good still between us. We just couldn't see it. No, I couldn't see it. Graham still did and he'd tried to clear my vision, but I gave up because I felt as if life had given up on me. God had. I was wrong, though. So very wrong.

"Yes. I realized on the day you drove away from our house for the last time that I was still in love with you despite all the heartache between us. I hated seeing you leave, Graham. I-I hated seeing the back of your truck loaded up with all those boxes of your belongings, but it was too late," I choked out.

Graham set down his glass on the coffee table and when he turned back to look at me, he reached up and cradled my face in his hands. His eyes were brimming with tears just like mine and he was breathing deep like I was too.

"Stevie, is it too late for us to try again? Would you be willing to give me a second chance?"

"I don't know. I mean..."

I looked down at Graham's lips, then leaned closer and pressed mine against them. Then I closed my eyes. Graham sighed and so did I, and then our gentle kiss quickly became more. It wasn't just our lips touching now. Our tongues were too and feeling the heat of Graham's entangled with mine made me want even more of him.

I remembered this kiss of his. I also remembered the taste of his tongue. Graham had always been a passionate kisser and he was also a passionate lover. The sex we used to have was good, but I was who shut all of that down between us. Not anymore, though. Right or wrong, I wanted my ex-husband. I wanted to feel him all over *and* inside me again. Having sex with him didn't equate to a "yes" for a second chance because I didn't know if I wanted that to happen. It just meant that I needed to be close to Graham tonight. I thought maybe if I could, then I'd stop visualizing Zac every time I looked at him.

I pulled my mouth away from Graham's and then reached for the hem of his t-shirt. He raised his arms into the air and after I dropped his shirt onto the living room floor, I ran my hands down the front of Graham's hairy chest and abs. He'd always had a good physique and I had always been attracted to his body.

When I reached for the snap on Graham's blue jeans, he grabbed my hand.

"Stevie, what are we doing?" he breathed out, staring straight at me.

"You know what we're doing."

"As much as I want you, the timing of this isn't right and we both know it. It's too fast."

"Was our kiss too fast?"

"No. Having sex would be, though."

"Why do you think that?"

"Because it wasn't that long ago that you ended your affair. Right?"

"Right."

"Being with me like this won't fix your heart. I can tell how much you're still hurting and you need more time to heal. Me getting a second chance with you is irrelevant at this point and my pushing the pause button is for both of us."

I looked down at Graham's chest and abs again and then met his gaze. "Okay. I'm sorry about all of this tonight. It's just that I..."

"Wanted to forget his memory for a little while?"

I swallowed hard. "Yes."

"I tried doing that too, with my memory of you, but it never worked. I always saw your face whenever I looked at Emma's."

Graham grabbed his t-shirt off the floor and put it back on. Then he pulled me into his arms and just held me. I rested my head on his shoulder while he rested his cheek against mine—and we both breathed. It wasn't long after that that he told me that he needed to leave. Before he did, though, he asked me about going on a Halloween hayride with him on Saturday in Georgetown.

"You know I love spooky stuff," I said.

"Yes, I do. We'll go as *old friends*. How does that sound?"

I smiled. "It sounds good to me. I know we'll have fun. We always used to."

"Yeah, we did. We'll need to leave here around six. Does that work for you?"

"Sure. I'll bring some blankets for us."

"And I'll make us a thermos of hot chocolate."

"And you know I love that too."

"I do."

Graham and I smiled at each other, then got up from the couch and I walked him to the front door of the parsonage. After stepping outside onto the front porch, he turned around and looked at me.

"I'll check on you tomorrow," he said. "Bye, old friend."

I watched him walk down the sidewalk and then make his way over to his truck parked in the driveway. After he'd driven a few yards down the street, he stopped in front of the parsonage, rolled down his window, and then stared at me. I shrugged my shoulders to ask him if something was wrong and he shook his head no. Then he gave me the "hang loose" sign with his hand. He hadn't forgotten it and neither had I.

It was something that we'd started doing in high school after we became friends. It was our personal sign for "hello" and "goodbye" and eventually became our sign for "I love you." I didn't know if Graham was telling me goodbye again or reminding me that he loved me right now, but I knew what I was saying to him when I raised my hand into the air and made the sign. I loved him and I always would.

54
#success

Stevie

"Dad, you're doing so well," I said.

"Between my physical therapist and you pushing me, of course I'm doing well. I have two drill sergeants here." He chuckled and so did I.

"I'm really proud of you."

"I appreciate it, daughter of mine."

"I'm really thankful that you've made it through all of this, too."

"So am I."

"Hey, before we go back home, how about we stop by Torchy's Tacos?"

"I'm all for it."

"Then let's go, old man."

He sighed out a grin and then stood up, using his walker. My dad's rehabilitation could be quantified as a success, although he still had lingering effects from the stroke and probably would for the rest of his life. Still—he was doing so wonderfully.

New Year's Eve was tonight and my dad and I had plans to ring in the new year in his parsonage living room in front of the big screen, watching the ball drop in Times Square while he enjoyed some Pinot Grigio and I enjoyed some Hendricks. My dad had always been one to celebrate the new year's arrival—always recounting his blessings from the previous year and already thanking God for the ones that he knew lay ahead. This time, I was going to do that too.

On our way over to grab some tacos, my dad brought up something that I'd struggled with saying yes to because I wasn't sure if he was in a place where I could say yes. Now, I felt at peace having said yes.

"Are you excited about going back to work on Monday?" he asked me.

I cut my eyes over him sitting in the passenger seat of my car and smiled. "Very excited."

"I know Melissa is excited to have her Joan of Arc back fighting for children around here."

"Now remember that I can come home at any time if you need me. Melissa has already assured me that it won't be a problem."

"Oh, I'll be fine while you're at work. I know I still have a little way to go before I can hop back in the saddle at my pulpit but it doesn't mean that I can't go ahead and prepare some sermons."

"You're right, it doesn't. Have you thought about what your 'welcome back' sermon is gonna be?"

"I have."

"And?"

"Redemptive love."

"God's love?"

"Yes—and also the redemptive love of another human being. It's what your mom's love was to me. She saved me in so many ways and now, your love has saved me."

I reached over and held my dad's hand. "I love you."

"I love you too, daughter."

"And I'm telling you right now that I'm gonna be sitting in the front pew to listen to your sermon on your first Sunday back."

My dad lifted my hand to his mouth and kissed it. "Good."

After we got back to the parsonage and devoured our tacos, my dad said he needed to take a nap because it was the only way that he was going to be able to stay awake until the new year rang in. He'd just started walking toward the hallway when he stopped, turned around, and looked at me.

"What time did you say Graham is coming over?" he asked.

"Around eight."

"Okay. I've really enjoyed getting to see him again."

"I know you have."

"You seem to have also."

"I have, Dad."

He slowly walked back over to me and studied my eyes.

"But there's something missing."

"What do you mean?"

"I can see how much Graham is still in love with you and I know you love him too, but what you and he are feeling for each other doesn't match. I know why—and so do you."

I looked down at the floor.

"Stevie?" my dad continued. "Stevie, look at me."

"Don't say it."

"I have to speak the truth and the truth that I see in you is you're still deeply in love with Zac Buchanan."

All at once, I felt the sting in my eyes and the lump in my throat, then I slowly nodded in agreement.

"I am still deeply in love with him," I choked out. "I've tried letting go of him and I just can't. I miss him so much. What am I supposed to do, Dad? I have to move on. You know Graham wants a second chance with me. He's just waiting for me to say yes."

My dad canted his head to the side and looked over my face. "I don't know what you're supposed to do, daughter, but God does. There's incredible power in a prayer that you make from the seat of your soul for direction in life. It beckons the universe to set in motion a chain of events that begins steering you in the right direction whether you realize it or not. Then, before you know it, you wake up one day, look around, and know

GINA MAGEE

beyond any doubt that you're exactly where you're supposed to be and with whom you're supposed to be."

"With whom?"

"Yes."

"You mean Graham or Zac?"

"Yes, I do."

"Dad, Zac does not factor into this other than I'm still in love with him. There is no future with him for me," I said, throwing my arms up into the air.

"All I know to tell you is to pray for God's direction in your life, cling to your faith with both hands and then hang on. It may get bumpy for a while but keep believing, keep going and keep looking up at the stars."

55
#ridingthewave

Stevie

"No, I haven't had any contact with Zac since the day he showed up at my house in Dallas to tell me goodbye before I moved here. Why do you ask?" I said to Melissa. We were eating lunch together at Cypress Grill in Austin.

"Because you and Zac have been on my mind for the past few days for some reason. Plus, haven't we all heard of old lovers reaching out to each other just to see how they're doing?"

"Sure, I've heard of that happening, but it hasn't happened between Zac and me. It doesn't need to, either."

"I'm not trying to upset you, Stevie."

"I know you're not, and really, I'm fine. I just wasn't expecting that kind of question is all. My mind is overloaded with my cases."

"Are they too much for you?"

"Not at all. I do better when I stay busy."

"Some people do that just to distract themselves from something else."

"Such as?"

Melissa shrugged. "It could be any number of things. Life. You know."

"Yeah, I know."

"So is it really a wrap with your counselor?"

"It is. She believes I'm mentally, emotionally, and spiritually good now with what happened back in Dallas. I believe I am too. I know I am."

"That makes me happy to hear. I was really worried about you for a while."

"Well, there's no need to worry anymore. So tell me how Haven's teacher conference went yesterday."

Melissa rolled her eyes. "As expected. I swear, my granddaughter..."

"She's not gonna put up with any boy's bullshit."

"I know, but she can't just punch one in the face for mouthing at her."

"Yes, she can and she did," I chuckled.

"She's in third grade, Stevie."

"And your point?"

"I'm just—hell, I don't know."

"I'm proud of her."

"Let's just hope it doesn't happen again. That was the second time. I don't want the school to kick her out."

"They're not gonna kick her out."

"It was challenging raising my kids during my twenties and thirties but I've gotta tell you, it's kicking my ass raising my granddaughter in my fifties. Don't get me wrong. I love her so much and would do anything for her. It's just really hard sometimes."

I reached across the table for Melissa's hand. "I know it is, but you're an amazing grandmother and mom-in-one. You're also an amazing friend to me."

"You're an amazing friend to me too. We've been through a lot, haven't we?"

"Yes, we have. Life has definitely seasoned us."

"That's one way to put it."

Our waiter walked up and asked if we wanted some more tea. We did, so he refilled our glasses and went to wait on his other customers. That was when Melissa asked me about Valentine's Day. It was coming up soon.

"Do you have plans with Graham?" she asked.

"Yes. We're going out to eat. I don't know where yet and it really doesn't matter to me. I just enjoy his company."

"I always liked Graham, but I hated him after finding out about his affair with Emma. I've learned to like him again now. As long as he keeps treating you like he has been ever since you moved back, then I'll keep liking him. If he fucks up again, then I'm gonna kill him."

"And you wonder where your granddaughter gets her fire?" I chuckled.

"Oh, God, I know."

"About Graham, though. Now that I've walked in his shoes concerning having an affair, I understand it. He and I had a long and positive talk about it, too. It was nice being able to lay all my cards on the table and let him see me for who I am today."

"What did he say to you after you told him about Zac?"

"Well, I never told Graham his name, but I did tell him about our affair, plus what I learned from it."

"What'd you learn?"

I smiled. "That I still care about and love Graham. I always will, too."

"Okay, I just have to say it. You two have been spending quite a bit of time together and you keep telling me that you're just friends. But really? There's gotta be more going on."

I sighed. "We've kissed."

"I knew it! How many times?"

"Several."

"What else have you done?"

"Well, we came really close to having sex not long after I moved back here. We'd just shared one hell of a kiss. As a matter of fact, it was our first kiss since we divorced. I took Graham's t-shirt off and was reaching for the snap on his jeans when he stopped me. He knew it was too soon for me to be that intimate with him. It'd only been a month since I ended my affair with Zac, and Graham could tell how much I was still hurting about it. He also knew that my wanting to have sex with him was to escape my memory of Zac for a little while. He was so right about that, but I also wanted to be with Graham because I am still very much attracted to him."

Melissa sat back in her chair and sighed. "First of all, wow about him being so insightful and understanding, and also for having that kind of restraint. Second of all—why are you just now telling me about all of this?"

"Because I'm judging myself again."

"You and Graham are both single, Stevie."

"I know. It's just that I really feel guilty sometimes when I'm with him and he's being so wonderful to me and while I'm looking at him, I'm imagining that he's Zac. I don't do it every time. There are days when I'm able to block out Zac and truly enjoy Graham for the good man that he is—and also the great kisser. And by the way, kissing *is* all that we've done since that night we almost had sex."

"Still... I'll bet Graham has the bluest pair of balls ever."

I threw my napkin across the table at Melissa and we both busted out laughing.

"You're awful!" I said.

"Yeah, but I'm honest. Granted, I'm brutally honest most of the time but you get me."

"Yes, I do and I love you."

"I love you too. Tell me something, though."

"What?"

"Do you see things with Graham ever getting more serious than they are now?"

"He asked me for a second chance, Melissa, but he pushed pause on it because he wants me to heal my Zac-wound first. It's only fair to Graham that I do."

"Yourself too."

"Yeah."

"And how is your Zac-wound?"

I blew out a heavy breath. "Still very much open and raw. Zac haunts me in every way. I still feel him on my skin and sometimes, I hear his voice calling out to me like he's in the next room. It's that clear. I know it's just my memories of us that are making all that happen. They constantly replay like a movie inside my head. I also see things that remind me of Zac whenever I'm out and about, running errands. And if you only knew the number of times that I've gotten into my car and turned on the radio only to hear a song that Zac and I both love. We used to always text songs back and forth to each other. I still have every one of them on a playlist on my phone, too. All except for one. It was the last one that he texted to me after we said goodbye."

"Okay, you're about to make me cry."

"Myself, as well."

"Stevie, I don't think you're ever gonna get over Zac."

"I know I'm not."

"So where does that leave things with you and Graham?"

I shrugged. "Today, I don't know. Tomorrow, I might. For now, I'm just gonna take in the blessing of this day, which includes getting to see Graham tonight and probably kissing those soft lips of his again. I'm gonna ride this thing out and keep waiting for a door to open that will show me beyond any doubt what I'm supposed to do concerning my heart. I can't take it being broken again by anyone."

"Hey, Dad! I'm home," I hollered as soon as I opened the front door of the parsonage.

He didn't say anything like he usually did, so I walked into the living room but he wasn't there, or in the kitchen, either. After setting down my purse and briefcase on the counter, I started walking toward his bedroom and called out for him again. He still didn't answer me. His bedroom door was closed so I cracked it open quietly, thinking my dad was probably taking a nap—but I was wrong. I was so damn wrong.

"Dad!" I screamed, running over to him.

He was laying on the floor, his eyes were closed, he was non-responsive and his skin was cold. I started shaking him and screaming his name over and over because this could not be happening. My oh-so-sweet dad could not be dead. He could not leave me like this.

I looked up and saw his cell phone on his nightstand, grabbed it and then dialed for help.

"911. What's your emergency?" the dispatcher asked.

"I-I need an ambulance at the First Methodist Church parsonage on Oak Street."

"Ma'am, please tell me what's wrong."

"It's my dad, the pastor of the church. He's not breathing. He's not doing anything. He's dead—he's dead—he's dead."

I didn't know how long it took for the ambulance to arrive but it didn't seem like it was very long. Ten minutes maybe. It really didn't matter, though, because my dad was gone and there was nothing that anybody could do about it.

When the paramedics rang the doorbell, I got up from the floor and looked back down at my dad laying there, with a pillow underneath his head and the blanket that my mom had crocheted for him covering him up to his chest. I couldn't stand seeing him in the shape that he was in when I first found him, so I'd provided the last little bit of human comfort that I could give him despite the life in his body no longer being there.

As the paramedics were checking for any trace of life in my dad, I stood back and watched them in a daze. After carefully loading Pastor Steven Sinclair onto a stretcher and then completely covering him with a white sheet, the paramedics began rolling him out of his bedroom. I followed them down the hallway and out the front door of the parsonage to the driveway, where some of my dad's neighbors had already gathered. They came running up to me and were moving their mouths, but I couldn't hear what they were saying. I could only see them. My head started spinning and then I felt someone grab me from behind. When I looked to my right, Graham was looking back at me and then everything went black.

56
#dusttodust

Zac

Brooke, Bash, and I arrived at Mr. Sinclair's church thirty minutes before his funeral was to begin. The building was packed with people who, I was certain, were church members, longtime friends of Mr. Sinclair's, and even new friends that the man had recently made.

I'd found out about his death through Brooke. Stevie's friend and boss, Melissa Landry, had called Brooke to let her know what happened. As soon as I heard Brooke say the words, all the emotions that I'd been holding inside ever since the day I told Stevie goodbye through a song came pouring out. All I could think about was how broken her heart had to be and also how much I wished I could be in Austin to hold her in my arms and let her cry.

When Brooke asked me about going to Mr. Sinclair's funeral, I immediately said yes. Nothing could stop me. When I called Bash and told him what happened, he said the same thing.

While Brooke was using the church restroom, Bash and I walked into the large sanctuary and stood to the side. I could see Mr. Sinclair's open casket sitting in front of the pulpit, countless sprays of flowers stretching out from both ends of it, plus displays of photos of him, his wife—and Stevie. The line of people walking past his casket was long and I already knew that I would not be joining it.

I felt a hand on my shoulder and looked over to see Brooke.

"What do you wanna do, Buchanan?" she asked.

"Stay right here. I don't want Stevie to see me and get even more upset, so I'm gonna pay my respects from afar. You and Bash go ahead, though. I know it'll do Stevie so much good to see both of you. She'll appreciate you being here."

"Okay then. I'm gonna go get in line to pay my own respect to Joan of Arc's pastor-dad and then I'm gonna go sit down in a church pew, hope that lightning doesn't strike me, say a prayer for the love of your life, and then cry my way through the rest of this damn funeral. Are you with me, Bash?" Brooke asked him.

All he could do was nod his head yes. He couldn't speak because he was a ball of emotions. Professionally, Bash was the boldest and could also be the meanest attorney there was. Personally, though, he was the kindest and biggest-hearted person that I knew other than my parents, Brooke Murphy—and Stevie Sinclair.

As the funeral began, people were still coming into the sanctuary to take their seats. Brooke and Bash were sitting about a third of the way down and I was still standing by one of the entryways. Then I saw Stevie enter her dad's church to the right of the choir loft, wearing a fitted black dress on her now rail-thin body.

A woman was walking beside her, holding her hand. I guessed her to be Melissa or another one of Stevie's Austin friends. On the other side of Stevie, there was a man and he was holding her hand too. I had no idea who he was but the thought immediately came to me that it was Stevie's ex-husband, Graham. Because of his long history with Stevie and her family, and also his being on cordial terms with Stevie, it made sense that he would be here today to help her.

As I was watching her walk over to the front pew that was marked for family, I choked back my tears because of the pain that I could see on her beautiful face and also the tremble in her body even from where I was standing. I wanted to run to her so badly. I wanted to take her into my arms, hold her so tight and tell her that everything was going to be okay. I didn't, though. I didn't move.

The assistant pastor, Kyle Hughes, was the first person to speak about Mr. Sinclair and while listening to him, I wondered if Stevie was going speak. I wondered if she was going to share some of her cherished memories of her dad and also her mom. The people here knew Mrs. Sinclair as well as they knew her husband. From what Stevie told me, they were two separate human beings yet they were one.

A few more people spoke after the assistant pastor, but Stevie wasn't one of them. She never got up from where she was sitting. Realizing she *couldn't* speak about her dad got to me even more. She was hurting so badly and if she had tried to make herself go stand at that pulpit, there was no telling what would've happened. My Joan of Arc was wounded and nearly fatally. She had a long road of healing ahead of her.

With all the talking and praying over with and a pianist now playing music, the funeral attendees began making their way up to the front of the church to see Stevie. When Brooke and Bash's row was told that it was their turn, though, the two of them walked back up to me.

"Buchanan?" Brooke said.

"What?"

"The *three* of us are going up front to see Stevie."

"No, we're not."

"Yes, we are."

"Brooke, I..."

She held up her hand for me to stop arguing with her.

"Zac, it's not only the right thing to do but Stevie needs to see you, even if she starts crying harder than she already is," Bash added. Then he pointed toward the receiving line. "You've gotta go up there."

I was in a back and forth stare-off with my best friend and my other mother. Several seconds passed and I still didn't agree with what they were insisting that I do.

"The time isn't right and both of you know it," I finally said to them.

"I think it is the right time for you to not only share your condolences with Stevie about her father's passing, but also to tell her about what's happened in *your* life," Brooke said, and Bash nodded in agreement. "You may not get to tell her about yourself when you see her in a few minutes, but Stevie being able to see the love that you still have for her shining in those blue eyes of yours could quite possibly open the door for you to let her in on the secret that you've been keeping. In fact, I'd bet on it."

I stared up at the ceiling, shook my head and then closed my eyes and sighed. My heart was about to beat out of my chest and the lump in my throat was already there because I knew what I was about to do. I was about to come face-to-face again with the one and only woman who my soul ached for. The woman who changed the course of my life. The woman who I still hoped had room for me in hers.

It was Brooke, first in line, then Bash and then me as we approached Stevie, who was still sitting in the front church pew with the same woman and man on either side of her and numerous other people surrounding them. I watched Stevie look up in a teary daze, and at the moment she realized it was Brooke standing in front of her, she slowly stood up and the two women hugged each other and started crying. We all were.

After Stevie and Brooke had somewhat composed themselves, Stevie thanked her old boss for coming to her dad's funeral, and then she saw Bash. She reached out for him and they held each other while mourning the loss of so much. It wasn't just Mr. Sinclair. Bash and Stevie had lost access to their incredible friendship when she moved away from Dallas. I knew how much it hurt Bash not having her around anymore and how much he missed her.

He and Stevie were standing only a few feet away from me, still hugging with their heads resting against each other's. I couldn't see Bash's face but I could see Stevie's and she had her eyes closed. Although I'd been this close to her all this time and I'd seen her open her eyes a few times since hugging Bash, she hadn't noticed me. Or rather, she couldn't see me. It was very apparent to me now that due to her emotional and physical state, she really could only see what was in front of her and barely a little to either side. Her vision wasn't only blurred, it was also tunneled.

When Stevie and Bash looked at each other again, she smiled a weary smile at him and he did the same. Then he kissed her cheek and stepped aside for me to have my turn with the woman whom my soul would always love.

As I was moving closer to her, I watched her slowly turn her head in my direction and then look up at me when I came to a standstill in front of her. Her eyes grew big and her lips parted. Then the bottom one began quivering so hard just like mine was. I couldn't hold myself back any longer, so I stepped up to Stevie and wrapped my arms around her trembling body. She melted into me, then buried her face in my chest and started wailing.

Things began to blur around me, so I leaned my head down and rested it on top of Stevie's, closing my eyes. I opened them again when I heard Stevie's crying begin to calm and I realized she and I were swaying back and forth. We weren't moving our feet. Just the upper part of our bodies. It was a sort of mourning slow dance that we were doing, rocking each other in this way, and it was so needed by both of us.

I raised my head back up when I felt Stevie start stirring in my arms but I didn't let go of her. I looked down at her as she looked up at me. Seconds passed and we just couldn't pull our eyes away from each other. I wanted to say something to her but my tongue was suddenly tied and hers seemed to be too. Then she nodded at me. She was telling me so many things at once without saying a word. She was letting me know that she was okay, that it was okay that I was here, and that she was glad I made it.

I knew it was time for me to move on and let the other people in the receiving line express their condolences to Stevie, so I unwrapped my arms from around her. Before I stepped away from her, though, I took her beautiful face into my hands and leaned down to kiss her cheek, but she turned her head last second and our lips met. It was brief but it still reignited everything inside me. When I looked back at Stevie, she searched my eyes while I tried to keep my bearings. A few seconds later, I walked away from her in a daze.

Bash came up to me, put his hand on my back and guided me over to Brooke standing a few yards away. She gave me a mother's smile, and then she, Bash, and I headed into the large foyer by the front doors of the church, where Brooke asked me if I was going to stick around and try to talk to Stevie one-on-one.

"No, I'm gonna have to wait. It's still not the right time," I told her.

"Are you sure about that?"

"Yes, I'm very sure."

"Okay. Then let's get back on the road to Dallas. We can stop somewhere along the way and eat if you guys want to. My treat."

As we were nearing the front doors of the church, a deep ache began filling my chest that made me stop right where I was. I took a deep breath and then another while looking back and forth at Brooke and Bash.

"Zac, what's wrong?" they asked at the same time.

I held up my finger and told them to give me a minute, then turned around and walked back to one of the entrances of the sanctuary. My eyes immediately found Stevie. She'd walked away from the line of people and had made it to about a quarter of the way up the aisle from them, coming in my direction. When she saw me, she stopped walking and started crying again. Through her tears and through mine, we smiled at each other then I lifted my hand to my chest and patted it twice above my heart. Stevie did too.

57
#youthere

Stevie

After my dad's funeral I spent two weeks in his parsonage, slowly going through his belongings, which included many items that had belonged to my mom. I didn't throw anything away; I couldn't yet. I just packed up all the things that I knew for certain I wanted to keep, such as my Dad's bible, the wine glass that he used whenever he drank Pinot Grigio, the canvas on which my mom had painted "Wait a minute, baby. Stay with me a while. Said you'd give me light but you never told me about the fire," and also my mom and dad's wedding photos.

During those two weeks, the assistant pastor, the church secretary, several other church members, and Melissa checked on me often to see how I was doing, and so did Graham. He actually spent the first three nights with me at my dad's parsonage. Knowing he was there was comforting to me, and I was able to sleep soundly.

On the first night, I didn't want to be alone in my bed and asked Graham if he'd just hold me—and he did. When I woke up in the middle of the night to use the bathroom he wasn't in my bed any longer, so I got up and walked into the living room to find him sleeping on the couch. I sat down on the floor and watched him while thinking about us, our history, our son, and my feelings toward Graham. During that time, I allowed myself to accept the fact that he and I weren't going to get a second chance, because I realized the love that I felt toward him was only that of a very good friend. That was all it was ever going to be.

When I talked to him about it a few days later, he took it well and told me that he was thankful we could at least be friends. Then he brought up Zac.

"The tall, muscular guy with the short beard and blue eyes in the receiving line at your dad's funeral, who didn't wanna let go of you, and whom you kissed on the lips, and also whom you went to go find after he left the receiving line—he's the man you had an affair with, isn't he?" he asked me.

I told Graham yes, and then he asked me another question about Zac. He wanted to know if I was going to get back together with him.

"No," I said.

"But you're still in love with him and he's still in love with you. It's so apparent."

"It doesn't matter that we're still in love with each other. It will never work between us as long as he's married...and he still is. He had on his wedding band. I saw it."

"It wasn't a wedding band, Stevie. It was your name in a Celtic design tattooed on his finger."

I didn't believe Graham at first. But then I remembered how everything was so blurry to me on that day unless it was right in front of me. As I kept thinking about Zac's third tattoo, I wondered why he'd gotten it and I wondered how that had gone over with Avery. Then I thought that maybe she and Zac were living separate lives underneath the same roof again and he just didn't give a damn about anything anymore. Having my name tattooed on his ring finger was like the last big middle finger that he could give to Avery about our relationship.

On the day before I was supposed to return to work, I called Melissa and asked her for more time off. I wasn't ready to go back. What I was ready to do was get far away from Austin to somewhere tropical. I needed to swim in an ocean and let it heal me. I needed the warmth of the sun on my skin and the salty air in my lungs. I couldn't go to Destin, though, because it would only remind me of Zac. I couldn't drink Hendricks gin again either and for the same reason.

Where I finally decided to go was the island of St. Croix in the U.S. Virgin Islands—2,247 miles away from my hometown. I bought a first-class ticket and sipped on Blue Chair Bay rum by Kenny Chesney while on my flight to paradise. Upon arrival, a taxi drove me over to the beach house I'd rented for the week and then I unpacked my suitcase, put on my new bikini, and went home to Mother Ocean to swim in her warmth while letting my tears fall.

Today was my fifth day on St. Croix, I was sitting on the beach and I was soaking up a few more rays. There was about an hour before it got dark but I wasn't planning to go inside anytime soon. I wanted to watch the sunset like I had on all the other nights. I also wanted to watch the sky fill with stars while listening to the new music playlist that I'd made.

I had just grabbed my cellphone off my beach towel to take another picture of the rolling ocean waves when it chimed. I was shocked when I saw who the text was from. It was Zac.

I couldn't imagine why he was reaching out to me. Surely he knew what this contact from him was already doing to me: throwing me for an emotional loop just like it did at my dad's funeral. It was worth it, though, just being able to see and touch Zac again—and kiss his lips. Hopefully, this unexpected contact from him was going to be worth it too.

My hands were trembling as I opened his message, then I shook my head when I saw a link to a song. I looked out at the ocean, closed my eyes, and said a prayer for the strength to make it through what I was about to do. What I had no choice but to do. And that was to listen to what Zac wanted to say to me through this song by Aquilo.

The opening line "You there, you're better off here" instantly had me in tears because Zac knew I was in St. Croix. It went without saying that Melissa had told Brooke about my plan to come to this tropical paradise and then Brooke passed along that info to Zac. He knew I was right where I needed to be to begin healing my heart over losing my dad. I was still trying to do the same thing about Zac and me ending. Would I ever get over losing either man? No. Not completely. They would always be part of me.

When I heard the line "Funny, it takes no time to fall back down. Funny, it takes the time to get back up" it made my tears start falling like rain. I made it through to the end of the song but the last line was what slayed my heart. Through those moving lyrics, Zac asked me to ask myself where my reflection was. It used to be in him. I saw myself in him whenever I looked into his eyes. I saw our future too—but not anymore.

I turned off my phone, tossed it onto my beach towel, and then wiped off my face. I was staring out at the ocean when I noticed out of the corner of my eye some people walking the shoreline, heading in my direction. With the angle of the sunlight, I could only see their silhouettes, but when they got closer, I found myself in a state of total disbelief.

I kept sitting where I was with my heart pounding and my mind still unable to accept what I was seeing, and then the two people stopped walking. One of them squatted down and said something to the other while pointing at me—and that's when Malcolm Buchanan saw me. He began jumping up and down on the sand and I rose to my feet. Malcolm started running toward me and then I started running toward him. As soon as we reached each other, I picked him up and hugged him to me as tightly as I could while looking over his shoulder at his daddy walking up to us. All three of us were crying and unable to say a word, but then Zac did.

"Hey, you," he choked out.

All I could do was nod at him. He stepped up to Malcolm and me and wrapped his arms around us while we all slowly got our composure back. When Zac looked at me again, I searched his sparkling sky-blue eyes while wondering what was about to take place here on this beach.

"Stevie Grace Sinclair, it's time for you to come back to Dallas, Texas," Zac said, brushing his fingertips up and down my arm. "It's just Malcolm and me now and we built a house for you. We love you and don't wanna live without you."

My head was spinning from not only seeing Zac and Malcolm again but also from hearing what Zac had just said. It was at the moment I heard those words come from his mouth that I realized the true meaning in the song by Aquilo. Zac wanted to tell me that I would be better off with him.

I was looking back and forth at Zac and Malcolm, still unable to speak, when Malcolm pressed his little hands against my cheeks, smiled at me, and then said, "Come home, Mommy." I still couldn't say anything but I already knew where I would soon be going.

58
#generations

Zac

On that sunset evening on the island of St. Croix, when Malcolm and I surprised Stevie, I felt everything come full circle for the three of us. The goodness of life had returned and so had peace.

After Malcolm told Stevie to come home with us, she didn't say anything at first. She just kept looking back and forth at us as tears continued falling from her beautiful eyes. It was apparent that she was in shock from seeing us and also from hearing what we said. A short while later, after she, Malcolm and I went over to her beach house, Stevie was shocked again by all that I shared with her about what'd been going on in my life.

Avery had gone back to Lubbock in mid-November without saying a word to me. I just came home from work and she was gone again. Up until that time, she'd still been pushing me to reconcile with her. I didn't know if Avery finally gave up on that happening or if she left because Justin came back into the picture. It wasn't long after that that I found out that was exactly what had happened. Justin was back...but there was more.

Avery sent a long text message to me that told the whole story. She confessed to her longtime affair with Justin, as well as her love for him, which had been there since their days in college together. Then she told me that she was pregnant with his baby. I asked her how far along she was and she replied by telling me that she was pregnant when she came home the last time. When I read that, I realized that was why Avery had pushed me to have sex with her. Because she believed she and Justin were over for good, I was all that she had left, and if she could get me to have sex with her, then she could say the baby was mine. When I asked her the truth about that, she confessed to it also.

I went on to ask Avery if she was going to keep the baby and she said yes. Having a child with Justin and being his wife was all that she'd ever wanted. I laughed but not in a humorous way when she texted me that reply. She didn't want my child, but she wanted Justin's. That was Avery, though, and I wished her a lot of luck. That was also when I let her know I was filing for divorce and full custody of Malcolm.

I told her if she tried to fight me on it, I was going to put her through the wringer with all the years of evidence that I had on not only her affair but also her violence, alcoholism, and neglect of Malcolm. She couldn't believe I'd known about her and Justin all that time, but then I reminded her that I was a Buchanan, and that underestimating me was one of her many mistakes.

There was a lull in Avery's texting for several minutes, and then she sent: Draw up the divorce papers. I'll sign them. I don't want you or Malcolm or anything from the house. I just want to be free to live my life with Justin. A week later, she'd signed the papers. Malcolm and I were finally free to live *our* lives, and that was when I started taking steps that I hoped would lead me back to Stevie.

Once I'd finished telling her all about Avery and our divorce, she pointed at my left hand.

"When did you get my name tattooed on your finger?" she asked.

"The same evening I came over to your house to tell you goodbye before you moved back to Austin—although I couldn't tell you goodbye. I wanted something symbolic of my unending love for you. There's something else you haven't seen, though."

I turned over my hand to show Stevie the other side of the tattoo and her lips parted in surprise.

"That's the date we saw each other the first time. On the running trail," she said.

"I know. That was the first door that opened for you and me. We just didn't know it at the time."

I glanced over at Malcolm laying on the floor in the living room, watching cartoons, then I got up from my chair at the dining room table and stepped over to Stevie sitting in hers. Then I held out my hand for her to take. She took it and slowly stood up while keeping her eyes glued to mine. Several seconds passed as we kept staring at each other, and then I reached up and held Stevie's face in my hands. Then I kissed her. She breathed into me as I breathed into her and our bodies pressed together. It was our first kiss in total freedom to be *us*. There would be no more hiding anything. There would be no more holding back. And if I had anything to do with it, there wasn't going to be any more sadness either. Only happiness and so much love.

After that kiss, Stevie and I sat back down at the dining room table, but I was still touching her. We held hands and just kept looking at each other and smiling. Then I asked her about coming home to Malcolm and me. The way she'd reacted on the beach to that invitation seemed to be a yes, although she never said the word. I needed to hear her say it—and then she did. She also told me that she loved me and I told her that I loved her too.

I had a pizza delivered for dinner and a short while later, Malcolm fell asleep on the couch. Stevie covered him with a light blanket, stroked his hair and then kissed his cheek. The way she was with him warmed my soul so much. She needed Malcolm as much as he needed her.

While he was sleeping, Stevie and I sat outside on the back deck with the ocean breeze blowing in. We continued catching up on our lives and we also talked about our future plans. Everything fell right back into an easy and natural rhythm with Stevie, and I was so thankful.

I had a surprise for her—something that I wanted to show her on my cellphone. I told her to close her eyes and then pulled up a picture.

"Okay, you can look now," I said.

Stevie's eyes moved across my phone screen, then she looked back at me. "Who are those people in that painting?"

"Our ancestors from the fifteen-hundreds. The first Buchanan/Sinclair marriage."

Stevie gasped. "No."

"Yes, it's them."

"How did you..."

"A professional genealogist is how. I hired one, and all he needed to begin journeying back in time down your ancestral line and mine were our full names, our dates of birth and our parents' names. It took him a while, because there were a lot of records to comb through, but he did it. He verified our connection. And that painting? I have a framed copy of it waiting for you to hang up wherever you want it."

Stevie grabbed my phone out of my hand and took a closer look at our ancestors. I was waiting for her to notice what I'd noticed about them the first time I saw them. My only guess as to why Stevie didn't immediately see what I did was because of how overwhelmed she was by everything that had happened.

When her lips parted again, I knew she finally recognized her face in her Sinclair ancestor and she also recognized my face in my Buchanan ancestor.

"Oh, wow," she whispered, looking back at me again.

"I know. It's pretty amazing, isn't it?"

"Yes. I'm covered in goosebumps."

Stevie grew quiet but kept her eyes on mine, searching them. Then she asked, "Zac, do you think it's possible that these two people are..."

She couldn't finish asking the question and I knew why. It seemed too outlandish to believe the man and woman in the painting were actually Stevie and me from lifetimes ago. But was it too outlandish? I didn't think so.

If the couple really was an earlier embodiment of Stevie and me, then it explained a lot. It explained why we were so familiar to each other the moment we made eye contact the first time. It explained why we were able to stray from our moral compasses and be each other's exception. It explained why we were drawn to each other and also why we could sense each other's emotions even when we were apart. It explained why I ached for Stevie and why I never could let go of her. We were soul mates. Although neither of us could prove it, we both knew it was true. We knew we'd traveled through time and found each other again.

I told Stevie my belief about our ancestors and us, and then she smiled and nodded in agreement. Then I pulled her into my arms and kissed her again. We were breathless in no time and wanted so much more from each other, so I looked around and saw where we could be alone. I carried my beautiful mermaid across the white sand to the warm tropical water of the Caribbean where she and I became one again with an ocean of stars above us.

Two days later, she, Malcolm and I flew back to Texas. We didn't part ways, though. Stevie didn't go to Austin alone. Malcolm and I went with her and helped her get packed up to come to Dallas with us to the new house we'd had built hoping Stevie would one day make it a home. In March, she finally did.

It was October now, I was wearing a gold band on my left hand, Stevie was wearing a beautiful diamond ring on hers and she had my last name. It was Sunday, she was in the kitchen preparing dinner, and Malcolm and I had just come inside from taking a swim in the pool. We walked over to Stevie, who was standing next to the kitchen counter, peeling an avocado, and we both hugged her. I got her upper half and Malcolm got her lower half and all three of us started giggling. Precious moments like this one had happened so many times over the past months and they always made me smile with so much gratitude.

After Malcolm and I changed into dry clothes, we walked back into the kitchen and Stevie looked up from the Mexican casserole that she'd just taken out of the oven. The expression on her face wasn't what it was only minutes ago. Now she looked nauseated, and when she covered her mouth and then took off running for the bathroom, I realized I was right. I also realized I was right about something else.

I gave Stevie a couple of minutes, and then Malcolm and I walked into the master bedroom and I tapped on the bathroom door. When Stevie opened it, I couldn't keep from grinning.

"It's not funny," she said, still looking so nauseated.

"I know it's not. I've just never seen you like this before is all."

"It was like a wave came over me in the kitchen, then I got hot and then I felt what was inside my stomach start coming up. Maybe it was the breakfast that we ate."

"I don't think so. Malcolm and I are fine."

Stevie looked down at him standing beside me and smiled through how badly she was feeling, then met my anxious gaze. That's when I gave her the box that I was holding behind my back. She frowned at first, but then her eyes grew big and I just kept grinning.

"I can't be," she whispered to me.

"Yes, you can and you are, but take the test anyway."

"But I..."

"Babe, go take the test."

I gently pushed her backward into the bathroom, closed the door, and waited for her to open it again and tell me that she was indeed pregnant.

One week after she moved in and began making this place a nurturing home, she and I had talked about our desire to have a child together. It wasn't just for us, though. It was for Malcolm too. We wanted to give him a little brother or sister to grow up with, so Stevie immediately got off the pill. Neither of us knew how long it was going to take for the birth control to leave her system but we were hoping it was quick. We were eager to begin living our life together to the fullest, and that included adding to our family.

On the day that Stevie and I discussed having a child, I asked her if she was fearful about it since she lost her Malcolm and she said no. She was at peace about it, as well as everything else in life. As she was telling me that, I just stared at her—once again blown away by the strength of her spirit. She had suffered so much loss in her life. She lost *everything* but she came out on the other side stronger than before and I didn't think my Joan of Arc could get any stronger.

Her transition from being a warrior-attorney to being everything that Malcolm and I needed and wanted was immediate. Her focus on us was 100% while her focus on herself took the backseat. While she became scattered about herself, I kept a close eye on her. I also did something else. I kept up with her monthly cycle because I knew she wasn't. That's how I knew Stevie was pregnant.

When she opened the bathroom door, she looked straight at me and nodded yes. I pulled her into my arms and held her while we both cried tears of joy. After a long emotional minute, I picked up Malcolm and told him that Stevie was going to have a baby. His response to the news was something that Stevie and I weren't expecting to hear. In fact, it shocked us.

"I know she's having a baby," he said to me, then he turned to Stevie and went on to say, "My sister told me in my dream that she was in your tummy but it was a secret."

After telling Stevie that, Malcolm reached out for her, and while the two of them were hugging, I just stood back and watched them while thanking God for this life-changing moment.

It was when Malcolm went to sleep for the night that Stevie said she wanted to talk to me about something, so we went outside and sat on the edge of the swimming pool while our legs dangled in the heated water. Stevie wanted to know if I would be okay with us *not* finding out the sex of our baby before he or she was born. Because of what Malcolm said about his "sister" in his dream, Stevie was curious about there being any validity to it, but wanted to wait to find out. She thought it'd be the best surprise ever if we really did have a little girl.

Of course I was fine with waiting until the day of our child's birth to find out, because I felt just like Stevie did. And on the day that our blond-haired, deep blue-eyed, beautiful little girl was born, my wife and I realized our little boy's dream was not only real but it was also right.

The Starry End

Love this author?
Read her other romantic suspense novels,
Twisted Roots and *Fall Into Me* today.

Acknowledgements

TO MY READERS—a great big Texas hug and thank you from me to y'all for loving my stories like you do. I had no idea how any of you would receive *Twisted Roots* or *Fall Into Me*, and was so dang nervous about releasing them because I was putting my heart out there into the world. I feared it'd be devoured...but it wasn't. You received Alex & Taylor's story with open minds and arms, as well as London & Sam's story. You loved them, too, and it is all of you who spur me on to continue writing rollercoaster romantic suspense books full of passion, intrigue, crime, justice, redemption, and magical endings. I hope Stevie & Zac's story in *Ocean of Stars* has touched you just as much as the others.

To my hubby, Gregg Magee—as always, thank you for your support of this author gig that I'm doing. Thank you for believing I could pull it off. You believed I could do it long before I ever did. And by the way, I greatly enjoyed writing you into the storyline of *Ocean of Stars*. You've been such a great father to our kids and you're the same kind of father to the hero, Zac Buchanan. I love you more and yes, it is absolutely possible.

To my son, Jordan Magee, and my precious daughter-in-law, Sammi Jo—it is you two who inspired me to write *Ocean of Stars*. No, Stevie & Zac's story isn't your story. I just borrowed the unique dynamic of how you met, as well as your profession. Thank you for not minding, and also for the informative legal chats we had when I first started writing *Ocean of Stars*. I wanted the story to be as accurate as possible and you helped to make it that way. XOXO.

To my fellow writing partners, Brittany Lammerts and Brooke Frachiseur—I love y'all. I'm so lucky to have you two Libra girls on my team. As with *Twisted Roots* and *Fall Into Me*, you tackled reading the rough draft of *Ocean of Stars* for me and caught holes in the storyline that I couldn't see because my mind was so overloaded with all-things-Stevie & Zac. Thank you a gazillon times over for taking the time to help to make their story even better. Y'all are so good at what you do!

Also, Brooke—I appreciate you not minding me making you one of the main characters in *Ocean of Stars*. Like I told you early on, *Brooke Murphy* is definitely you but she's also your amazing momma-bear/my soul sister, Debbie VanDeman. I grabbed onto your strengths and hers to bring Dallas's district attorney to life. Her role within the story moved me tremendously, and I could easily see you AND your mom "taking care of business" the same as *Brooke Murphy*. All of you are badass women.

To my awesome little-big brother, Mike Smith—thank you for jumping into the pages of the rough draft of *Ocean of Stars*, and then giving me your "dude perspective" on the story. You helped me keep the testosterone level right up there where it needed to be with Zac Buchanan's alpha male character. You also did that with Taylor Kingston in *Twisted Roots*, and then with Sam Hunter in *Fall Into Me*. Those three men are very well-rounded due to your eyes having been on the early version of their individual stories. Thank you again for doing that for me, and also for not minding me including you in *Ocean of Stars* just like I did in *Twisted Roots*. It's been super fun writing you into my books—first as an attorney, and then as a judge. You're a fantastic fictional one just as you are in real life. Hugs to you for being YOU and also for all your legal pointers in my third book baby.

To my spitfire little sister, Melissa Madden—Ohhh, how I enjoyed making you one of the lead female characters in *Ocean of Stars*! I laughed so many times while typing out your dialogue, because I could hear you talking inside my head. Your personality stands out BIG TIME within Stevie & Zac's story. Thank you for being all for me immortalizing you in it, as well as your sweet grand-girl.

To my family and friends—Brittany, Jason, Ellie, Jennifer, David, Misty, Evan, Macie, and Jackson—I borrowed your names to create some of the minor characters in *Ocean of Stars*. It was so fun doing it too. And Misty, you made for the best nurse ever just like you do in real life. XOXO.

To my incredible book cover artist, Murphy Rae—the *Ocean of Stars* cover that you created still takes my breath away whenever I look at it. It's beautiful. It's perfect. And I just love seeing Stevie Sinclair & Zac Buchanan standing in the ocean, in that sweet embrace, with a night sky full of stars above them. Thank you!

Lilly Schneider—my stellar editor... I appreciate you so very much. You've taken each of my books and streamlined the story with your suggested edits. You've also helped to improve my writing ability via those edits. I've learned a huge amount from you in the past year and half, and creating my romantic suspense stories comes easier now because of you.

To my wonderful book formatter, Elaine York—yeah, I'm sending you a great big Texas hug and thank you for getting the *Ocean of Stars* manuscript "just right" for uploading online/ publishing. I also want you to know how much I appreciate all the little artistic touches you've added to the interior of all three of my books. My readers have let me know how much THEY love the pretty pages that you design.

Acknowledgements

GINA MAGEE is a romantic suspense author who sprinkles the supernatural into the storyline of the books she writes. Her first book, *Twisted Roots*, embraces the world of practical magic while her second book, *Fall Into Me*, explores the supernatural once again via superstitions. Gina's third book, *Ocean of Stars*, plunges deep into the topics of soul mates and past lives. She's currently working on her fourth romantic suspense book and is enjoying making it just as magical as the others. The East Texas Piney Woods is where Gina resides with her husband and two very spoiled Pembroke Welsh Corgis—Gypsy Willow and Sir Chesney.

Follow me:

Instagram: @ginamagee_author (https://www.instagram.com/ginamagee_author/)
TikTok: ginamagee_author (https://www.tiktok.com/@ginamagee_author)
www.facebook.com/ginamageeauthor
www.amazon.com/author/ginamagee